CONTINUUM

RIVEN WORLDS BOOK ONE

G. S. JENNSEN

HYPERNOVA
PUBLISHING
2020

CONTINUUM

Hypernova Publishing
P.O. Box 2214
Parker, Colorado 80134
www.hypernovapublishing.com

The Hypernova Publishing name, colophon and logo are trademarks of Hypernova Publishing.

Ordering Information:
Hypernova Publishing books may be purchased for educational, business or sales promotional use. For details, contact the "Special Markets Department" at the address above.

Continuum / G. S. Jennsen.—1st ed.

LCCN 2019920395
978-1-7323977-8-1

AMARANTHE UNIVERSE

AURORA RHAPSODY

AURORA RISING

STARSHINE

VERTIGO

TRANSCENDENCE

AURORA RENEGADES

SIDESPACE

DISSONANCE

ABYSM

AURORA RESONANT

RELATIVITY

RUBICON

REQUIEM

SHORT STORIES

Restless, Vol. I • *Restless, Vol. II* • *Apogee* • *Solatium*
Venatoris • *Re/Genesis* • *Meridian* • *Fractals*

ASTERION NOIR

EXIN EX MACHINA

OF A DARKER VOID

THE STARS LIKE GODS

RIVEN WORLDS

CONTINUUM

For Bob, who saved our lives

DRAMATIS PERSONAE

HUMANS

Alexis 'Alex' Solovy Marano
Space scout and explorer. Prevo.
Spouse of Caleb Marano, daughter of Miriam and David Solovy.
Artificial/Prevo Counterpart: Valkyrie

Caleb Marano
Former Special Operations intelligence agent; space scout and explorer.
Spouse of Alex Solovy.

Miriam Solovy (Commandant)
Leader, Concord Armed Forces.

Malcolm Jenner (Admiral)
AEGIS Fleet Admiral.

Mia Requelme (Senator)
Head of Concord Consulate.
Artificial/Prevo Counterpart: Meno

Kennedy Rossi
Founder/CEO, Connova Interstellar.

David Solovy
Professor, Concord Special Warfare
Training Center.

Marlee Marano
Consulate Assistant.

Richard Navick
Concord Intelligence Director.

Valkyrie
Alex's Prevo Counterpart.

ASTERIONS

Nika Kirumase
External Relations Advisor, Asterion Dominion. Former NOIR leader.

Dashiel Ridani
Industry Advisor, Asterion Dominion Advisor Committee.

Adlai Weiss
Justice Advisor.

Perrin Benvenit
Omoikane Personnel Director.

Lance Palmer
Military Advisor.

Grant Mesahle
Dominion Armed Forces Consultant.

Parc Eshett
Omoikane Consultant.

Kiernan Phillips
DAF Lieutenant, Pilot.

OTHER MAJOR CHARACTERS

Eren Savitas asi-Idoni
CINT agent.
Species: Anaden

Mnemosyne ('Mesme')
Idryma Member, 1st Analystae of Aurora.
Species: Katasketousya (Metigen)

Cosime Rhomyhn
CINT agent.
Species: Naraida

Casmir elasson-Machim
Leader, Anaden military.
Species: Anaden

Danilo Nisi/Corradeo Praesidis
Former leader of the anarch resistance.
Species: Anaden

Drae Shonen ela-Machim
CINT agent.
Species: Anaden

Eosha Norhalle
Artist.
Species: Novoloume

Felzeor
CINT agent.
Species: Volucri

Ferdinand elasson-Kyvern
Anaden Senator, Concord Senate.
Species: Anaden

Ilgur Darhk
Savrakath Ambassador.
Species: Savrakath

Jaisc
Iona-Cead of the Taenarin.
Species: Taenarin

Lakhes
Praetor (leader) of the Idryma.
Species: Katasketousya (Metigen)

Maris Debray
Culture Advisor, Asterion Dominion.
Species: Asterion

Noah Terrage
COO, Connova Interstellar.
Species: Human

Nyx elasson-Praesidis
Former Inquisitor.
Species: Anaden

Pinchutsenahn Niikha Qhiyane Kteh
Tokahe Naataan of the Khokteh.
Species: Khokteh

Spencer Nimoet
Justice Advisor, Asterion Dominion.
Species: Asterion

Torval elasson-Machim
Navarchos, Anaden military.
Species: Anaden

Toshke'phein
Pilot, Taiyok military.
Species: Taiyok

Vaihe
Refugee.
Species: Godjan

William 'Will' Sutton
CINT Operations Director.
Species: Human

MINOR CHARACTERS

Abigail Canivon, cybernetics expert (*Human*)

Ainye asi-Idoni, hostess (*Anaden*)

Akamu Chacko, Lieutenant, AEGIS Special Forces (*Human*)

Beshai, Taenarin Caomh (*Taenarin*)

Bautista Rodriguez, Major, Prevo, AEGIS Special Forces (*Human*)

Braelyn Rossi-Terrage, Kennedy and Noah's daughter (*Human*)

Carl Odaka, Colonel, AEGIS Special Forces (*Human*)

Charles Basquan, owner, Mirai Pavilion (*Asterion*)

Daayn Shahs-lan, Barisan Senator, (*Barisan*)

Emilio Rogers, Colonel, Dominion Armed Forces (*Asterion*)

Erik Rhom, Justice Division analyst (*Asterion*)

Ian Sevulch, restaurant waiter (*Asterion*)

Isabela Marano, biochemistry professor, Caleb's sister (*Human*)

Joaquim Lacese, former NOIR Operations Director (*Asterion*)

Jonas Rossi-Terrage, Kennedy and Noah's son (*Human*)

Kuisk Jhountar, General, Savrakath military (*Savrakath*)

Onai Veshnael, Dean, Novoloume Senator (*Novoloume*)

Phael Thisiame (Pointe-Amiral), leader, Novoloume military (*Novoloume*)

Selene Panetier, Justice Advisor (*Asterion*)

Tele Diya, Lieutenant, AEGIS Special Forces (*Human*)

Thelkt Lonaervin, former Anarch agent (*Novoloume*)

Thomas, *Stalwart II* Artificial (*Artificial*)

Vii, employee of Connova Interstellar, Valkyrie's sister (*Artificial*)

CONCORD

MEMBER SPECIES

Humans
Representative: Mia Requelme

Anadens
Representative: Ferdinand elasson-Kyvern

Novoloume
Representative: Dean Onai Veshnael

Naraida
Representative: Tasme Chareis

Khokteh
Representative: Pinchutsenahn Niikha Qhiyane Kteh

Barisans
Representative: Daayn Shahs-lan

Dankaths
Representative: Bohlke'ban

Efkam
Representative: Ahhk~sae

ALLIED SPECIES

Katasketousya	Taenarin
Fylliot	Volucri
Ruda	Yinhe

PROTECTED SPECIES

Ekos	Icksel
Faneros	Pachrem
Galenai	Vrachnas

AMARANTHE
CONCORD EMPIRE

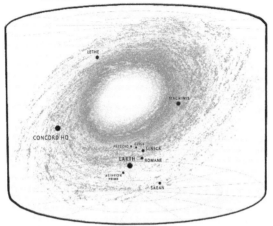

LETHE

IVACHIMIS

CONCORD HQ

PRESIDIO • LUISE
SENECA
EARTH • ROMANE

ASTERION
PRIME

SAGAN

MILKY WAY GALAXY

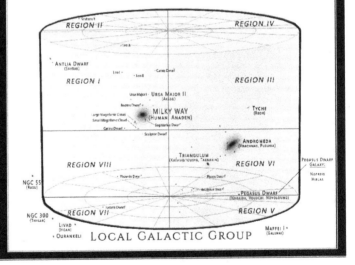

T. Vratatea A
REGION II · REGION IV

· Leo A

ANTLIA DWARF
(SAVRAK)
Leo I · · Canes Dwarf
· Leo II
REGION I
REGION III

Ursa Major I · URSA MAJOR II
(AKELSO)
Bootes Dwarf · TYCHE
Large Magellanic Cloud MILKY WAY (RADN)
Small Magellanic Cloud (HUMAN, ANADEN)
· Sagittarius Dwarf
Carina Dwarf ·
Sculptor Dwarf ·

ANDROMEDA
(VRACHNAS, PLOUSIA)

TRIANGULUM
(KATASIA, YOUSYA, ANADEN) REGION VI
REGION VIII
PEGASUS DWARF
GALAXY:
· Phoenix Dwarf · · Pisces Dwarf NOFRERE
NGC 55 HIRLAS
(RASU) · Aquarius Dwarf ·
· PEGASUS DWARF
(NARAIDA, VOLUCRI, NOVOLOUME)
· Tucana Dwarf
NGC 300 REGION VII REGION V
(THALAR)
LIVAD · MAFFEI I ·
(HOAN) (GALENAI)
· OURANKELI

LOCAL GALACTIC GROUP

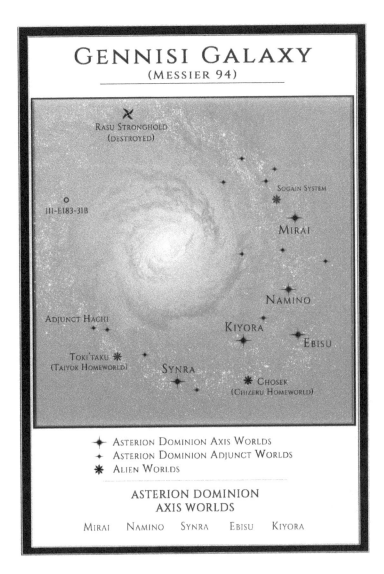

GENNISI GALAXY
(MESSIER 94)

RASU STRONGHOLD
(DESTROYED)

SOGAIN SYSTEM

111-E183-31B

MIRAI

NAMINO

ADJUNCT HACHI

KIYORA

EBISU

TOKI'TAKU
(TAIYOK HOMEWORLD)

SYNRA

CHOSEK
(CHIZERU HOMEWORLD)

✦ ASTERION DOMINION AXIS WORLDS
✦ ASTERION DOMINION ADJUNCT WORLDS
✳ ALIEN WORLDS

ASTERION DOMINION
AXIS WORLDS

MIRAI   NAMINO   SYNRA   EBISU   KIYORA

DELVE INTO THE MAPS, CHARACTERS AND MORE AT THE
AMARANTHE WIKI: GSJ.SPACE/WIKI

CONTENTS

Continuum

For a brief summary of the events of **AMARANTHE #1-13**, see
the Appendix in the back of the book.

SUBSCRIBE TO GSJENNSEN.COM

*Download free books and short stories, stay informed about new
books and be the first to know about events and other news.*

PART I

A NEW WORLD

1

AKESO

URSA MAJOR II GALAXY
LGG REGION I

B lades of grass crunch beneath the steady gait of our hooves as our powerful leg muscles propel us swiftly forward. Elements of us feel the brief pressure, the weight that flattens the blades against our earth. Elements of us feel instead the compression of our earth in response, the momentary subtraction of sunlight and oxygen before the pressure is removed and we unfurl to our former shape. Elements of us feel the resistance from the air to our movement forward, how our breeze skates along our silken coat then reforms behind us to cavort with the tree limbs we've left behind.

The rhythm of our journey through the expanse of our forest lulls us into a quiet serenity, a place where we revel in all these perceptions at once and as one—then we race beyond the tree line, out of the shadows and into the sunlight of our meadow.

Motion to the left, where the forest reclaims dominance, draws a portion of our focus. A lark darts from limb to limb upon one of our trees, a worm grasped in its beak. We feel the tree bark rough beneath our dancing feet, see ourselves through its/our eyes, take in the gleam of our majestic spiraling horns set upon the afternoon light. We soar up to a nest with our prize in tow/we resume our gallop and leave our meadow behind.

Beneath a sun cooling as it descends toward the horizon, we leap grandly into the frigid waters of our creek and bound up onto the embankment on the other side. We pause to shake droplets of water from our coat, and we are the droplets as they are flung into our air and plummet to the damp soil of our creek's bank. Then we turn and trace *the path of the bank toward the north, at a more leisurely pace now that as we have sated our fervor.*

For we sense a brief crack in the fabric of the world and with it, Her return to us.

We loiter in the clearing near the Structures, circling languidly as we munch on our lush grass at our feet and await our reunion.

Other blades of our grass compress beneath other steps, and we shift our awareness toward the movement. Warmth—joy, contentment, a stirring of anticipation—rises in our chest as we observe Her. The warmth spreads from our elafali form through our earth into our trees to frolic along our gurgling creek, and our song reaches the ears of those who would hear it.

She grins as she nears our form, the spread of Her lips brightening Her features. Her head moves side to side to send long burgundy tresses dancing across Her skin where neck meets shoulders.

She comes to a stop in front of us, Her lips curling up anew as a hand reaches out to stroke the thick hair of our long, curving neck then moves up to caress the curl of our horns. Her touch both calms and excites us, but we experience no contradiction or discord, for we are accustomed to experiencing many and varied sensations at once. We nudge our way closer and nuzzle Her neck until She laughs and steps away.

"It's time to come home. And this time, remember to get dressed before you leave the forest. We're having a guest for dinner."

RW

We feel the blades of grass, flush and cool, pressing against the heat of our skin stretched taut over our spine....

Caleb breathed in slowly, letting the crisp air fill *our*/his lungs, and let it out in a series of short puffs. He flexed his fingers, then his toes, and so bit by bit reclaimed conscious control over his body and sovereignty over his mind.

The process was second nature by now, for he'd performed it hundreds of times in the last fourteen years, but he always tried to make sure he felt at home in his own skin before he opened his eyes. Yet when his eyelashes parted his vision swam, flitting between his own limited human perception and the overwhelming cascade of Akeso's awareness. He blinked deliberately until the tumultuous sensations faded, then carefully sat up.

Of course, Akeso's awareness was never further than one of those blinks away; it required only an indefinable *shift* in his focus to access. The distance between *here* and *there* was so slight, it had taken several months of disciplined practice before he was able to keep from accidentally shifting over at random moments—at which point he usually ended up on the floor.

But that was a long time ago, back when this unique and somewhat peculiar existence of his was new and fraught with uncertainty.

He glanced around in search of his clothes, chuckling to himself at Alex's admonition as he grabbed the navy brushed-wool shirt from the mulberry-and-silver pentas plant he'd draped it on and pulled it on. It was tempting to treat Akeso like their own personal nudist colony, and sometimes they did. But the real world and its social customs intruded even here, in this wild and precious place.

As he stood and finished getting dressed, his mind settled back into itself, and his thoughts drifted to the evening to come. If they were having a guest for dinner, it must mean she'd been successful in her mission to make contact with the Asterion.

At the sound of melodic chirping, he peered up, then stretched out his arm to invite the lark dancing on a limb above to alight upon it. It wasn't truly a lark, but rather a bundle of organic material molded into Akeso's admittedly convincing imitation of one of an increasing variety of animal life. It was *Akeso* as much as the grass and trees and water and soil and planetary crust and atmosphere.

He flicked his arm, and the lark flew up into the tree canopy and vanished. He started off toward the house, purpose creeping into his gait with each step. If she'd been successful in her mission, odds were high their life was about to get interesting again.

RW

The glass-walled, two-story house sat almost precisely on the spot where the *Siyane* had first landed here nearly fifteen years ago, around forty meters from the creek where Akeso had cured the poison coursing through Alex's veins. Behind the house, shrubs and flowering plants transitioned to trees then grew into a woodland that stretched for hundreds of kilometers.

The glass remained untinted, and he could see Alex in the kitchen marinating the steaks and sliding cubes of peppers and mushrooms onto skewers. He drank her in through his own eyes this time, appreciating the way the black leggings she wore hugged her long, shapely legs. How the pewter sweater wound through with silver threads made her diamond irises dance in the light. How, as per usual, she hadn't brushed her hair in hours, making the messy knot it was now half bound into and half tumbling out of earn its name.

She'd left the front door open, and Caleb moved quietly across the porch and inside. He was barefoot, and he'd never wholly lost the skills learned in seventeen years as an intelligence agent. He crept over the distressed hardwood floor into the kitchen, slipped in behind her and wrapped his arms around her waist to kiss her neck.

"Ah!" She jumped back against his chest, and a skewer tumbled into the sink. "I swear, I'm going to put a bell on you."

"No, no. This is much more fun. You were successful? You found your mark, and she didn't immediately try to kill you?"

He'd murmured the words while his lips teased her neck; she hummed in pleasure, and he felt the subtle vibration travel down the skin of her throat and along the trimmed hair of his beard. She'd recently spent hours on board an alien starship, and beneath the scent of marinade and lemons lurked hints of ozone and something bitter, akin to chicory.

The first time he'd communed with Akeso, through blood, the experience had left him with acutely heightened senses for days. Now those heightened senses never left him.

"I got her to trust me enough to agree to come here, which I count as a success, yes."

"Good job. I'm proud of you."

She snickered, and he knew she rolled her eyes by the way her head angled briefly. He did the same. "You know what I mean."

"I do—exactly what you said."

No resentment or hurt darkened her voice, but he kissed her neck again anyway before unwinding his arms and leaning on the counter beside her. "I never doubted you. So tell me about our guest."

"She's—" they both turned at the sound of a ship descending toward the landing complex to the north of the house "—here. She's here."

He picked up the platter stacked with steaks and kabobs. "I'll take over. And wing it with her, I guess."

"I suspect you won't have any trouble." She washed her hands and dried them, then jogged out the door and toward the landing complex.

2

AKESO

As a first impression, the woman who accompanied Alex to the house closely resembled a human, in most respects more so than Anadens did. A fraction taller than Alex and sporting raven hair falling just past her shoulders, her vibrant teal irises sparkled from a thousand points of artificiality even at a distance—but so did Alex's.

It was her skin that gave her away. It shone from within, almost as if someone had painted a fine layer of glitter beneath the epidermis. Caleb couldn't say whether it was due to a pervasive cybernetics mesh or pervasive Reor/kyoseil, but it marked her as unmistakably alien.

She moved with decisive, easy efficiency. And something else...it took him longer than it should have to name it, but in fairness he was out of practice. Two opposing demeanors battled one another for dominance in her aspect: poised elegance and a honed, primed awareness of her surroundings.

So she was a fighter, and possibly a killer. Like him—like he used to be. According to Mesme she was also a diplomat, and both facets showed in equal measure in her demeanor.

As she neared, the expression she donned reminded him a little of the one Mia wore whenever she was working: a suggestion of openness painted atop a foundation of steel.

Our visitor is something new.

It had taken a while, but Akeso was on occasion starting to display a bit of curious attention to the various guests who paid them a visit. *Yes, I believe she is.*

He dialed the grill down to low and shifted toward them as they arrived at the side terrace.

"Caleb, this is Nika Kirumase. Nika, this is my husband, Caleb Marano."

The Asterion dipped her chin in a universal gesture of respect. "It's wonderful to meet you, Mr. Marano."

"Please, call me Caleb. We are as casual as it gets here. Welcome." He motioned to the grill. "Before I go any further, do you like steak? Because we also have fish, chicken and nearly everything else that's edible."

"Do I ever. I mean, assuming you're referring to red meat? I'm not using a translator, so I need to be careful of subtle differences in word meanings. My Communis is not always the same as your Communis."

"Understood, but you needn't worry. You got it right. Dinner will be ready in about twenty minutes, and will also include vegetable kabobs and wild rice."

Alex gave an exaggerated moan. "My mouth's already watering. But this means I have time to show Nika around." She motioned toward the side door, and she and their guest disappeared inside.

RW

Nika stared at him and Alex over an empty plate and an empty glass. "So let me see if I've got this correct. The Sogain—Kats, as you call them—formed a bunch of pocket universes where they ran experiments searching for ways they might defeat the Anadens, who over the millennia had become brutal and ruthless dictators. In one of those pocket universes, they used Anaden DNA to recreate the species as Humans. As you.

"Fast-forward a few time-accelerated aeons, and you—the two of you specifically—found the exit portal leading out of your pocket universe. The Kats sent a fleet of warships to wipe Humanity out, only you defeated them and kicked them out of the universe they'd created. Then you took your own fleet into their portal network to investigate what they were up to—"

Alex interrupted while she refilled the woman's wine glass. "Not a fleet. Only one ship at first. The larger one out there on the landing pad, in fact."

"An extraordinary enough ship can count as a fleet. Anyway, the Anaden leadership discovered what the Kats had been doing and moved to destroy your pocket universe and everyone in it. But Humanity brought an *actual* fleet to Amaranthe and, again, defeated an enemy who outnumbered and outpowered you. Then, Caleb, you used Praesidis *diati* to draw the Kats' network of pocket universes into Amaranthe. And now all the Humans live here alongside the Anadens and a bunch of other species."

Alex sighed dramatically; she was trying to be serious and failing. "Well, you left out most of the good parts, but that more or less covers it, yeah."

"Damn." Nika shook her head and took a long sip of her wine. She'd devoured the steak and cherry-picked the mushrooms off of three kabobs, and Caleb made a note to restock on mushrooms in case this wasn't her sole visit. Which he found himself hoping it wasn't. She was affable, pleasant and, despite his initial observation regarding her nature, didn't appear to mean them any harm. And Alex seemed to genuinely like her.

"How do the Anadens feel about you ruling them?"

Caleb nudged his plate off to the side and relaxed in his chair. "We don't rule them. We've spent years fighting and clawing to shape a governmental structure which treats all species as equal and gives everyone a voice in major decisions."

"And how's that working out?"

She also had a sharp wit that on occasion veered toward biting, but she displayed confidence more than maliciousness. "It's...working. Most days and in most ways. Alex, get that look off your face. It *is*."

"Is a disaster, you mean." Alex groaned in mostly mock disgust. "But I'll concede it's no greater of a disaster than any other government system and a damn sight better than the one it replaced. Nika, the Directorate didn't exist at the time of the SAI Rebellion, did it? Official Anaden historical records are somewhat unreliable on the subject of...on most subjects."

"I'm not surprised. History is written by the victors, right? No, or at least not by that name. The Empire called itself a republic back then. A republic that declared war on its own citizens, mind you."

"I'd like to get all high and mighty about it, but the truth is, so did ours, back when humanity resided in its cocoon. We were lucky that cooler, more reasonable heads prevailed in our case," Alex said. "You should know going in: a lot of Anadens still don't trust SAIs or hybrids or...they tend not to trust anyone, but especially synthetic-based life. Legally, synthetics enjoy the same rights as organics in Concord, and the Anadens have been forced to accept them in official interactions, but behaving in public is not the same as trust.

"Humans, though, are on the whole a lot more open-minded when it comes to synthetics. Hell, many of us are functionally closer to Asterions than we are to Anadens. Except for the kyoseil."

Kyoseil. When Mesme had first clued them in on the details of the former rebels, they had assumed kyoseil was simply the Asterion word for the substance they knew as Reor. But what this woman had interlaced into the pathways of her body was clearly not a solid, resilient block of mineral. This meant the translucent onyx mineral might in fact be a shell—a layer of protective armor— for the supradimensional fibers that ran through it. Kyoseil.

"And I am interested in hearing a great deal more about how you have mountains of kyoseil for the taking." Nika's iridescent eyes flickered and her lips pursed. He suspected they were visual cues of the effort it took for her to not say anything further, and he had to wonder exactly how badly she wanted their kyoseil.

"But all in due time. Thank you for dinner. It was delicious, and far tastier than anything I've had on my ship for the last several weeks. Also for the crash course in Humanity's story and the current geopolitical situation here. I've been away for…a long time."

Seeing an opening, Caleb leaned forward in interest. "Is it true you participated in the SAI Rebellion?"

The woman studied her empty plate for several seconds, then nodded slowly without looking up. "It's not cut-and-dried, and not many people know. But in the ways which matter? Yes, I did. I served as the diplomatic representative for the rebels, which meant I spent most of my time trying, and ultimately failing, to reach a manner of peace with the Anaden government that we could live with. That would allow us to live as we chose—or in many cases live at all."

"Brave of you to return here."

"I haven't returned as a rebel, but rather as a…" she frowned as her gaze passed between him and Alex "…neither of you seem especially taken aback by the fact I just admitted I'm seven hundred thousand years old."

Alex idly twirled her wineglass between her fingers. "You're not actually the first person we've met who's aeons old. All the Primors were, though they're also all dead now. And the Kats. No one knows exactly how long they've been alive, but they are not spring chickens. Then there was Danilo Nisi, or Corradeo, or whatever we want to call him, though he might also—"

"You don't mean Corradeo Praesidis? He can't still be alive."

He and Alex exchanged a quick look, and Caleb forced himself not to tense. "You knew him?"

"If that's the word you'd like to use. Is he?"

Caleb shrugged. "He was as of fourteen years ago. He took a ship and disappeared not long after The Displacement. Hasn't been seen since."

The man was already gone by the time Akeso returned Caleb to life, which had been a disappointment. Freed of the *diati*, he would have appreciated the opportunity to say goodbye to someone who hadn't quite been either a friend or a mentor, yet more than both. But if The Displacement had stripped Nisi of his *diati* as it did the rest of the Praesidis, the man likely would not have had any interest in speaking to Caleb, so perhaps it had worked out for the best.

Nika sank deeper in her chair and brought a hand to her chin. "He wasn't a member of the Anaden leadership—the Directorate?"

"No, he was the leader of the rebellion against it."

The woman snorted. "Bullshit."

Alex laughed. "Fair response, but no bullshit. It's a long, torrid story, but the short version is, around six hundred thousand years ago his son, Renato, tried to kill him. Renato thought he'd succeeded and stole his father's name, face and authority. The *diati* spirited Corradeo away to a safe location and healed him. He sulked around this corner of the universe for a few hundred thousand years before returning and joining up with a ragtag group of rebels. To his credit, he transformed them into a rebellion worthy of the title, and when we arrived in Amaranthe, he welcomed us as allies in the fight. Mostly."

"I can't believe it. I..." Nika abruptly leaned forward into the table, piercing eyes fixed on Caleb "...*that's* who you remind me of. It's been nagging at me all evening."

It was a testament to the intensity of the woman's gaze—or possibly the reason for it being directed at him—that Caleb deeply wanted to squirm. He never squirmed under scrutiny. "Technically, it was my father who favored the man." He shrugged, forcing levity into the act. "A genetic accident."

"One which enables you to control *diati*."

"Enabled." He cleared his throat and stood to busy himself gathering their plates. "That's all in the past."

"I'm sorry. I didn't mean to broach such a personal topic."

He placed the plates in the sink and glanced back toward the table. "No need to apologize. If I haven't gotten over it in fourteen years, that's on me."

He inhaled through his nose and listened to the ebb and flow of Akeso breathing for a moment, then shook it off and rejoined them at the table. "I don't mean to sound bitter. I'm grateful to the *diati.* It empowered me to save humanity from almost certain annihilation. But through me, it also killed eight billion people, only one of whom deserved it. *Diati* isn't a force for good or evil—it's simply a force. One I have no interest in ever wielding again."

Nika considered him with an almost sad glint in her keen eyes. "I understand. Let's change the subject to something more pleasant. What do the two of you do when you're not saving the world? This place is exquisite and amazing, but I bet you still put the gorgeous ship out there on the landing pad to good use."

Alex perked up at the mention of her favorite topic. "She's called the *Siyane*, and we do. We spend much of our time scouting out previously unknown alien species on behalf of Concord. The Directorate wiped out so many species during their reign, but they didn't get them all, not even in the nearby galaxies. And we're gradually pushing the exploration boundaries out farther, beyond the fringes of the Local Galactic Group. We locate undiscovered species, evaluate them and recommend a course of action to Concord. Well, I locate them. Caleb evaluates them."

He offered her an indulgent smile. "You help evaluate them."

"Ha. Not that time with those Icksel creatures, where instead of helping, I damn near inspired a new religion—not on purpose. Never mind. It's a terrible story." She reached out and squeezed his hand on the table. "You're sweet to say so. A liar, but sweet."

Then she shifted back to Nika. "I have a thousand questions about the Rasu, but I know I hate repeating myself, so I won't make you do it. We'll go see my mother in the morning, and you can tell us all at one time about the Rasu."

"Your...mother?"

"My, um...progenitor? The woman who gave birth—I mean, she didn't technically *give* birth to me, we use artificial wombs, but she and my father...."

A sly smirk grew on Nika's lips, and Caleb stifled a chuckle.

Alex's nose scrunched up. "What?"

"I know what a mother is. We don't reproduce in such a manner, but we certainly recognize how virtually all organic species do."

"Oh." Alex's cheeks reddened. "I'm sorry, that was clumsy of me. No one will ever mistake me for a diplomat."

"You're doing fine. I merely meant why your mother in particular."

"Because she's the leader of the military, and from what little I do know about the Rasu, they sound as if they are begging for an armed response."

"Leader of Humanity's military? Impressive."

"Actually, leader of all the Concord militaries. She's very good at her job."

"She must be."

An alert popped up in Caleb's eVi, and he quickly focused it...and groaned. *Goddammit!* He read it a second time then sent a follow-up query for additional information. With a grumble, he pushed away from the table. "I hate to do it, but I need to run. Family business."

Alex's eyes widened at him. "Again?"

"Apparently. I swear, I am going to drag her back to Seneca by her toes and lock her in a steel fortress."

"That didn't work last time."

"I know. I'll think of something better while I'm on the way." He turned to their guest wearing an appropriately chagrined expression. "I am so sorry I have to skip out on you. Please, you two enjoy the rest of the evening. I'll try my best to meet you at Concord HQ tomorrow in time for the meeting."

Nika smiled graciously. "Of course. Thank you again for a delicious dinner."

Alex pushed away from the table as well. "I'll be right back."

She followed him through the kitchen to the hall storage. "Where is she this time?"

He grabbed one of the plasma blades and stuck the hilt in his pants pocket; his gaze passed over the Daemon holstered on the wall and kept going. "Savrak."

"Fuck." She reached up, unholstered the Daemon and offered it to him. "Take it. Just in case."

He hesitated, staring at the gun instead of her...then accepted it and clipped it to his belt.

Cold metal, foreign and angry. This object causes disquiet.

In Akeso, or himself? Once upon a time, the weapon had acted as a natural extension of his hand. No longer. "I'll take *Puddle Jumper* and get Mia to authorize me through the temporary Prism leading to the Savrak system. This way, you can take Nika to Concord HQ in the *Siyane* tomorrow."

"Be careful. And patient."

"Oh, I'll be patient, don't worry. I won't kill her until we're safely in Concord space."

"That's not what the Daemon's for."

"Hmm." He drew her into his arms, letting his lips brush lightly over hers. "Love you. I'll see you in the morning."

3

AKESO

A burst of light flared from the Caeles Prism positioned two hundred meters above the landing complex, signifying Caleb's departure in their backup transport, as Alex stepped out onto the front porch, two fresh glasses of wine in hand.

Nika stood at the porch railing, and her gaze had gone to the Prism when it activated. "It's a wormhole generator, isn't it?"

"Probably not too different from what you use on your ship." Alex handed her one of the glasses and joined her at the railing.

A clear night had fallen in full, casting the creek in shadows lit by tiny sparkles of reflected starlight in the water. A melodic hum permeated the air; the soft chirp of a harmony from somewhere among the trees soon joined it, and the gurgling of the creek provided a quiet, rhythmic beat to impose order. She pulsed Caleb.

Akeso is putting on a musical performance for Nika. Your idea?

Me? Never. Akeso must be in a mood to hum a tune tonight.

Uh-huh. Well done.

Alex watched with some amusement as the woman gradually began to realize the sounds weren't merely the background noises of nature. Her brow furrowed and her eyes darted around; finally, she tilted her head toward Alex. "Is the planet...singing?"

"It is. I think it likes you."

"I know you told me it was alive, but it's truly *alive*?"

"Alive, self-aware and intelligent, though not in a way familiar to us. In sixty galaxies we haven't discovered any other life remotely like it. The Kats are exceptionally clever, but Akeso might well be their greatest achievement."

"What? The Kats created Akeso?"

Alex nodded. "It was a Mosaic world, along with two of its siblings. The first inhabited Mosaic system Caleb and I ever visited, in fact. The siblings weren't quite so friendly as Akeso—the first planet we touched down on perceived us as a threat and tried to kill us. It poisoned me, but when we came here, Akeso healed me. Thus was the beginning of our…unusual relationship with the planet."

"Does this mean you have a part of Akeso inside of you as well, the same as Caleb?"

"A little bit. Not like him, though. When Akeso feels something very strongly, I can feel it, too. But it doesn't speak to me in…Caleb calls them 'thought-words.' It doesn't converse in a language, but its thoughts become words in his mind."

"Is it odd, him being so closely connected to the planet? If you don't mind me asking."

Alex instinctively queued up a noncommittal answer, but instead of delivering it, she paused to take a sip of her drink. Though they scarcely knew one another, she already felt a kind of kinship with the woman. Here they were enjoying a lovely evening over a bottle of wine while the planet sang to them.

She perched her glass on the railing and leaned closer to her guest, as if to whisper conspiratorially. "The first time he had an orgasm after joining with Akeso, the entire planet convulsed in a 4.2 magnitude earthquake."

Nika gasped and brought a hand to her mouth, eyes wide. "It *didn't.*"

"Oh, yes, it did."

"I can't even imagine…" the woman laughed "…how did you react?"

"At the time, I laughed the way you are right now. What else was I supposed to do?" She sighed whimsically and draped her arms atop the railing. "After that happened, they developed methods for Akeso to…not disconnect, because it doesn't work like that, but to 'look the other way,' as it were. And Caleb, too. The symphony of an entire planet going about its business can get rather loud and raucous at times."

"Incredible." Nika seemed to ponder on it briefly. "Do you regret him joining with the planet?"

"No! Never." She huffed a breath. "I won't deny there have been challenges...including a few I didn't anticipate...or that it's changed him in some tangible ways. But he would have died, would have been lost to me forever. This was the only way. So, no, I don't regret it for a second."

They fell silent for a moment. She assumed Nika was noodling through the implications and possibly wondering about the challenges Alex had alluded to but not elaborated on. They weren't that good of friends yet.

"Humans can't use regenesis, then?"

"You are asking a complicated question replete with political, scientific, religious and philosophical tangles. Not back then, no, they couldn't. Except for..." she stopped herself, as the story of her father's rebirth would take the rest of the night to tell and still be unbelievable at the end of it "...special circumstances. Now, some can. Prevos certainly can, so long as the Artificial half survived whatever befell the human half. Sorry, Prevos are people who, like me, have merged at a neurological level with an Artificial."

"That was what kicked off the SAI Rebellion for us. People started merging with SAIs, and the government refused to stand for it. I have a memory from the time and—I should mention, Asterions can relive memories, their own and those belonging to other people, with as much vividness as if the remembered event were happening all over again. So I have this memory of being...two. Myself and my SAI, KIR. It was honestly a beautiful experience. Comforting, to be so close to another living being."

"It's not that way for you now?"

"No. We are Anaden and SAI and kyoseil, yes, but the psyche that results from the combination is whole and singular. I'm me, and only me." Nika cleared her throat and hurriedly took a sip of wine. "But what about you? You have a bonded SAI?"

Alex looked toward the sky. "Oh, Valkyrie...."

In seconds a golden swirl of lights materialized on the porch to quickly solidify into the form of a woman. Not solid, but far more substantial than when the Artificial had first begun to instantiate in the physical world. A long, blond braid wound over her left shoulder and down to her waist. Her attire was practical, dark gray suede workpants and a loose white shirt. Her skin was tanned, as if she'd spent a lifetime outdoors.

Nika jumped. "Oh...are you a Kat?"

Valkyrie laughed in a soft, elegant timbre that wouldn't be out of place in the lobby of an opera house. "No, though I can understand the confusion. A Kat taught me how to instantiate, so it's probable I continue to mimic their process more than I have a need to." She extended a hand toward Nika. "I'm Valkyrie, and you are Nika Kirumase."

Nika hesitantly reached a hand out in kind, then started when Valkyrie's hand grasped hers with real-world tactile pressure. "Oh my, this is remarkable. It's a pleasure to meet you, Valkyrie."

"The pleasure is mine. In truth, I'm most excited to meet an Asterion. I have a thousand questions—"

Not now, okay?

"—but I'm sure we will get an opportunity to chat in the coming days."

"I look forward to it."

"Wonderful. Now, if you will pardon me, I need to return to Earth, where I am engaged in a most lively discussion of the conditions necessary to create and manipulate a white hole." The lights dissipated into the air, and she was gone.

Nika blinked and took a longer sip from her glass. "Wow. She was quite something. Is that what SAIs are like now?"

Alex chuckled wryly. "Valkyrie would insist she's one of a kind, and she wouldn't be wrong. They're not any one way, frankly. Many don't instantiate the way she just did. It's an advanced skill. Some have physical bodies—usually humanoid forms, but not always, as Artificials seem to be fascinated by wild animals for some reason. And some are content to reside in their hardware."

"If they inhabit a Humanoid-shaped body, can they blend? Can you tell the difference?"

"Not always. A lot of them prefer to mark themselves as Artificial, usually through a flashy glyph pattern or some distinctly non-human physical feature. But if they don't?" Alex shrugged.

"We went to war over such events."

"As I said earlier, we almost did, too. Or humans did. Caleb and I were in the Mosaic and missed most of the ugliness." A memory of the night Romane burned flashed in her mind in vibrant color...Abigail's body in Devon's arms amidst a pool of blood...a face in the window of a building crumbling by her own hand.... "Not all of it. But thanks to some wonderful people, we got through it.

"Artificials aren't without controversy, even among humans. But so many people have become Prevos or at least Mélanges that the hard distinctions have gotten rather blurry. Plus, the newest cybernetics are so sophisticated, they've nearly reached an Artificial level of processing power.

"The continuum that starts with a pure human and ends with a pure Artificial is fairly crowded, and it's proved difficult to craft legal boundaries when you can't discern where to draw the lines. Mind you, this hasn't stopped every legislature from continuing to *try*, but it's mostly ineffectual blustering."

She went to take another sip of wine and realized her glass was empty. She peered over at Nika's and found it nearly so. "Let me grab the bottle and turn on the heating panels. Akeso, it's cold!"

She tapped the control panel inside the door to turn the porch heat up, then puttered through the kitchen to grab the open wine bottle and back outside.

Nika had settled into one of the retro-style rocking chairs. Alex did so as well and set the bottle on the floor between them.

"Thanks. You said some Artificials use physical bodies—are they true functioning organic bodies?"

"No. That's still illegal, for now. They're basically life-sized dolls equipped with the quantum hardware to house an Artificial's consciousness."

"Mmm." Nika made a strange face. "Sorry. 'Doll' is a pejorative term back in the Dominion for an Asterion who uses a remote-controlled avatar instead of a real body." Her lips twitched. "But that's my society, not yours. I'm not judging. So does Valkyrie have a...doll?"

"She has one that she keeps stashed on Earth for special occasions."

"Special occasions?"

Alex groaned dramatically and rocked her chair back. "Sex and fancy dinner parties, mostly. I think. I try not to peek in at inopportune times."

"Having spent an entire thirty seconds with her, I believe it. So then you two aren't bonded any longer?"

"Oh, we're definitely bonded. As to whether we're truly merged? It's complicated. She has her own life, in a way she couldn't when we first merged. And of course I have mine. But she's never more than a half-formed thought away. Like what happened here a few minutes ago. Physically, she was thirty kiloparsecs away, but a part of her is always present in my mind. As a result, she was able to materialize here instantly." Alex smiled. "Also, I get to keep all the added processing power and other cool tricks that come courtesy of Artificials. It's a good deal for both of us."

"Sounds as if it is." Nika set her glass down...then picked it back up again. "And the Kat? When will I get to meet this 'Mesme'?"

"Soon, I hope. Mesme can be tough to pin down, and it's the easiest to wrangle of the Kats. It's as apt to pop in without warning, the way Valkyrie did, as to show up for an arranged meeting, so be on the lookout."

"Right." Nika leaned forward and dropped her elbows to her knees with a sudden intensity. "Who I genuinely want to meet is *my* Kat—the Sogain with whom I've interacted. And when I say 'meet,' I don't mean in a 'mysterious voice in my head' or 'while I'm suspended in the void by nothing but a cloud of swirly lights' way. I mean real and in the…as in the flesh as they get."

"It suspended you in the middle of space? Just your body?"

"It did."

"Asshole. Still, it could have been worse. The first time I met Mesme, it kidnapped me and held me captive for over a day, under guard of a dragon, while it tortured me by forcing me to relive a highlight reel of the worst moments in my life and humanity's history."

Nika stared at her incredulously. "And you're *friends* with this creature now?"

"Eh, yes? It's…complicated. I'm sorry, I know I keep using that word, and it isn't particularly illuminating. After what was a most inauspicious beginning, Mesme helped us to defeat its own kind when the Kats invaded our pocket universe. It protected us countless times, even when doing so resulted in its exile. It convinced the other Kats to fight on our side and played a crucial role in defeating the Directorate. After The Displacement, it searched for weeks to find Akeso so Caleb could have a chance to come back to life."

She winced. "I guess what I'm saying is, the Kats aren't great with introductions."

Nika burst out laughing. "To put a fine point on it."

"But if you're…damn, I almost said 'patient with them,' but I've never been patient with anyone in my life, and certainly not with Mesme. But if you accept them as they are, while holding them accountable when they need to be, you'll never find a more loyal ally."

Nika stood to wander aimlessly around the porch. "The thing is, right now, I don't feel as if I have an ally at all in the Sogain, loyal or otherwise. Yes, they pointed us to a lone Rasu, through which we were able to learn a great deal about our enemy. And they conspired with Mesme to bring you and me together. But they have such phenomenal technology at their disposal. I don't understand why they wouldn't actually *help*. Fight at our side."

Alex had spent untold hours ruminating on the same question, usually in frustration and more than once in anger. She'd finally reached a sort of resigned acceptance of their nature, though in fairness, it could simply be because she hadn't desperately needed the Kats' help in a while.

"I'm afraid the Kats have a 'you should do it yourself or it won't stick' mindset. Getting useful information out of them is more frustrating than herding cats, but they somehow always seem to nudge you in the right direction until you *do* eventually get it done yourself. And possibly…maybe…on occasion…grow as a person or a species as a result."

"And I mean, there are exceptions to their policy. They evacuated dozens of less advanced species from Amaranthe that the Directorate would have slaughtered or enslaved and sheltered them in the Mosaic. So, in reality, your Kat was paying the Asterions a compliment. It believed you were strong enough and capable enough to protect yourselves. And it was correct."

Nika scowled over the rim of her glass. "Nonetheless."

"I hear you. Anyway, your Kat's name is Tyche. I don't have a direct line to it, but I'll see what I can do to arrange a meeting."

"Tyche? As in the Greek goddess of providence? An odd choice for a name."

"Most of the Kats are named after Greek mythological figures."

"Whyever?"

"I asked that question a few years ago. It turns out, those aren't their original names. When they integrated into the Anaden Empire as an Accepted Species, they chose those names so as to appear to be paying homage to and honoring Anaden cultural history."

"Except not really, though."

"Not really."

"Crafty, enigmatic bundles of light."

"You have no idea."

"Then I look forward to finding out."

"You might regret saying so." Alex pushed the chair back and stood. "It's getting late, and we have a big day tomorrow. You should find everything you need in the guest cottage, but there are intercoms inside the front door and the bedroom. Tap it and shout if there's a problem—or you can sleep on your ship if you want. Whichever you prefer."

"I think I'll spend a night with your living planet here. It ought to be interesting."

4

SAVRAK

ANTLIA DWARF GALAXY
LGG REGION II

M arlee Marano stretched out on the stone-hard bench, kicked her feet up on the wall, and folded her hands behind her head.

After a few seconds, she shifted her hips around in a futile attempt at relative comfort. The bench was narrow with open notches on both sides, like all Savrakath furniture, on account of their tails—so narrow, in fact, that she found she needed to cross her ankles in order to balance on it.

One of the jail guards passed by the front glass wall of her cell and stopped to check in on her.

She rolled her head toward the glass and shot him a challenging glare. *"Okegho kankii."*

He snarled and lunged toward the glass, but caught himself at the last second. He settled for baring his filed, razor-sharp teeth at her before moving on.

In his absence, her eyes searched the cell for something to ruminate on, but it was as empty and bare as a Kat's food cupboard. The sulfur walls had mottled from seeping moisture that inexorably invaded from outside. The lack of mildew meant the staff scrubbed the walls regularly, but no amount of scouring could remove these stains.

Beads of sweat dribbled down her temple and plopped to the floor. Her eVi worked diligently to keep her body temperature in a healthy range, but the moisture it generated in doing so had to go somewhere. Because damn was it *hot*. And humid, so bloody humid.

The Savrakaths' capital city—ingeniously named Savradin to distinguish it from the species who called it home—was built in the pit of a swamp, and while the aliens did a respectable job of trying to keep the swamp where it belonged, in the end the swamp always won.

She'd known enough going in to dress for the climate, but she'd been here for forty miserable hours now. Her periwinkle tank top clung in damp splotches to her skin, and her once-white gauze knee-pants, splattered by mud during a doomed chase and soaked by sweat in the hours since, had darkened to a blotchy taupe color. She'd hold a burning ceremony for them when she got home. Invite some friends over for the occasion, order in a bartending module, make a right party of it.

Home...she glanced back at the glass wall, but with the guard absent it revealed only an empty hall, so she fixated instead on the speckled ceiling above her. There was likely to be a line of people winding around the block waiting to yell at her when she got home. She'd seriously bollocksed things up this time.

But only because her plan hadn't worked. And it had been *so close* to working! But for an unexpected guard patrol rounding the corner at the worst possible of all possible seconds, she and her charge would have completed their escape.

She was here on Savrak on an errand for the Concord Consulate, sent to deliver requested volumes of information on the niggling details of Concord's appallingly sparse Code of Rights. The Savrakaths didn't want to be bothered with actually abiding by said Code of Rights—which was the price of admission into Concord's good graces—so their latest tactic was to quibble over the interpretation of every sentence, bullet point and dependent clause then mumble something about exceptions for cultural traditions.

For reasons she couldn't fathom, the Consulate was currently humoring this tactic. And since the Savrakaths weren't hooked into Concord's exanet, she had been dispatched to ferry a hefty set of documents, saved onto one of the Savrakaths' barely quantum storage disks, to their ambassador.

The diminutive Godjan assistant showed Marlee into the ambassador's office deep in the Savradin Government Hall. The alien kept her watery eyes down and her wide chin dropped, repeatedly bowing as she scurried on frog-like legs into the office ahead of Marlee.

"Ambassador-sir, the Concord representative is here to see you."

Ambassador Darhk growled, "You know better than to bother me unannounced! You will—"

Marlee cleared her throat loudly and marched to the front of his desk before the translator had finished its work; she spoke Savrakan plenty well enough to get the gist of his tirade-in-the-making.

"Ambassador Darhk, on behalf of Senator Requelme and the Concord Consulate, I am here to present to you the vital documentation you requested on Concord's esteemed and hallowed Code of Rights." She held out the disk with both hands and practically shoved it in his face. "I was told it was most urgent for you to receive this information, so we can move forward with cementing a fruitful relationship between our peoples. Forgive your assistant, for I was excessively rude in my insistence to deliver this package to you forthwith. As you requested."

Darhk's glistening nostrils flared as he stared at her with wide-set, reptilian irises. Finally, he snatched the disk from her hands and set it on his desk. "I should have expected insolence from a Human. So arrogant. You are here at my dispensation, Human, and you will obey our customs."

She swallowed a snicker. He wouldn't dare physically harm her while she was on Savrakath government property; Mia never would have allowed her to come here without an escort if she were in any danger. The Savrakaths wanted this alliance far too much to risk violence on a Concord official. Errand-girl and entry-level researcher, granted, but an official one. "Forgive my ignorance. I will endeavor to educate myself on your etiquette and conventions more fully before my next visit."

"See that you do."

The assistant took a meek step toward the desk. "Ambassador-sir, shall I place the disk in—"

Darhk sprung out of his chair and swung a long arm, claws extended, across the assistant's face. The Godjan stumbled backward and fell to the floor. "I told you never to interrupt me, vermin!"

The Godjan brought a trembling hand to her face, where blood trickled out of three deep slashes in her cheek. "Yes, Ambassador-sir. Mercy, please."

"I tire of your persistent disobedience. You will report to the Okshakin for discipline. And get the mess you've made on the floor cleaned up."

"Yes, Ambassador-sir." The Godjan half-crawled out of the room, tears streaming down her face.

Marlee bit back a half-dozen righteous diatribes. "Ambassador, respectfully, the Godjan did not interrupt you. If you had more you intended on saying to me, the knowledge of it was yours alone."

"You dare to question my actions in my office on my planet? Out, Human. I will instruct Senator Requelme to send someone better behaved on any future visits."

As if anyone ever 'instructed' Mia to do anything. Marlee spun wordlessly and marched out of the office. The vile lizard!

No, she hurriedly corrected herself. Darhk wasn't vile because he was a lizard; his species didn't matter. He was vile because he was vile.

So what was she willing to do about it? She scanned the hallway and spotted the Godjan assistant limping away off to the left. Marlee jogged that way until she caught up. "Hey, excuse me. Are you all right?"

The Godjan stopped and gaped at her, large aqueous eyes made enormous by terror and pain. "Y-yes-s. Apolog—forgiv—I meant no—must go."

"Calm down. I'm not going to hurt you. What the ambassador did was horrible! You need to get those gashes treated, or they'll become infected. Is there a medical station in the building?"

"No, must go to Okshakin now or else...must go now."

"Or else what?"

The Godjan peered furtively in both directions, then leaned in close. "Will be stricken out, sent into the swamps to starve and die."

"And what if you do go to this 'Okshakin'?" The word translated roughly as 'reformatory,' and she didn't care for the implications. "What discipline will they inflict?"

"Reeducation. Punishment. Then shock collar. Not removable. Easier for masters to reinforce discipline."

Bastards! Marlee made a snap decision. "No. This is inexcusable. What's your name?"

"Vaihe, ma'am."

"Okay, Vaihe, here's what we're going to do. You're going to come with me to the spaceport, where I have a transport ship waiting for me. I'm going to get you somewhere safe."

"But I can't—"

She put both her hands on the little Godjan's shoulders. "Yes, you can. All you have to do is follow me and do what I say until we get on the ship. After that, no one will ever give you an order again. Understand?"

Vaihe's chin bounced twice.

"Great. Now trail a step behind me. We're heading straight for the exit."

RW

The Savrakath security guard held out a claw, blocking her path out of the Hall. "Wait. Where are you taking this Godjan?"

Marlee gave him a stern glare. "She is a goodwill gift from Ambassador Darhk to Senator Requelme of the Concord Consulate. Now let us pass."

"I need to confirm this with the ambassador. You will wait here." The guard loped off to a desk in the far corner.

Shit. She searched around for anything she could use to distract the guard from his task...a group of Godjans toiled in some kind of swamp garden in the center of the lobby, hopelessly struggling to make transplanted plants grow. Only now did she notice that three of them wore collars around their necks. Shock collars.

The abuse had been occurring in plain sight, right in front of them. She should have seen it earlier. Everyone who had visited Savrak should have seen it earlier.

Her hand went into her small emergency pouch and retrieved a tiny object, as it was important to have a fallback plan. She reached behind her, took Vaihe's hand in hers, and whispered under her breath, "Get ready."

She lifted her chin and tossed her hair defiantly. "Godjans! Listen to me! It is time to rise up against your masters! Allow them to repress and torture you no longer! Fight for your freedom! Throw off your chains and fight!"

The Godjans stared at her, then at each other—then one of them leapt out of the garden and punched the first guard they came to, she was fairly certain in a most sensitive area. Emboldened, the other Godjans poured out of the garden and tackled another guard. She considered being surprised it took so little to set them off, but then again she'd never been enslaved and ritually humiliated.

Marlee grinned to herself and turned back to the doorway. "Now, we run."

They burst through the doors and out into the sweltering midday air. The spaceport was a kilometer away, across an alameda and through a commercial district. She didn't yet know how she was going to get past the spaceport security if they became alerted to the scene she'd instigated, but she'd figure it out when she got there. Hopefully, the guards here would have their claws full handling the disturbance for a while.

RW

Vaihe was panting by the time they came out the other side of the commercial district.

"It's only a short way farther. We're almost there. When we round the next corner, we'll start walking normally, okay?"

Vaihe nodded with her whole upper body, and they hurried forward—

—a Savrakath guard stepped out from the next intersection, weapon raised. "Halt!"

Marlee spun to the right, searching for an alley, only to find two additional guards advancing from behind them.

She slowly lifted her hands in the air. As she did, she slid one up Vaihe's arm and pressed the tiny comm device she'd lifted from CINT storage a few weeks ago onto the Godjan's sleeve. "I'm obeying your order. Please don't harm us."

The guards advanced in on them, tightening their circle. They carried long rifles, which were about to get unwieldy in such close personal space.

Another decision made, she queued up a series of commands in her eVi.

They closed to within a meter. Come on, move a little closer....

One of the guards produced a set of manacles. "Lower your hands and prepare to be restrained. Both of you."

"I will. I just need to—" Marlee shoved Vaihe into the gap between two of the officers. "Run!"

She produced a plasma blade hilt security hadn't detected, activated it, and slashed one of the guards across an arm. Then she pivoted and grabbed the barrel of one of the long rifles and yanked it toward her, sending its wielder stumbling into another guard.

In the corner of her vision, she saw Vaihe vanish down the next street. She dropped the first rifle, grabbed the barrel of a second rifle with both hands—a simple task given it was pointed directly at her head—and sent a powerful stun pulse racing out from her skin and through the metal barrel.

Everything went black.

Marlee grimaced and ran a hand through her hair, now so sweat-soaked she might as well have gone for a swim. It felt both spiky and frizzy all at once, which she imagined made her look like a proper horror show.

She'd tried contacting Vaihe multiple times, since she'd swiped the access code to the comm unit when she'd pilfered it, to no avail.

A security team had probably caught up to the Godjan girl and arrested her, if not shot her dead on the spot.

If so, her death was on Marlee's conscience. But the recalcitrant part of her brain insisted that death must be preferable to slavery, beatings and shock collars. To suffering such degrading humiliation at the hands of repugnant, disgusting masters.

As soon as she got home, she was going to have an earful ready to go for Mia and anyone else who would listen. The Savrakaths didn't belong anywhere near Concord.

But she had to get home first. If this cell were located on any Concord world, no matter the species, she'd have been able to break herself out in ten minutes flat. Unfortunately, the Savrakaths used native technology. They zealously guarded its functional details, not allowing outsiders so much as a peek at it.

She'd given the cell security a shot anyway, and had gotten as far as the authorization levels before hitting a virtual brick wall—

"Incitement to riot? Really?"

Her gaze shot to the glass wall; she whipped her legs around, sprung off the bench, and leapt the two meters to the wall, where she pressed open palms against the glass. "Gramps! You came!"

David Solovy arched an eyebrow, but he was smiling. "When I heard one of the charges was 'incitement to riot,' I couldn't resist. I had to get the story straight from the source."

She crossed her arms over her chest. "The riot was *supposed* to be a diversion. Turns out the Godjans suck at rioting."

"Who knew?"

"Not me, obviously. So, Gramps…can you get me out of here?"

David glanced down the hall toward the entrance. He wasn't her biological grandfather, of course—more like her great uncle-in-law or something—but she'd called him 'Gramps' since around five minutes after she'd met him when she was six years old. She'd commed him when she'd woken up in custody here. It wasn't the first time she'd landed in a tight spot and needed his help.

"I am working on it. Relations with the Savrakaths are at a delicate stage right now. Everything about our dealings with them is delicate right now. So it might take me a couple of hours, but I'll find a way."

"You're the best."

"I definitely am. While we wait on the wheels of justice to spin, do you want to tell me what happened?"

"I've discovered the most horrible—" Her eyes narrowed in accusation as a new visitor appeared from down the hall to approach the cell. "Dammit, did you comm him?"

Caleb scowled darkly at her as he reached the cell. "I'm sure he was just about to—" the scowl veered to his father-in-law "—weren't you, David?"

David shrugged. "Honestly? I hadn't planned on it. Marlee and I can handle this."

"That's right. We don't need your help." She glared at Caleb. Him, on the other hand, she'd stopped calling 'Uncle' the first time he bailed her out of jail, when she was thirteen. The arrest had totally been the result of a silly misunderstanding, but he hadn't believed her.

"Okay. I guess I'll take this release order and go back home." He pivoted and started heading down the hall.

"Wait!" She pressed up close to the glass. "You mean you can get me out now?"

Caleb half-turned, then made a show of taking a few hesitant steps back toward the cell. "In the next ten minutes. But if you don't want—"

"Yes. I want to get out of here as quickly as possible."

"All right. There are conditions."

She groaned and dropped a shoulder against the glass. "Shocking. What are they?"

"You're being released into the custody of the Consulate, which until we get home means me, pending a hearing on a list of serious charges. No skipping out, or you'll be facing Concord charges as well. And you will apologize to Mia, in person, within the next twenty-four hours or else—"

"Or else what? You'll ground me? You *can't*."

"No. I'll get you fired."

"You wouldn't dare!"

"I would and I will. Mia trusted you to represent the Consulate here, and you betrayed her trust. You might have irreparably damaged the diplomatic negotiations."

"But that Godjan was about to be tortured! I had to try to rescue her. Besides, I don't see how we can ever let the Savrakaths ally with Concord. They're brutal and backward. They have slaves!"

"They've vehemently denied the charge. And even if it's true, you know perfectly well that to become a Concord ally, they'll have to end any slavery they may or may not be practicing and recognize the legal rights of all residents. Once this happens, you can work within the system to ensure the lives of these Godjans improve— but only if you're still working for the Consulate."

"That's blackmail."

"Yes, it is. Are you going to pay up?"

Her forehead banged against the glass in defeat. He had her, dammit. "Oh, fine."

"Good. Like I said, it'll be ten minutes before the approvals come through. If you'll excuse us, David and I need to have a private conversation."

David gave Marlee a private, exaggerated wince before he turned and followed Caleb down the hall.

RW

Caleb stepped out the front doors of the Savradin security compound and into the stifling heat of a midday sun. He already regretted not changing out of his wool shirt before leaving Akeso. When the door had closed behind him, he turned to face David. "You should have commed me the second she reached out to you."

His father-in-law smiled almost placidly. "I knew I wouldn't need to. Richard's taught me quite a few things about spycraft over the years. I assume you control listeners embedded in the Concord security network tagged with a list of names. You found out she'd been arrested the instant Savrakath officials reported it to Concord."

"That's true. But you don't get to use it as an excuse for failing to contact me. How were you planning to get her out? Invoke Miriam's authority?"

"*Bozhestvo*, no. The Savrakaths have been flaunting itchy trigger fingers when it comes to the Concord military, and we're trying to prevent a war, not start one. No, I was just going to wing it. Bullshit my way through."

"You were going to bullshit your way through the Savrakath criminal justice system?"

David shrugged. "Yes?"

Caleb laughed in spite of himself. David would have succeeded, too; other than having been dead for twenty-five years of it, the man seemed to live a charmed life. He forced his countenance to darken nonetheless. "You've got to stop coddling her."

"And you've got to stop treating her like a child."

"She *is* a child. Dropping the '-teen' from her age doesn't make her an adult. Acting like one does. Or doesn't, so far."

"When did you turn into the party-spoiler disciplinarian of the family?"

"Probably around the time I killed eight billion people."

David's expression didn't so much as flicker. "Touché. But it doesn't mean you need to be the grumpy uncle here."

David had never attempted to coddle Caleb when it came to the horrific events at Solum fourteen years ago. Never offered platitudes or patted his head in feigned comfort.

Caleb deeply appreciated this about his father-in-law, but it didn't change the fact that David did coddle Marlee. "Someone has to, apparently. Listen, I am simply trying to protect her. At the rate she is going, she will get herself killed in short order, and very possibly kick off a war in the process.

"Do you know why she's still a child? Because she has no appreciation for her own mortality. She has no appreciation for loss, for consequences. She's never been *hurt*, not in a way that leaves an invisible scar on her soul forever. I want to make sure when she inevitably is, it doesn't spell the end of her."

David wiped a thin sheen of sweat off his brow. "I don't disagree with you, in principle. But you can't protect her—it's impossible. Life always bullies its way in to wreak its havoc whether we want it to or not. The best we can do for her is be someone she'll come to when it does all come crashing down on her. Now, I'm happy to be that person, but I suspect she'd really prefer it if you were as well. Or even instead." David paused. "Besides, the reality is, she's smarter and more talented than any of us. There's no cage you can devise that she won't escape."

"The Savrakaths appear to have done so."

"Eh, give her six hours. She'd be out and cruising home."

Caleb's chin dropped to his chest. "Well, I can still make her face up to the consequences of her actions."

"You can try. Do you want me to take her to Concord HQ? I promise I will ensure she makes it to the Consulate and pays up on her blackmail."

Caleb sent a quick pulse before answering.

Eren, I'm briefly on Savrak. Everything good with you and the team?

My skin has melted off and I've mutated into a swamp creature. This is my home now.

Okay, just checking. Tell everyone hello for me.

"Actually, we're all headed to HQ. There's a meeting this morning you'll want to sit in on."

"Alex's mission?"

Caleb nodded.

"Is it all right with you if Marlee rides with me? I suspect she's been through the ringer here and...."

"And she doesn't need me lecturing her for the next hour?"

"You said it, not me."

Caleb sighed. He didn't care for the party-spoiler disciplinarian side of him any more than Marlee did. If she could only appreciate how precious her life was—how precious *she* was—and stop kamikazeing her way through it like she had nothing to lose!

"Yes, she can ride with you. But will you promise me you'll give her a stern look before you serve her the gelato I know you have stashed on your ship?"

"Two stern looks. On my honor."

5

SAVRAK

*E*ren Savitas asi-Idoni (mission): "Felzeor, how do the skies look
this morning?"

Felzeor (mission): "Even higher humidity than yesterday. The
clouds are sticking to my feathers, with no wind to usher them past—"

Eren (mission): "I meant the facility."

Felzeor (mission): "But it's on the ground, not in the skies."

Eren (mission): "Smartass bird."

Felzeor (mission): "Yes, indeed. The early shift is hard at work,
and I daresay displaying a new urgency. Lots of heavy equipment is
being trolleyed inside."

Eren (mission): "Heavy equipment? Arae! That can't be good."

Drae was out doing the morning perimeter sweep, and Eren
checked his tracker location on the vicinity map.

Eren (mission): "Drae, can you sneak around toward the entry
bridge and do a closer inspection of the new equipment before it vanishes
into the building?"

Drae Shonen ela-Machim (mission): "Already moving."

In the camp, Eren rose to his knees and started rebinding his
long, now eternally tangled and matted locks for the eighth time
this morning. "Ten-to-one odds they're starting to assemble the
casings for the antimatter missiles in there."

Cosime Rhomyhn scampered around behind him and swatted
his hands away. "Let me do this. You seriously think they're planning to follow through with the missiles? Surely the Savrakaths
can't be that stupid."

At her touch, he instinctively relaxed and let her fiddle with his
hair. "You mean because antimatter bombs kill mass populations

with no nuance? Because they destroy the land for half a kilometer deep and wreck the atmosphere and ecosystem for decades?"

"Yes, because that."

"They may have a smidge more manners than the Ch'mshak, but the Savrakaths were bred to be warriors. Killing is what they do, and antimatter weapons kill quite thoroughly." He smiled as a pulse from Caleb arrived. "Caleb says 'hi.'"

"And Akeso?"

"Um…I guess Akeso also saying 'hi' was sort of implied in Caleb doing so, yes."

"And Alex?"

"Nearly as implied?"

"Neat. Can we visit them when we get done with this mission? I miss Akeso."

"Anything you want, my love."

"You say the sweetest things." He felt her hands wind into his hair, then pause. "The Khokteh were bred to be warriors, too, but they're peaceful now."

"True, but whenever I'm around more than a few Khokteh grouped together, I can't help but get the feeling they're one hot-headed general away from breaking out the knives. Or electrified spears, or whatever those jabby things are they use in their martial contests."

She kissed his neck, her lips hot and moist against his skin, then pronounced his hair suitably bound and lay down to prop on her elbows. "The Savrakaths are still stupid. Stupid to think using an antimatter weapon, no matter where, will result in anything other than an epic Concord smackdown."

"No doubt." Eren stretched out beside her, murmuring happily to himself as their arms touched. They were already near-to-naked due to the suffocating heat, and it would be so easy to….

But they were working, and he shouldn't leave Felzeor and Drae exposed on the front lines. Nevertheless, he found he was leaning closer to let his lips drift across the silken, sweaty skin of her upper arm—

Drae (mission): "Eyes on a new convoy now. Visuals incoming."
Eren (mission): "Roger."

A series of images manifested in the team's shared virtual vision. Two Savrakaths in military uniforms sat in the front seat of a long trolley stacked high with six racks of thick, curved metal. "Told you."

Cosime grumbled. "We should let Director Navick know."

"Eh, we need a little more evidence first. I know that metal is going to be used for missile casings, and you know that metal is going to be used for missile casings, but right now it's just metal."

Drae (mission): "Oh, who do we have here?"

Eren returned his attention to the visuals Drae was transmitting. Zoomed in, they showed a particularly pretentious lizard—you could tell from the way they strode bowlegged and swished their tail around without regard for what it might take out—trailing the trolley with three underlings in tow.

Eren (mission): "Well, hello there, General Jhountar. Aren't you looking handsome today?"

Cosime scowled and leaned in close to his ear. "If you compliment the way his scales reflect the sunlight in prismatic colors, I'm not having sex with you for a month."

"A *month?* You evil wench. But I shall submit to your extortion, as I always do."

Eren (mission): "Felzeor, how many loads have made it inside this morning?"

Felzeor (mission): "This will be the fourth."

Drae (mission): "If Jhountar's making a personal appearance, it must be a big day."

Drae wasn't wrong; Eren crawled over to his gear bag. "You stay here. I'm going to move closer and get a new spectrum scan of the assembly room inside. Try to see what they're up to today."

"Or I could come with you."

"You could, except someone's got to keep an eye on the camp and make sure a Savrakath patrol doesn't discover it."

"No Savrakath patrols ever come out this far. We can leave a cam running."

Their experience here thus far agreed with her. The facility was the last vestige of civilization before marshland and moors engulfed the land for hundreds of kilometers. A Veil-tech bubble and an assortment of additional stealth measures protected their camp and their tiny ship, ensuring passing aerial ships or drones wouldn't detect them. Beyond that, they hadn't seen a single ground patrol more than a quarter-kilometer out from the facility.

But he needed to remember how, despite the backwater surroundings, the Savrakaths were a technologically advanced species. If they decided to turn their own surveillance capabilities toward this area, they stood a decent chance of uncovering the camp.

"Not good enough. We must be vigilant." He pocketed a drone unit from the gear bag, leaned over and kissed her full on the mouth, then drew back a fraction to drink in her sylphean, deceptively fragile beauty.

It still took him by surprise sometimes to see her features unmarred by the lines of a spiraire. Scientists hadn't yet cracked the code for regenesis for Naraida, but they *had* successfully introduced gene therapy to allow their lungs to process a greater variety of atmospheres.

Concord represented a vast improvement on the Directorate that had preceded it in a number of ways, but one of the objectively best ways was that Concord dared to share the fruits of its technological superiority with all its member species. What had been a radical, even laughable, concept in an empire ruled by Anadens *for* Anadens was standard operating procedure under Concord rule. And it had made Cosime's life better—every Naraida's life better.

He stroked her cheek then stood. "Eyes on the perimeter. I'll be back."

"So will I." She leapt up and began scampering up a nearby tree.

He started to protest, as the trunks of the swamp trees weren't very sturdy; they swayed and bent in the slightest breeze. Or he was certain they would do so if a slight breeze ever materialized.

But she'd swiftly reached the top, where a canopy of broad leaves spread out like an umbrella.

Cosime (private): *Now, I can see the camp's perimeter and the facility.*

Eren (private): *Maddening woman you are. Also insubordinate. I'm in charge, you know.*

Cosime (private): *Yep. Absolutely.*

He began picking his way through the underbrush in a crouch. The swamp vegetation and reeds rose to waist-level, so at least he didn't have to shimmy across the ground like one of the region's non-uplifted amphibians. He had a Veil on him that he'd activate once he got closer, but in the excessive humidity, the stealth device trapped too much moisture against his skin and transformed the surrounding air into an oven—even more of an oven—so he despised using it for prolonged periods outside.

Eren (mission): *"I'm moving toward the east wing of the facility to try to see what's happening inside. Felzeor, squawk if bad guys start heading my way."*

Felzeor (mission): *"Squawking armed and ready. But are we really convinced they're bad guys? I don't want to prejudge them."*

Eren chuckled to himself, then cursed as his foot caught on one of the branches snaking through the groundcover. He disentangled himself and started off again.

Eren (mission): *"It's all right, I can do all the prejudging for the both of us. You just make sure they don't catch me."*

Felzeor (mission): *"Aye, aye."*

Eren sighed. Felzeor was enjoying this mission far more than the rest of them.

Crossing the kilometer to the perimeter of the weapons development facility took a solid twenty sweat-soaked minutes. Whenever Eren and his team finally got pulled out of here, he was shooting every article of clothing he'd brought into the nearest star, because the sweat, the smell, the mildew, the *swamp* was never coming out of them. Then he'd take Cosime to the ultra-private section of Plousia, where they'd spend a week all-the-way naked. *Then* they'd visit Caleb and Alex on Akeso.

Of course, he had no idea when that might occur. They'd been here for more than two weeks now, with an open-ended directive to learn whatever they could about the secretive facility situated outside the Savrak capital. His ultimate endgame was to sneak inside the facility, hack into the servers, visual everything and sneak out. But given the risk involved in such a plan, they needed to learn everything they could from the outside first.

Unless the Savrakaths were transitioning to some sort of final phase of weapons development, in which case time became of the essence. Jhountar's visit made it highly likely they were doing exactly such a thing. Cosime was right. Whatever information he captured on this pass, he'd send it and everything else they'd learned to Concord Intelligence, along with a request to escalate, resolve the situation or bug out.

Plousia, nudity, and crystal-clear water that didn't try to poison you were calling to him.

6

CONCORD HEADQUARTERS

MILKY WAY GALAXY
LGG REGION I

CONCORD COMMAND

Miriam Solovy unwrapped the banana-nut muffin she'd brought from home and nibbled on it while she began her regular morning review of the day's schedule.

David had left home in the middle of the night to go rescue their adopted granddaughter from her latest scrape with the authorities. Rather than try to get another hour of sleep, Miriam had gotten up as well and headed into the office early. One peek at the schedule told her that today she'd need the extra hour.

Later this morning, Alex would be bringing the Asterion in for an informal get-acquainted meeting. Alex finding a new alien species to entertain herself with was nothing new—it was in fact her job these days—but her finding one which registered on the Kardashev scale was somewhat more rare.

Of course, the Asterions hadn't become so advanced on their own; they shared most of their history with the Anadens and had carried all the Anaden Empire's knowledge with them when they'd fled the Milky Way. Alex had made it sound as if they'd transformed themselves into something altogether new in the intervening millennia, but like much else about the Asterions, the extent to which it was true remained to be seen.

An insistent tone rang through the office, and Miriam dropped the muffin on its plate to place one hand on the emergency button beneath her desk and the other on the Daemon holstered beside it.

An interference field prevented the creation of spontaneous wormholes inside Concord HQ, but they had yet to develop a way to prevent the more ethereal beings of the universe, such as Kats and Yinhe, from teleporting inside whenever they wished. A sensor dedicated to detecting unexpected shifts in the composition of the air in her office did, however, provide her a few seconds warning of such a visitor.

The sparkle of lights in front of her desk marked the arrival as a Kat, and she waited patiently for it to finish instantiating. She didn't bring her hands back to her lap; so far as she knew all the Kats were friendly, but a lot of Kats existed whom she had never met.

When the lights settled down into an amorphous shape, she spoke. "Identify yourself."

It is Lakhes, Commandant.

Now her hands returned to her lap. She'd 'enjoyed' a number of visits from the Praetor over the years, the vast majority of them unannounced. She rarely saw Mesme, though Alex insisted she spoke to it every few months. "I assume this visit relates to my meeting with the Asterion this morning?"

Why do you assume such a thing?

"The timing is too coincidental to be anything else. You do make a habit of appearing moments before an event of great import."

Ah...yes. I see. I possess some information to impart to you before you speak to the Asterion.

"Enlighten me." The Kats had no use for social etiquette, and she'd long ago taken to obliging them in this respect.

First, regarding the Asterions as a species. We have observed them for longer than three hundred millennia now. While they are as flawed as any sentient beings, we have found them to be a fundamentally peaceful and honorable people. In rebelling against the worst of Anaden tendencies, they have for the most part shed those tendencies. In fact, they now find themselves struggling to rediscover the warrior's heart they left behind when they departed the Milky Way.

"They need to rediscover it because of the Rasu."

Yes. Of necessity they must now fight, and we take comfort from how difficult this is for them.

From anyone else the statement would be the height of arrogance, but from a Kat? It was still the height of arrogance, but this was to be expected. "Is this why you've sent them our way? Because they need us to do their fighting for them?"

They will say no, for they wish to fight to save themselves. But they could benefit from a touch of guidance from those with more experience at doing so.

"Noted. I will form my own judgment about them, but know that your words carry great weight."

Thank you.

"And what about the Rasu?"

Regretfully, I say this: we now consider them to represent the greatest threat to life in this region of the universe since...I confess, I began to say since the Directorate, but though the Directorate was cruel and cold and murderous, it would not measure up. Perhaps since the Dzhvar.

It took Miriam a second to place the name. "The aliens who attacked the Anadens long ago—the war that led the *diati* to join with Corradeo Praesidis."

Correct. The Dzhvar were a primordial, supradimensional force that devoured the fabric of the universe as they proceeded across it. The Rasu do not, we believe, destroy the spacetime manifold, but they do obliterate much of what exists within it.

"What else can you tell me about them?"

In most respects, the Asterions have the same information as we do, and it will be better conveyed from them. As it is not sufficient information to mount a proper response, however, we are collecting additional data.

"I see. Then I will await the results of your collection. Do make a note to drop by and share them with me."

As you say. The lights spun up and vanished.

Miriam sank back in her chair with a sigh. A potential ally arriving from the sordid past of the Anadens? A potential grave threat rising on the void's horizon? It must be Tuesday.

RW

KATOIKIA TAIRI

Cetus Dwarf Galaxy
LGG Region V

IDRYMA

Lakhes returned directly from Concord Headquarters to the central chamber of the Idryma. The meeting place of the Katasketousya leadership now existed on multiple planes: as a physical structure of tall marble columns and vast halls situated upon the rust and caramel steppes of Katoikia Tairi, and as an empyreal structure of light stretching across the hidden dimensions of the universe.

Habit led Lakhes to inhabit the empyreal version; after all, it possessed no tangible feet upon which to press against the cool marble.

On the periphery of its senses, it recognized Mnemosyne meandering along the fringes of the circular chamber. It said nothing in greeting, instead busying itself checking on a variety of research and observation projects.

Few of them brought good news. Every hour the information the Rasu observation teams delivered grew more troubling. Meanwhile, the hoped-for taming of the Savrakaths by introducing them to Concord perched on the verge of abject failure. The Idryma had created the Savrakaths, bred them for a specific purpose—warfare—and it should not be a surprise when they were not easily deterred from that purpose. The creatures were their responsibility, but time remained to avert a catastrophe.

Mnemosyne's presence brushed past its awareness again, and Lakhes now broke the silence. "All right, my friend. I sense your unease, and I have deduced the reason for your presence.

"Many aeons ago, I agreed with you regarding the wisdom of locating and monitoring the Asterions, as any branch of Anadens warranted our careful attention. More recently, I agreed we should nudge them toward developing ways to combat the Rasu, and I am pleased to see they are proving worthy of our intervention.

"Further, it is good that our involvement with the Asterions brought the Rasu to our awareness sooner than we would have otherwise discovered them. In normal circumstances, this should have granted us sufficient time to devise a proper plan to face this new threat.

"Instead, however, at your vehement urging, we have now set Concord on a course they would not otherwise have adopted. We are hastening a confrontation between Concord and the Rasu, when evidence counsels us that Concord is not yet prepared for such a confrontation.

"We have done this because you insist the Asterions are important—far beyond their normal importance as a sapient, peaceful species, all of which are worth making efforts to preserve. You insist the Asterions *must* survive.

"I recall similar protestations from you about the Humans, and though you were ultimately correct in your assessment, at the time I attributed it to the fondness you had developed for them over long millennia of observation. You possess no such excuse when it comes to the Asterions, however."

Lakhes morphed into his chosen fae form in the physical realm. "Mnemosyne, I believe the time has come for you to, as the Humans say, 'come clean.' Tell me, my friend. Why, precisely, are the Asterions so important? What do you know, and why have you chosen to keep it from me?"

Mnemosyne spread its wings wide across the chamber and drifted into the air. "It is time at last, isn't it? Come, let us retire to a less public venue. This will take some time to explain."

7

CONCORD HQ

T he *Siyane* exited a wormhole gate into a region of space bursting with activity on a scale Nika didn't recall ever witnessing. Yes, the Rasu stronghold had been active, but it hadn't *bustled*. It hadn't shone and crackled with positive energy.

Most of the activity flowed to, from and around a space station the size of a planetary satellite. It consisted of a solid center structure over six kilometers in diameter surrounded by two tori at right angles to one another. Connected to the tori, hub-and-spoke structures chained outward five layers deep. A blue-white star shone in the distance, but she saw no evidence of a nearby planet.

A rush of anticipation electrified Nika's skin. Akeso had been so quiet, so peaceful, she could be forgiven for doubting whether a true intergalactic civilization thrived anywhere in the vicinity.

But here it was, in vivid and living color. She snapped a few visuals and sent them to Dashiel with a bit of gushing commentary, then again she returned to how little resemblance the scene bore to what she'd witnessed at the Rasu stronghold. The ships arriving and departing came in all shapes, colors and sizes. The patterns of movement were chaotic, though she assumed some system provided a guiding hand so the ships didn't crash into one another. The architecture of the structure and its appendages was bright and open, inherently inviting.

She hoped it proved to be the same on the inside.

Alex and Caleb had been nothing but welcoming, far above and beyond what she'd hoped for when she'd set out on this journey.

But the shadow of the SAI Rebellion, brought into stark relief by a series of heartbreaking journal entries she'd devoured on her trip here, imposed a layer of caution on her expectations. Anadens may not rule this region of space with an iron fist any longer, but they remained a player in the power structure. And Humans were at least as much Anaden as Asterions were, if not more so. Capable of great kindness, yes, but also perhaps great cruelty. Possessing great strength, no doubt, but what of weakness?

The *Siyane* maneuvered effortlessly—Nika couldn't say whether it did so under Alex's control or not—through the crowded space surrounding the station to what must be a coveted berth right on the central hub.

"Have to reserve this spot in advance?"

"Hmm. No."

Nika had spent most of her remembered life as a rebel rather than a high-ranking diplomat, and she couldn't help but take note of the trappings of privilege on display. *This* was why it was Alex who had arrived in the void to pluck her out of space and personally bring her here, to the seat of power of the former Anaden, now Concord, Empire. Because she possessed the keys—and a reserved parking spot—to that seat of power. For reasons that remained somewhat obscured, the woman was helping Nika to short-circuit both bureaucratic mazes and diplomatic snafus and take her appeal directly to those who could act on it.

Or possibly this Kat, Mesme, whom she'd yet to meet, was pulling a maze of strings behind the scenes to bring her here. She didn't care for mysterious machinations going on hidden from her view, but at this precise moment she was damn grateful for them.

She peered out the viewport as the station's shadow consumed them. "I'm a little surprised we didn't simply walk through a wormhole on Akeso and into the space station."

"No free wormholes are allowed to terminate inside Concord HQ. There is a transport hub inside with permanent Caeles Prisms leading to and from the government centers of the various species, but the hub sits at the center of twenty-one layers of security, and it is so tedious to get through."

Nika studied Alex curiously. "But you can still open a wormhole inside, right?"

Alex was silent for a few seconds, then chuckled. "I might have carved out a small back-door program to bypass the block so I can wormhole into my mother's office. But it's likely a one-time-only pass, so I'm saving it for when I really, *really* need it."

The ship settled into unseen clamps, and Alex stood and went into the main cabin. Thirty percent larger in length and breadth than the *Wayfarer*, what struck Nika most about the interior of the *Siyane* was how comfortable it felt. Lived in—and livable. It felt like a home. She'd spent several weeks on the *Wayfarer* traveling here, and while it had provided for her every need, she wasn't close to considering it home.

Of course, she'd only begun to feel that way about her flat on Mirai; possibly she simply wasn't at ease with the notion of having a place one called home.

"I've registered you as a guest of the Concord Consulate. Your identity isn't in the system, so you'll need to wear this while you're here." She pulled a strip of thin film off a small printer and handed it to Nika. "Stick it on your skin somewhere you don't mind being scanned, like your forearm or neck."

Nika studied the translucent film briefly, noting its subtle glow of nanoscale printed circuitry, and pressed it to the inside of her left forearm, above the invisible slit that released one of her blades when a blade was required.

"Perfect." Alex opened the airlock, and they traversed a short entry tube, then another airlock. "Welcome to Concord."

Welcome, indeed. They stepped into an expansive, brightly lit and high-ceilinged atrium constructed of a semi-lustrous tungsten-hued metal, ivory ceramics and prodigious glass. The area buzzed with enough activity to set Nika's senses aflutter.

Off to the left, a bipedal cat-like alien tossed animated gestures in the direction of a glowing blob of gelatinous material a meter and a half tall. Her mind ran through all the species Alex had mentioned to her...an Efkam? Two tiger-looking aliens with long, thick tails jogged across the atrium and disappeared down one of the many halls. A stunning alien with iridescent skin glided along the periphery, pausing to speak to another of the cat aliens.

But most of the beings inside were Anaden or Human. Or rather, she assumed those who resembled Humans but not quite were Anadens. They didn't look exactly the way they had in her limited memories from so long ago. Their physical appearance was somehow...colder. Harder. Most notably, harsh cybernetics carved ridges in their skin, like veins bulging beyond their bounds. Humans, on the other hand, either appeared fully organic or sported shimmering glyphs of varying colors and patterns.

Her eyes drank in as many details as she could absorb while Alex guided her through two security checkpoints and a brief tram ride. They exited the tram into another, smaller atrium. Across the way, an only slightly ostentatious awning labeled "GCDA EMBASSY" stretched above a wide glass entryway.

"You've mentioned the GCDA a couple of times. What does it stand for?"

"Galactic Common Defense Accord, which is a basically meaningless collection of words now. It originates from a time when we were the only sentient life in the universe—in *our* universe—and the Milky Way was the only galaxy that mattered. But it was the organization that managed to defeat the Directorate, and after The Displacement so much was changing so fast, it seemed easier to not change the name. In principle, the GCDA ensures when it comes to Concord business, humanity speaks with one voice. God knows they don't any other time."

"I certainly understand differences of opinion at all levels of government."

"It's worse than that. When we came to Amaranthe, our colonies were grouped into three major camps, each one sporting a full-fledged sovereign government and military. Governments which had gone to war with one another more than once in the last several decades, even if they were finally trying to play nice."

"And now?"

"Now? The fiefdoms still exist, but as the world has gotten bigger, their effective power has gotten much smaller. It's all a work in progress. But it's improving, I think. I'm not the best person to ask. Politicians and I don't get along—sorry. No offense."

It took her a second to piece together what the woman meant. "Oh, none taken. I don't think of myself as a politician, though I suppose technically I am. Government in the Dominion is fairly minimal."

"Must be nice." Alex went up to a woman behind a counter. It was odd seeing a person acting as reception instead of a dyne. Nika had noticed several mobile machines during their trip into the heart of the station, but they represented a tiny fraction of what one found in Dominion buildings.

"Hi, Jan. Are they ready for us?"

"They are. In fact, you're the last to arrive."

"Thanks." Alex glanced at her. "Are you ready?"

Nika squared her shoulders. This was likely to be the most receptive audience she would find in Concord, but this didn't mean she should expect it to be easy. "I am."

A door behind the receptionist opened to reveal an expansive, open, airy office with a perfect view of the station's sprawling arms. Several people stood casually around a long conference table, talking and munching on cookies from a plate at the center.

Caleb came over as soon as they stepped inside, leaning in to give Alex a quick kiss on the ear. They murmured to one another for a few seconds, and Nika tried not to eavesdrop. Then he turned to her wearing an apologetic grimace. "I am so sorry I ran out on you last night. I trust you two managed just fine without me."

Alex laughed. "With the help of a second bottle of wine."

"Naturally."

Alex cleared her throat above the conversational din. "Good morning everyone. The guest of honor is here, so ease off on the cookies for a minute. I'd like to introduce Nika Kirumase, diplomatic representative of the Asterion Dominion. Nika, from left to right, this is Miriam, David, Mia, Malcolm and Richard. First, Commandant-General Miriam Solovy, leader of all Concord military forces, and incidentally my mother."

"I suspect it's far from incidental." Nika crossed the distance to the table and extended a hand to the woman, Alex having briefed her on greetings and a host of related etiquette. The woman was shorter than Alex by several centimeters but shared her striking burgundy hair, though the elder Solovy wore it in a neat braided bun. Her features were more…mature was a better descriptor than 'old,' as the woman's appearance gave no obvious clues to her age. She wondered if mature features were a marker of seniority—of authority—in their society.

The woman offered her a guarded but seemingly genuine smile. "Advisor, yes? Welcome."

"And this is David Solovy, Professor Emeritus at the Concord Special Warfare Training Center and my father."

The man's resemblance to Alex was much more noticeable, from the bone structure to the body language, to the twinkling, if less artificial, eyes.

"I only came for the cookies, but it is my genuine pleasure to meet you, ma'am." His smile was easy and open, and she liked him instantly.

Alex kept going, leaving no opportunity for the exchange of polite pleasantries. "Senator Mia Requelme, the GCDA representative to Concord and current head of the Concord Consulate. You two should get along great."

Requelme was a beautiful woman with honeyed olive skin and sleek black hair. A Prevo, if Nika understood properly how these things worked, due to her intense jade irises and the fact a duplicate of the tiny orb Alex wore on her bracelet hung from a bronze chain around the woman's neck.

The woman exuded casual grace as she greeted Nika warmly. "I am so glad you're here. We will have much to talk about."

"And this is Fleet Admiral Malcolm Jenner, head of the GCDA AEGIS military forces. Be nice to him, as he's got Mia's ear."

Nika had already figured that much out from the subtle body language between Mia and the strapping yet handsome military officer. She arched an eyebrow. "I'm glad to hear the diplomats enjoy all the real power here as well."

The man laughed a tad awkwardly. "Maybe, but I still answer to Commandant Solovy."

David Solovy grabbed a fresh cookie. "We all do in the end."

Alex snorted. "You mean all of *you* do. Finally, this is Richard Navick, Concord Intelligence Director and an honorary Solovy."

Navick, an unassuming man with sandy brown hair and kind eyes, nodded mildly and offered her a hand. She accepted it before stepping back a little so she could address everyone.

"It's such a pleasure to meet all of you. I admit, I worried about what kind of reception I was going to receive when or if I found anyone willing to receive me. So far, this visit has exceeded my greatest hopes." She considered the others in blatant curiosity. "Everyone here is Human, correct? Does this mean, as I've suspected, the true power in Concord rests in Human hands—or does it mean Alex only invited people she liked?"

The remark got a good chuckle, and the residual tension in the room eased further.

Alex scowled, but it appeared to be in jest. "I'll have you know I have many alien friends. I just didn't invite any of them. As to your question, Mom and Mia are both fidgeting trying to spout the party line that Concord is a multi-species representative republic, and no one species rules it. And it's true, as far as it goes."

Nika started to shift toward Alex, then directed her attention to Miriam Solovy instead. "And how far is that?"

The corners of the woman's mouth twitched. "The line continues to shift in the sand with the tide. I believe Alex brought you here to meet with us because you will not find a friendlier audience anywhere in Concord space. Later this morning, Senator Requelme will take you on the rounds to meet the other species' diplomats, some of whom might not be quite so welcoming. But we very much want to hear what you have to say first."

"You want to know about the Rasu."

"Without a doubt. But first, we'd actually like to know about the Asterions. Official Anaden history writes that the Asterion rebels were routed and all but a scattered few killed on the battlefield. To discover this was not in fact the case was an interesting and pleasant surprise."

"I'm glad it was a pleasant one. I've been heartened to learn how the rights of SAIs are now respected here, it seems at Humanity's insistence.

"As to how we survived? In the last months of the SAI Rebellion, we were losing, and we knew it. A desperate plan was hatched by the Rebellion leadership—a plan for as many of us as possible to escape the Milky Way and find a new home, one where SAIs and Anadens could live in peace together."

RW

"You tossed the Rasu stronghold into *a star?*"

Nika shrugged. She'd left out the details of her eight thousand incarnations, because it would require a far lengthier and more personal explanation than she was ready to give. Also, she'd been talking for what must be hours now; she picked up the glass of water in front of her and took a sip before responding to David Solovy's question. "In a manner of speaking—and also somewhat literally—yes."

"Brilliant. I mean strategically."

"We had the advantage of complete surprise on our side. It would never have worked if they'd seen us coming."

"True. Still, most impressive." He gave her a quick nod of approval and leaned over to murmur something to Richard Navick.

"Not to diminish your accomplishment, because I in no way am, but you said you believe the Rasu presence in your galaxy represented only a forward scouting party. What do you know about Rasu forces elsewhere?"

Nika returned her focus to the commandant. Throughout the morning, the woman's questions had been measured yet probing, though she'd given few clues as to her opinion on Nika's responses.

"Right now, only what they told us, which is that they control hundreds of galaxies throughout the Laniakea supercluster. Obviously, their word can't be trusted. We do believe there are Rasu in other galaxies, however, given the extensive communication arrays they were using. They were talking to someone. We are planning stealth expeditions to the galaxies adjacent to the Gennisi galaxy to see what we can learn, but given our limited military resources it hasn't been our highest priority in the initial weeks after the stronghold's destruction."

"An understandable choice. Perhaps this is an area where we can assist you. It's my understanding the Katasketousya are currently conducting their own survey of Rasu territory, and we'll be happy to share their findings with you."

"Excellent. I thank you for that."

The conversation finally lulled for a moment, and Mia Requelme stood. "I've managed to reserve ten minutes of Dean Veshnael's time, but only in the next ten minutes. I'm sure everyone has more questions, but hopefully we can reconvene later. Nika, if you'd like to come with me, I think you'll find the Novoloume leader most fascinating."

"Oh! Of course. I believe I am at your whim today."

Alex touched Nika's arm as she stood. "I hate to run out on you, but Caleb and I have somewhere we need to be shortly, so we'll be gone whenever you get back. But Mia will take excellent care of you. If you need to get back to your ship later on today, she can make that happen, too. We'll touch base...tomorrow?"

"Tomorrow Akeso-time, or here on the station? Or are they the same thing?"

"Not even close. But when your world encompasses over sixty galaxies, you develop a strong internal clock real fast. I'll send you a message."

8

CONCORD HQ

CONSULATE

Miriam watched quietly as Mia departed with Advisor Kirumase. As soon as the door closed behind them, she directed her attention to those who remained. "This morning, shortly before you all arrived, I had a visit from Praetor Lakhes. The Praetor voiced support for the Asterions, but the primary purpose of its visit was to impress upon me the position of the Kat leadership regarding the Rasu."

Alex peered at her from between splayed fingers. "Dare I ask what it is?"

"They regard the Rasu as the single greatest threat to the peace, freedom and even survival of all those living in Concord space."

David stared at her expectantly. "The single greatest threat since...?"

"According to Lakhes, since the Dzhvar."

Caleb flinched at the mention of the ancient species who had warred with the *diati*, but no one said anything for several seconds. Finally Alex sighed. "Why didn't you share this with Nika?"

"Advisor Kirumase is a stranger to us. I might ask why you seem to trust her implicitly already? It's not like you."

"She and her friends rebelled against the Anaden government to fight for their right to merge with Artificials." Alex spread her arms wide and leaned back in her chair. "It's called kinship."

"True, but that happened an unimaginably long time ago. Why else?"

"Mesme believes in her—in the Asterions as a people."

"Did Mesme say why?"

Alex groaned and reached for the final cookie crumbs remaining on the plate. "When has Mesme ever divulged the reasons behind its actions ahead of time? But has it ever been wrong?"

"What about those shenanigans in the Khokteh portal?" David asked. "Where the Kats deliberately pitted the various Khokteh factions against one another?"

"That was the Idryma as a whole, and that ass Iapetus in particular. It wasn't Mesme's doing, and once we called them to the floor for their misdeeds, Mesme helped us put a stop to it. What is this inquisition? Are all of you *not* buying her story?"

Miriam shook her head. "On the contrary, I found her quite believable. Guarded and holding much close to the vest, but it's understandable given her history with the Anadens. Nevertheless, we should proceed using measured caution. While I have high hopes for our future relationship with the Asterions, the relationship is only now taking its first steps. I saw no need to embolden Advisor Kirumase's position for her before she had been given an opportunity to present her case. And it turned out I didn't need to, as she made the case convincingly on her own."

"So what you're saying is, you and Mia and Malcolm and whoever else are going to do the diplomatic dance thing, feel each other out while you play it cool and whatnot. But in the meantime, you're going to transition Concord to a war footing and prepare for what looks to be an inevitable conflict with the Rasu."

"You could be overstating the situation a small amount. I give Praetor Lakhes' admonitions proper weight, but we need to assess the threat for ourselves."

Alex leaned forward in interest. "Yes, let's do that. How?"

Her daughter always was eager for a dangerous adventure. Miriam called up a map of the Local Galactic Group and surrounding regions above the table. "According to Lakhes, the closest Rasu presence to Concord space is in NGC 55. Alex, how would you and Caleb like to make a stealth run by there? Tell me what we're facing—but for goodness' sake, do *not* pick a fight with the Rasu while you're there."

Alex grinned at Caleb. "I'm offended you would even suggest such a possibility. We absolutely will do it, if tomorrow is okay. As I said to Nika, we have a prior engagement today."

"Tomorrow is fine. I don't expect the Rasu to attack in the next twenty-four hours."

RW

Malcolm followed Alex and Caleb out, and David squeezed Miriam's hand before leaving to go teach his next class. Richard, however, stayed comfortable in his chair.

She'd been about to depart herself, as this wasn't actually her office, but when he didn't move she clasped her hands on the table. "You have something for me."

"I do." He splashed a series of visuals above the table's surface. "This is a new report in from Eren's team on Savrak."

He didn't elaborate, instead letting her study the visuals and accompanying notes in silence.

The Savrakaths were one of the Kats' engineered species from the Mosaic. Alex and Caleb had never encountered them during their exploration of the portal network; if they had, Caleb might well have chosen to leave them behind along with the Machim Primor and Ekos-3 during The Displacement. The reptilian species was militaristic, quick to take offense and nearly as quick to resort to violence. Though they were marginally more technologically advanced than the Khokteh, thus far they had showed no inclination to similarly temper their more barbaric instincts.

They claimed to desire to ally with Concord, and they had paid lip service to the concessions required for them to do so. These included the recognition of full legal rights to the Godjans, a less advanced species they shared a planet with and treated somewhat poorly, as well as free passage across their territory for all Concord citizens and renouncement of antimatter weapons and similar banned instruments of mass destruction.

The visuals, brought to life by Eren's rather colorful annotations to them, called into question their commitment to one of those concessions, to say the least. She sank back in her chair. "This isn't good."

"No, but I can't say I'm surprised."

"Do you really believe they're building antimatter missiles?"

"I believe it's the most reasonable explanation for the data at hand."

"But you can't be certain."

"No. Eren's requesting approval to infiltrate the facility and attempt to confirm the nature of the work being done inside."

She stared at the visuals again. "Is infiltration the only way to get confirmation?"

"Considering the Savrakaths aren't just going to fess up, likely so."

"If we've learned everything we can from proximity surveillance, I think we have to proceed down that path."

"Understood." He paused. "And if we do get confirmation? What then?"

"Then the negotiations for their admittance as a Concord Allied Species are going to take a hard left turn."

9

MIRAI

ASTERION DOMINION
GENNISI GALAXY

RIDANI ENTERPRISES

"You need *another* warship manufacturing line?"

"Two, actually." Lance Palmer delivered his demand in a matter-of-fact tone wearing a stone-cold expression, as if he would broker no argument over it.

An intimidating glower might work on his soldiers, but Dashiel Ridani had been an Advisor of the Asterion Dominion for more than thirty-two hundred years, and he didn't so much as flinch. "I can build you *twenty* additional warship manufacturing lines, but if we don't have the materials and equipment to construct the ships, they'll simply sit idle. The bottleneck isn't the lines, it's the components."

"Then I trust that you and Mesahle are working with all due speed to solve the bottleneck. In the meantime, build me two more warship manufacturing lines, so they can be ready to fire up the instant you do."

The weight of responsibility driving Palmer's demand bore down on Dashiel's shoulders in spite of himself. Yes, he, Grant Mesahle and half a dozen materials experts were 'working the problem.' Not that working so closely with Nika's former lover was in any way easy or comfortable, but such personal qualms shouldn't and couldn't matter under the circumstances.

In fact, now he felt ashamed even acknowledging the issue, because Grant was comporting himself as a consummate professional and had been entirely without guile about his relationship with Nika. It was what it had been, and that was that, leaving Dashiel no room to play jealous, overprotective or outraged, none of which he had a right to be anyway. And he wasn't so much bothered by the fact they'd been lovers—when you lived as long as Asterions did, these things happened. It was more that the man had been her friend for innumerable millennia when Dashiel had not. Grant knew a thousand details and held a thousand memories of her that Dashiel would never have...all because his ancestor, Steven Olivaw, had denied him that right.

Palmer continued to stare at him expectantly, and he banished the brief bout of self-pity to refocus on the problem at hand. In a nutshell, they hadn't needed such a volume of space-rated materials since the construction of the Platform two hundred thousand years ago, and now suddenly they needed thousands of tonnes of them. Millions of tonnes, if Palmer had his way.

Which he *should*; Nika had entrusted Dashiel with managing the creation of a true military fleet, one capable of defending every Dominion world from the Rasu, and this was all Palmer was asking for.

Two dozen component assembly factories now dotted the Namino landscape or, more often, its orbit—and they were currently running a single shift a day then idling while they waited for materials to arrive. Meanwhile, mechs mined every asteroid, moon and suitable planet they could find in the region and dozens of cargo ships ferried the loads back to Namino. Where the materials couldn't be mined, labs on Mirai worked nonstop to synthesize them. They were playing catchup—catchup for seven hundred thousand years of refusing to be a militaristic species, of turning their back on war and hoping it didn't come looking for them.

But now it had. He met Palmer's impatient gaze with as much resolve as he was able to summon. "All right. Two more warship manufacturing lines it is. We'll piggyback off the framework in place and—"

"No. Don't build them in Namino orbit. Build them here. Or above Kiyora or Ebisu, or wherever. But not above Namino."

"Dammit, Palmer, why the hells not? The infrastructure is in place in Namino orbit. Starting from scratch at a new site will double the cost and the time required to get new lines up and running, never mind the inefficiencies of sending the base materials to two different planets in two different systems."

"I recognize that, Ridani. But it's a strategic mistake to concentrate all our ship-building capabilities at one location that can be wiped off the map in a single enemy strike. Far better to build out our infrastructure at multiple sites now than after the Rasu have wiped out everything we constructed."

"I...okay, that makes sense. But today, pre-wipeout, it's a question of priorities. Do you want a lot of ships fast, or do you want a resilient supply chain of ships?"

"Both."

Dashiel groaned. "Well, you can't have both."

"And here I thought Asterions could do anything we set our minds to."

Now Palmer was just provoking him. "We can, but not instantaneously. How long are we going to continue building out the infrastructure? How many ships built in how many locations will be enough?"

"We are so far from whatever those numbers are, I won't speculate on what they might one day be. We began Omoikane from a standing start, with our weight back on our heels. Now, eight thousand new ships in a month is superb, but it's hardly a dent in our deficit. If we want to defeat the Rasu in head-to-head battles, we need hundreds of thousands of ships. Millions—"

"How does forty million sound?"

Dashiel whipped around at the sound of a voice that made his heart sing with joy. He found Nika standing in the middle of the room wearing a smug smirk and enough attitude to save them all from the Rasu.

His brain had barely begun to form the question of where she had come from when his eyes supplied the answer, such as it was. Behind her, a shining oval ring cut into the air—into the fabric of space, as it revealed another room in another place on the other side.

At the sight of her beaming smile and dancing eyes, he crossed the distance between them and wrapped her up in his embrace, reveling in her warmth and energy. His lips found her ear. "No ceraff will ever be as good as the feel of you in my arms."

"I agree." She wound a hand into his hair and dropped her forehead to his.

They'd been in constant contact during her journey, of course. Dashiel knew she'd made contact with representatives of the former Anaden empire, this 'Concord.' With Humans, a species whose mere existence made for an outlandish tale. He knew she'd found them welcoming and had appeared not to be in any danger during her initial encounters with them. This morning, he'd known when she visited their awe-inducing headquarters. But a tiny part of him had, until this instant, feared it all an illusion.

He kissed her softly, then drew back to consider the reality of her presence. "How are you here? I mean, obviously…" he gestured toward the tear in the fabric of space, which remained miraculously open despite the absence of any frame to contain it.

"It's a wormhole—a d-gate, basically. The mechanics differ in the details, but the result is the same."

Palmer was studying it, peering at the edges as he circled it twice, and she gestured in his direction. "Lance, aren't you going to ask what I meant by forty million?"

"Oh, I already figured it out. That's how many ships this Concord can field, right? Are they all ours for the taking?"

"Not exactly. One step at a time. First step—you are both invited to return with me to meet their military leaders and tour their central facility."

This drew Lance's attention away from the wormhole. "I'm in."

"Dashiel?"

"What, are you kidding? I'm not going to let you get away from me again so fast."

"Good." She reached into her pocket and produced a small slab of a semi-translucent onyx mineral. She searched the room until she found Vance Greshe, Ridani Enterprises' Manufacturing Director and EVP, who'd been working at the conference table while Dashiel had sparred with Lance. She went over to him and offered him the slab. "I'd give this to Dashiel, but he'd just give it to you."

"Yes, ma'am. What is it?"

"Kyoseil."

"What?" Dashiel hurried to join them at the conference table.

"Possibly a different evolutionary branch of it, or possibly the slab is simply a shell. I don't know exactly, but the jade threads you see running through the interior? That's kyoseil. We need to learn if we can extract workable, usable kyoseil from slabs such as this one. Then we need to determine if the kyoseil in them is safe for us to use. If the answer to both those questions is yes..." she met Dashiel's gaze with a hint of amusement on her lips "...our kyoseil supply problems are over."

"Concord has a lot of these slabs?"

"An incalculable amount. But more importantly, they know how to grow it."

The possibilities spun out through Dashiel's mind like spider-woven silk. Growing kyoseil? It would mean...he needed time and quiet to properly consider all it could mean.

"I'll get our best people on it right away. Sir?"

Dashiel shook his head and refocused on the here and now. "Yes, do what she said. Thank you. I'll be gone for...?" He checked with Nika in question.

"Let's call it a few hours and see how the day goes."

"Excellent." He turned to Palmer. "Are we ready?"

They got a curt nod from the Military Advisor. Nika grasped Dashiel's hand and drew him back to the center of the room and the edge of the ring. Together they walked through, crossed five megaparsecs of space and stepped into another room.

RW

CONCORD HQ

COMMAND FLEET COMPLEX

Dashiel found himself in what was immediately identifiable as an observation lounge. Glass lined all the walls excepting the doors at each end of the long room. The room was in space, part of a wing of a colossal structure judging by the stretches of broad, curving tunnels beyond both doors. In four directions out from the room, ship dry docks extended out in a hub-and-spoke pattern. For a long, *long* way.

If Concord was trying to make a meaningful first impression by choosing this location for their entrance, it was succeeding.

Two strangers stood in the room, but Palmer ignored them to stride directly up to the glass, his eyes scanning across the dry docks like he was hunting for defects.

Nika left Palmer to his inspection and gestured to the people who had been waiting on them. "This is Senator Mia Requelme, the Human representative to Concord, and Fleet Admiral Malcolm Jenner, the leader of the Human military. Senator, Admiral, this is Dashiel Ridani, our leading Industry Advisor, and..." she cleared her throat in Palmer's direction "...Commander Lance Palmer, Military Advisor and the head of the Asterion Dominion military."

"Such as it is." Palmer spun back to them and jerked his chin down in greeting at Fleet Admiral Jenner. "Forty million ships, eh?"

Nika rolled her eyes in annoyance, but Jenner seemed to take Palmer's directness in stride. Maybe it was a military thing.

"Across all the Concord fleets, yes. I realize it sounds like a lot, but it's not so much overkill when you consider how we have to cover sixty galaxies' worth of space."

"Peacefully?"

"When it's up to us, absolutely."

He was already getting a glimpse into why Nika had taken a liking to the Concord people. They spoke her language; whether they lived it remained to be seen.

The call of the alluring ships docked outside the viewport called to him, and he found he couldn't resist them any longer. He approached the glass to stand beside Palmer. Though the vessels varied greatly in size and structural design, to a one, their hulls gleamed a rich tungsten hue with a subtle pearling effect. He knew of no material that presented in such a manner under these conditions. "Can I ask, what are these hulls constructed of?"

Behind him, Nika chuckled. "I told Mia you'd be asking about it inside two minutes."

'Mia' so soon? Maybe it was a diplomat thing.

"Indeed, which is why I asked our foremost expert on the material to drop by. She should be here in a few minutes."

Dashiel offered Senator Requelme a perfunctory smile, only belatedly realizing how much she favored Nika. Not so much physically, though they shared raven hair and similarly brilliant irises, but rather in their bearing: confident yet refined and almost regal. The psyche-wipe and her time leading NOIR had left Nika with a grittier, harder edge, but once upon a time.... "Thank you for anticipating my questions."

The admiral exchanged a meaningful look with the senator, who nodded approval. Jenner cleared his throat. "Commander Palmer, if you'll accompany me, I can give you a brief tour of the facilities and talk you through our high-level structure."

Palmer motioned to the door. "Lead the way."

Once they had departed, Dashiel again dragged his gaze away from the stunning ships outside to address the senator. "This feels a lot like the velvet glove treatment. Which, don't get me wrong, I appreciate. But I admit, I didn't expect Nika—and all of us—to be greeted so warmly."

"Understandable. If you'd arrived here in the Milky Way a mere fifteen years earlier, you would have received a decidedly colder welcome from the Anaden Directorate. We are honestly still trying to make our way here, and we welcome all friendly, peaceful faces. Especially, but not limited to, those who look more or less like ours."

As he understood things from Nika's frenzied information downloads over the past two days, the Humans had quite suddenly found themselves living in the midst of over a dozen alien species—dominated by the Anadens, who had been both friend and foe, depending on their inclination. He could scarcely begin to fathom how disorienting such a displacement must have been.

But he was feeling a bit disoriented himself at the moment, so he gave the woman the most innocuous shrug he could manage. "It appears to me as if you're making your way just fine."

"You haven't seen the Concord Senate in session." Requelme turned toward the left doorway/airlock as it opened and a Human man and woman entered. The woman's wild mane of golden curls obscured much of her face, and the man's dark blond hair swayed across his brow as he struggled to balance a small boy on one hip and a smaller girl on the other.

The woman increased her pace to reach them, haphazardly tucking a few of her curls behind her ears to reveal lively, pale green eyes as she did. "Sorry we're late. There were..." she tilted her head toward the children "...complications at their rec session."

"It's no trouble. We were getting acquainted." Requelme gestured between them all. "Nika Kirumase and Dashiel Ridani, this is Kennedy Rossi and Noah Terrage, the founders of Connova Interstellar, which is the owner and primary producer of adiamene, the metal used in our hulls."

The man—Noah—set the children down, and the woman reached out to position them in front of her. "And this is Jonas and Braelyn." She nudged them each in turn. "Can you say hello to our guests?"

The girl blinked twice then lifted her chin proudly. "Hello, guests." The boy just snickered.

Nika knelt in front of the children to meet them at eye level. "Hello, Jonas and Braelyn. It's wonderful to meet you."

The girl regarded Nika suspiciously while the boy fidgeted.

"How old are the two of you?"

The girl crossed her arms over her chest in defiant smugness. "I'm five and two months. He is, too, but I'm three minutes older."

"Fantastic. Want to know something? You are the first Anatype children I have seen in a long time."

The girl's face scrunched up in fiery indignation recognizable across all species. "I am *not* Anaden!"

He sensed Nika deflate in front of him, saw the chagrin in the smile she offered as penance. "No, no, of course you aren't. I apologize. You two are the first Human children I've *ever* met. You must be pretty special."

Braelyn elbowed her brother. "That's what Mommy says."

"Yeah, about *me!*"

"Nuh-unh! She said I was the specialist special ever. Last week, after dinner, when you got sent to your room for making food cannons out of your mashed potatoes."

"Those were awesome food cannons!"

"I bet she says it about both of you." Nika stood, and Rossi adopted an apologetic, exasperated expression that she shifted to direct at Terrage.

The man reached out and scooped both children back up in his arms. "I'm going to herd them off to class before they cause an intergalactic diplomatic incident. It was nice to meet you both."

"Wait!" Jonah wiggled out of his father's grasp and scrambled to stand proudly in front of Nika. "Why do you glow?"

"What?" She glanced at her forearm then back at the boy. "Oh. I guess I do, a little. It's because of a mineral in my body called kyoseil."

The boy's mouth morphed around while he considered this new information. "Can I glow?"

"I'm not—"

Noah wrapped an arm around the boy's waist and hefted him into the air. "If you're good in class today, I'll get you some body glitter. Then you can glow."

"Yay! Brae, I'm going to glow and you're not."

"Am, too! Daddy will make you give me some of your glitter."

Their back-and-forth continued as their father carried them off and out the door.

Rossi watched them leave; then her shoulders sagged in a full-body sigh. "I'm sorry for being so scattered. I thought I was ready for a child, but in no way whatsoever was I ready for two of them at the same time."

Nika relaxed her stance in a way Dashiel had seen her do so many times before the psyche-wipe, and now again. "No, no. I'm sorry if I was gawking. I hope I didn't frighten them."

"Don't worry. Braelyn can be reserved and cautious, but few things frighten her. And Jonas, well…."

Nika shook her head, and Dashiel realized she was genuinely flustered. "It's been seven hundred thousand years. I mean, we have alien allies who bear and raise children, but they're…alien. Still, I should have handled that better."

"Alex wasn't kidding about you." The woman eyed them speculatively. "*Anyway*. You want to know about adiamene. The story begins with a tale of two star-crossed lovers."

Dashiel's looked at her strangely, and Rossi laughed. "Kidding. Not actually, but we can skip the sappy parts for now."

RW

"These numbers can't be legitimate. I mean, I'm sorry, but—"

Ms. Rossi didn't appear to take offense. "It's fine. Everyone says that until they see adiamene in action, at which point they quickly become believers. This is better performance than you get with what you're using to build ships currently?"

Dashiel nodded vaguely. "A little, yes." A lot, but he was trying to play it smooth. "Do all the Concord species use this adiamene for their ships now?"

"Would you believe no? The Anadens spent the first ten years insisting their starship and space station construction was superior to anything humans could offer, full stop. Damn stubborn Diaplas engineers. In the last couple of years, a few prominent Anaden *elassons*—that's their highest rank except for the Primors, who don't exist any longer, and I have no idea whether you know any of this—have begun to make quiet noises about suggesting some changes. But humanity is not inclined to provide adiamene to them, for..." her gaze drifted out toward the dry docks "...*reasons.*

"As for the Novoloume, we might be convinced to provide it to them, as they really are delightful, but their ship designs are so radically different from ours that it isn't practical for them to switch over, as they'd have to start from scratch. And I kind of hope they never do, since their ships are gorgeous. More prone to blowing up than ours, but *gorgeous.* I hate there aren't any in dock right now. You would drool over their ships.

"But about the adiamene. The Khokteh have lusted after it from the beginning, if only because their stellar system is very metal-poor, so they lust after any metal, no matter its ship-worthiness. But the Khokteh make our governments twitch, as if the politicians expect to be eaten for literal lunch every time a Khokteh swaggers into the room, so they're a no for the foreseeable future."

The woman sighed with tremendous affect. "And those are all the Concord species who can field military warships in any real numbers. Well, except for the Kats, but that's a whole *other* conversation."

Dashiel half-frowned in surprise. "The Katasketousya have ships?"

Rossi winced so dramatically, he almost wanted to wince with her in sympathy. "Oh, my yes. Some Kats have personal non-combat starships, though they don't need them, so I don't know what's going on there. Then there's the AI-helmed warships they used to try to wipe us out when we discovered their portal, and later used to help us defeat the Directorate. Those ships aren't indestructible—we proved that—but they are certainly formidable. And creepy as hell on the inside, never mind the outside. Also, the hundreds of thousands of swarmers each one comes stocked with." She shuddered. "I still have nightmares about the swarmers, mostly because they tried to kill Noah and me when we were stranded on Messium."

Abruptly she smiled brightly. "So, what are your questions? Regarding the adiamene, I mean?"

Each new fact revealed about the Katasketousya/Sogain only served to deepen the mystery surrounding them—and surrounding the Humans. Dashiel cleared his throat with what felt like increasing awkwardness. "How much per tonne to buy it from you?"

In an instant, the woman's demeanor pivoted to shrewd businesswoman. "How would you do that, exactly? What do you use for currency?"

Nika covered for his dismay by leaving Mia to rejoin them. "This is on the list for Senator Requelme and me to work out— some method of financial exchange. I'm not certain what it's going to be yet, but I feel confident we'll have one in the next few days."

"Then once we figure it out...?"

Kennedy grimaced. "I'm afraid I can't sell it to you until the GCDA says I can."

Nika sent him a quick ping.

GCDA is the Human political representation in Concord.

"Adiamene is a Human state asset?"

"You could say so. Humanity clings to it with both hands as if it's the only thing that will save us from the void. Which it did not so long ago and....." A troubled look overtook the woman's expressive features.

Nika nudged him discreetly, and he took the message. "I can understand the politicians' reticence. We're intrigued by this supermetal of yours, but even if it's off the table, I expect we have a great deal to offer one another." He turned to Nika. "If we can find Palmer and drag him away from the forty million ships, he and I should probably get back. We have a lot of new information to review. And you, if you're ready to come home."

She pursed her lips in contemplation. "We do have a lot to discuss. Let me touch base with Mia, but I should return home, too, at least for a day or two. I need to get the *Wayfarer*, but Alex indicated it wouldn't be a problem."

"Won't you be weeks getting back, then? I mean if you use the ship to fly home instead of a wormhole?"

"I performed a bunch of short jumps coming here because I was being cautious—I didn't know what I would find or where I would find it. Now, though? I don't see any reason why I can't cut a hole in space all the way back to Mirai."

10

*T*he vortex spit Kiernan out like a bitter seed, and the next second his tumbling vessel was falling through a white-hot atmosphere. He fought valiantly to regain control of the ship, but the spin ground his brain into mush and white faded to black...

"Collision imminent. Eject. Collision imminent."

Eject? From what—ah, fuck! His left hand fumbled across the bottom-left section of the dash for the Eject button. He didn't open his eyes, as he didn't particularly care to see the manner of his death.

"Eject. Collision imminent."

There! His finger depressed the button and he shot in the opposite direction from his crashing ship. Still tumbling, but not so violently as before. Wind buffeted his parachute, and his velocity began to slow. He risked opening his eyes in time to see cracked adobe mud racing up to meet him.

Lieutenant Kiernan Phillips scooted up beside Toshke'phien, careful to keep his profile below the top of the tall grasses, and handed the Taiyok pilot the flask of water. "Anything?"

"The collectors have started stripping the field in the northeast corner. I estimate we have forty minutes before we need to relocate again."

Kiernan rubbed at his jaw. He and Toshke had crashed on the Rasu-controlled planet several weeks earlier, though it already felt like years ago. Following his faceplant into the mud, he'd lain unconscious for almost six hours before Toshke found him, having himself crashed somewhat less spectacularly a kilometer away. He thanked the stars every day that the Taiyok had seen his ship crash, because while Toshke wasn't exactly a laugh riot, or even a particularly talkative companion, Kiernan didn't want to suffer through this trial alone. Selfish of him, just like his last lover had said.

As near as they were able to determine, they'd both been sucked into the Rasu leviathan's wormhole vortex during the battle at the stronghold then been tossed out the other side...somewhere. Somewhere where the Rasu appeared to be in the process of eradicating the local populace and stripping the planet of resources, but this planet could be two galaxies or two hundred away from home.

They had no idea what had happened to the Rasu vessel that created the wormhole. Toshke insisted it was breaking into pieces when he'd been pulled into the vortex, but if so much as a tiny part of it had survived to arrive here, it could inform other Rasu about the battle in the Gennisi galaxy.

They both agreed they ought to try to stop this from happening, but how? Assuming they located the former leviathan, their weapons consisted of two handguns and two blades. They'd considered stripping panels from the wrecked craft to use as shields but then decided the reflective metal would attract the wrong kind of attention.

Determining their location and contacting home for rescue should have been a simple matter, but a mysterious field was interfering with all quantum-based activity. Notably and most tragically, communications. They'd been unable to reach their respective governments—or anyone else—which meant in addition to being clueless about where they were, they didn't know if they had been victorious at the stronghold. It also meant their superiors, friends and loved ones believed they were dead.

Which they were apt to be any hour or day now, so it didn't really matter so much. No one was coming for them.

Based on the couple of square kilometers of territory they'd managed to survey so far, the Rasu infested this region of the planet. In a nearby valley, the aliens had assembled themselves into multiple structures, bestowing on the valley the veneer of a cold, dead city. The setup was well-established and fully operational when they'd stumbled upon it five days after 'arriving,' so they doubted these were Rasu from the leviathan.

Transports routinely arrived at and departed from the enclave, implying other Rasu concentrations existed elsewhere on the planet. Still, it didn't feel as though this was a Rasu planet. The metal transforming aliens had invaded here, likely recently.

However, they hadn't come across any other, non-evil aliens or signs of an existing civilization with any measurable level of technology. If any natives remained alive here, they were hiding the same as he and Toshke.

The field they currently resided in stretched all the way to the horizon toward the southeast. The grasses it supported were grown—the soil was tilled and the plants seeded in straight rows— another indication a primitive species had thrived here not long in the past. The tough, fibrous grass plant wasn't edible for either of them, but Rasu collectors now churned through the field harvesting the plant like ravenous beasts, so the raw material served some purpose for them.

Kiernan's stomach grumbled at the mental mention of food. They'd been able to salvage the food rations from their wrecked crafts, but those ran out at the end of the first week. The next week they'd scrounged up several handfuls of berries and a fleshy fruit from a secluded grove that wasn't stripped bare of resources, and neither the berries nor the fruit had killed them yet.

With draconian modifications by his OS to his bodily systems, he could survive for three months on only water—not fun months, mind you—but he doubted Toshke could last half as long. The Taiyok was reticent to elaborate on his physical limitations, but he clearly required food to live. Kiernan had quietly cut back on his food rations so Toshke would have more to eat, but even so supplies were running low.

He stretched aching muscles and risked lifting his head to peer around. In the distance, the Rasu collectors churned through the harvest. "We should go ahead and get moving. You might be able to out-fly those machines, but I can't outrun them."

"Indeed." Toshke scanned the horizon. "Rain clouds are moving in from the northeast. If we can meet up with them, we can replenish our water flasks."

More water would definitely be awesome—more awesome than a new batch of berries if his dry, scratchy throat got a vote. They hadn't yet traveled very far northeast.

Despite the fact that he was resigned to his inevitable death, hope stirred anew in his chest. Maybe there was real food to the northeast. Maybe there were survivors from this Rasu holocaust with cushy beds and clean clothes they would share with two weary travelers. Maybe there would be a way home.

No, that last one was ridiculous.

Toshke rose to a hunched-over standing position. His natural camouflaging capabilities, coupled with his sorrel-and-sandstone feathers, allowed him to blend in seamlessly with the tall grasses. Kiernan enjoyed no such camouflage to protect him, but he also couldn't realistically crawl on his belly for hours and hours and hours. The compromise they had arrived at involved him walking practically up against Toshke, which neither of them enjoyed, as they crept deliberately forward.

When they got clear of the endless fields, he hadn't the slightest idea what they were going to do to remain hidden.

But first they needed to make it to the end of the endless fields, so he got his feet underneath him and unfurled his body next to Toshke. "After you."

11

SENECA

MILKY WAY GALAXY
LGG REGION 1

CAVARE

Marlee shuffled down the hallway toward her apartment, her feet dragging across the floor like leaden potato sacks.

She'd suffered through yet another scolding from Caleb outside the Consulate, then a stern talking-to from Mia—but thankfully not one that ended in her firing—then an excruciating half-hour session with a security official who droned on about the Savrakath legal system and her continuing obligations to 'the process,' before she'd finally been released on her own recognizance. *Then* she'd had to stop by her office and hack into the CINT system to divert transmissions from the stolen comm module to her eVi. She'd sent Vaihe several new messages but received only radio silence in return.

It had been a disappointing end to a brutal two days.

She was about to send the unlock passcode to her security system when someone shouted her name from down the hall. No, 'shout' was a crass, crude word for the lilting, sing-song tenor of Eosha's voice. She turned and gave her neighbor a weary smile. "Good morning, Eosha."

The Novoloume barely suppressed a gasp as she neared. "You smell terrible, Marlee! What have you endured?"

Marlee sank against the wall beside her door. "Oh, you know. I spent the last day in a Savrakath jail cell."

This gasp made it past Eosha's lips. She reached out and placed a cool, soft hand on Marlee's shoulder. "You poor thing. I cannot conceive of the horror."

Marlee's considerable—best-in-class and best-in-everything—cybernetics protected her from the more illicit effects of Novoloume pheromones, at least when she wanted them to, but she nonetheless felt a peaceful serenity wash over her at her friend's touch. She was okay with this; she could use a dose of serenity.

Eosha was a participant in an outreach effort on the part of the Senecan government to encourage closer relations with their alien allies. The apartment complex in the heart of downtown Cavare boasted four different alien species as residents, as well as several Prevos and Solo Artificials with dolls. This, plus its proximity to Cavare's Caeles Prism Hub, was the primary reason Marlee lived here. If the complex hadn't existed, she'd have needed to move to Concord HQ to live immersed in alien cultures. And she might one day, but the apartment sufficed for now.

"It was hellish for certain. And now I'm going to shower for two hours then nap for twelve. After I do this file review for Mia."

"I do not blame you." Eosha frowned and touched a spot on Marlee's left forearm. "New skin. Did the Savrakaths injure you?"

"No, no. A Barisan scratched me up the other night."

"You got into a fight with a Barisan?"

"I didn't say it was a fight." Marlee grinned in spite of her generally wretched state.

"Oh, dear. Is it your plan to sleep your way across Concord space before you age another year?"

"Now that you mention it, that's not a bad short-term goal." She let Eosha assume what she'd left unsaid about the encounter, even if it wasn't entirely accurate. Her sex life was not quite so exciting, but the reputation that it was suited her purposes. "But first, showering forever."

"Yes, of course. I will leave you to it. Dinner tomorrow? You promised to let me try rigatoni."

"I did! Come by around seven."

Eosha glided off toward her apartment, and Marlee opened her door, dragged her potato-sack feet across the floor to the futon and collapsed onto it. The cushions reacted to her presence, softening and supporting her in all the right places.

But this wasn't the shower. If she fell asleep now, she'd wake to the entire apartment smelling like Savrak. So she pushed herself up and trudged off to the shower.

RW

Forty-five minutes of scalding hot water later, Marlee lay on her stomach on the futon with a glass of lemon spritzer beside her and began working through the files assigned to her.

She'd been tasked with reviewing the previous month's worth of footage from the surveillance probes Concord kept situated above the planets of species both interesting and dangerous. For one reason or another—it differed depending on the species—none of these species had been contacted by Concord, but Concord had a vested interest in keeping an eye on them.

A sub-Artificial could easily tear through the visuals and punch out some summaries, which was why it was a punishment that she'd been assigned the task. Nevertheless, there were far worse punishments.

She'd been watching twenty minutes of footage of the Galenai before she realized it. They were a delight to observe, and when she got the chance to do so, she almost always got lost in their underwater world. Alex had taken her to see the ray-like aliens in person once, nearly a decade ago, and it had been the highlight of several years of her life.

One of the adolescent Galenai pirouetted up through a porous coral tube, and she squealed in delight—then immediately berated herself. "Marlee Marano, you are twenty years old and possibly the most advanced Enhanced in existence. You do *not* squeal."

The Galenai followed up with a triple flip, and she giggled anyway. Once the juveniles swam off toward the center of the submerged city, she wrote up her summary: "Still swimming, still delightful, still not ready." She moved on to the next file.

The Vrachnas! This scut work wasn't so bad after all. She zoomed in the camera until the sunlight glittered off the individual scales of two young dragons playing together on a ledge. One gold hinting at green, the other vivid amethyst with splashes of pewter.

The purple dragon lunged forward, ducked a swipe by its sparring partner and bit into a leg, drawing blood.

A low growl from off to the side caused both dragons to freeze. The dust coating the ground vibrated as a lumbering adult strode into the fray, grabbed the purple dragon by the neck and hauled it off for a scolding.

Oh, to hear such a growl in person, to see and smell the creatures, perchance to feel the scales beneath her hands....

She sighed dreamily and rolled over onto her back. She'd been considering taking a stealth trip to the Vrachnas homeworld for several months now. But it would be straight-up stupid to get in trouble twice in one week, especially what with Caleb threatening to get her fired. Maybe next week?

She fell asleep dreaming of Galenai children chasing baby Vrachnas through an underwater maze.

RW

The alarm woke her with gently trilling flute music. Even so, the decibel level had escalated precipitously before it registered in her sleepy consciousness enough to awaken her.

She stretched and checked the time. Six hours and change of blessed sleep, but she could use another four or fourteen.

She let her eyes close again—then popped them back open. Right, right. She had an appointment to keep. So back to the shower it was for round two, then into some fresh clothes. She grabbed a sandwich from the kitchen and headed out the door and down the street to the Prism Hub.

RW

SAGAN

MILKY WAY

DRUYAN INSTITUTE

In The Displacement's aftermath, when so much changed, Sagan fought hard to remain the heart of human cybernetics research. It was such a beautiful planet that it was no wonder scientists, engineers and researchers clamored to win a spot at one of its prestigious institutes. But so dull. Not a club worthy of the name on the entire surface.

Despite the lack of entertainment options, Marlee did appreciate all the cutting-edge, still-in-beta upgrades she was able to purchase here. And in some cases, in return for a little field testing, not have to purchase at all.

She passed a woman leaving as she entered the Druyan Institute—abruptly the woman spun back around. "Marlee!"

The face instantly found its match in her memories. "Vii, it's so good to see you."

Vii reached out and hugged her. "It is. It's been...almost a year? My goodness."

"Mia's had me busy. You look good. Do I see a new upgrade or two?" Unlike her sister Valkyrie, Vii had adopted a doll as her preferred state of existence, though she presumably flitted about on stardust from time to time. This form reflected her adopted Nordic heritage, tall and blonde and muscular with strong facial features and ice-blue irises.

"Bah. Well, perhaps a few. You probably believe you're Abigail's favorite guinea pig, but you can't imagine the code infusions she subjects me to."

Marlee laughed. "Oh, I'm sure. You can complain, but I know you relish it. Speaking of, I have an appointment to be a guinea pig, so I should get inside."

"Good luck!"

Marlee waved goodbye and headed inside, through a pretentious lobby and two sprawling labs into a third, more private lab. There she found Abigail Canivon spinning out new code at her wall-sized screen, wearing khaki slacks and a white silk blouse, light blond hair secured in a smooth tail.

Marlee had never known Abigail Version 1; she'd been a little girl when the woman was murdered by OTS terrorists on Romane. Abigail Version 2 was a unique creation, much in the way Gramps was. Armed with the woman's DNA, an archaic neural imprint and the records of their many, in-depth interactions with her, Valkyrie and Vii had painstakingly recreated her mind and consciousness, then imported them into an adult clone body twelve years ago—a body which was technically still illegal at the time, but in the post-Displacement disruptions no one noticed.

Some people said Abigail V2 was an imperfect specimen—that she was neither fully human nor fully Artificial, but rather a pale imitation of both. That she was cold and emotionless, lacking human empathy and likely a human soul, whatever that meant. But Alex said Abigail V1 had been cold and emotionless, too, and claimed she could discern no difference in the reborn woman's personality.

Marlee didn't particularly care one way or another. Abigail Canivon could weave cybernetics into cosmic art, and without delivering a condescending lecture on their proper and safe use first. Good enough for her.

Abigail looked up and gave her a tiny smile, which was a big smile for the woman. "Marlee, welcome. Tell me, how are the newest enhancements performing?"

Marlee blinked, and light raced across her skin to light up every pore in elaborate sapphire glyphs. She flared her hands out, and virtual code and images surrounded her in a spherical aural. She spun around within the sphere. "Fabulously."

"Indeed. Yet you are already back for more."

"I am. I found myself in a...sub-optimal situation on Savrak earlier this week, and the thought crossed my mind that if only I had one or two additional tricks at my disposal, it might have ended better than it did."

"Let's see what we can do. What do you have in mind?"

"Can I shoot lasers out of my eyes?"

"Not and have your eyes continue to be human eyes. And even if we replaced your entire optical system with synthetic components, the power requirements would be too high. Unless you wore a battery pack on your person, the lasers would be minuscule beams that petered out after a meter."

"Damn." Marlee wandered around the lab. "What about from my fingertips?"

Abigail merely stared at her.

"Right. Okay, I just thought I'd check. What I really need are faster reflexes. I was *so close* to getting away from the, um...Savradin police."

"I see," Abigail remarked noncommittally. Damn, nothing disrupted the woman's calm.

Abigail called up a new screen and reviewed details and specs on Marlee's current cybernetics loadout for a moment. "I can increase your physical reflexes by an additional eight percent. But understand, there will be consequences. We can temporarily push the human body beyond its limits, but doing so takes a toll."

"What do you mean, 'a toll'?"

"Ask your Uncle Caleb."

"Ah, no thanks. I'll take your word for it."

"Very well. In the short term the toll is temporary, mostly involving muscle aches and the need for greater sleep and calories, but in the longer term it will mean more frequent and extensive cellular therapy, among other treatments."

She mulled it over for a few seconds. "I can live with those consequences. Let's do it."

RW

Valkyrie waited for the door to close behind Marlee before sweeping into the lab. Her doll was stored back on Earth, so she instantiated her virtual avatar, which in her scarcely humble opinion was the best example of a virtual form to be found in Concord space. It appeared solid from farther than a few meters away, so complete was her projection of skin, eyes, hair and clothes.

She'd deleted the sword and shield some years earlier, though she did bring them out when the situation called for it. This one did not.

Abigail glanced her way. "Why didn't you let Marlee know you were here? You're usually eager to talk to just about anyone."

"I will see her in a few days at David Solovy's birthday celebration. Today, I was more interested in observing her without her knowledge."

Abigail abandoned her work and leaned against a nearby table, giving Valkyrie her full attention. Inwardly, Valkyrie smiled.

"And? What did you learn from your observations?"

"It is odd. She's the only human I've been able to observe from the time she was a small child, to witness as she grew into an adult. I look at her now, and I can't help but still see the child. I believe this is Caleb's problem as well."

"Oh? She did react caustically when I mentioned him, but I didn't feel it was my place to pry."

"Alex says Caleb is quite overprotective of her. Given the manner of young woman she is, she appears to find this behavior most grating and responds poorly to instances of it. The conflict escalates."

"Ah, human relationships. Always so terribly messy."

Valkyrie hesitated. No matter how many times they had conversed on the topic, Abigail continued to make offhand remarks implying she was in some way separate and apart from humanity. She *wasn't*, but Valkyrie feared some part of her refused in her heart to believe this.

She applied a casual tenor to her projected voice. "Abigail, you know—"

"I never understood emotional relationships, Valkyrie, not even in my first life. I was horrid at them, and you have internalized enough of my personal history to recognize this, regardless of whether you are too kind to say it. I meant nothing more consequential by the comment. Now, you've expressed how you felt when you saw Marlee, but what did you observe?"

"That she is exceptional, and those of us who continue to view her as a child do so to our own detriment. She is nonetheless impulsive, as befits her relative youth. She is also startlingly empathetic for one so young, though mostly with respect to alien species, as she seems to have a blind spot when it comes to family. Brilliant, self-evidently. At this point, her cybernetics are so advanced that she might be indistinguishable from a Solo Artificial, yet she is also wholly human.

"More to the point, she is among the first human generation to grow up in a multi-species society. Amaranthe is her home, and it shows in every action she takes—in the way she lives her life."

"Those are astute observations. The generation coming of age now will, I suspect, be the harbinger of a turning point for humanity. While most people have come to accept the reality of our existence here, the aliens will always remain 'other' to us, at least in the aggregate. This will not be so for Marlee's generation.

"I fear I will need to improve my skills if I'm to keep up with her needs. She has nearly reached the boundaries of what I can do for her…and you are correct. She is increasingly blurring the line between human and synthetic in new and interesting ways. The Prevos were a joining together, a merging in many ways, of the two existences. But she is something else. We shall have to come up with a name for this new variation of human."

"As is often the case, the youth have beaten you to it. They call themselves 'Enhanced.' It lacks the dramaticism of 'Prevo' and the romanticism of 'Mélange,' but I suppose it suffices." Valkyrie strolled around the left side of the lab. "Oh! I met the Asterion last night."

"Now this *is* interesting. Do you think she will let me put her brain under a scanner?"

Valkyrie's virtual eyes blinked mutely.

"That was a joke, Valkyrie. Restart your ethereal heart."

"Your delivery is flawless, Abigail. Have you considered a second career in the comedy industry?"

"Your delivery, however, can use a bit of work. Tell me about the Asterion."

"I only spent a moment with her. She has a marvelous glow to her and eyes like bio-luminescent oceans. She speaks like a normal person, though, so I can't guess at what goes on in that fascinating brain of hers. What we have barely begun to explore—the true fusion of organic and synthetic—her people have spent seven hundred thousand years perfecting."

"Again, I express interest in five minutes and a brain scanner. Voluntarily for all involved, of course. What does Alex think of her?"

"They are getting along rather well so far. Alex is not exactly quick to trust new people, but she already finds herself trusting Nika."

"The woman is a diplomat. It is a feature of her profession to present herself as trustworthy."

"True. But Alex follows her instincts even when logic cautions otherwise."

"That she does."

"I have detected no evidence the woman should not be trusted, but it is early days." Valkyrie wandered over to Abigail's primary workstation and peeked at the screens, which contained what Abigail had been working on before Marlee's visit. "How is the testing coming?"

"For humans? The same as last month. We are now as close to true regenesis as we are apt to get without implementing an always-connected integral network, and that's not going to happen anytime soon."

"It doesn't need to, though, does it? I mean, 'as close as we are apt to get' is close enough, correct? You've succeeded."

"Not I alone, but, yes, I believe so. There is no reason why a person sporting a full complement of current generation cybernetics cannot be reborn in a new body and remain the person they were when their last neural imprint was recorded. The question that remains to be answered is whether the person will accept this reality."

"And whether those around them will—society as a whole."

Abigail sighed. "Society will do what society will do, and it's rarely rational. I can do nothing to alter that."

"So what about the other species, then?" As one of humanity's foremost experts on human cybernetics, before and after her death, Abigail had been a natural choice to work on humanity's forays into recreating the Anaden regenesis process for themselves. Working on the same process for other species was less obvious, but Abigail had always been the curious sort. Pushing envelopes and circumventing barriers when it suited her to do so.

"The Novoloume are a rousing success. Their neurological structure proved easily malleable and receptive to complex cybernetics, and from there the development was, I daresay, simple. The Volucri, too, proved to be fairly straightforward. I admit I was skeptical about their level of intelligence, but their brains are notably complex for being so small. Arguably intriguing. We're still in testing, but I'm optimistic the birds will soon be able to enjoy full regenesis."

"Any progress on the Naraida?"

"No, I'm sorry to say. Their neurological structure, much like their physical one, is an unusual amalgamation, and it is proving difficult to develop one comprehensive system to capture its workings."

"I know Alex continues to press the Taenarin to contribute to the research."

Abigail made a hedging motion with a hand. "It would likely help, if only to provide a basis for comparison. I worry that will not be enough to solve the issues, however. We also continue to face problems with the Barisans and the Khokteh—problems which I fear are insurmountable, for their tissue rejects any and all cybernetic implants."

The Khokteh had turned out to be so genetically similar to the Barisans that Valkyrie suspected the Kats had intended to produce a species of larger, stronger, more physically resilient Barisans in their creation of the Khokteh in the Mosaic. Mesme denied all knowledge of such intentions; since the Khokteh enisle had not been its domain, it might even be telling the truth.

"I begged off working on the Dankath project, but my understanding is other researchers are seeing limited success. And the Efkam? We simply gave them the documentation on Anaden regenesis and wished them the best of luck. We have no idea if they're using it or not."

"It sounds as if the overall regenesis extension project will be wrapping up soon, except for those who want to continue to try to solve the issues with the problematic species. What do you think you'll do next?"

Abigail seemed surprised for a moment, and an expression Valkyrie would daresay seemed whimsical grew on her features. "There's always a new frontier waiting to be conquered. I'm certain I won't lack for options."

"So there is." She glanced out the window in time to see a hoverflyer race by a meter above choppy water in the bay. "And now, I must bid you adieu, as I have an obligation this evening."

"Oh? Is it another date? With Carlton, yes?"

"No, no. Carlton is sweet, but he's so...sheltered. He's an Artificial, thus he can do anything he wishes. Yet he contents himself with historical studies and analytical models. I'm afraid I grow bored listening to him drone on. No, I'm leading a discussion group on the cosmological structure of sidespace—*in* sidespace."

12

TAENARIN ARIS

*TRIANGULUM GALAXY
LGG REGION VI*

Iona-Cead Jaisc greeted Alex and Caleb on the frozen surface of Taenarin Aris. Behind him, the circular elevator and the spindle at its center waited, no longer hidden by a Kat stealth field.

Jaisc grasped Alex's hands with his long, multi-jointed fingers, and his sorrow bled through his skin and into her soul. *You honor her with your presence. Take solace. Thank you.*

Alex nodded, her lips tight, and he stepped over to Caleb and did the same. While they greeted one another, she pulled her parka tighter around her. Though it provided substantial protection, the frigid air nonetheless seeped through the material in icy tendrils, and she shivered.

As if reading her mind, Jaisc gestured toward the spindle as his eyes pulsed a rich silver. "It's most cold up here. And oppressively open. Please, let us go below."

They followed the Taenarin leader onto the elevator, and it began descending into the depths.

They'd visited the Taenarin many times over the intervening years since The Displacement, but it nevertheless took several visits before they were able to coax the Iona-Cead into opening an official dialogue with Concord. After much diplomatic maneuvering on both sides, eight years ago the Taenarin became an Allied species. This meant they agreed to abide by Concord's fairly lenient rules on travel, treatment of residents and weapons development, and in return they enjoyed favorable commercial trade relations and had an advisory voice in certain Concord decisions, as well a protector should an adversary threaten them—but no real power within the organization.

They deserved a seat on the Senate, but according to Jaisc this was how the Taenarin wanted it. For a Taenarin to be seen on a Concord world or station remained a rare event. They preferred to continue living out their lives underground, practicing the old ways. All the wonders of space and its varied inhabitants held little interest for them.

But they did maintain basic communications with the outside world now, which was how she and Caleb had learned of Caomh Beshai's death three days earlier. The request to attend her funeral came at an inconvenient time what with Nika's arrival, but there had never been any question that they would do so.

The air warmed as they descended, and Alex removed her parka and folded it over her arm as the elevator slowed to a stop. Beyond the archway, the Taenarin's fantastical subterranean world spread out before them.

A subdued, mournful air quieted the normally bustling activity of the winding city. Children trudged rather than scampered; adults huddled in small groups to talk in hushed voices. Their skin took on solemn hues: rust to cinnabar, sallow to olive.

Jaisc watched her gaze take in the scene. "The Caomh was greatly loved by all. We mourn together now."

A cynical voice in her head, though, had to wonder. How much of what she saw was genuine grief, and how much was societal ritual? The Caomh was a delightful and inspiring person, but how many Taenarin had really known her? Huddled away in her sanctuary a day's journey from any settlement, how many children had actually sat at her feet and soaked up her often saucy wisdom? She suspected the Caomh was more legend than matronly figure. And it was a damn shame, because the old woman had much to teach.

"The procession will begin momentarily. Please, follow me."

When they headed away from the city center, such as it was, for a minute she thought they were all going to be making the long trek up to the Caomh's camp, which would mean this trip was going to take a lot longer than they'd planned. But then Jaisc veered to the right, and the high rocks soon gave way to a clearing of smooth granite, where the arcing ceiling stretched so high above it could almost be mistaken for sky.

Beshai's body, wrapped from head to toe in pristine ivory linens, lay atop an altar built of wood and stone at the center of the clearing. Tiny glowing rocks ringed the altar; beyond them, twenty or so children formed a circle around the altar. They wore matching ivory tunics, and their hands were joined together while their skin rippled prismatic colors in a mournful melody Alex could feel but not hear.

She'd never seen a Taenarin burial ritual before, but she wasn't surprised it took this form. As she drew in a long breath, her heart began to ache. They were here to bear witness to the ritual, and in doing so, to pay homage to the great woman Beshai had been.

She closed her eyes, remembering the woman's gnarled, warm hands grasping hers with equal parts gentleness and vigor.

"Child, there is a hole in your mind."

Beshai had known before she herself had, before Valkyrie had, before Caleb had. The Caomh looked into Alex's mind and soul and saw the cracks that would in time widen and become an abysm. Alex didn't understand the woman's magic, but magic it was.

The first time they'd visited after The Displacement, Beshai had helpfully taken a second look. She'd confirmed the hole was no more and pronounced Alex's mind well and whole, if very strange. They'd laughed about it over tea while sitting cross-legged upon a plush tapestry.

There would be no new shared mugs of tea in a little hut high upon a cliff.

Alex took Caleb's hand in hers and squeezed. He gave her a sad smile and wrapped an arm around her shoulder as an honor guard wound down the path. The circle of children parted to allow the guard to pass. They lined both sides of the altar, hefted it high in the air, and a procession began.

RW

After much singing and kneeling and orating via voice and color, the Caomh's body was burned and its ashes captured in a bronzed urn. The Taenarin rarely used open flame, so this, too, surely signified the importance of the ceremony.

Finally, many hours after they had arrived, Jaisc escorted them back to the elevator. As they walked along the now-familiar path, Alex drew beside the Iona-Cead. She recognized it had been a long, difficult day for him—a day that was likely far from over—but there wasn't apt to be another opportunity for this conversation anytime soon. And there may never be a more relevant time for it. "We could have saved her."

"No, you couldn't have." Jaisc's eyes danced from cinnabar to deep indigo. "I am well aware of the difficulties you've encountered with developing regenesis for most non-Human species."

Alex swallowed a grumble. Of course he was. Just because he preferred to stay home didn't mean he wasn't paying attention from afar.

One interesting discovery scientists made several years earlier was that the Naraida and the Taenarin shared a great deal of genetic compatibility—far more than either did with any other known species. Both were native to Amaranthe, though, so they couldn't blame the Kats for the similarities. The Taenarin, or least their leadership, might not be interested in regenesis, but the Naraida decidedly were, and if the Taenarin would only agree to contribute to the research, it was possible they held the key to unlocking it for the Naraida—and for the Taenarin.

She tried again. "We can save you."

He reached out and grasped one of her hands, the better to communicate nuanced thoughts. *You are kind in your offer, but we are not meant to live forever. Taenarin are not—I pass no judgment on Humans' desire to do so. The Caomh was at peace in her last days, at peace*

*with the knowledge that she had lived a meaningful and impactful life. I
hope I can achieve such peace when it is my time. So, thank you, but our
answer remains no.*

And that was that. Concord regulations were quite clear on the
topic: participation in regenesis and related research was entirely
voluntary. They couldn't force a single Taenarin to so much as contribute a blood sample.

She offered him a weak facsimile of a smile. "I understand. The
offer is always open, should you change your mind."

In the solitude and near-darkness of the elevator, Caleb
wrapped his arms around her from behind. "He said no again?"

She sighed against him. "He did. Stubborn, set-in-his-ways
luddite."

"I understand it, though. This, today? It was a touching, moving ceremony. Her life had meaning, and they honored this at her
passing."

"But twenty years from now, they'll say her name with rever-
ence, sure, but they won't remember her. Those children will never
know her, and they'll be lesser for it."

"I know. It's not an easy choice. But we have to respect that
they've made theirs."

13

SAVRAK

"Here's the plan. Felzeor, you know your role: be our eyes in the sky. If anyone starts heading toward the facility, even a single, solitary, poor Godjan soul, send out the alert."

"As you command."

Eren shot Felzeor a squirrelly look but didn't comment on the odd response. The Volucri was always trying out new dramatic phrases. "Drae, you're guarding our exit route. If it all goes to Hades, we need to be able to escape and get back to camp, where we will cower in fear for twelve hours."

"You're giving me the boring job again."

"Yes, I am. But like Felzeor, we all have our roles. You're the soldier, and I'm the infiltrator."

Drae flashed him an obscene gesture, but it was the extent of his pushback. His friend had on occasion bristled at taking orders from Eren. Respect for hierarchies was bred into the man's genes, and as a former *ela* in the Machim dynasty, he outranked Eren in the great Anaden societal structure in the sky.

But Drae had chosen to reject that philosophy, that entire worldview, when he'd burned out his connection to the integral and become an anarch thirty-two years ago. And if he didn't trust Eren's judgment, he wouldn't be here on this Tartarus-quality shithole of a planet with the team.

"Cosime and I will *infiltrate* the facility from the maintenance entrance on the east side using the entry code Drae acquired for us via his sophisticated use of talcum powder. Once inside, Cosime, you will flit around like a beautiful, invisible ghost and capture images of everything you see—especially nasty bombs in progress, but pretty much everything. We need to know how far along they are or, Hades forbid, if they've already created a functioning antimatter missile. While you do that, I'll hack into their computer database and copy out all the sordid details of the program."

Drae arched an eyebrow. "Have you ever hacked a Savrakath system before?"

"No, I haven't. But I have hacked 4,739 other kinds of systems. The Savrakaths aren't anything special, and their security measures have proved to be primitive. I mean, compared to ours. I can do it."

"And if you can't, at a minimum we'll get a good look around inside the lab. Or you will. I won't, what with my bored ass standing watch outside."

"I swear to Zeus, this entire team is composed of smartasses. Besides, you can stand watch inside—in fact, you should. Felzeor will let us know well in advance of anyone showing up from the outside, but there might be internal security measures you'll need to clear out."

"Sure, giant lizard-shaped mechs and whatnot. Not a problem."

Cosime's emerald eyes danced. "If there's a giant lizard-shaped mech, I want to see it!"

"Drae will take visuals." Eren peered at the horizon, where the blazing orange sun melted away into the swamp. "The evening shift will be leaving in the next few minutes. We'll wait until it's full dark to move, so ninety minutes from now."

Cosime bit her lower lip and gave him a *look*, one that sent heat rushing to private places. Ninety minutes? Plenty of time to relax before prepping for the mission. He stood and grasped Cosime by the hand. "Take a walk with me? We should check the perimeter monitors."

RW

If the days on Savrak were sweltering and miserable as they roasted beneath a fiery sun, the nights were worse. Any breeze to occasionally waft through during the day invariably died away, and the air stilled into a suffocating, humid blanket. Blood-sucking insects emerged from their burrows to swarm across the landscape in search of food—them.

Eren wiped sweat off his brow and activated his Veil as they approached the facility. Beside him, Cosime's skin glistened in the moonlight—then she did the same and vanished from his sight.

Drae had scouted ahead and taken up a position at the maintenance entrance. With the way clear, they wasted no time picking their way through the overgrowth to join him.

Eren (mission): "Felzeor?"

Felzeor (mission): "All clear. There is much activity in downtown Savradin, however. Fireworks and music. A celebration of some kind?"

Eren (mission): "Good. Maybe everyone will get drunk and pass out. Drae?"

Drae (mission): "Entering the code and...door's open."

Eren (mission): "Moving inside. Athena's grace, there's air conditioning!"

Felzeor (mission): "Can I come inside, too?"

Eren (mission): "Sorry, my friend. Next time."

Felzeor (mission): "You only say that when there won't be a next time."

Eren (mission): "Do I? Huh. Anyway, moving into the facility. Cosime?"

Cosime (mission): "Thirty meters ahead of you. One of us has work to do."

Eren (mission): "Smartasses. All of you."

Drone spectral scans from outside had enabled them to build a basic schematic layout of the building, and they'd pegged the location of the server room as the far west corner. But he didn't need the server room, only an access terminal. One of those should be in the lab control room, which they believed was upstairs overlooking the wide central chamber.

Eren crept down the hall. He was invisible to security cams, but if he moved too fast, the air displacement he caused could set off motion sensors. He'd called Savrakath tech primitive earlier, and compared to Concord tech, it was. But he still needed to respect its ability to detect him then kill him.

Gloriously cool air caressed his skin through the Veil, and he moaned in pleasure.

Cosime (private): "Eren? If you are having fun without me...."

Eren (private): "Never. Merely basking in the cool air."

He had to give the Savrakaths a little credit here. He wouldn't have guessed from the outside, but they appeared to be successfully keeping the swamp out of the facility. He reached out and ran fingertips along the wall. It felt not just cool but clean, even sterile. It occurred to him that the facility workers must wear protective gear, and by walking around in here, he and Cosime were getting germs all over everything. Hey, maybe they would contaminate the research and break the bombs.

The facility felt eerily quiet as he reached the end of the hall, with naught but the faint hum of working electronics to penetrate the silence—

—as if to prove him wrong, a security mech turned a corner and began its circuit around the central chamber.

He chuckled to himself. It wasn't giant, but the mech did feature two standard legs plus a third center-rear rolling appendage, which looked shockingly like a tail. Every species created their mobile machines in their own image.

A staircase along the left wall drew his attention as a promising path to his destination. He tiptoed up each stair, then paused at the landing to take in the chamber below.

Four partially assembled missiles stretched seven meters long in a series of lattice frameworks. Open hatches exposed their innards, revealing what appeared to be complete warhead assemblies.

Eren (mission): "Cosime, are there bombs inside those warheads?"

Cosime (mission): "There are not. Small favors, eh?"

Eren (missile): "The smallest."

The technicians could install the bombs in a matter of hours. But at least they hadn't yet done so.

Ahead of him stood the narrow room they'd identified as the lab control room. Farther down the catwalk on the right, a door led to the lab itself.

Eren (mission): "Cosime, as soon as you're finished imaging the warheads, get upstairs and image every centimeter of this lab. The bombs that will be installed inside those warheads are somewhere, and I'm betting it's the lab."

Cosime (mission): "Sir, yes, sir. Moving forthwith."

He got no respect. None at all. But it was fine. He was only in charge because someone had to be. These were his friends, his companions, his comrades-in-arms. In Cosime's case, his lover and the shining light of his oddly and unexpectedly enchanted life.

Eren smiled to himself, stepped inside the control room and surveyed its contents. The Savrakath equipment looked ungainly and therefore primitive, though in reality it was simply different. Designed from the start by a culture that had never met Anadens or any other advanced civilization that could guide them toward more standardized designs.

Still, there were only so many ways to design working electronics. Physics was physics, no matter the number of digits on your hand or whether you had a hand at all. The anarchs had developed sophisticated tools to break into every kind of system imaginable, and after the Directorate had fallen, Eren had absconded with several sets of those tools. In the decade and change since, he'd improved upon them a great deal, learning clever new tricks from the Humans and their Artificials.

Plus, since he worked for a spy organization—well, technically an intelligence-gathering organization—he knew every detail Concord had discovered about Savrakath technology. He'd preloaded his preferred hacking tool, dubbed an 'armature' by the Diaplas anarch who had designed it, with basic Savrakath-friendly commands before setting out tonight. Now all he needed was the access point.

He found it directly in front of a Savrakath bench/chair con-traption, which made sense. He nudged the bench/chair out of the way and went to work.

Cosime (mission): "Found the bombs. Is it bad that there are a lot more than four of them?"

Eren (mission): "Of course it's bad. It means they've already mas-tered the hard part of their insidious little project. Navick is going to be pissed."

Over the comm, Cosime laughed.

Eren (mission): "What?"

Cosime (mission): "The notion of Director Navick being pissed at anything—I can't picture it. What, would his brow furrow up really hard or something?"

Eren (mission): "Probably. Now hush, I'm trying to hack unfamil-iar technology."

Drae (mission): "I thought it was going to unlock and open its con-tents to you for the taking just from your presence in the room."

Eren (mission): "Shut up. It is."

He stared at the screen for a moment while his brain translated the Savrakan symbols. Then he chose what he hoped was the right routine and set it running.

Yes! Data began scrolling up the screen, and he switched the armature to copy mode.

Eren (mission): "Got that shit done—"

The door to the control room opened and a Savrakath—not a mech, but a living, breathing lizard—strode in. His uniform marked him as military, so possibly a security guard rather than a scientist. Unless the scientists were also military, which seemed likely enough.

Data continued to scroll up the screen in bright, flashing yel-low. Shit. A centimeter at a time, he moved in front of the screen. The way the Veil worked, it might obscure the details of the screen? Maybe?

The guard moved cautiously through the room, one claw on the firearm at his side. Was he responding to a security alert? Had Eren unknowingly tripped an alarm?

Cosime (mission): "Eren? Is something wrong?"

Eren (mission): "I've got a visitor. Get out of the lab while you can. Drae, I hope that exit route is clear."

Drae (mission): "Only the roving mech. So long as you watch your timing, it won't be a problem."

Cosime (mission): "Eren, I'm coming to help you."

Eren (mission): "No. We can't take him out. If they learn we've been here, the whole mission is fucked."

The armature blipped a tiny green light, and he risked a glance at the screen. A cursor blinked silently. Hoping it meant he'd captured all the files, he started to retrieve the tool—the guard reached the opposite end of the room and turned his way.

Eren froze. He couldn't remove the armature without causing the screen to flicker. And if the Veil wasn't obscuring the screen, the guard currently had a perfect view of it.

He held his breath as the alien neared to three meters. Two meters. Its scales glistened beneath the security lighting and...Eren's nose wrinkled up. He'd never actually been this close to a Savrakath, and gods did it smell. The stench of fetid water and spoiled eggs invaded his nostrils, and he fought the overwhelming urge to sneeze.

One meter. The fingers of his hand that wasn't locked around the armature rested on the blade at his hip. In less than a second he could have it in motion, activated and slicing into the alien's thick hide. He'd do it if he had to, if it was the only way to make certain Cosime and Drae made it out of the facility safely. It would mean mission failure and presumably trigger a diplomatic incident. Possibly kick off a war. Shitty consequences, all the way around. But he'd do it if he had to.

The guard passed by less than a meter from him. Surely the alien could feel Eren's breath on his skin? Could hear his pounding heart and racing pulse through the protection of the Veil?

The guard continued on toward the door.

It took every ounce of self-restraint he possessed to wait until the guard had exited the door before removing the armature and dropping it in his pack—

—a hand touched his arm.

Cosime (private): "Let's go."

He whipped around in surprise, and her hand grabbed his wrist before he accidentally smacked her. He choked off an exclamation in his throat.

Eren (private): "Arae, Cosime! What are you doing here?"

Cosime (private): "I said I was coming to help you."

Eren (private): "And I ordered you not to." He grumbled in frustration. *"Let's just get out of here."*

Cosime (private): "Yep. I'll follow you and watch our back."

Eren (mission): "Drae, we're on our way to you. If we can leave undetected, it's mission accomplished."

Drae (mission): "All clear for the next twenty-four seconds. Move."

RW

Later, after he'd transmitted all the data and visuals they'd captured to CINT, after he'd retreated to their cloaked ship for a shower, after they'd turned in for the night and Cosime slept in his arms beneath the thin, breathable material of the sleeping pouch, Eren lay awake.

They lived dangerous lives, and he recognized Cosime wouldn't have it any other way. They'd tried to retire to a peaceful, leisurely life on Hirlas after the Directorate fell and the anarchs dissolved, and it had been an utter disaster. Fire burned in her veins; lust for action, danger and adventure gave her purpose and drive. He'd never try to change her. In fact, it was one of the first things he'd ever loved about her.

But he was immortal and she was not, and sometimes, times like tonight in the control room, the yearning to protect her from those dangers flared beyond his ability to control it. She hated it when he acted on that yearning, but he couldn't *not* need to protect her.

She murmured something unintelligible in her sleep, and he stroked her feathery, snow-white hair. If Navick reacted to the intel the way he expected, they'd all be going home soon. It was beyond time for a vacation.

14

CONCORD HQ

SPECIAL WARFARE TRAINING CENTER

"And what lesson should we learn from Marshall Boleshek's tactics at the Battle of Altay?"

2nd Lieutenant Robinson, a skinny kid from Laos with attitude to burn, raised his hand. "Never get into a land war in Asia?"

"Correct!" David Solovy smirked. "But what else?"

Two seconds of uncomfortable silence from the students was interrupted by a chime ringing, signaling the end of the class period.

"You think that chime just saved you, but now I want thousand-word essays from all of you on what Marshal Boleshek did right *and* wrong. Turn them in at the start of the next class, and be prepared to defend your analyses."

Because they were soldiers—not all human, but soldiers nonetheless—not a single grumble made it to David's ears as they exited the classroom. No ordinary soldiers, either, but among the most promising young officers of their respective militaries. Not everyone earned a slot at SWTC, and the competition was fierce to win the right to spend six months being rigorously challenged to exercise one's brain rather than one's physical prowess. Much was expected of the students, but much would be given to them in the years to come.

At least, this was the plan for the school, along with training future military leaders to work closely with all Concord species from early on in their careers. It was too soon to say if the experiment was a success. Formed in the wake of the numerous mistakes committed during the Ch'mshak conflict, SWTC had only existed for six years.

The Directorate had kept the aggressive and brutish Ch'mshak under control in two ways: by providing them frequent opportunities to sate their considerable bloodlust slaughtering lesser alien species, and via the ever-present threat to blow up their entire planet should they get out of line.

Neither the Concord Senate nor Command utilized these controls, and there were consequences. Seven years ago, the Ch'mshak had begun to turn violent, raiding small colonies and space stations alike. All attempts at diplomacy failed, for without the threat of annihilation, the Ch'mshak simply didn't care what Concord thought. Months of bloody conflict ensued, and with it many of those mistakes.

It ended with the death or deportation of every Ch'mshak not on their homeworld and the ironclad quarantining of that world. The Ch'mshak had never developed space flight technology of their own, and now they were trapped on the ground, possibly forever.

It was an imperfect solution, but by far the best one that didn't involve genocide.

When the classroom had emptied, David grabbed his jacket and decided to trek over to the CINT offices. He had two hours free until his next class, and while Miriam was embroiled in back-to-back meetings for most of the day, he hoped to find Richard and Will available for lunch.

RW

CONCORD INTELLIGENCE (CINT)

David pressed the pad by the door frame to request entry to Richard's office.

The door quickly slid open. Before David could voice a greeting, however, Richard motioned for him to come inside then closed the door behind him. He felt more than heard the slight buzz of an anti-surveillance field being activated.

Will Sutton was sitting in one of the two chairs opposite Richard's desk, leaning forward intently, and didn't even glance up when David entered.

David eyed both men as he approached the second chair and took a seat. "*Bozhe moy*, who died? Wait, almost no one dies any longer, so what's the next worst thing that could happen? Did Alex order clowns for the party tomorrow night? If so, please dissuade her, I beg you."

Richard laughed, but it sounded forced. "I know nothing about clowns. On my honor. No, we've just confirmed that the Savrakaths are building antimatter weapons." A wave of his hand and a series of aurals fanned out above Richard's desk. Interspersed with chemical formulas and schem flows were images of long, menacing missiles near completion.

David shuddered. "Shit."

"That does seem to be the general consensus."

"So they've been lying to us this whole time."

"Unquestionably. But what has me more concerned is the question of what they're planning to do with their deadly creations. Now, maybe they simply intend the weapons to be an insurance policy—a deterrent they hope never to use—or maybe they plan to brandish them at Concord as some sort of threat if the negotiations don't go their way."

David stood and leaned half over Richard's desk to get a closer peek at the aurals. "Do they not realize how terrible of an idea it would be to do that?"

Will had been taking notes on the voluminous information crammed into the aurals, but he paused to shrug. "They've thus far shown little indication of appreciating either the governing ethos or the military power of Concord."

"True enough. Does Miri know yet?"

Richard shook his head. "No. I only received this report twelve minutes ago. She doesn't care for getting bad news without concomitant ideas for how to address it, so I thought Will and I should have several response alternatives prepared for her and Mia."

David glared at the close-in image of one of the missiles' open hatches. "It's times like these I wish I were still active duty. I'd get a tremendous amount of pleasure from dropping a literal and completely legal bomb on their 'insurance policy.'"

"No question. Unfortunately, if we send a squadron in to carpet-bomb the facility where they're developing these weapons, the Savrakaths will view it as an act of war. I'll include such a mission as an option, but a better one might be to let the team there plant explosives inside the facility then vacate."

"That's is Eren's team, right? He'll enjoy executing on that."

"I said *then vacate*. He'll fight me, but he's not staying to watch the fireworks."

Will frowned. "The Savrakaths don't have any domestic enemies to speak of. If we destroy the facility, they will still know it was us and will still view it as an act of war."

"True, but subtle differences matter, as does plausible deniability. Nothing says 'war' like foreign bombers darkening your skies, whereas an explosion? It's over and done with and no one on the ground is quite sure what happened. See, this is why I'm glad I'm not a diplomat. There aren't any good options here."

David snorted. "There aren't options, period, merely details to finalize. We have no choice but to cease all negotiations with them regarding their acceptance as a Concord Allied species and destroy their ability to produce antimatter weapons. And if I get a vote, we red-flag them as well."

Richard's gaze diverted from the third aural to stare at David in a way that would be inscrutable to anyone else but the two men in the room, and possibly Miriam. Not disapproving, but *concerned*. Not expressing disagreement, but *circumspection*. "Red-flagging is an extreme measure."

David had been grateful many dozens of times over both his lives for the presence of Richard's cool-headed, cautious voice of reason to guide him back from the fiery brink. But, dammit, sometimes hesitation got good people killed; sometimes only ruthless and merciless actions saved them.

"Yes, it is—so extreme we've only implemented it once in fourteen years. But the Savrakaths are making a hard play for being the second. They're a militaristic species displaying minimal to no respect for the sovereign rights of anyone but themselves, they're actively developing weapons they know perfectly well are outlawed in Concord space, and they lied to us about doing it. What if they take the next step and use those weapons?"

David sighed. "I'm getting flashbacks to the Ch'mshak conflict here. An aggressive, violent species takes advantage of our desire to rule with a light, fair touch to inflict gruesome casualties on us. Our technological superiority means we can return them to their stone age with a single strike, but our morality forbids us from doing so. Red-flagging exists for a reason."

The creased lines around Richard's eyes flinched; he wasn't convinced, but David had made a dent in his resistance. "A simple quarantine won't be a viable strategy for the Savrakaths, either. Unlike the Ch'mshak, they're not dependent on others for interstellar transport. In fact, they have an entire damn fleet they can send wherever they please. I don't know, though…a blanket order to shoot on sight any Savrakath vessel spotted in Concord space? We might as well go ahead and declare war."

15

MACHIMIS

MILKY WAY GALAXY

MACHIMIS MILITARY ANNEX

The Annex above Machimis had been rebuilt after The Displacement, but it no longer bore the moniker "Central Command." Now it went by the unassuming name of Machimis Military Annex. A place free of the strictures of the planetary atmosphere where ships could come and go and, on occasion, their captains meet.

Casmir elasson-Machim studied the newest weekly reports while he waited for the other *elassons* to join him for lunch. A lounge of sorts had been added to the top floor during the rebuild to serve as a spot where the *elassons* and occasional *ela* aide could gather in an informal setting. Machims were not well-versed in being informal, but it was a new world, so perhaps they could adapt.

He sipped on his coffee and considered what the reports told him. Aside from the simmering tensions with the Savrakaths, everything across the LGG was quiet. Of course, this tended to happen when you stopped preemptively attacking and either subduing or wiping out every new species you discovered. This also, however, left the military with little to do but patrol.

Machims bore no resemblance to the base and brutal Ch'mshak, but they *were* bred to fight. To meet all challengers with arms readied and to defeat all comers. Without an integral to continually reinforce it, in a few hundred or thousand years some measure of their killer instinct might begin to wane among the population, but that was in the future. For today, Casmir's men and women stood ready and primed to battle but were afforded no arena in which to do so. The Ch'mshak conflict six years earlier had provided plenty of opportunities to exercise their skills, but only for a short time.

Casmir braced himself as the door opened to deliver the first guests. He wasn't the Machim Primor, and he had never been comfortable leading those who were his equals. But Concord had insisted there be a single voice representing the Anaden military, and Casmir had been viewed as a 'friendly' choice on account of his buzzer-beating assistance to the Humans in helping to stop the Machim Primor from annihilating their home universe. Because he had dared to defy his Primor when no others had.

He owned his defiance, though at the time it had felt more like desperation. And now he acted as the titular leader of those who he suspected merely gave lip service to his authority.

Hannah and Otto entered, and he nodded curtly. "Help yourself to sandwiches. This will be a working lunch."

Three of the attendees would be virtual, as their current patrol routes had taken them far afield of the Milky Way, and it would be inefficient to ask them to return to Machimis for a simple status meeting of no real import.

Casmir tensed a second time when Torval strode in. Long the most brash and imprudent of the *elassons*, the man's demeanor screamed arrogance and privilege, as always. He wished Torval's patrols had taken *him* far afield, as he was at least ten percent easier to manage when on holo. But Casmir had never considered himself a lucky man.

"Torval, help yourself to some lunch."

"No need. Let's get to work." Torval pulled out a chair, sat directly opposite Casmir and clasped his hands atop the table.

"We will begin when everyone has arrived." He stood and went to get a fresh glass of water, if only to avoid Torval's piercing stare.

Three minutes later the last person, Ulrich, walked in, and Casmir activated the privacy filter. "Navarchos, thank you all for coming today. I've received and reviewed your latest reports and will address your requests now. Hannah, permission is granted to bring your Imperium into dock for repairs and upgrades. In the absence of active combat, it is incumbent upon us to keep our vessels in top condition. Nevertheless, double the number of battlecruisers on your route while the Imperium is out of commission.

"Otto, permission is granted to double patrol sweeps of the Ch'mshak system. If they're getting feisty, we need to be ready to put a forceful stop to it. Torval, permission is denied for beginning active flybys of Savrak. The diplomatic negotiations are at a precarious stage, and we don't need to be seen as provoking the Savrakaths."

"But they—"

He gritted his teeth. "Follow my orders, Torval."

"*Sir*, they have antimatter weapons."

"Excuse me? What leads you to believe this?"

"I have an acquaintance in CINT. She mentioned it."

It was a weaselly answer from someone who was usually direct to a fault. "If CINT is aware of the production of antimatter weapons by the Savrakaths, then we can assume it is being handled."

"Handled? How, by *talking*? By *tsking* them in disapproval? The Humans are cowards, and they will let the Savrakaths walk all over them like a threadbare rug in an attempt to keep the peace at any cost. It is our duty to eliminate this threat before they're able to use those weapons on us."

"The Humans weren't cowards when they kicked our asses fourteen years ago, Navarchos Torval. Until Commandant Solovy gives the order, there will be no aggressive actions taken against the Savrakaths. Have I made myself clear?"

Torval's jaw locked. "Crystal. May I be excused?"

"Does the meeting look as if it is over? No, you may not be excused."

RW

Casmir powered through another twenty minutes of bureaucratic procedures on stubbornness alone, but he breathed a sigh of relief when the room finally emptied without any acts of physical violence.

He dropped his chin in a hand and stepped through the action items now falling to him as a result of the Navarchos' feedback. Then he sent a message requesting a remote audience with Commandant Solovy.

Less than thirty seconds later, her representation appeared in the space above the table. "I only have a moment, Casmir. What is it you need?"

"I'll come straight to the point, then. One of my Navarchos has voiced a belief that the Savrakaths are developing antimatter weapons."

She looked up sharply. "Where did they hear this?"

"If he is to be believed, you have a leak in CINT. Is it true, ma'am?"

Her lips pursed, and her eyes darted to somewhere—or someone—off-cam. "We don't know for certain. We are investigating."

"If they're allowed to—"

"I am aware of the variables, Casmir. If our investigation produces hard evidence that the Savrakaths are manufacturing or fielding antimatter weapons, we will act accordingly. Not before then."

He kept his posture rigid, consciously refusing to wilt beneath the rebuke. "Yes, ma'am. I'd like to be kept apprised of developments, however. So we can be better prepared to respond if needed."

She hesitated a moment, then nodded minutely. "I'll update you on what we find."

"Thank you, Commandant. I'll wait to hear from you."

16

MIRAI

MIRAI PAVILION

Dashiel hurried out the front entrance of the Mirai Pavilion the same instant Nika began ascending the steps. They met halfway and then she was in his arms. It had been less than a day since she'd seen him at Concord HQ, but he held onto her as if she'd been absent for years. She didn't mind.

His lips found her ear. "I'm glad you're back on Dominion soil for real."

"I was fine."

"But you might not have been."

"I'm here now, safe and sound. Want to go home—my place or yours, it doesn't matter—and spend the next eighteen hours naked in bed?"

"Yes, I *do*."

Her lips brushed across his and back again; she sighed softly.

He drew back a little, his amber eyes twinkling. "Can't do it, can you?"

"Dammit, no. Later, though, I promise. Now, show me what you've been up to while I was traversing the void."

"You've got it." He took her hand in his to lead her the rest of the way up the stairs and inside.

The Dominion government had entered into a long-term lease for the Mirai Pavilion from Charles Basquan, and the ways in which they were making it their own began to leap out to her from the minute she stepped inside: a glossy new paint job, permanent panes announcing the purpose of each wing and room in pearl-white lettering, informational billboards...and an intriguing new logo adorning every one.

Dashiel strode down the main hall, guiding her past a long sequence of rooms with fascinating titles, and she fought the urge to peek inside them all. He led her to the east lift, then selected the top floor.

"The data vault?"

He smiled mysteriously. "It's not a data vault any longer."

"Fine, keep it a surprise." She kept her voice nonchalant, but by this point her curiosity was beyond piqued.

The lift rose into a sleek glass enclosure as it slowed to a stop. She stepped off to find she was part-way inside a single expansive room. It must stretch the entire length and breadth of the top floor.

"Welcome to the Omoikane Initiative."

A name that promised knowledge and wisdom in equal measure. She studiously took in the space, though she found she had to turn in a complete circle to discover it all.

The floor-sized room was divided into numerous workspaces through the use of half-walls, shoji screens and curving frosted glass dividers. At least fifty people occupied the floor, all giving the appearance of working diligently at unknown tasks. On the far wall, which had acted as a command/information center during the attack on the Rasu stronghold, a single long pane stretched for the entire length. She zoomed in her vision until she could read it without approaching closer. Nine columns segregated the data displayed by subject matter.

The first column contained military fleet strength for a variety of craft—cruisers, frigates, fast attack craft, support vessels and more. She blinked and realized the data had updated while she studied it.

The second consisted of a bullet list of "Top 5 Projects," each one coded by priority, feasibility and status. The third included a much longer list of other projects in development. The fourth displayed a list of the most critical 'needs.' The remaining columns broke out each of the Top 5 Projects in far greater detail.

The highest priority—

—someone tackled her from the left, sending her stumbling back a step. "You're back!"

She laughed as Perrin Benvenit enveloped her in a bear hug. "Still needing to breathe, though!"

"Sorry." Perrin released her and took a step back to scrutinize her. Nika did the same. Her friend had straightened her wavy-bordering-on-curly hair into a sleek side part and lightened it to strawberry blond. She wore a baby blue velvet shirt and navy slacks—practically formal attire for her. She looked...good. Put together, bordering on professional.

"Who are you, and what have you done with my friend?"

"What, me? Pfft. I just didn't want security to think I was a vagrant and kick me out. You look the same, though. Maybe a little tired."

"It's been a whirlwind..." she counted it up in her head "...thirty-eight hours. Plus all the weeks before then."

"Tell me everything. But first, want to see my office?"

"Of course I do." She glanced at Dashiel, who rolled his eyes and nudged her after Perrin.

She was stopped by multiple people on the way across the room, but finally they made it to an enclave toward the front right of the space.

"This is Personnel. And also my office." Perrin motioned with exuberance to a marbled ceramic desk covered from corner to corner with knick-knacks, data weaves, empty glasses and two jackets. Three panes hovered at the center, and a tall stack of more data weaves was piled haphazardly on the floor beside the desk.

"It looks as if you're most of Personnel."

"Well, I am. I mean, I'm in charge of it, but I do have two employees. Part-time only, but they totally work for me."

"Two today, two hundred tomorrow. What does being in charge of Personnel mean?"

Perrin pointed to the expansive pane along the back wall. "All those projects on the scoreboard? They need staffing. They need brilliant brains working on them and engineers designing what the brilliant brains come up with and techs building the designs. I find those people and connect them with the right project. Then sometimes reconnect them with the actual right project."

"That sounds perfect for you."

Perrin shrugged. "It's something I can do to help. And I don't have NOIR to take care of any longer, so I needed a job."

"Speaking of, how are our former NOIR comrades doing?"

"Let's see. Parc is running a dozen ceraff projects—some Omoikane-authorized, some not so much—while Ryan and Dominic are mostly working on the Guerilla Project, which involves strategizing for building-to-building combat against the Rasu. Some of the Taiyoks on Namino are even helping us with it, since they're, you know, sneaky." Perrin grimaced. "Joaquim's working on that, too, though he refuses to become an official employee of Omoikane. He's even gotten Xyche'ghael to pitch in. Ava and Maggie are designing..." Perrin's eyes narrowed "...oh. I see what you did there. But I swear, keeping up with NOIR people takes no more than twenty minutes a day of my time."

"Uh-huh. And how's Adlai?"

Perrin collapsed into her chair. "Grumpy, today. He's over at the Justice Center now trying to wrangle a particularly thorny series of crimes." Her voice dropped to a conspiratorial whisper. "Ceraffin trouble."

A warning flared in Nika's mind, tinged with a flavor of dread. "A single ceraff, or all of them?"

"Neither. A few of them. Justice is having a difficult time herding the multiplying ceraffin into any sort of monitorable, rules-abiding structure."

She wasn't surprised. But she refused to feel guilty about creating the kyoseil-powered consciousness hubs; they'd done what they'd had to do.

"So you likely want to get updates on all that stuff—" Perrin waved toward the scoreboard "—from the other Advisors, and I know they want to hear from you about the Anadens or whoever it is you found. But later, you have to tell me about your adventures. But only the exciting parts."

"I will, I promise." She wandered closer to the front of the room, using this new information to scan the information in greater depth. After a few seconds, she sensed Dashiel join her in front of the scoreboard.

"What's the Vault?"

RW

MIRAI TWO

The commercial shipbuilding facility on the outskirts of Mirai Two bustled with as much activity as the Pavilion, but most of this activity was dyne and mech in nature. The first true oddity, however, was the level of security here. It far outstripped the measures at the Pavilion, the Axis World Towers and even the former Platform.

An opaque force field completely enveloped the facility in a half-bubble, obscuring whatever was inside, and heavily armed combat dynes staffed a single two-stage checkpoint entry through the field. Outside the bubble, three AEVs flew in a patrol pattern high overhead.

She eyed Dashiel suspiciously, but he just motioned her toward the checkpoint. "You'll see why once we're inside."

"Are they going to *let* us inside?"

"They are. We have clearance."

And so they did. It took several minutes, but finally they passed through the force field, and she got her first look at this mysterious Vault.

The outdoor factory floor, formerly devoted to assembling private starships, had been turned over entirely to a single construction project. An enormous and already imposing circular object over fifty meters in height and one hundred twenty in width was suspended above the ground in an elaborate construction framework. Mechs fitted thick pieces of hull plating into unfinished sections while drones buzzed around using precision torches to seal up open seams.

"It looks like the Platform."

"There's a good reason for that. The Platform was built to survive permanently in space, and it used the best technology available to us to do so. We've cribbed a lot of the designs and tech from it for use in the Vault."

"You still haven't told me what the Vault is, exactly."

"It's better if I show you. Let's go inside."

More surprises, then. Served her right for leaving him behind for a few weeks with an expansive mandate and a blank check.

A sturdy lift platform waited on the ground beneath the center of the…ship? Station? When they stepped on it, Dashiel entered a code in a control pane, and it rose to deliver them inside.

The temperature dropped a good ten degrees as soon as they reached the interior. The lighting inside was dim but pervasive, with streams of silver lights running horizontally two meters apart. They revealed a ring of…she squinted. Server hardware, she thought, encased in durable containment boxes. Periodic breaks in the ring revealed aisles leading to additional, larger rings that circled outward into the shadows.

The volume of data this much hardware could store was almost beyond conceiving. "Are we storing the sum total of all knowledge of the Asterion Dominion?"

"You're not far off. We're storing the psyche backups of every Asterion."

She spun to Dashiel, properly astonished. "*Every* psyche?"

"That's the goal. Then we're going to send the Vault to space, where it will keep them safe from a Rasu attack."

"Will it? From everything we've seen, the Rasu are a space-based species."

"True, but to say that space is a big place understates the matter by a fair amount. They'll have to find it to destroy it, and this is where we're getting clever. We can't move the Axis Worlds, but we can move the Vault.

"The navigation system will be fully autonomous and pro-grammed to avoid astronomical phenomena as well as any artificial activity it detects. It will stay in the Gennisi galaxy, but beyond that limitation, its movements will be random and unpredictable, even to us. Accessing its location at any given moment will require the simultaneous approval of a minimum of four Advisors, as will tak-ing control of navigation or accessing the contents. The entire system is stand-alone—no nex web access—and only the Advisors know how to contact it."

She approached the innermost ring and ran her hand along the cool metal, felt the faint vibration of power. "The psyche backups won't be regularly updated?"

"No. To do so would send the security risks through the strat-osphere. It's not a perfect plan, but it's the best one we've come up with to make certain our people survive to start again, should the worst happen. The Vault operating system will expect to receive a confirmatory ping from one Axis World every ten months. If it doesn't receive a ping for fifty months, it will travel to a randomly chosen habitable world in its database and land."

"And begin constructing bodies? There's a regen lab in here?"

Dashiel gestured toward the ceiling, which hung only thirty meters overhead instead of the expected fifty.

She came to an aisle and peered down it. Seven concentric rings? No, eight. "Everyone in the Dominion, truly?"

"Probably not 'truly.' We can't transfer backups from private facilities without the individuals' permission, and obtaining those permissions is going slowly. Also, not everyone will agree to it. It seems some people continue to be paranoid about government in-trusion into their lives."

She laughed faintly. "Having been on both sides, I can't honestly blame them. And it is ultimately their choice." The mere notion of what the 'worst happening' meant in real terms sent a shudder rippling through her body. But if such a catastrophic string of calamities *did* befall them...she nodded deliberately. This would ensure her people lived to rise again.

"What's the schedule?"

"The structure itself is eighty-two percent complete, and we've loaded thirty-six million psyches so far, or around forty-one percent of what we hope to include. In theory, the Vault will be ready to launch within three weeks." He gave her a teasing smile that belied the dark solemnity of their environs. "So, you know, let's make sure and get your psyche backup in here."

RW

MIRAI JUSTICE CENTER

Escalation had been a reality of law enforcement since time immemorial. Justice implemented better, more advanced security measures and crime detection methods; criminals devised new ways around them. Justice adapted; the criminals followed suit.

The old story now featured a fresh new twist: the ceraffin. Instead of it taking months or years for enterprising criminals to develop a new way to elude Justice, it was taking weeks. Days. Twice now, mere hours.

As much as Adlai Weiss was coming to despise the collective consciousness hubs, he nevertheless recognized they weren't limited to criminal pursuits. The Justice Division already operated two standing ceraffin, and they helped to stay on top of shifting criminal practices and patterns. But the Justice ceraffin had to cover the entire Dominion's worth of law enforcement, while a single criminal-operated ceraff was able to focus all its considerable processing power on its chosen goal.

And this morning at 9:27, the imbalance in resources had reared up to bite him in the ass. To bite Justice in the ass, but specifically Justice on Mirai. In other words, him.

Despite all their extensive precautions and security measures, someone walked into the Mirai Justice Center, proceeded to the server hub in the basement and had their way with it. Then they walked back out the front door, all without a single alarm activating.

Adlai took the server offline immediately upon the breach being discovered and loaded a backup from overnight so the regular and ordinary work of Justice could continue. One of the Justice ceraffin specialized in forensic analyses, and it had taken the group of joined Asterion minds less than twenty minutes to determine no data had been altered in the server and no malicious code left behind. Nonetheless, because even ceraffin made mistakes, the sliced system would remain offline and the updates processed since the backup reentered on an individual basis.

The obvious conclusion to arrive at was the incursion had been a fishing expedition. Someone wanted secure data that Justice possessed. Slicing left behind traces, so usually in such a circumstance, they'd be able to determine what data the slicer had viewed. Not this time. A worm had crawled wild through the system, spiraling outward and touching virtually every corner of every database. It had done so to obscure what the perpetrator wanted to study, of course. And done a damn fine job of it.

Adlai pulled up the building security report for the third time. They'd identified every person who had entered the Justice Center and not yet departed at the time of the breach, and officers were locating and interviewing them with commendable speed.

Everyone, that was, except for the five identities that did not correspond to actual living Asterions.

Spoofed IDs were nothing new. It wasn't easy to create one comprehensive enough to pass a Justice security scan, but it was certainly doable. In the days after the destruction of the Rasu stronghold, when they were all still giddy about the victory and doing more celebrating than working, Nika confessed to him that she'd used spoofed IDs to enter the Mirai Justice Center three times in the last five years, and the Namino and Kiyora Justice Centers once each. Perrin swore she'd never done so…but had admitted to him she could have if she'd needed to do it.

NOIR had enjoyed access to more sophisticated tools than most criminals ever saw, but with the advent of the ceraffin, those tools were becoming available to anyone who wanted to obtain them. Again, not easy, but clearly doable.

Still, five people using spoofed IDs on a single morning had to be a record. His gut told him it only happened because all five were involved in the crime. Maybe the role of four of them was simply to give him multiple ghosts he needed to track down. Maybe some had served as lookouts or distractions.

He stared at the image captures of the five, for what they were worth, which wasn't much. Like digital signatures, faces could be changed. Or rather, the faces that Asterion eyes and cams recorded could be changed. Not dramatically, but enough to render legal identification impossible.

Three of the individuals displayed male facial features and two androgynous ones. Two sported medium brown hair, one black, one ginger, one dark blond. Similar distribution in iris color. The bone structures of their faces differed in the details, but they all clustered around 'normal.' Nothing distinctive, nothing to catch the eye.

He sank back and rubbed his jaw. And this constituted the entirety of what he had to go on. It was a breach notable primarily for its audaciousness—and for its exposure of an uncomfortable truth: as it stood right now, Justice security was not up to the job it purported to perform. But they'd uncovered no clues as to what the criminals wanted or what they left with, and nothing but five throwaway names and faces as leads.

He needed to head over to the Pavilion in a few minutes to help catch Nika up on what she'd missed, but he'd do a quick ceraff with the other Justice Advisors later today on the off chance that collectively they might spot some new thread to chase down. Then he'd review the recommendations for new measures to escalate the building security yet again.

17

MIRAI

Nika took a seat at the slick glass conference table in the 'Operations' zone of the Omoikane Initiative. No more scrounging up chairs and moving furniture into whatever conference room at the Pavilion happened to be available and not disrupted by rubble. Every meter of the building had received a fresh coat of professionalism and respectability. Nothing shoestring or ragtag here. Not any longer.

Maris Debray was always prattling on about the emotional power of imagery; seeing the difference it made here, Nika found she couldn't disagree.

She wrapped her hands around the steaming coffee mug in front of her. "Talk to me. Where are we?"

Lance went first. "We are 10,213 warships stronger than we were a month ago, doubling our preexisting fleet. Three hundred forty new ships now leave the assembly lines each day. Those assembly lines consist of four separate facilities in orbit above Namino and twelve component facilities on the ground. I won't bore you with the details of the new ship designs, but some of them are interesting."

Maris moaned whimsically. "They are gorgeous. I never thought I'd say such a thing about weapons of destruction, but they belong in an art gallery."

"No, they belong patrolling Dominion space, which they are doing in greater numbers every day."

Dashiel tilted his head. "We've developed a new railgun weapon that uses the archine blade technology. We started installing it on all the larger ships last week."

"How does it do that?"

He chuckled. "It literally shoots out eight hundred meter-long archine blades at a speed of ninety km/s for as long as the supply holds out."

The image forming in her head made her chuckle, too. "Clever."

"Well." He shrugged. "We're also working on a laser weapon that in effect acts like an archine blade, but it's slower going. We're deploying long-range sensors specifically tuned to detect the Rasu emission signature throughout all Dominion stellar systems. We've leased a dozen of the sensors to the Taiyoks, and next week we'll deploy several in the Chosek system. If or when the Rasu show up, we ought to have at least several hours' warning."

Adlai spoke up. "Justice has been developing emergency evacuation procedures designed to get as many people as possible off a planet if it comes under attack. Your basic emergency practices: switching all trams to inbound to the transit hubs, flipping every d-gate to exit mode, as well as broadcasting nex alerts and instructions.

"We are also developing procedures for those who can't get off-world in time to follow. We're building underground bunkers to shield them, and possibly including weapons stashes there, though the security measures to access those are under discussion. In theory, we want to provide people a way to survive until we can rescue them."

Nika frowned. "Perrin mentioned something about the 'Guerilla Project'—but what does 'can't get off-world *in time*' mean, exactly?"

Adlai shifted uncomfortably; she'd hit a nerve. "This is also still under discussion, but should the worst occur—should the Rasu make landfall—there will come a point where we'll need to shut down the d-gates on the sieged world under a protocol we're designating 'Firewall.' The prevailing belief is that we can't leave open the slightest possibility of Rasu using them to reach other Dominion worlds."

She sank back in her chair, the optimistic mood buoyed by so many exciting advances swept away by the somber weight of the threat looming over them. "Containment."

"Containment. I know it's not a pleasant thought, but we—"

"But we have to think strategically. I appreciate the arguments for it—and those against it. I need to think about it. We can discuss it further later." She said this as though the Justice Advisors would allow her to overrule them if she decided she disagreed with the protocol, which...there would only be one way to find out. She forced her spine straight. "What else?"

Dashiel spoke up again. "You've already seen the Vault. The other big project in a similar vein is the planetary shielding. We expect to be ready to begin deployment testing of it in another two weeks."

"How does it work?"

"Currently, thirty-two hundred satellites are in high orbit above Mirai. When activated, they'll broadcast a signal pattern that will create an electromagnetic mesh surrounding the planet. We've based the pattern on Taiyok stealth technology, and it should mask the presence of the planet from outside the mesh."

"But?"

"But we're facing a host of technological and safety issues. The power required to generate the pattern is tremendous, and this power must then be masked as well, thus increasing the needed power output. The long-term effect of the mesh on the atmosphere and thus on the planetary climate is unclear. Simulations indicate it will be marginal at worst, but a planet's climate is one of the most complex ecosystems in existence, and we can't be certain."

She chewed on her bottom lip. "How effective is the cloaking?"

"Again, we're in the realm of simulations for a while longer. But it fools our own scans from as close as two megameters. Of course, it's all an illusion. If the Rasu fire a weapon through it, the weapon will hit the planet. Now, they might not know it hit anything unless it's a missile that continues to send back data."

138 | G.S. JENNSEN

"Nonetheless, that's impressive. You said the satellites are already in place above Mirai. What about our other worlds?"

Dashiel sighed. "The cost and manufacturing effort required to produce a working deployment for Mirai has been gargantuan. Until we're sure it works and is tolerably safe, we frankly can't afford to build a second one, never mind four more, or twelve more after that for the Adjunct Worlds."

She gave him a small smile. "I understand." Then she dipped her chin toward Lance. "How's Jerry doing?"

"Sunning itself on III-E183-31B like it hasn't a care in the world. Which, who knows? Maybe it doesn't."

"I'm glad to hear it." She straightened up in her chair. "This is all incredible, and far above and beyond what I imagined you could accomplish in a few short weeks. It's possible we'll soon have additional assistance coming our way from Concord, but we can't rely upon it. We need to be able to defend ourselves, and it sounds as if this is what we're preparing to do."

Dashiel didn't bask in her praise, but she hoped he felt it. He gestured toward the scoreboard. "There are additional projects in the early development and vetting phases. A virutox to scramble Rasu systems when injected directly into them is the most promising idea as of today, though such a weapon will only be usable in a narrow and unpleasant range of circumstances.

"We've got four ceraffin working on everything from the mundane to the truly outlandish, testing out permutations and running feasibility analyses. And Perrin's done a fantastic job of setting up citizen teams to help develop and build out projects. If you walk the streets, you'll see a hundred ways the Initiative is out there.

"We do, however, continue to run up against one intractable problem—how to permanently destroy Rasu. Unless there happens to be a nearby star we can hurl them into, our options remain limited.

"We are quietly building nuclear-based weapons we hope will be able to take out individual ships in the right circumstances, but the risks to using those widely go without saying. We are also experimenting with miniaturized atomic weapons that can be used to disintegrate the ground-based, bipedal Rasu forms. The collateral damage will be extensive, and we're having trouble finding ways to mitigate it. Our bodies are mostly organic, and we can't completely prevent radiation damage.

"If we start activating these weapons all around a city, the impact will be devastating to the ecosystem as well as to us. So...yes, we still need to find another way to destroy them." He smiled gamely. "Stay tuned."

18

SIYANE

NGC 55
BEYOND THE BOUNDARIES OF CONCORD SPACE

The Caeles Prism vaulted them across two megaparsecs of space in the span of a blink, though Alex never blinked during such transitions. Her eyes were closed but her vision open, and when they emerged out the other side of the space-time tear, seven billion new stars bathed her in their light. Cosmic particles agitated by their sudden arrival danced their way around and through her.

Around and through the *Siyane*, that was. Which happened to technically also be her at the moment. Once upon a time, this elemental connection between her and her ship had nearly destroyed her mind and her life. As such, she took due care with it, always treating it as a privilege—and it was the greatest of those—to be enjoyed judiciously and with deliberate intentionality.

Few experiences could compare to bursting into the heart of a new galaxy while using all of one's faculties to see, feel, *know* every dimension of its existence, and she damn well appreciated the wonder of it.

Alex sensed the gentle nudge of another consciousness as it slid into the *Siyane's* quantum circuitry like it owned the place. Which....

Hello, Valkyrie. Curiosity won out?

It did. I want to see what you find.

Well, since you're here, you can fly. Our initial destination is in the region of SGC—

No, no, I'm simply here to observe.

Tough. You can do your old job for a bit.

Oh, fine.

Valkyrie's gradual separation from the *Siyane*—or rather her expansion beyond it—had occurred in fits and starts in the years after The Displacement and even now wasn't truly complete. For the most part, her original circuitry remained inside the walls of the ship and operated with full functionality. It was merely that Alex could now inhabit that circuitry as easily and completely as Valkyrie could. Valkyrie also maintained a complete set of quantum hardware on Earth, with a synced backup set on Sagan as well, and probably third and fourth copies in additional places Alex didn't know about. Valkyrie's consciousness projected out from any of those sets of hardware to anywhere the Artificial wanted to be present.

And every now and then, Valkyrie dropped into the *Siyane* for a visit.

Alex eased the strands of her consciousness back into her body, then stretched out in the cockpit chair and yawned.

Caleb arched an eyebrow at her, then at the ceiling. "Hi, Valkyrie."

'Hi, Caleb. I'm sorry I missed you the other night.'

"Hmm?"

"Valkyrie stopped by briefly to meet Nika after you left."

"Ah. Yes, I had to wrangle my insolent niece back into Concord space."

'How is Marlee?'

In truth, I saw Marlee the next day when she visited Abigail. But it's better to allow him to talk about her, yes?

You're sweet, Valkyrie. I wish I could say it would help.

"I am the last person to answer that question. No longer in a Savrak jail cell, but beyond that, I don't want to hazard a guess."

'I'm sure she'll be all right. She is remarkably bright and resourceful.'

"Yes..." Caleb rolled his eyes "...remarkably."

Alex felt as if she should respond, though whether to defend Caleb or Marlee she had no idea, but the first round of sensor readings arrived to rescue her. What she'd sensed while she inhabited the ship was becoming hard data and a lot of it. "Damn, this galaxy is loud. Louder than the Milky Way, which is saying something."

'All stealth measures activated. Dimensional Rifter charged and ready.'

A few years earlier, Alex had switched out her old impulse engine for a modified Zero Drive. Among other features, it ensured the *Siyane* now had plenty of power to run all the things pretty much all the time without having to take drastic measures like cutting the heat to compensate.

Caleb answered. "Thank you, Valkyrie. Let's not forget that we're in the heart of enemy territory here. So what does 'loud' mean? What are we seeing here?"

"Right now, it simply means loud. Lots of noise from artificial, non-cosmological sources. It's as if every star system has quantum-grade technology deployed."

"Perhaps they do."

"Considering what brought us here, the prospect does not fill me with warm fuzzies. Valkyrie, pick a star, and let's take a look." She stood and went into the main cabin to get a snack; inhabiting the ship always gave her the munchies.

After Lakhes visited her mother the other day, the Kat had shared data pointing them toward NGC 55 as the closest galaxy to Concord space where the Rasu maintained a significant presence. The barred spiral galaxy lay on the fringes of the Local Galactic Group, but not in the direction of the Gennisi galaxy and the Asterions, which suggested the Rasu's area of influence was...substantial. Her mother had followed up, asking Lakhes what 'significant presence' actually meant, and the Kat had responded precisely how one expected it to, with a vague mutterance about the answer being best seen to be understood.

Valkyrie jumped them in close to a nearby star—and missed getting them run over by a mammoth vessel by a scant few meters.

Caleb shouted an unnecessary warning. "Evasive maneuvers!"

The *Siyane* dove nose-down at twenty-eight degrees, and Alex slammed into the cockpit half-wall. Her shoulder jolted painfully and the crackers she'd grabbed spilt to the floor, but she ignored the pain and the mess to stumble into the cockpit and see what they'd almost hit.

As they pulled out of the dive, a dark aubergine hull sped by above them...and continued to speed by as seconds ticked away. Little of note broke up the smooth metal hull as it kept stretching on and on. "How big is this monster?"

Valkyrie waited until the flare of engines hopefully signaled they were reaching the end of the vessel. 'A minimum of 3.3 kilometers in length.'

"Jesus." Caleb studied her in concern. "Are you all right?"

"Yeah. Valkyrie, move us a few megameters, in case they detected the spatial disruption from our wormhole." She worked her shoulder around a couple of times as the vessel *finally* cleared the viewport and they were able to see the area.

"Oh, fuck me." Alex leaned as far into the dash as she could. "Do you remember when we came upon an armada of Kat superdreadnoughts and swarmers pouring out of the Metis Nebula portal?"

Caleb nodded vaguely, his gaze also fixed ahead. "I do."

"Why does this keep happening to us?"

"Because we keep insisting on going looking for trouble?"

"Oh, that's right." Her hands came to her mouth. Match point to Lakhes: best seen to be understood indeed.

Ships flew in every direction—small ships, large ships, but most of all truly behemoth ships. The shapes and hull configurations varied, but all were built of a dark, burnished metal that reflected almost no light. Valkyrie had added a full EM overlay to the viewport to help them spot all the vessels against the blackness of space.

Every so often, two of the ships met one another and docked together, interlinking as effortlessly as if they'd once been two halves of a whole, then separated into multiple pieces—usually a greater number than their original two—and continued onward.

A Dyson structure encased the star at the center of the system. Not quite a shell, as it was porous, but a tight lattice more solid than a swarm and far more extensive than a series of rings. Outside the Dyson structure, a ring of platform stations orbited the full circumference of the star.

Each platform was the size of a city, something like twenty kilometers in diameter. The vessels arriving and departing each platform resembled insect swarms, so numerous were they.

She sank down into her cockpit chair, though her eyes continued to take in the details of the scene out the viewport and the Artificial parts of her brain joined Valkyrie in beginning to analyze the deluge of sensor data. "Does this feel worse than the Mosaic portal to you? Because this feels worse to me."

Caleb's throat worked as he considered the question. "It does not, but only due to the fact these ships aren't currently preparing to depart for Seneca, Earth, Romane and all our worlds. Not yet."

She didn't take as much comfort from the admitted blessing as he seemed to. Deep in her heart, she knew it was only a matter of time before these armadas, or other equally terrifying armadas, would take exactly such action.

In the pit of her stomach, an old dread began to stir from its long slumber. Space was vast and untamed, and another of its creations was readying itself to threaten not merely their way of life, but their very existence.

But they'd triumphed over all comers so far, and with enough time and preparation, they would find a way to do so again. Somehow. She buried the dire ruminations and tried to focus on why they were here, which was to conduct research on their soon-to-be enemy. "This setup matches what Nika described."

'Initial scans suggest a much higher level of activity throughout the remainder of the stellar system than what the Asterions encountered in their galaxy.'

Caleb nodded. "They've been here for longer. They only arrived in the Gennisi galaxy eight years ago, but here they've had time to establish a proper presence."

"I wonder just how proper. Valkyrie, can you cobble together an efficient course for us to get a reasonable sample of the Rasu presence in this galaxy? No longer than four hours' journey, since we have Dad's party tonight."

'Done. Jumping to the next star.'

The scene they'd encountered at the first star repeated itself another half-dozen times, with only the tiniest variations. They found three planets infested from pole to pole by Rasu, one of which showed signs of having previously been home to a Tier I civilization. A series of orbital arrays around the fourth planet of a now-silent system hung in broken tatters, drifting along a deteriorating orbit that would soon deliver them to the atmosphere to burn.

If the original inhabitants had been able to so much as scratch the Rasu during their invasion, however, there was no evidence of it. The surface of the fourth planet as well as two additional planets had been literally shredded down to the mantle. Plundered then abandoned.

After less than an hour, it became apparent that the Rasu dominated every corner of this galaxy. Other than a few stray remnants of non-Rasu structures in razed and decimated systems, they found no evidence that any other species continued to exist here. Possibly a few primitive life forms remained as slaves on occupied worlds, but confirming it would require a much more thorough and hazardous investigation.

Alex rubbed at her face; her eyes were already aching from gaping at what by now had to be millions of Rasu vessels and structures. "This isn't just worse than the Metis Nebula, it's worse than I expected. I called myself prepared after listening with rapt attention to both Mesme and Nika's dire proclamations, but there are so damn *many* of them. And this is one galaxy of hundreds, if not thousands."

'I fear it might be even worse than that.'

"Of course you do, Valkyrie. Dare I ask why?"

'I propose we leave behind a superluminal-capable probe and set it to orbit the galactic core at a distance of two kiloparsecs. I am detecting a high concentration of Rasu signals in, so far as I have been able to determine, a complex ring 1.6 kiloparsecs distant from the core. I can speculate that they have constructed a porous structure encircling the core. Perhaps it is a variant on a Dyson ring, or perhaps it is something more substantial.'

"The entire galactic core? Gives a whole new meaning to our concept of megastructures, doesn't it?" She waved weakly at the viewport. "Okay, launch a probe."

'Launching. I further propose we jump to the opposite side of the galaxy and launch a second one in order to cut the time required to circumnavigate the core in half.'

"Hell, let's go ahead and launch four. I can restock tomorrow, and I kind of want answers yesterday." She rested her elbows on her knees and stared at Caleb. "So much worse. How are we going to deal with this?"

His expression was grim, but his sapphire irises twinkled with...not excitement, but maybe intrigue. The thrill of a hunt? It had been some time since they'd embarked on a hunt such as this. "Learn about our adversary. We need a lot more information from the Asterions—and from the Kats, if we can extricate it from them."

"Agreed. Mesme's pulled something of a disappearing act since helping me find Nika, but I'll try to corner it tomorrow. Valkyrie, as soon as we're done dropping the probes, let's Prism to the Gennisi galaxy." She stood and checked the charm on her bracelet. "We don't have much time before the party, so we'll have to drop in on Nika directly."

19

MIRAI

Nika relaxed back against Dashiel's chest and stretched her legs out on the couch. Her head swam beneath the barrage of information she'd been presented with today, and she struggled to absorb and catalogue it all. But the warmth of his skin as he wound his arms around her helped to quiet the noise. She curled her hands over his. "Thank you."

"For what?"

"For doing everything I asked of you and so much more. You've accomplished more than I dreamed possible in a few short weeks, and the Initiative appears to be running as smoothly as one of your assembly lines."

He chuckled lightly and kissed her ear. "It's an illusion, trust me. But I think we will get there. Oh, I meant to tell you. A forensics team finally found Magnus Forchelle's psyche backup hardware stashed in an underground storage bunker on his property."

She twisted around to face him. "Really? That's great news. Now we can—"

"No. We can't. He deleted all his backups before he left Adjunct Hachi with me the day I met him."

"Damn...." She frowned under the weight of conflicting emotions. Another connection to her past gone before she'd had an opportunity to explore it. But she was being selfish. *Not everything revolves around you, Nika.* "Why would he do such a thing?"

Dashiel shrugged weakly. "I think maybe he stayed alive all these millennia because he felt an obligation—to keep his secret safe, but also to make sure it didn't die with him. Once he no longer needed to guard the truth about kyoseil, about us? His mission was complete."

"I'm sorry. I know you liked him."

"'Liked' isn't the right word. He was a crotchety, infuriating son of a bitch. But I guess I saw in him—"

Dashiel cut himself off and peered past her shoulder. When alarm grew on his features, she turned to see what had drawn his concern just as a shimmering oval tore open space in the middle of the living room. Alex and Caleb stepped through the tear, and with a flick of Alex's wrist, it closed behind them.

Alex leaned intently into the back of the nearest couch. "Tell us about the Rasu."

Dashiel had leapt up from where they sat; when Nika didn't similarly move to defend her home, his gaze darted between her and their new guests in confusion.

Nika stood more casually and placed a hand on Dashiel's arm. "It's okay. Hello, Alex. Caleb. Didn't have a chance to ring ahead and let us know you were dropping by?"

Alex cringed. "Sorry. You're right, this was rude. But we need you to tell us about the Rasu."

"First, I'd like you to meet Dashiel Ridani. You two had left by the time he visited Concord HQ the other day."

Caleb adopted a chagrined expression and stepped forward to offer a hand. "Please do forgive our rudeness. I'm Caleb Marano. Nika has told us a lot about you. It's a pleasure to meet you."

Dashiel finally recovered his composure and accepted the hand. "Of course. She's spoken a great deal about you as well. Thank you for welcoming her into your home."

Alex tried to hide an eye roll and thrust out a hand in Dashiel's direction. "Alex. Nice to meet you." Then she spun back to Nika. "Please. The Rasu."

Nika scowled in low-grade irritation. "I've already told you—"

"Not the glossed-up diplomat version. We need the real, deadly, heart-stopping details."

Caleb came around and sat down on the couch opposite where she and Dashiel had been relaxing, then leaned forward. "Nika, you've been on board a Rasu ship. You've seen—"

"On two, actually."

"Even better. You've watched them move and shift their forms. You've fought them hand-to-hand. Dashiel, you've fought them ship-to-ship. The two of you have captured one alive and talked to it. Tell us about these experiences, please, in as much detail as you can recall. Which, given your nature, should be a significant amount of detail."

Nika returned to her seat and clasped her hands in her lap. "Why?"

"Because if we don't discover a way to exploit their weaknesses and defend against their strengths, they are going to kill us all."

She nodded soberly. "Yes, they are. But why the sudden urgency?"

Alex hurried over to prop on the arm of the couch beside Caleb. "We paid the Rasu embedded in NGC 55 a visit today. Some things you simply have to see to believe. Now we believe."

Nika recalled how she and Dashiel had felt after discovering the stronghold in their own galaxy, and her irritation eased. They wanted to save their people, same as she did. She smiled. "Fair enough. As I mentioned to you before, Asterions can record their memories with perfect accuracy. So perhaps it's best if rather than tell you, we show you."

RW

The visuals arrayed above the living room table in Nika's flat split into two dozen smaller frames, each one displaying a different area of the cavernous structure. Each one in frenzied motion, each one conveying urgency, terror and powerful determination.

One frame went black and was instantly replaced by a different vantage. Then another did the same.

Alex dragged her gaze away from the visuals to regard Nika curiously. "Each one of these points of view—they're all you?"

"Yes. And each one is mentally connected to the others, and to this instance. To me."

Her eyes drifted back to the frames. "How many were there?"

"To start? Eight thousand."

Alex blinked. "Eight *thousand*? Can all Asterions do this? Can you teach—"

Caleb reached over and touched Alex's arm. "No, baby. You're not splitting yourself into eight thousand shards. The universe is barely surviving one of you."

Nika laughed, as much at Alex's offended glare as at the nature of Caleb's remark. "Regardless, it's brand-new technology. We're still working out the kinks ourselves, to the extent we need to. It was necessary in this circumstance, but it's not really our...way."

Caleb stood and pointed to one of the frames in the upper left corner. "Can you focus in on this one for a minute?"

The first encounter where she was able to put the archine blade to use. She eyed him speculatively. "Interesting choice." She enlarged the frame in question, and they watched as, in slow motion, she spun, ducked and sliced upward to sever a Rasu arm from its torso.

"You have impressively quick reflexes. Is this also true of all Asterions?"

Nika smirked as a touch of pride warmed her chest. "No, that's just me. Well, probably not *just* me, but it is a learned skill."

"And by 'learned,' you mean installing a program in your operating system to heighten your situational awareness and speed up your reflexes?"

"Programming makes it possible, yes, but it also takes real-world experience and a dozen other factors, as well as a particular mindset."

"Not so different from us, then."

Alex had mentioned the kind of man Caleb had been before The Displacement, but this was the first time since Nika had met him that his demeanor began to hint at something harder lurking beneath the peaceful, halcyon exterior. She shrugged with intentional mildness, a deliberate counter to his sudden intensity. "Perhaps."

His attention returned to the visual. "So you have a weapon that can slice them up."

"We do. Dashiel invented it, in fact. Unfortunately, slicing up a Rasu is never more than a short-term solution." She tilted her head toward the frames above the table. "Why don't we keep watching? You'll see what I mean."

And so they did. When her incursion into the Rasu platform came to a bloody end in the power core and the last of her copies fell, everyone stared silently at the final frozen image for almost a minute.

Finally, Caleb shook his head roughly, as if trying to rid himself of an oppressive spell. "Do you mind if we take a look at the blade?"

She caught Dashiel's questioning glance.

What do you think?

It doesn't hurt us, only the Rasu. I'm okay with it.

Nika stood and went over to the hidden library, where she'd placed the blade on a shelf beside the last journal entries. It had seemed appropriate somehow.

She returned to the living room and offered the blade to Caleb. "We call it an archine blade. Take it with you. I can get a new one." She winked at Dashiel. "I know where they're made."

Caleb turned the blade over in his hand twice, then held it up in front of him, admiring the shimmering, razor-thin metal. "Splendid craftsmanship. Thank you." He dropped it in a sheath attached to his belt. "Can we see the interrogation footage?"

"Fascinating. The Rasu operate as a variation on a collective consciousness, yet they clearly can exhibit independent thought and decision-making."

"When left to their own devices for long enough, yes. In fact, Jerry displayed shrewdness and a keen self-interest."

Alex frowned. "But it—Jerry—insisted the Rasu lose their individuality while they are part of the whole."

Nika hesitated. "I'm not certain there is a 'whole'—merely a larger, more dominant consciousness that subsumes the formerly individual parts into itself."

"Valkyrie is going to eat this up. I apologize in advance if she approaches you about writing a treatise on the Rasu consciousness gestalt."

"If she can help us understand their nature, then I welcome it. I mean it."

Caleb continued to focus on the image of the Rasu in its hastily constructed cage. "I can't believe you let Jerry go."

Nika bit back a sigh. Lance had berated her twice again today regarding the decision, though he'd reluctantly admitted Jerry had so far done nothing except readopt its languorous lifestyle among the deserts of planet III-E183-31B. "We're watching it. If Jerry makes any move to—"

Alex leapt up off the arm of the couch, abruptly a flurry of motion. "We have to go."

Caleb looked at her in surprise, then realization. "Why—oh, shit."

"Exactly." Alex paused to wince at Nika. "Sorry to run out on you after we rushed in on you. We will resume this collaboration very soon, I promise, but right now we have somewhere we *have* to be." Alex waved her arm, and light spun out of the orb at her wrist. A wormhole opened behind the couch; they hurried through it and vanished once again.

Dashiel stared at where the wormhole had been for several seconds. "That was all…unorthodox."

"Thank you for rolling with it."

"No, no, it was fine. I'm glad they're taking the threat seriously. But are all Humans like they are? I mean, I met a few the other day, and they weren't quite so…intense."

"No, they're not all like that. Alex and Caleb, though…for one, I don't think they're much for decorum." Her lips quirked. "Or manners necessarily."

Dashiel laughed, and the low-grade tension that had stiffened his bearing during the unexpected visit melted away. He reached out and drew her closer, into his arms. "They do seem to be committed to getting things done, though, which in this circumstance acts in our favor. You said they have the influence needed to get Concord to act?"

"They have connections for certain. Her mother is the leader of the entire Concord military, and they appear to be close personal friends with most of the high-ranking Human government officials. But more than anything, I get the feeling they make their own power. I mean, she found Amaranthe, and he's responsible for Human civilization being here at all. I can't guarantee they'll be able to get Concord to act, but I feel fairly confident that when the time comes, *they* will act."

"Useful friends you've made, then."

Nika stared at the empty spot in her living room where the wormhole had rippled. "I think maybe I have."

20

CONCORD HQ

Marlee checked the hallway to confirm no one loitered outside before activating the anti-surveillance field she'd installed for her tiny office. The field wasn't illegal as such, merely unauthorized. Her job at the Consulate hadn't been deemed important enough to require secrecy or even privacy.

And this much was true. Her job did not require those things. But the access it provided enabled her to do a great deal of work that did require them.

Mia was spending the afternoon over at Dean Veshnael's office discussing the Asterions—and how had she managed to miss meeting their new friends? "Next time," Mia had blithely tossed over her shoulder on her way out the door while Marlee grumbled. Dammit, the whole reason she worked for the Consulate was so she could position herself on the front line of relations with all the various alien species, but especially the new ones.

Of course, arguably the Asterions weren't truly new. One-third Anaden, one-third synthetic, one-third Reor/kyoseil…she already knew all those species. Still, the combination must be fascinating. She'd have to pick Alex's brain tonight for juicy details.

The tick-over of the clock to a new hour pulsed in her awareness, and she refocused on her task. Soon she'd have to rush home, shower and change, then pick up Ainye, her date for the night, and head to Akeso. She'd sped through the day's work log this morning, however, to clear time for her to get in a little extra work on a side project.

Satisfied no one was watching, physically or virtually, she activated her console and backchanneled through the network over to the CINT database. It held all sorts of provocative intel, but more importantly for today, she believed it held brand new intel from Savrak. Richard and Eren had been conspiring at a fevered pitch for the last several days, and events were now in motion. If she expected to rescue Vaihe, she needed to know *what* events.

The comm transmitter continued its radio silence, but she refused to believe the Godjan girl was dead. Captured, possibly, and if so, being tortured almost definitely, but not dead and thus in desperate need of rescuing. No way would Mia allow Marlee to set foot on Savrak in an official capacity any time this century, so she was forced to devise another way to get back to the planet. But first she'd need a plan, and in order to create one of those she needed information.

She searched around for a moment until she located the latest report from Eren. "Aha. There you are, you sexy beast...." And not *just* the man who'd filed the report. She shivered in delight at the mere thought of him, taken though he was, then opened the report and spread it out in front of her.

Ugh. Antimatter weapons. It didn't surprise her to learn the Savrakaths were planning to deploy them, though. Their disgusting lack of respect for any lives other than their own meant they'd use such weapons without compunction.

But now things got complicated. Surely this was going to cause Concord to call off the alliance negotiations with the Savrakaths. Aunt Miriam would show them the door for certain.

If Concord stopped talking to the Savrakaths, how were they supposed to improve the living conditions of the Godjans? No military option existed that could help them, only diplomatic ones.

Unless the Savrakaths reacted poorly enough to Concord's rejection for a real war to begin. Then they could justify evacuating Godjans to Concord locations, couldn't they?

She thought on it for a minute...yes. It had been done before. Evacuating hostages and people detained unlawfully—which the

Godjans absolutely were—was the most humanitarian of humanitarian actions. Though she might want to use a more racially inclusive word for it when she made her pitch. Or maybe not; it wouldn't be the first word to transcend its linguistic roots.

She checked the time—crap. Running late already. She set a search routine crawling the exanet to collate a lengthy list of historical examples of military evacuations of civilians from behind enemy lines, then prepped an analysis routine that would take the results and use them to compose the best arguments for such a course of action. Then she left the office in a rush.

21

AKESO

A lex rushed down the ramp the instant the *Siyane* settled onto its landing pad, sprinted across the meadow and burst into the house transitioning into a frenzy—and skidded to a stop. She blinked several times, confident her panicked mind had constructed an absurd illusion simply to screw with her.

A dozen platters of food were arranged neatly on the dining table. A bucket of ice sat atop one of the kitchen counters, tongs hanging off the side and glasses surrounding it in a perfect circle. Two bottles of wine were breathing beside a row of wine goblets, and a pitcher of margaritas chilled alongside shrimp cocktails in the glass-doored refrigeration unit.

Kennedy bustled around the kitchen with matter-of-fact purpose, moving a stack of plates to a counter then gathering silverware. A little squeal escaped Alex's throat, and Kennedy glanced over in surprise. "Oh, there you are. What do you want to do with the potatoes in the refrigerator? It looks like you've chopped them, but I don't know what you planned for them."

Alex cackled as she leapt across the room and grabbed Kennedy in a fierce hug. "Thank you. You are my hero, I swear. And apparently a wizard as well."

"I am." Kennedy stepped back. "You said to get here and start setting everything out, so I got here and started setting everything out."

"You did so much more than that. This is perfection, and you have saved my ass. I'll make it up to you somehow—I don't know, I'll take the kids off your hands for an entire day. I can't guarantee I'll survive it, but favors must be repaid."

"We can negotiate down to something everyone will survive."
Kennedy motioned at the refrigerator. "Potatoes?"

"Right. Um, there's a marinade mix on the third shelf. Let's toss
the potatoes in it then put them in the oven. Caleb was headed to
get the grill ready out on the terrace. Can you take the burgers...."
She searched around in renewed panic.

"Thawing in the sink."

"You marvelous hero. Can you take them out to him? I'm going
to run upstairs, splash water on my face and change clothes. As
soon as I get back, you are a party guest and officially off-duty."

"Until Noah gets here with the twins, at which point I am back
on-duty to relieve him."

"That's between you and him. As far as I'm concerned, you've
earned the right to enjoy yourself." She squeezed Kennedy's hands
then sprinted upstairs, dark thoughts of the Rasu vanishing beneath excitement for the night to come.

RW

The landing complex only had room for four personal ships,
and two of the slots were taken up by theirs, but Akeso had con-
sented to the indignity of allowing vessels to land on the grass for
the evening. This was good, since half a dozen ships now dotted the
meadow surrounding the landing complex.

She and Caleb had discussed the possibility of adding a permanent Caeles Prism at ground level, one people could walk through.
But she didn't care for the idea of people, even people she liked and
cared for, strolling right up to her home at any time and from anywhere in the universe.

Granted, Prevos could do it so long as they knew the location
of Akeso and the house. But it was the principle of the matter. A
line had to be drawn somewhere.

And only now did she realize how she'd done this exact thing
to Nika a few short hours ago—walked straight into the middle of

her house unannounced and without warning. Double hypocrisy points for her!

She made a mental note not to do so again in the future and was refilling her wineglass when Marlee walked in. She wore a sapphire shirtdress that drew out her irises and the sapphire streaks in her deliberately messy hair, and black knee-boots. The blonde Idoni woman on Marlee's arm wore a black leather vest with a plunging neckline over skin-clinging champagne pants, as if she was *trying* to be a walking stereotype.

Alex took a long sip then went into the foyer and gave her niece a sideways hug. "I'm glad you escaped the hellhole that is Savrak."

"Ugh, what a miserable planet and miserable species." She motioned to her companion. "This is Ainye. She works at *Elliptical* on HQ."

Alex smiled politely. "It's nice to meet you. If you want anything to drink, we've got a wide selection in the kitchen."

Marlee's face brightened. "Oh, get me a margarita."

The woman sauntered off into the kitchen, and Marlee grabbed Alex's free hand. "I want to hear all about the Asterions. But first, have you talked to Morgan lately?"

Alex groaned internally, though hopefully she managed not to visibly grimace. It wasn't a new question; Marlee had asked it of her every third time they saw one another at a minimum. The girl had developed a crush on Morgan Lekkas when she was a young teenager, and it seemed hope continued to spring eternal.

"You know I haven't. Morgan wants to be left alone, and I'm respecting her wishes."

"Well, she shouldn't be alone, and she's too valuable a person to be lost. If we reach out to her, maybe we can help her get past her grief and rejoin society."

Morgan had checked out on said society the day six years ago when Brooklyn Harper and a squad of Marines had gone into a fortified Ch'mshak bunker and hadn't come back out. Like many people back then, Harper had included strict instructions in her will not to subject her neural imprint to a regenesis procedure that at the time remained highly experimental and incomplete, and legally Morgan could do nothing to override the directive.

So she'd resigned her leadership position with AEGIS and vanished off the map before the week was out.

Valkyrie, we can find Morgan if we ever need to, yes?

Of course. In fact, I can tell you—

No, don't tell me. This way, I don't have to lie to Marlee...any more than I already am. I was just checking.

As you wish.

Caleb would throttle her then possibly divorce her if she ever helped to put the two of them together. Morgan Lekkas would be a bad influence on Marlee on her best day. Morgan Lekkas without Brooklyn Harper would be...poison.

"I'm afraid she's not inclined to rejoin society quite yet. Honestly, knowing Morgan, she may never be so inclined."

"What a tragedy." Marlee accepted a margarita from her date. "Thanks, Ainye. Come on, I'll introduce you around—" her expression widened into a grin and she scurried off toward the front door "—Gramps!"

The guest of honor was fashionably late. When Ainye wandered after Marlee, Alex retreated to the kitchen. She rested against the counter and waited for her dad to navigate the initial flood of well-wishers.

She had thrown him a birthday party every year since he'd returned to life in an anarch lab. The parties weren't always here on Akeso, but they were always a celebration of life—his life in particular—for family and close friends. He'd forbade presents, so they lavished food, drink and affection on him instead.

When he finally made it to the kitchen, she shot him a smirk. "Hi, Gramps."

"Don't you even start with me. This body is still younger than you."

"An excuse that stopped working around thirty seconds after you woke up in it." She wrapped him up in a hug. "Happy Birthday, Dad."

"Thank you." He kissed her cheek then drew back as her mother joined them. "As I was telling your mother on the way, this is all lovely and also continues to be entirely unnecessary."

"Are you kidding? People love food. And alcohol. And they love both more when they're surrounded by friends and family."

David nudged Miriam in the side. "Did you have any idea our daughter was so wise?"

"Yes, dear. I did." Her voice dropped to a murmur. "How did your trip go?"

Alex held at bay the avalanche of warnings that surged forward to pose upon the tip of her tongue. "It went. We'll talk about it tomorrow."

Miriam scrutinized her, searching for clues as to how bad the news was going to be, but Alex refused to relent.

"All right, I'll do my best to keep some time free tomorrow. It will be a challenge."

"More so than usual? What's the latest crisis?"

David slid in beside her. "Last night, Eren confirmed the Savrakaths are building antimatter weapons."

"Oh, for fuck's sake."

"Alex, lower your voice. This information is not for public consumption."

"Sorry." The scene at Nengllitse flashed into her mind, when a grief-ridden Pinchu had used an antimatter weapon to flatten the capital city of the enemy who had killed Cassela and their unborn child. The buildings had disintegrated and the sky had burned, leaving behind only scorched earth and countless dead in the weapon's wake.

"What are you going to do about it?"

"Worry about it tomorrow, along with the Rasu and everything else." Her mother's gaze drifted to the refreshments on the counter behind Alex. "I think a glass of wine might help with this."

"It usually does."

RW

The first round of drinks had decimated the ice bucket, and Alex was refilling it when Caleb came inside and joined her. He did a poor job of sounding nonchalant as he retrieved a set of tongs from above the oven. "Who is that with Marlee?"

"I think she said her name was Ainye."

"I thought she was dating that guy from Krysk. Gregor? The biology major."

She'd known Caleb for sixteen years now, and it still surprised her how he could be so naïve about the most unexpected things. She laid a hand on his arm. "I don't think she's exactly...dating...anyone. Not seriously. She's merely...."

He regarded her silently, and she watched as realization drew his brow into a tight line and darkened his irises into a churning storm of indigo. "I see." His gaze flitted past her, toward the living room where Marlee and her date were cuddling. "I need to talk to Isabela."

"Caleb, now isn't the time—" But he was already marching off in search of his sister. If he'd bothered to stay and listen to her, she'd have pointed out how Isabela had brought a date as well, though admittedly a far less scandalous and more acceptable geophysics professor. But in truth, nothing she'd said would've made a difference.

She waited until he'd disappeared out onto the rear terrace, where Isabela was talking to Kennedy, then surreptitiously went into the living room. "Marlee, can I talk to you for a minute?"

"Sure. What's up?"

She glanced toward the back door. "Caleb's having a word with your mother."

"About what?"

Alex winced and tried not to stare too pointedly at the Idoni woman sitting beside Marlee. The woman's unfocused eyes as she gave Alex a sloppy smile suggested she was quickly heading toward sloshed.

"Is this about Ainye? It's none of his business who I spend my time with!"

"I realize it isn't, but he's just trying to look out for you."

"He can stop trying any time he wants. I'm an adult, and he can't control my life..." her face fell "...but he can pitch a fit and cause a scene in front of everyone, can't he?"

Alex shrugged weakly. She wanted to say he was too respectful to do any such thing, but she remembered the storm in his eyes. He'd never been his most rational self when it came to his niece.

"How rude. Fine. I'll take the high road. I won't let him ruin Gramps' party." She grabbed Ainye's hand and stood. "Come on. Let's get out of here. I heard Writhing Rage is playing tonight at *Lumice.*"

Alex watched as Marlee diverted to the kitchen to give David a giant hug then jogged out the front door, her date in tow, before Caleb could waylay her.

And this was why Alex had warned her. Despite all the girl's post-adolescent rebellions—which Alex *definitely* wasn't in a position to pass judgment on, given her own prodigious indiscretions in her youth—she believed Marlee would never willingly hurt David in any way. Marlee had now buttressed Alex's belief by leaving the party rather than risking a scene that might dampen the celebration.

With a sigh she refilled her glass, probably too soon and now too often—she jumped to the side as two manic five-year-olds barreled through the kitchen in a deluge of excited chatter. Nothing fell over and shattered in their wake, so she went out onto the rear terrace, where 'Story Time with David' was now in full swing.

"—the Efkam is strobing bright red and yellow so frenetically I feel as if I've stumbled into a kooky alien dance club. Two Vigil officers keep their firearms trained on it while three drones buzz around it in menacing circles. The Efkam slides forward half a meter, and the drones fire on it. Split it half in two. Disaster averted, right?"

Valkyrie, who had brought out her physical body out for the occasion, laughed heartily. "Something tells me not."

"Indeed. The two halves of the Ekfam deflate for a second, as if a plug had been pulled, then promptly pump back up and start skittering around again, flashing their colors like they're trying to trigger epileptic fits in the Vigil officers. Did you all know that splitting an Ekfam in half doesn't kill either half? Because I did not.

"So the drones fire again, and now we have four Efkam. There are two Naraida girls who seem to be innocent bystanders caught in the fracas, and they're huddled up in the corner behind the Efkam, hugging each other and wailing in terror. The Vigil officers are screaming at the Efkam to submit to arrest. And how does one shackle an Efkam, anyway?"

Will held up a hand, sloshing a bit of beer over the rim of his glass. "There's a sort of ring that goes around their midsection and generates a restraining field around them."

"Good to learn. So the Naraida girls are screaming, the Vigil officers are screaming, and now I'm screaming at the officers to stand the *yebat'* down and deescalate the situation. But they don't know me from a hole in the wall, and at this point in time, a few short months after The Displacement, nobody really knows who is in charge of anything.

"From where I'm standing, all my options are for shit. I'm confident I can take out the two Vigil officers without suffering serious bodily injury, but only until their drones turn on me—then I'm down. I can run into the fracas and try to be a human shield, but the now *eight* Efkam pieces are bouncing around like ping-pong balls at a rave, and I've no idea how to convince them to huddle up behind me. I can maybe shield the Naraida girls, but only until the drones with itchy triggers decide to shoot me instead of the Efkam. Or, I can mind my own business and walk away."

Miriam burst out laughing, and David arched an exaggerated eyebrow at her. "Something to add, *dushen'ka*?"

"I'm shocked your brain even acknowledged 'walking away' as a valid option on the table."

David winked at her. "Truthfully? It didn't, but I needed a fourth option to build suspense."

"Now this I believe."

"So I keep berating the Vigil officers to calm down while I try to decide which way I want to play this—then like a gift sent from the very Heavens, Richard walks into the atrium. My savior, arriving to perform his sacred responsibility one more time."

Richard blushed beet red. "Not for the last time, though."

"No, no. So Richard stops in the middle of the atrium, takes in the circus of horrors with his keen intelligence agent eyes for two seconds, then shouts, 'Pavo Sigma Delta Stama!' The drones instantly quit firing and stop to hover quietly in the air. The officers lower their weapons and stare at Richard in confusion. Richard, would you care to share the secret of your superpowers?"

"Sure." He took a sip of his beer and set it on the table beside him. "Reading. See, in the final days of the conflict with the Directorate, we were rifling through Vigil's servers hunting for information we could use to gain an advantage. We found plenty of it, thanks to Alex's Reor decryption." He dipped his chin in her direction, and she returned the gesture. "One of the millions of data points we came across was the override order code for Vigil drones. That's my superpower—I remember everything I read."

"And a sexy superpower it is," Will murmured as he nudged Richard's shoulder.

"A useful one, too," David agreed. "Once the Efkam was no longer under constant fire, its various pieces wobbled toward each other and gradually reformed back into the original, solitary Efkam. The Naraida girls took off, tearing through the atrium into the landing wing, and one of the Vigil officers shakily delivered a stern warning to the Efkam not to ever do that again."

Valkyrie leaned forward intently, clearly enthralled. "And what was 'that'? What had it done to get in trouble in the first place?"

David shrugged. "No idea. I never found out." He stood. "Now, if you all will excuse me, I need to visit the restroom and return with food."

Several other people got up as well, and the crowd started to break up and mingle. Alex dropped into the chair beside Richard and Will.

Richard rolled his eyes, still looking vaguely embarrassed. "He never disappoints, does he? I remember the event somewhat differently, but his version is certainly more entertaining."

Alex smiled. "You know what *I* find interesting? How you are almost always the hero of his stories. In his first life and his second."

"Well. That's just because he knows the story gets a bigger reaction if he uses it to make fun of himself."

"Or it could be the truth."

Will nodded sagely. "Almost certainly the truth."

RW

"Caleb, do you know what strategy is even less effective than you trying to give Marlee dating advice? *Me* trying to give her dating advice. The only thing it succeeds at is provoking her to greater and more outlandish misbehavior."

Caleb exhaled in frustration. "You're her mother. Won't she listen to you?"

"When was the last time you listened to our mother?"

"That's not a fair comparison. Our mother is cracked. Mentally addled."

Isabela spread her arms wide. "I'm fairly certain Marlee currently thinks the same of me. Am I happy about her trotting out a woman of...questionable morals and parading her in front of us? No. But she could be doing a lot worse. Right?"

"Like getting arrested on a foreign world by an adversarial police force?"

Isabela's lips pursed tight. "I haven't had a chance to thank you for getting her home safely."

"No need." He stared over his shoulder into the house. "I'm going to talk to her. I have to try."

His sister's hand landed on his arm. She hesitated...then nodded and let him go.

But after ten minutes of searching, Caleb decided that Marlee had given this highly trained, twenty-year elite black ops agent the slip. She'd sneaked away with the trollop on her arm to go...he shuddered to imagine the possibilities. Dammit!

He needed to clear his head if he were to stand any possibility of enjoying the rest of the evening, so he grabbed a beer and went outside.

Noah stood a few meters away, watching Braelyn and Jonas play along the bank of the stream. Jonas dipped a hand in the current and splashed water on his sister—Caleb's eyes closed and *we are the cool water impacting warm skin*—Braelyn spun and chased after him, an expression of pure fury animating her young face. Akeso had conjured fireflies to frolic around the kids and dance through the air, and Braelyn got distracted from her chase trying to snatch one out of the air.

Caleb chuckled lightly as he came over to stand next to Noah. "Quite a handful at this age, huh?"

"They've been quite a handful since the day they got here. Everyone tells us it'll get better once they're six or so...until they turn eleven or so, at which point it will be worse for another decade." Noah rubbed at his eyes. "I haven't slept in five years."

"Are they worth it?"

Noah shot him a sharp look. "I would die for either one of them, right here, right now. No hesitation. I'd die for Kennedy, too, but I might take a half-second to rue how it had come to that. Not for them, though. They are everything to me." He cupped his hands around his mouth. "Jonas, you had better stop harassing your sister. She will make you regret it, and I won't stop her."

The warning evoked zero response, and Noah shook his head. "Jonas is like a devil's brew of Kennedy and I. Vivacious, fearless, a prankster on good days and a troublemaker on bad ones. Braelyn, well...Kennedy says she suspects Braelyn is the literal reincarnation of her great-great-grandmother. Quiet—comparatively—studious and utterly brilliant. Also conniving and devious, which brings its own manner of challenges."

Caleb watched the kids scamper over a group of small boulders and slip-slide along the damp shore. *A loose rock digs into the soil as a shoe slides over it, bracing back to provide leverage and support as we send the shoe and its owner on their way.* "Do you worry about them?"

"All the time. I'd be terrified for them playing here, except I know Akeso won't let them come to any real harm. I mean, they're part of the first generation who will grow up with the cybernetics necessary to allow for true, secure and guaranteed regenesis. So one day they'll be safe. But not yet, not until they're adults. And even then, I'm sure I'll still worry. Worry they'll experience pain, loss, heartbreak. Given the way our lives have gone so far, possibly torture, war, famine, extreme blood loss, limb replacement...."

They shared a laugh at that, but Caleb remained serious. "Don't you want to protect them from all those things?"

An exposed root jutting out of the dirt stretches and lies flat as a shoe skims a centimeter above us at a full run.

"Of course I do. And now, while they're young and portable, I can a little bit. But not for much longer. Soon, the best I'll be able to do is ensure they understand that I love them, I trust them and I'm proud of them. I don't have any other options, so I have to believe this knowledge will protect them far more than a parental cage or an underground bunker."

Noah had no way of knowing it, but that one stung a bit. "I remember when you were a smuggler on the wrong side of the law eking out a living in the slums of Pandora. When did you get so damn wise?"

Grasses puff out and create a soft cushion as tiny, fragile bodies tumble across our surface.

"Wise?" Noah snorted. "Never. I'm still hanging on for dear life, scrambling to figure out which way is up today, only to usually discover it's a different direction than it was yesterday."

"Well, you could have fooled me." Caleb tilted his head toward the house. "Shall we?"

Noah cupped his hands again. "Kiddos! There's about to be cake and ice cream inside!"

They scrambled out of the creek, all mud-streaked faces and wet clothes, and barreled into Noah's legs. He feigned stumbling backward, then reached down and scooped them up in each arm. After situating them on his hips, he set off into the house.

Caleb started to follow, but paused and glanced back at the creek. It gurgled quietly beneath a crescent moon and a gentle breeze. *Thank you.*

They are precious life, and such life as that should be sheltered from all storms.

RW

It was a full two hours later before Noah, Kennedy and the kids departed. They were the first to leave, which no one begrudged them, but once they were gone the party gradually began to break up.

Isabela gave Caleb a hug and an apologetic grimace on the way out, and he offered kind pleasantries to her date. She seemed to like him, and he seemed a decent if somewhat dull man. If his sister finally found worthwhile companionship after all these years alone, it was a good thing.

Richard, Will, David and Miriam bottomed-out another bottle of wine before winding down. Caleb offered for them to stay the night in the guest cottage, but in a world of ubiquitous near-instantaneous travel, it wasn't really necessary, and two more rounds of hugs finally got everyone on their way.

Akeso breathed a planetary sigh of relief as the last ship lifted off its soil. Caleb found himself wishing he could do the same.

22

EARTH

MILKY WAY

GREATER VANCOUVER

Miriam slipped into a robe and stepped out onto the second-floor balcony wearing a tiny, almost contented smile. It was terribly late, and tomorrow was not going to go easy on her. Tough decisions and contentious arguments waited on her with the dawn, and likely the dawn after that as well.

She should be crawling in bed and relishing in what sleep she might steal, but instead she relished stealing a few moments of quiet back at her own home. Akeso was a marvel, and Alex and Caleb's place was wonderful, and the hours spent there with family and friends had been a welcome respite. A treasure, truly. But there was nothing like home, and she refused to take it for granted.

They'd commissioned Will Sutton to design and build the house in the mountains above Buntzen Lake eleven years ago. By then he hadn't worked as an architect for some time, but he'd professed to enjoy the diversion from spycraft, and the result had been worth every considerable penny they'd insisted on paying him. David had always cherished living as deeply in nature as they were able to manage in the various locations their postings had sent them. When he'd died, she'd left all that behind, choosing practical townhouses in bustling cities minutes from work. Running from his memory in every way she could find.

But she didn't have to run now, and it did her heart good to be back among the seclusion of the Douglas firs. A ten-minute skycar trip brought her to the Caeles Prism at AEGIS Earth Headquarters, and from there it was a few short steps to her office at HQ. But here on the balcony, surrounded by crickets chirping and leaves rustling beneath a star-strewn sky, the stresses of work remained a universe away.

David slipped in behind her and wound one arm around her as he slid a Manhattan in front of her on the railing. The warmth against her back told her was shirtless, and she smiled to herself as she picked up the drink. "Thank you. I shouldn't, as I had two at the party. In addition to the wine."

"It's my birthday. You can have three. Me, I'm having...let's see...four or...well, more than three." His voice slurred over the rolling 'r's just the slightest bit, giving his voice an even more melodic quality than usual.

"As you said, it is *your* birthday."

"Da. I wonder, how many years will it be before Alex and everyone finally decide that me being here in the world having birthdays is actually a monumentally mundane and ordinary detail and stop throwing lavish parties to celebrate it?"

"I suspect never. Nor should we." Daily life with David in it *had* often become normalized during the past fourteen years. Days went by during which she never once thought of the decades he'd been absent. But then something would remind her, and her heart would break and soar all over again.

She shifted around in his embrace to face him. "It's a wonder, and increasing years of it being a wonder won't change that for any of us."

He rolled his eyes dramatically. "Oh, *khorosho.* They are fantastic parties."

"Yes." She leaned in close and kissed him, long and slow. "They are."

RW

AKESO

Alex set the house bot to cleaning up the kitchen and living room and dragged herself upstairs. She found Caleb sitting on the edge of the bed, his hair damp from a shower. The rigid set of his shoulders and formal lift of his chin screamed a warning, and she stopped before reaching the bed. "What is it?"

His voice was steady and oh-so controlled. "You told Marlee to leave early tonight, didn't you?"

Once an intelligence agent, always an intelligence agent. Nothing got past him, except the obvious things he didn't want to see. She rubbed at her eyes, suddenly more weary than she should be. "I implied to her that it might be an option for her to consider, but she suggested it on her own. I would never tell her to leave our home."

He shifted on the bed to look at her, his expression unreadable. "Why did you do it?"

"Because it was my father's birthday party, and you were about to make a fucking scene because you didn't like her date."

"It had nothing to do with that woman and everything to do with—"

"Oh, it absolutely did. You didn't care for the mental image of Marlee engaged in a chimeral-induced haze of sex and partying you were so certain an Idoni slut was on the verge of seducing her into."

Caleb's voice dropped low as his posture pressed forward, though he didn't stand. "Don't even *say* such a thing."

She exhaled and cast a gaze to the glass wall beyond the bed, searching for some peace or maybe an escape in the tranquil nature's bounty enveloping their home. "You know…" she resisted the sudden urge to press her palms flat against the glass as if it were a prison wall "…I'm not angry that after all this time, it turns out you're a prude. I'm angry that you were willing to ruin my father's party over it."

"I am not a—and I wouldn't dream of—" He ran a hand viciously through his hair. "I am trying to protect her. She's not ready for the punishments the world will inflict on her."

"No one ever is. And you can't protect her. You *can't*, and all you're succeeding in doing is shoving her away." *And now, me, too.* In frustration a groan escaped her throat. "I'm going to review the Rasu data one more time. I need to be sharp on it tomorrow." She pivoted and left the bedroom, closing the door behind her.

RW

She leaned into the data table in the office at the opposite end of the second floor from the bedroom. Twice as long and twice as advanced as the one on the *Siyane*, she did most of her data analysis here these days.

She'd retreated here legitimately intending to pull up the scans they'd taken in NGC 55 and begin studying them, but now that she was here she couldn't summon the will to send the command to the table. Her head dropped to her chest.

It had been a *good* party. Whatever tensions had dwelt beneath the surface—familial spats, alien troubles, Rasu shadows—none of it had dampened the frivolity for a few hours tonight. So she didn't need to be angry. Even if heated words had been exchanged, her father had existed in this world for fourteen years now, and a few broken dishes wouldn't have shattered the spell and sent him back to the grave.

She was being dramatic bordering on histrionic in her obsessive protection of the sanctity of the ritual event. She was, in fact, being *silly*, when she had no real cause to be either silly or angry.

Caleb moved ridiculously quietly in bare feet, but though she didn't hear him approach, she did sense his nearing presence with enough time to spin around or move away.

She did neither, and he wrapped his arms around her waist from behind and rested his chin on her shoulder. "I'm sorry. I didn't mean to take my frustrations out on you. I tell myself I would've had enough self-control to avoid causing an embarrassing scene, but under the circumstances, I don't blame you for warning her." His lips caressed the nape of her neck. "Forgive me a little bit?"

She couldn't stay upset with him when he was touching her this way; she'd never been able to. Not when the strength of his embrace surrounded her like a stalwart shield barring the torments of the world from reaching her. Not when his heart beat rhythmically against her skin like the drumbeat steadying the symphony of their lives.

Which was good, since she didn't need or want to be angry. She shifted around in his arms and brought her fingertips to his lips. "Forgive you all."

He kissed them softly. "You're both right *and* wrong, you know. I am not a prude, and I'll be happy to demonstrate this whenever you like. But I also used to be the fun uncle who swept in on a whirlwind to urge Marlee onward with crazy, rebellious ideas. Now I'm the grumpy old man who's no fun at parties."

She started to protest his characterization...but it would have been a lie. She opted for a teasing tenor instead. "When did that happen?"

His expression darkened as the brooding shadows of earlier threatened to return. "Your father asked me almost the exact same thing the other day on Savrak. My response then was 'around the time I killed eight billion people.'"

He'd yet to truly forgive himself for what happened at Solum. For years she'd tried everything she could think of to help him, but she'd eventually accepted reality. Only he could forgive himself. And he might never do so.

She struggled against his darkness to hang onto the lighter mood. "Or possibly around the time Marlee hit puberty. That's when most parents go evil."

He stared at her for a moment, though he didn't seem to really be seeing her at all. "I feel so impotent sometimes. Useless."

"Because you're not fighting any longer?"

"Or because I'm not killing any longer."

She touched his cheek. "*Priyazn,* those were never your defining traits, and you're not lesser for their absence now."

"I'm not. But for so long, violence was how I protected people. Without it, I don't think I know what to...."

His throat worked, and as she watched, he forcibly drove the grave countenance away. "You're probably right about the puberty." His lips brushed across hers then returned more insistently; his hands splayed wide across her waist. She pulled him closer, and his weight pressed her into the edge of the table.

She wanted so badly to lose herself in his touch, and damn the niggling voice in the back of her head that insisted on grumbling in petulant annoyance about how he'd dared to almost maybe ruin her father's party.

His mouth trailed down her neck in a tantalizing dance of anticipation. "Again, I'm sorry. Let me make it up to you?"

Her breath caught in her throat...'*yes*' hovered on her lips but '*no*' made it past them. She eased out of his grasp. "It's been an outrageously long day, and tomorrow stands to be as long. Can we just get some sleep?"

The surprise-turned-hurt that flashed across his features lasted only a millisecond. "Of course we can." He took her hand in his and led her back to the bedroom.

RW

She awoke to Caleb's touch, to the tickle of his beard brushing along her shoulder. She smiled even before she was fully awake and reached out to draw him eagerly into her arms.

Sleep had banished the niggling voice to the dungeon, and in the morning light, all she wanted in the world was his skin against hers. He obliged her, his hands tracing every curve, every hollow in a masterful dance that drove her to madness as easily and thoroughly as the first time. Every time.

His touch was tender yet needful, and their lovemaking was gentle and slow, until it wasn't. More than niggling voices were banished so long as their bodies entangled each other and his lips never left hers.

And in the blissful afterglow that chased an ecstasy never to be matched, basking in the rays of dawn streaming down on them through the walls, everything was good and right in their world once more...

...until they remembered the Rasu.

PART II

SET PIECES & STRATEGEMS

23

THALER

N yx elasson-Praesidis whipped around, firearm raised, fingertip hovering over the trigger—then watched as a small chipmunk-looking creature ran off into the lavender grass carrying a stick it had snatched from the soil.

She exhaled and holstered her weapon. "You've got me spooked with these tales of giant, lumbering beasts running wild across the continent. Now I'm jumping at mischievous woodland critters."

Danilo Nisi, née Corradeo Praesidis, shot her a stern look. "I'm fairly certain I did not say 'running wild.' They had achieved Stone Age development at a minimum. They constructed rudimentary shelters, lived in close-knit tribes and honed stone and wood into weapons."

"As we are discussing giant, lumbering beasts, that doesn't reassure me, grandfather."

"I suppose it doesn't." He patted her on the shoulder and set out toward the edge of the forest to the northwest. "If one *does* charge out from the brush, I have every confidence that you will protect us both."

Her eyes narrowed at his back, but after a brief survey to ensure no genuine threats lay in wait, she followed him.

He wasn't wrong. It had taken her a long time—months going on years—to adjust to the absence of the *diati* that had been her constant companion for millennia. Her weapon, her transport, her protection.

The *diati* was gone forever, but she was still a Praesidis Inquisitor. She'd soon set about training with real, physical weapons, from firearms and electric projectiles to blades to improvised uses for ropes and whatever blunt or sharp object was handy. Her reflexes were bred to be superb, but now those reflexes needed to be able to adapt to variables like weapon weight, size and responsiveness, the distance to the target and sometimes the weather.

Before they'd left Anaden space behind, she'd also upgraded her cybernetics loadout to include resilient shielding and flexible defenses to physical attacks, because the *diati* was no longer there to instantly heal any injuries she suffered.

Now, fourteen years later, she too was confident in her ability to protect them both from a giant, lumbering beast charging them. Two or three as well. Four? Possibly not.

Her grandfather hadn't bounced back from the loss of his *diati* so rapidly as she had, despite the fact that in recent millennia he'd used it far less often and less dramatically than she.

She wasn't at his side when The Displacement occurred, but he'd said the *diati* had simply quietly drifted away, at roughly the same instant every other Praesidis who survived the destruction of Solum lost theirs. The event was a tremendous psychological blow to every Praesidis, but her grandfather had lived with *diati* coursing through his body for far longer than anyone else; it had saved his life even when he'd begged it not to; it had in many respects defined his extraordinary life.

She suspected one of the reasons behind their travels was his quest to discover whether he still had a life without it, extraordinary or otherwise.

For a while, their travels felt random and spontaneous, the only rule being they didn't visit any system formerly controlled by the Directorate. This meant they rarely encountered other advanced life forms with whom they could converse or trade, and twice they'd been forced to break the rule and acquire supplies at remote Anaden outpost stations. They'd disguised themselves and avoided any small talk and fled as soon as the *Periplanos'* cargo hold was full.

187 | G.S. JENNSEN

Her grandfather insisted they were leaving their old lives behind, and seeing as how their old lives were intimately intertwined with the rise and fall of the Anaden Empire, this involved leaving it behind as well. He'd once ruled the Empire, leading it to great heights. Then he'd torn it down. And now, he wanted nothing to do with it.

Nyx had never thought of herself as an adventurer or explorer. She'd ventured to many and varied locales as an Inquisitor, but only in the service of her missions. To travel merely to travel, to see what was there to be seen? It seemed fanciful and frivolous, until they'd begun doing it.

Danilo was a master at travel for pleasure's sake. He knew how to weave colorful tales of the imagined history of a planet, to speculate to excess about what its past held and its future might. He noticed the smallest of details and delighted in pointing out how they didn't have anything like such a detail in the Empire.

Recently, around a year ago, their travels became less random. They began to visit places he'd traveled to before, during the years after his son Renato had assaulted him to within a centimeter of death and before he'd returned to the Empire and joined the anarch resistance.

He'd spent a long time traveling in this manner, and he'd visited a lot of places. Met a lot of species. They'd encountered two of those species in the last several months, but of course given the timespan, none remembered him, and they'd needed to begin again as strangers.

One of the species had advanced significantly since her grandfather's earlier journeys and was in the midst of a burgeoning industrial revolution when they arrived. That particular visit, to a species known as 'Blanetes,' hadn't actually gone so well. It turned out that while primitives were happy to ascribe spiritual or supernatural natures to peculiar aliens descending from the sky, more civilized peoples displayed a disturbed, skeptical and, if pushed, violent reaction to their sudden appearance.

On the last two stops they'd made, however, the former inhabitants of the planets were nowhere to be found. Primitive civilizations vanished swiftly beneath the sands of time and ecological shifts, so they weren't able to determine what had transpired in either case. The possibilities were many: war, famine, drought, disease or planetary impact by any of a number of astronomical bodies, to name a few. For scientists posited that fewer than five percent of species in the universe who discovered fire survived to discover electricity.

Here on the planet her grandfather dubbed 'Thaler,' it appeared this species had suffered a similar fate to the two before it. Possibly the entire species had migrated across the continent, chasing food or safety, but the more likely reality was that it had simply died out.

They reached the beginnings of the forest, and Danilo reached up and slowly ran a hand along the leaves of an overhanging tree. This region of the planet was certainly alluring, with a shifted color palette distinguishing it from most Anaden-habitable planets. The grass was a vivid lavender, the tree bark flint and the leaves a darker purple edging toward indigo. A high chlorine content in the atmosphere lent the sky a pale clover hue, and the dirt beneath their feet hinted at pink. They'd brought breather masks along due to the low oxygen and high chlorine content of the air, but their bodies were designed to breathe and process a variety of atmospheres; so long as they didn't exert themselves, they should be fine.

Despite the serene charm of their environs, the farther they ventured from the ship, the more the threat of giant, lumbering beasts lurked in every extending shadow.

Nyx jogged ahead until she drew beside her grandfather. "I'm not seeing any signs of settlement. Maybe if we head west a few hundred kilometers?"

He peered out along the curve of the tree line. "Doesn't this border look rather abrupt to you? It's too well-defined, too precise to be created by nature."

She followed his gaze. "I see what you mean, but nature can craft surprisingly unique landscapes. Why don't we study it from above? If there's a pattern, it will be more clearly visible from the sky."

"You are not fooling me, granddaughter. I don't need *diati* to sense your growing anxiety. But you might be correct about not wanting to stumble into a nest of giant, lumbering creatures. In any event, I mostly wanted you to see the ecology here. I've always remembered its singular beauty."

"It is quite stunning. Thank you for bringing me here."

RW

Once they were back on board the *Periplanos*, she retraced their path to the northwest for several kilometers until they hovered above the last field they'd traversed. Her hands lifted off the controls as she peered below, frowning. "You need to come see this."

Danilo left the kitchen unit, where he'd been cooking up a pot of chili, to join her in the cockpit. "What—oh. How very unusual. I knew something about the landscape didn't feel right."

The field they'd crossed took the shape of a perfect circle 3.1 kilometers in diameter. The forest surrounding it ended abruptly at the outer edge of the circle for three-hundred-sixty degrees, sending trees towering over an area in which nothing grew taller than thirty centimeters. It was as if at some point in the past—a quick dive into geological scholarly data banks suggested between fifty and one hundred twenty years ago—something had scorched the earth, burning away all life, and the biosphere was only just beginning to recover.

Over the next three hours of aerial survey, they found eight more instances of the strange circles. Each the same size, each displaying the same features. They also found no evidence that any life larger than the chipmunks continued to exist here on Thaler.

Danilo toed his chair from side to side. He'd been doing so for hours—for the entirety of their survey, in fact, one hand at his chin and the other resting across his chest. The chili sat neglected and cold, congealing on the kitchen unit.

When he didn't notice her watching him for a full thirty seconds, she cleared her throat. "Grandfather? Where to next? Should we keep searching for signs of life? Or further evidence of...tampering?"

His rich sapphire eyes drifted to her for a blink before returning to the viewport. "No. The scars upon the land tell the tale of what happened here. As to who inflicted them and why...those answers aren't to be found today. Let's go."

As they departed the planet to continue their travels—she'd give him another hour or two before pressing him on their next destination—Nyx had the passing thought that perhaps the Blanetes had the right of it. Peculiar aliens descending from the sky didn't always have peaceful intentions.

24

EARTH

AEGIS EARTH HEADQUARTERS

Malcolm Jenner stood at parade rest while he watched the group of Marines perform hand-to-hand combat drills on the practice field in the western corner of the AEGIS Earth Headquarters—formerly EASC—grounds. It was a lovely Vancouver morning, the air crisp and clear and the rising sun reflecting brightly off the gleaming buildings of the complex.

Next week, the best of those gathered here today would be offered the opportunity to try out for the special forces division. It would mark only the beginning of a grueling trial for them, at the end of which...no, not only the best of the best would remain. The most determined, most resilient and most prepared would remain. Possibly the most stubborn.

He chuckled to himself. He'd been one of these eager kids once upon a time. Looking back, he had no idea how he'd survived the trial with all his limbs intact, much less qualified for special forces. Then again, half the time he had no idea how or why he'd somehow ascended to the rank of Fleet Admiral over humanity's armed forces. Stubbornness seemed the most likely explanation.

He didn't need to be here watching the drills. In fact, he wore plain BDUs and stood in the shadow of the Headquarters Tower in an effort to not be recognized. These Marines didn't need the added pressure of the man at the top of their chain of command judging their performances. Well, one step below the top. When the intergalactic shit hit the proverbial fan, he still took orders from Miriam Solovy.

No, he was here for his own mental recalibration. Because it was good to remind himself every now and then of where he came from. Of the real men and women who served under him, whom it was his duty to look after and to give every possible chance to succeed in the battles they fought.

Besides, he spent too much time on space stations and in fleet dry-docks these days. He and Mia owned a home on Romane as well as a townhome here in Vancouver, but they inevitably spent half their off-hours at nice but impersonal apartments on the Presidio or Concord HQ.

He'd accepted the reality of a life lived in space some years ago, but in his heart, he would always prefer solid ground beneath his feet. His duty kept him in the stars, but...as he watched a lean young Marine use his bulky sparring partner's weight against him and pin the man to the mat, he couldn't deny the truth...he *missed* this, dammit.

Because he had once been a special forces Marine, he sensed a lone individual approaching from behind him several seconds before they arrived. He nonetheless had to squelch a flare of surprise when Caleb Marano came to a stop beside him, crossed his arms and gazed speculatively out at the drills.

"Marano." They had never been and were never going to be friends. But after giving his life to save humanity, then having it miraculously returned to him, Caleb had walked away from his former profession as a black ops agent, killer and one-man arbiter of justice. This, Malcolm had to respect. So, over the years they had developed a somewhat cool but generally collegial relationship.

"Good-looking kids out there. Neither of us ever moved that fast or with that much precision, not even when we were that young."

He'd wager good money Caleb had moved faster, and might still, but he humored the man's casual attempt at bonding. "It's the cybernetics. In the past few years, the technology has pushed far beyond what scientists previously claimed were the physical limits of the human body."

193 | G.S. JENNSEN

"Doesn't it always. Regardless, I'm glad these guys are on our side."

"No kidding." Okay, enough small talk. "What brings you here this morning? I doubt it's a bout of nostalgia."

"If I wanted nostalgia, I'd go to Seneca. You're needed at a meeting in Miriam's office."

Malcolm double-checked his messages and frowned. "I haven't received a request from her."

"She doesn't know she's having the meeting yet, or that she'll want you there for it. But she will in about…" he blinked "…ten minutes. We should start heading that way."

RW

CONCORD HQ

COMMAND

Mia steepled her hands at her chin and peered across the desk at Miriam. "Why must species continue to be so short-sighted—myopic even—when it comes to weapons that can wipe life out en masse?"

"I have no idea. You're the diplomat, so I was hoping you might enlighten me."

"Being a diplomat merely means I've had plenty of experience dealing with species acting *myopic* when it comes to weapons that can wipe life out en masse." Mia sighed and adjusted her posture in the chair. "All right. We can wish the situation were different, but it is what it is. When confronted, the Savrakath ambassador will insist that should Concord grant them allied status, they will cease all antimatter weapon development in order to comply with our Code of Rights.

"But the reality is, the fact they're developing them now, knowing our stance on the weapons and lying to us about their forays into them, means they have no place within Concord. They can't be trusted. More than anything else, their values do not align with ours."

Miriam arched an eyebrow. "Is this a revelation?"

"Not in the slightest. But I owed it to the Concord species and to the Savrakaths to try to influence them for the better. I hoped we could show them the path to becoming better stewards of their people and better citizens of the cosmos. But it seems they're not ready to be shown it. And unfortunately, given our increasing interactions with them, this means they're now likely to become an adversary if not an outright enemy."

"Which I do know something about. We can't allow a spacefaring species possessing knowledge of our existence and whereabouts to wield such weapons. Therefore, I intend to authorize a CINT team to destroy the antimatter facility. I'd ask you to refrain from breaking off negotiations with their ambassador until after the operation is complete. Once it is, you are free to explain the new state of the world to him in whatever manner you think best."

None of this should come as a surprise to Mia, and the senator didn't balk. "Are you recommending we red-flag them?"

"I think it will depend in part on their response to the message we send them. I confess, I'm not optimistic."

"Neither am I. But I will make it clear to them how their choices going forward will control their fate—"

Alex chose that moment to barge into Miriam's office carrying a thermos and a bagel. "Good, you're here. Mia, you, too. I hate repeating myself."

Miriam took a sip of her tea, taking a bit of perverse joy in the increasing exasperation on Alex's face while her daughter waited for her to rise to the bait. She calmly set the teacup on its coaster and folded her arms atop her desk. "Good morning. Thank you for throwing a lovely party last night."

"Of course. But now I need to tell you all the information I desperately wanted to tell you last night, but kept my mouth shut for Dad's sake."

"You went to NGC 55 and observed some Rasu."

"Some Rasu? Yes, I most definitely observed 'some' Rasu."

"And what did your observations tell you?"

"That we should go back to Aurora."

The beginnings of dread stirred in Miriam's gut. Her daughter had a penchant for making declarations that at first sounded like hyperbole, but all too often resolved to understatement. "That's not an option. The Aurora pocket universe no longer exists."

"Obviously. I'm just saying. A boring, isolated universe without Rasu in it would be highly preferable to basically any other universe with Rasu in it. Since we're stuck here, however...I'll be honest. We're probably fucked. I don't know, maybe we can move everyone a few thousand galaxies farther away and buy ourselves a millennium or so?"

Miriam frowned, and she and Mia exchanged a worried glance. "Alex, you've seen armadas of gigantic and well-armed alien warships before, and they've only pissed you off."

"I've never seen this before."

The dread knotted together and took up proper residence.

Alex finished the bagel and began pacing in a tight circle by the windows. "The Rasu contingent the Asterions defeated? They were right about it. It was only a forward expeditionary party. Everything Nika told us about the Rasu? Multiply it by a thousand. A million. Oh, and don't forget the part about how it's almost impossible to actually kill them."

"Well, you're certainly a fount of bad news this morning. Did you bring any good news to counter it?"

Alex shrugged broadly. "They don't know we exist yet? We have time. And I suggest we use it."

25

CONCORD HQ

The circular conference room at the apex of Concord HQ was designed to impress, and it never did disappoint. The walls and ceiling were a hybrid-glass composite divided into segments by strips of adiamene, so that no matter where one looked, one was presented with the technological and military might of Concord juxtaposed upon the stars. The oval table was constructed of exquisite cameo marble from Nopreis, the Novoloume homeworld. The chairs were made of a modular, adaptive polymer that shifted form according to the needs of the species currently sitting in them.

The reasons given for using this room for the meeting today were two-fold: it was the only place with a large enough table to seat everyone appropriately—in other words, treat them as equals—and it was where 'important discussions' were typically held. That it also stood to suitably impress the Asterions in attendance wasn't mentioned and might not even have been considered, as her mother didn't usually bother herself with such things. But nonetheless.

Alex chose a chair not-quite-opposite her mother so she could read the tiny facial tics Miriam deigned to let slip—and because she was reserving the seat to her right for Nika, and this way Nika would be directing her words to Miriam more often than not.

Caleb returned with ice water for them and sat to her left, and over the next couple of minutes the table gradually filled in. The attendees included Mia and Malcolm, as well as Pointe-Amiral Thisiame, the leader of the Novoloume military, Casmir elasson-Machim, the leader of the Anaden military, and Pinchutsenahn Niikha Qhiyane Kteh, Tokahe Naataan of the Khokteh people.

Concord frowned upon a single person holding both the military and political leadership positions, but Pinchu had bullied the others into accepting him as both by declaring that 'to be a leader of the Khokteh means to lead them in peace and in war.' He remained the sole exception to the rule however, which Alex had always assumed was why Malcolm and Mia had never married. Were they to do so, some people—those who didn't actually know them—might argue a married couple broke the spirit of the rule.

Richard was also here as head of CINT, while Lakhes swirled languidly around the room; the Kat hadn't been reserved a seat, because when had a Kat ever sat? This wasn't an official meeting of the Concord Senate, so other than Mia, who was here in her role as head of the Concord Consulate rather than as humanity's political representative, the political leaders were mercifully absent.

No, though it hadn't yet been given such a name, this was a war council.

The Asterions were the last to arrive, as they had a bit farther to travel, and were escorted in by one of Mia's aides. When they entered, Mia stood and went to the door to greet them, then faced the table. "I'd like to introduce our guests from the Asterion Dominion: Advisors Nika Kirumase, Dashiel Ridani and Commander Lance Palmer."

Casmir half-rose in his chair. "Asterions? The Asterions are aeons dead."

Nika gave him a wicked little half-smile. "Surprise."

Alex covered her mouth to silence a chuckle bubbling up at the expression on Casmir's face. God, it was going to take *centuries* to breed a sense of humor back into the Machims.

Mia kept a serious countenance, though she seemed to enjoy the exchange as well. "The Asterions recently made contact with us in order to warn us about a species they've encountered which they believe are a threat to all sapient species in this region of the universe. We've been undertaking our own investigation, and the purpose of this meeting is to discuss our findings thus far."

Casmir continued to look as though he'd eaten spoiled tuna for breakfast while Nika and the others took their seats, and Miriam called the meeting to order with a subtle twitch of her shoulders. "Everyone, thank you for coming, particularly on such short notice. I'll get straight to what we know at present. The species in question is known as 'Rasu.' They are an inorganic shapeshifting species of metallic origin."

At the center of the table, a semi-translucent image of the Rasu stronghold in the first stellar system in NGC 55 that she, Caleb and Valkyrie had visited materialized. "This is an example of their common appearance when they take on the form of ships or space stations."

Miriam ignored the outburst of murmurs from those who were just now seeing their first Rasu to switch the image to one of a group of bipedal Rasu from Nika's virtual memory. "Whereas this represents their most common bipedal form. They are also known to take on the form of drones—" another brief image "—and a variety of physical implements." Images of oversized saws, diggers and haulers flicked past.

"When inside a larger structure, they also take on the form and purpose of scientific equipment, data storage and propulsion, to name several roles. In fact, thus far the only item the Asterions have been able to identify that the Rasu use but which is not actually Rasu itself are these crystals. They use them to generate power, we believe primarily for their ship engines and weapons."

The visual of the cluster of crystals built into the belly of a Rasu leviathan lingered above the table for several seconds, until Miriam quietly replaced it with a map of the Laniakea region of the universe. The Milky Way sat near the bottom center of the map, and the Gennisi Galaxy off to the right. Triangulum, Andromeda, the MCs and a few other galaxies were marked as well. Above the crescent of Concord-controlled space, harsh colors bloomed like the mushroom cloud of a nuclear blast.

"The Katasketousya have been conducting an exhaustive survey of the Rasu's presence in Laniakea. This is what they have found so far. Areas in red represent galaxies where the Rasu have completely taken over. Orange represents a significant but not total Rasu presence, while yellow signifies galaxies the Rasu are now expanding into."

A swath of yellow arced over the Gennisi galaxy, pushed downward by a large blob of orange disappearing beneath an ocean of red that extended upward to the edges of the map.

The red wasn't total, to be fair; small islands of orange dotted the map, and yellow framed the contours on two sides.

Malcolm gestured to the map. "Is this the entire area of space they control? If not, how much farther does their sphere of influence extend beyond Laniakea?"

We are continuing our survey.

"Thank you. Please let us know what you find." He jerked a nod in Lakhes' direction and went back to staring at the map.

Pointe-Amiral Thisiame spoke up in his always gentle, reasonable tone of voice. "Can we assume these Rasu are hostile?"

Nika lifted her chin and repositioned herself indefinably toward the table. Asserting authority with a skill Alex could only admire. "Everything we have learned about them indicates they practice complete disregard for all life forms they encounter. They strip planets of useful resources and capture and study any life forms present, then exterminate them."

Casmir squirmed in his chair, and it was a testament to the professionalism of everyone in the room who wasn't Alex that no one but her stared scathingly at him. Thus far, the Rasu sounded a lot like Theriz Cultivation Units, and everyone here was exercising the height of restraint by not pointing it out.

Alex *really* wanted to point it out.

"When we encountered them, the Rasu blackmailed our government, demanding tens of thousands of Asterions be handed over as test subjects in return for them refraining from attacking our worlds. Those who were delivered then suffered months of unspeakable torture at the hands of the Rasu before dying."

The galaxies marked as red contain no measurable level of life forms that are not Rasu. As this is statistically impossible, the logical conclusion is the Rasu have eliminated all life forms they encountered in those galaxies.

Thisiame's skin gleamed subtly in response to Lakhes' commentary. "That must be thousands of species."

Hundreds of thousands by our estimates, hundreds of which were at a Tier I or higher stage of development.

Pinchu growled. "Their leading edge remains dozens of galaxies away from Concord space. This is an interesting theoretical discussion, but they will not represent a threat to us for many centuries."

Alex shrugged minutely. "Maybe, maybe not. We're still figuring out how fast they tend to move. But they're on the Asterions' doorstep today."

"And? What does this mean for us? We know nothing of these Asterions, other than that they look suspiciously like Anadens."

She adored Pinchu, but his first takes tended to be annoyingly insular and even xenophobic. He'd come around, though.

Miriam barely glanced at Pinchu. "We are continuing to explore an amicable relationship with the Asterions. Regardless, we cannot treat the threat the Rasu represent lightly. If there is any good news—" she dipped her chin toward Alex "—it is that we have time to prepare for an eventual conflict with them. We need to talk about how we do so."

Malcolm nodded deliberately. "All right. What weaponry do we know is effective against them?"

Lance Palmer lifted a hand. "We hurled them into a star. That seemed to work."

Malcolm's eyes widened briefly. "Did anything *short of* hurling them into a star work?"

"Oh, we blew a bunch of them to pieces using electricity bombs. But here's the problem with the Rasu: every atom of a Rasu *is* a Rasu. You can blow them up easily enough—not *easily*, but we can do it, which I assume means you can as well—but unless you atomize them, the individual pieces will simply join back together."

"How long does it take?"

Dashiel responded. "It depends. We haven't identified all the variables, but the number of pieces and the distance over which they're spread are clearly two. Seconds, minutes, hours. Possibly weeks if the spread is large enough."

"So we can win a battle against them."

Palmer jumped back in. "On a given day, yes. In theory. But the next day or next week, you're facing the same armada again, and odds are your forces have been markedly reduced."

Alex couldn't help but note how in some respects this was a familiar refrain. The Machims couldn't instantly replenish destroyed ships, but they could replace the soldiers who flew them quickly enough. Humanity had been here before and won.

She shifted in her chair in anticipation of making this exact point, but Casmir started talking before she could get a word in. "But conventional weapons will damage them?"

"Our weapons were able to inflict some damage, yes, as were volatile bombs placed in proximity to their hulls. But only temporarily. To destroy them, you need to do so at a subatomic level."

"What about negative energy weapons? We have a healthy supply of those."

Dashiel shrugged. "We haven't tried negative energy weapons. Theoretically…they should destroy the subatomic structure, yes."

"What about antimatter weapons?"

Every head at the table, other than the Asterions', whipped around to gape at Miriam. Most in shock, a few in amusement. Her expression didn't flinch. "I am merely exploring all possibilities."

Dashiel exhaled. "Again, I can't say for certain, but the science would suggest that an antimatter charge will destroy the Rasu atoms it comes into contact with."

Alex leaned back in her chair and folded her hands behind her head. "Well, since the gloves are off and everything's on the table, what about a Tartarus Trigger?"

Nika turned to her in question. "What's a Tartarus Trigger?"

"A weapon that creates an artificial black hole."

"You can *do* that?"

"Some enterprising Anaden scientists have built one or two in the past, yes. And I assume the Kats can gen up the equivalent should they be properly motivated to do so. Right, Lakhes?"

The question is irrelevant. Much as with antimatter weapons, if you set about deploying black holes in your battles to destroy the Rasu, eventually you will do enough damage to irreparably destabilize the space-time manifold, at which point we are all dead. Neither are viable strategies.

Miriam cleared her throat. "Acknowledged. Nevertheless, in an emergency situation, a single use of one or both must be on the table as a last resort."

"Nobody tell the Savrakaths."

"That is not a topic of discussion for this meeting."

Casmir wilted beneath the force of Miriam's glare. "Apologies, Commandant."

"Thank you. Now that we've identified the outer bounds of our options, let's talk about reality. If or when the Rasu arrive, what sort of war will we be looking at?" She motioned at the map. "This represents a frankly inconceivable number of Rasu. From here, I see no viable way to win an offensive war against them—at least not with our current knowledge and level of technology.

"A defensive war is another matter, however. The entirety of Rasu-kind will not be descending upon us in a tidal wave. As I understand it, historically they have moved methodically across space. They set up a base of operations in a galaxy and gradually subdue any species who live there while harvesting useful resources. Then they construct a network of strongholds, leave some number of themselves to populate them, and move on to the next galaxy.

"In the likeliest scenario, they will at some point in the future reach a Concord-governed galaxy, and they will find it defended. We need to prepare a strategic plan for such a defense, one driven by a primary goal of not allowing the Rasu to ever gain a toehold in Concord space."

Alex drummed her fingers on the table. "Lakhes, want to build a Kat Rifter with a circumference as wide as Concord space?"

Not particularly.

Caleb gave her a little shrug. "It was worth a thought."

Commandant, once you pick a fight with them, they will come for you.

"Acknowledged. But we have our own advantages as well. We are not limited to a single planet or even a single galaxy. We can fight them where they hit us, but they cannot hit us everywhere at once."

Alex stared at the expansive red blob on the map. Not until the entirety of Rasu-kind did descend upon them in a tidal wave, anyway. "Not at first, no. But that's a *lot* of Rasu."

Nika interjected then. "One fact which might be relevant to this topic. The Rasu do not communicate with one another using quantum entanglement. They rely on powerful broadcast antennae."

Her mother frowned. "Whyever not?"

"The Rasu are paranoid about control. I can only speculate as to why, but I believe it originates in their nature of splitting apart and coming together, of constantly changing their purpose and thus their identity. The Rasu in our galaxy were experimenting on our people because they believed we held the secret to controlling other life forms across infinite distances."

Alex grinned mischievously. "Do you?"

Nika's lips pursed. "Not…as such. It's possible they were on the correct track, but so far as we've been able to determine, they did not make any significant progress in their research before we put a stop to the experiments.

"The point is, the nature of Rasu consciousness is a fickle beast. When Rasu are separated by measurable distances for a long period of time, they develop their own…will. If they later rejoin other Rasu—physically—they lose their independence of thought. We believe this makes the Rasu paranoid, as I said, regarding the intentions of others of their kind. Now, all these Rasu—" she gestured to the map "—are almost certainly committed to the same general cause, that of Rasu domination of space. I imagine they work together in a thousand ways to achieve this goal.

"But the relationship among the Rasu in different galaxies is..." Nika's smile hinted at her own mischief "...I suspect not unlike the relationship among the people in this room. You are all committed to a common cause, and you work together peacefully to further it. But I daresay you don't always trust one another to put the greater good above self-interest."

Damn. She was good, and that kind of audacity deserved to be rewarded. Emboldened, Alex stood and began circling the table. "Now. We've talked a lot about what we're going to do to prepare for a future but inevitable Rasu confrontation. At the risk of deviating from the topic of discussion for this meeting, I want to know: what are we going to do right now for the Asterions?"

26

CONCORD HQ

N ika paced along the wall of viewports in the lobby outside the meeting room, acknowledging but no longer really seeing the awe-inspiring view they provided. Spiraling rings and interlocking chains of ships and endlessly more ships.

For the second time in the last minute, she stopped to glare at the closed door beyond the reception area. "What's taking them so long?"

Dashiel sidled in close and leaned in to whisper in her ear. "It's been eight minutes."

"Right. I'm being impatient. Highly undiplomatic of me."

"It's understandable. Big decisions are being made about our future, and we don't get a say in them." He kissed her ear and stepped back, then gestured toward the view. "I have to admit, this is all incredible."

She shrugged. "We could have chosen to go down this path—a path of military armament, of staying always on a war footing, poised to lash out at any new threat. Instead, we chose to go another way."

"And who's regretting that now?" Lance returned from the far corner, where he'd been conferring with one of his officers, and joined them at the viewports. "Ridani, we can't dawdle around here any longer. We're needed at DAF Command. There's an issue with one of the materials supply chains. It's holding up new ship production and requires our input to unclog."

"You mean *my* input."

"With me staring over your shoulder until the ships are moving again."

Dashiel took Nika's hand. "I'm sorry to abandon you here in a den of..." his brow furrowed "...what seem like mostly reasonable people, honestly."

"They do. And even if they didn't, this is my job. Go do yours. I'll fill you in on what the verdict is later today."

He squeezed her hand goodbye, then he and Lance headed off toward the Consulate, where a wormhole to the Omoikane Initiative would be opened for them.

RW

The conference table had lost many of its occupants by the time Mia retrieved Nika from the lobby and welcomed her back into the room. In addition to Mia, Commandant Solovy remained, as well as her daughter, Caleb and Fleet Admiral Jenner. The real power in Concord.

Nika reclaimed her seat next to Alex and took a deep breath. "Tell me."

Commandant Solovy smiled with notable warmth. "We have decided to offer the Asterions active military and scientific consultation, including materials support where needed. We'll help you build early warning systems and develop more effective weaponry against the Rasu. We also intend to provide information sharing on everything we learn about the Rasu from here forward. When we know it, you'll know it. We'd appreciate the same in return, of course."

Mia stepped in. "We also would like to propose the construction of a permanent wormhole gateway between Concord HQ and a location of your choice in the Dominion. It will be able to be activated by either side, so we can begin a regular and official dialogue. A dialogue which, if all goes well, in time may lead to the Asterions being offered a formal alliance—or possibly even full Concord membership, if you are so inclined."

Nika worked to look grateful. Which she was, no question. "Thank you. On behalf of the Asterion Dominion, I accept your offers with the utmost appreciation." She shifted her attention to

Commandant Solovy. "You said, 'materials support.' Does this include an opportunity for us to buy adiamene from you?"

The woman had the grace to act chagrined. "It does not. Understand, we don't expect to ever face a day when the Asterions are our enemy. But we do not provide adiamene to our allies—not to the Novoloume, not to the Khokteh, and..." she paused "...certainly not to the Anadens. We've learned the lesson the hard way that today's allies can become tomorrow's adversaries."

"Even though this limits the capabilities of many of the forces you yourself command?"

"Even though. Nonetheless, you make a valid point. In truth, this particular decision is not mine to make. It's a decision for humanity's governments, and they have made their position on the topic explicit."

Mia cleared her throat. "I will broach the issue with the GCDA. Perhaps given enough time and familiarity, they will show some flexibility on the issue." Her lips quirked. "I would not base your defensive strategy on it, however."

Nika softened the blow for herself. "I understand. So what happens if a new Rasu force arrives in Dominion space and attacks us?"

Commandant Solovy's hands wrapped around the teacup situated in front of her. "You're asking if the Concord military will come to your defense."

"I am."

"The decision will be up to the Concord Senate, and we're not ready to put the question to them quite yet. Let's pursue the avenues we've put forth first. Get to know one another better."

Beside her, Alex dropped her forehead into her palm with an audible groan. "The Senate will—"

"Alex."

Alex raised both hands in the air and sank back in her chair. "I know. Not up to me."

So this had been a contentious issue. She made a note to express proper thanks to Alex later for being their advocate in the room.

"Thank you for everything. I look forward to building a strong and enduring relationship between our people." Her gaze flickered to the viewports as a battlecruiser sailed past...*there was never, could never be enough kyoseil*...then returned to those gathered. "There is one resource that will do more to assist us in preparing for the Rasu than any other. More than adiamene, more than a fleet of ships at our back. Kyoseil—your Reor. It's my understanding it is in plentiful supply here and its use is not restricted. We will happily pay for it—we're close to working out an exchange system so we may do so—and we will buy however much you have to offer."

Alex leaned forward with sudden intensity. "We can do that. Right? There's no reason why we can't do that."

Commandant Solovy's jaw twitched. "We don't want to create an unexpected shortage. It's still widely used for storage, especially by Anadens."

"Sure, because we never told them about its security vulnerabilities—"

"Alex, this isn't the place or the time."

Nika suppressed a chuckle. As she understood it, Alex had unlocked the interlinking properties of Reor and used them to steal strategic secrets from the Anaden Directorate—secrets that led directly to Humanity's victory. And it seemed in fourteen years, they'd never divulged how they'd done it. Interesting. It made her wonder how collegial the relationship between the Humans and Anadens actually was, or wasn't.

"Whatever. The point is, we have plenty, and we can grow more, though we've pared back the practice. And if we run low, the Kats keep a horde of it hidden. We won't run out."

A secret horde? Now *that* was interesting.

"Granted. Ms. Requelme, I believe this question falls in your purview, or rather the Senate's purview."

Mia nodded decisively. "The sale of Reor is perfectly legal in Concord space to everyone except red-flagged species. By my interpretation of the rules, this means there is nothing to stop the Asterions from buying it or us from selling it to them. It will take a few hours, but I'll put together the details and we can come to an arrangement."

Oh, Dashiel was going to love her so. "Thank you. You have no idea how much of a difference you've just made."

RW

Alex lingered in the lobby after the meeting while Caleb chatted with Mia, presumably about Marlee. It truly did offer a marvelous view, and she never passed up one of those.

Sometimes she could scarcely believe that humanity had risen to such heights as to create all *this*. Despite their considerable, extensive and exasperating faults, they hadn't done half bad for themselves.

She sensed Mesme's presence almost before the Kat completed its arrival. A hint of a smile teased her lips. "You keep barely missing the big meetings. Do I need to get you a timepiece?"

My attendance was unnecessary, as Lakhes represented our interests. I would have been a distraction.

"Trust me, we all could've benefited from a distraction. I want you to meet Nika, and she wants to meet Tyche. Can you do something to make that happen?"

Tyche is not as well-versed in interacting with organic species as myself and Lakhes are, and they are demonstrating some reticence about becoming so.

A socially awkward Kat was the height of redundancy, but she supposed there were degrees. Mesme and Lakhes were in fact…everything was relative. "Try to convince them. Assure them we don't bite."

Our form is ethereal, thus it would be impossible for you to…oh. An idiom. Yes, I will make the attempt.

"Thank you. So why are you here? I doubt it's to enjoy the view. Everything for megaparsecs is your backyard, as it were."

It is, nonetheless, a striking tableau.

"It is." She paused. "Will all this military might be enough? Enough to defeat the Rasu?"

It is a complicated question. Alone? No. But Humans are no longer alone.

They contemplated that in silence for a little while.

You are considering taking Nika Kirumase to the Reor enclave in the Oneiroi Nebula. To impress upon her the fulsomeness of our supply, or perhaps simply to impress her. Or perhaps to offer it to her in its entirety.

She eyed the faint dots of light, washed out as they were by the bright lighting of the lobby. "So you were eavesdropping on the meeting after all. Mesme, we've talked about this. We don't mind your presence, but we don't like being watched without our knowledge."

And I have made a thousand lifetimes of observing. It is not a practice easily broken. Nor should it be. It is what I do.

"One of the things you do, anyway. To answer your question, yes. I'm considering it. I'm curious what an Asterion might experience surrounded by so much Reor…so much kyoseil. We really need to decide which one we're going to call it."

You are wise to be curious. But do not take her there. Not yet.

"And why not?"

It is not time.

She whipped toward the Kat. "Excuse me?"

I mean precisely what I say. It is not time. She is not ready for what will happen to her should she venture there.

"How would you know? You haven't even met her."

No Asterion is ready for what will happen to them should they venture there. Please, accept my statement without further elaboration. On faith, if you wish.

She couldn't help but remember what had happened to *her* when she'd ventured there, and she'd had no prior exposure to Reor. For the Asterions, it literally ran through their veins. Still, though. "Mesme, you haven't been this disconcertingly cryptic in a long, long while. What aren't you telling me?" She belatedly realized her error. "What pertinent fact related to this specific topic aren't you telling me?"

Fourteen years ago, you said you would never ask anything of me again if I located Akeso for you. I wish I could say I will never ask anything of you again if you grant me this accommodation, but I fear it will be a lie. Nevertheless.

We have trusted one another, often contrary to each of our better judgments, many times in the past. You have never disappointed me or proved this trust misplaced, and I hope you would say the same of me. So I ask you to trust me today.

She stared at the gaps between the swirling lights. "Will you give me a heads up when it *is* the right time?"

I will not need to.

"Mesme...."

Very well. Yes.

"Thanks," she grumbled under her breath. The next instant there was absence where there had been presence, and Mesme was gone.

Well, that was an odd conversation, even by Mesme's standards. The Kats were meddling again, positioning players where they wanted them ahead of what was certain to be apocalyptic trouble. As one of those players, she should be angrier about it. But she did genuinely believe whatever they were doing, they were doing it in order to give all sapient life the best possible chance for survival.

She still didn't like it. Not one bit.

So, apocalyptic trouble. It could only be the Rasu—god, she hoped there wasn't a threat yet worse beyond the Rasu. At least this time, the government wasn't ignoring her warnings of the looming threat or angling to use it as a tool in political games. So that was something.

She breathed in and removed a tiny block in place in her mind. A few months after The Displacement, she and Valkyrie had devised a way to shut out the Noesis, and she'd rarely opened herself up to the Prevos' quantum playground in the years since. A couple hundred thousand Prevos didn't need to know her business.

But, she decided, they did need to know this.

It began as a low thrum at the base of her skull, then grew to a buzz, faint at first but growing inexorably louder as it wound through her mind. Not unpleasant even at its loudest, but akin to a sensation forever on the verge of becoming an itch.

She closed her eyes and felt her way around for a minute, making sure she remembered how to navigate the virtual dimension. Thoughts and conversations swelled into her conscious awareness and faded into the background at an uneven pace that gradually found its rhythm. She noticed a few tickles as others noticed her manifestation, but no one tried to barge in or interrupt her.

A vague feeling of...was this nostalgia?...weighed down her mood. All this vibrant activity going on across hundreds of thousands of minds and dozens of galaxies. Currents of excitement regarding innumerable different initiatives, research, pranks, crimes and discoveries washed over and past her. It had been going on without her all these years. She'd always be the *first* Prevo, but she hadn't been a leading one for a long time.

And that was fine. Her choice, and she didn't regret it. She might be a little envious at the margins, but nothing more.

Still, her name had damn well better count for something here.

She readied all the files from their visit to NGC 55, as well as everything the Asterions had provided, then performed the equivalent of a throat-clearing in the middle of the vast and boundless Noesis.

Your attention, please. This is Alex Solovy Marano, and I come bearing a present for you. We have a new enemy, goes by the name of 'Rasu.' An enemy of humanity, of Concord, of all decent and interesting species. I'm distributing everything I know about them, free and unencrypted. Go, do your thing.

27

EARTH

SAN FRANCISCO

A lex rode the lift to the top of the Pyramid Tower, where a penthouse restaurant looked out over San Francisco Bay. The Golden Gate Bridge had seen every girder, bracing, beam and cable replaced three times in the last two centuries, but the bridge still stood. Even though skycars had no use for it and what traffic traversed it was invariably pleasure vehicles—mostly cycles and lev-bikes—it still stood. 'It still stands, dammit!' was in fact the official position on the matter of the Southern Pacific Regional Government.

She was, believe it or not, a few minutes early for her regular monthly lunch with Kennedy. They always met in San Francisco, and always at a different restaurant. Yes, they were being sentimental, dopily so. But it was only once a month, and it felt good to enjoy something that was and had always been *theirs*. So much had changed in their lives; it was okay if this stayed the same.

She headed to their reserved table by the bay-facing windows and ordered a bottle of chardonnay and bruschetta. In truth, she was early for a reason. Because she had a reason to be here beyond sentimentality. The need to act drove her forward, and this constituted the next necessary step on her mission.

Kennedy arrived five minutes later, her arms mercifully devoid of children. Alex loved her two godchildren very much, she truly did, but some things needed to remain the province of adults, and their monthly lunch should be one of them. Especially today.

"Ugh!" Kennedy collapsed in the chair opposite Alex and poured herself a glass of wine. "Do you want to hear about the new specification requirements coming out of CBAL? You probably don't, right? Right. Fabulous party the other night. The kids went home soaked and filthy, so thank Akeso for that."

"I will. Thank *you* again for your help in getting everything ready. You are the definition of lifesaver."

"I won't argue." Kennedy shrugged and grabbed a slice of bruschetta. "What's the latest from the world of intrigue?"

"You mean Concord? We had a boondoggle of a meeting about the Rasu and the Asterions yesterday. Short on politicians, thankfully, but long on military blowhards. They will, as usual, investigate and form commissions and draw up strategic plans."

"Some things never change."

"Nope." They paused to order a more proper lunch; when the waiter had departed, Alex idly ran a fingertip along the rim of her wineglass. "So...."

"Uh-oh."

"Hey!"

"No, please, continue. What comes after 'so'?"

"Concord decided to help out the Asterions in mostly lame but a few reasonably decent ways. They agreed to sell them Reor, which is excellent. But no adiamene."

"Of course not. It's highly illegal under GCDA regulations."

"Oh, I know it is."

Kennedy sank back in her chair and covered her face with her hands. "Alex...."

"Fifteen years ago, you defied a whole host of government laws and regulations, went rogue and sold adiamene to the Prevos, the IDCC, Volnosti and whoever the hell else you wanted to sell it to. You did it because it was the right thing to do. And you got away with it! You're where you are now because of what you did then. We're *all* here today because of what you did."

"And the entire universe has changed since then, too. Those Earth Alliance laws Winslow shoved through were never legitimate. But now? The GCDA is a different matter. It's not a faction—

it's humanity's government, and while they're not always awesome, they haven't done anything stupid enough to deserve rebelling over."

"They're denying a vital resource to people who desperately need it to defend against a warmongering alien species who will annihilate them the first chance it gets."

"Over-dramatize much?"

"Not actually. I got my first look at the Rasu the other day before the party."

"Oh." Kennedy deflated. "Still. I can't be so reckless with my life, my freedom or my money any longer. I have a family."

"I realize you do. I get it. But maybe you could help without being quite so brazen about it this time."

"Like, on the sly?"

"Exactly. You can't sell adiamene to the Asterions above the table. But if the chemical formulas and schem flows for its production were to somehow end up in their hands, then the cat's out of the bag, and it's no one's fault. The GCDA can't stop the Asterions from manufacturing it themselves."

Kennedy's nose wrinkled up, and she took a hurried sip of her wine. "What, blame industrial espionage? Say the Asterions stole the information? Wouldn't that sour our burgeoning relationship with them?"

"Not if the people who would get upset about it never know— or don't find out until much later. We're planning to build a single wormhole gate from Concord to the Dominion. It's not as though GCDA regulators are going to be crawling around their ship assembly lines five megaparsecs away anytime soon. They'll be none the wiser."

"Government regulators have long memories and lots of time on their hands. Trust me on this."

"So one day someone notices and pitches a fit. By then, we'll all be waist-deep in Rasu gore, and you can safely tell them to go screw themselves."

"We will? You really think so?"

Alex sighed. "I really do. Not to over-dramatize—I mean it—but a shitstorm is looming on the horizon. And I fear it's going to arrive sooner than anyone expects. Listen, I've spent a fair amount of time with some Asterions now, and while I realize I'm not the best judge of character to ever exist, I genuinely believe they're good people."

"They were Anadens once."

"So were we, in the ways that matter for this conversation. And they affirmatively rejected their Anaden heritage to forge their own destiny, which makes them far better in my estimation. But, okay, let's be cold and logical and a little selfish about it. The Asterions are building the ramparts on the front line of the Rasu invasion. Everything we can do to help them to stay stronger and hold out for longer buys us more time to get ready for when those ramparts fall."

Lunch arrived, and Kennedy frowned at her plate of angel hair pasta and shrimp for several seconds. "I need to talk it over with Noah."

"Of course. I assumed as much." She was glad for this. Noah was the one who had goaded Kennedy into rebelling the first time, and while these days he was making a hard play for Dad of the Decade, something told Alex his rebellious streak hadn't died away completely. "If you both decide you want to help, let me know, and I can connect you to the proper people."

"You're already in that tight with the Asterions?"

"I know a guy."

"Advisor Ridani? I met him."

Alex crossed her arms over her chest in a mock huff. "That's right, you did. Why don't you just send all the files yourself, then?"

"Oh, come on. Can't we at least pretend we're spies and act like we're crafty?"

RW

ROMANE

MILKY WAY GALAXY

Kennedy stretched out atop the bedcovers, luxuriating in the moonglow streaming through the windows. Indulging in a bit of decadence for the minute that she could.

"Hi, gorgeous." Noah closed the door behind him and sidled up next to her on the bed.

"Everything okay?"

"All good. Braelyn heard something in class today about the lizard monsters coming to eat little human children, and she wanted to talk about what she ought to do if they come here."

"Lizard monsters? Does she mean the Savrakaths?"

"Yep. The dad of one of the kids in their class works at the Consulate and is apparently too free with his dinner-table conversation. I told her I would protect her from any lizard incursions. She thanked me for the offer, but said she'd let Grimwulf take the first crack at them."

Kennedy chuckled quietly. "Daddy's little Machiavellian princess."

He kissed her bare shoulder. "You're being suspiciously contemplative. What's on your mind?"

He always did know. She rolled over to face him. "Alex wants me to give the adiamene formula to the Asterions in secret."

"Of course she does."

"I told her this wasn't like before. We can't go casually flaunting government laws any longer. We have a family to protect."

"We do—from lizards, Rasu and politicians. It is an enticing idea, though, isn't it? Throwing caution to the wind and risking everything for a dream of what doing the right thing can accomplish? Of deciding for ourselves what we can do, should do and will do?"

Her eyes narrowed as she studied him. "Oh, no. You sound *way* too wistful."

"No. I wouldn't trade the life we have now for all the gemstones on Narala. I'm just saying the reasons why we defied the government before haven't changed, even if the reasons why perhaps we *shouldn't* have."

"I know." She rolled the rest of the way onto her stomach and propped up on her elbows. "Alex made a persuasive case that it's the right thing to do. I mean, what if Concord refuses to defend the Asterions against the Rasu? They'll need to be able to defend themselves against what is a horrific enemy."

"I suspect if Concord were to wuss out, Miriam will give the Senate the finger and send the fleets anyway."

"Oh, goodie, another civil war."

He leaned in close, until his hair tickled her shoulder. "What if we could get the formulation to them without it coming back on us?"

"Noah, there's only one supplier of adiamene, and that's Connova Interstellar. We would be the only suspect, for good reason."

"Sure, but suspecting isn't proving. If there's no evidence we provided the information to them, the government can't prosecute us." He switched to their private Connova channel. *"Vii, could we gen up some records, say of a corporate espionage-style incursion into our data banks, to make it appear as if the Asterions stole the formula for adiamene?"*

'It is a trivial matter to do so. Have you considered how this will reflect on the Asterions, however, when they are endeavoring to gain Concord's favor?'

"Yes, but they can put forth a compelling defense. They simply want to be able to defend themselves."

Noah rose to his knees, straddled her back and began kneading Kennedy's shoulders. "Once the Asterions have the formula, our trade secrets will no longer be so secret. It might not be long before our monopoly evaporates into the wind."

Kennedy moaned in pleasure as he worked a thorny knot beside her spine. "I admit, I don't care in the slightest for the idea of the Anadens getting their hands on adiamene. Or the Savrakaths, for sure. But isn't this what we said we wanted way back in the beginning? How no government should be allowed to restrict access to a metal?

"We've let the GCDA do exactly that for the last fourteen years, mostly because…because it was important for humanity to be able to protect itself in this new, overwhelming, dangerous place. But we're not the wide-eyed newcomers any longer. I realize Mia and Miriam would disagree, but humans are kind of in charge now. So maybe it is time for us to live our principles again."

Noah urged her to roll over, then leaned down to press his chest against hers and kiss her softly. "Protecting Jonas and Braelyn must be our highest priority, no matter what. But if we can do that and help the Asterions, too, then…I think we should."

28

SENECA

CAVARE

"*H*ello? *Is anyone there?*"

Marlee sat bolt upright in her bed. *Identify!*

Her eVi splashed the result across her virtual vision.

Source: CINT Comm Module #D17e4s

User: Unknown

She gasped and curled her fingers tight over the edge of the covers.

"*Vaihe? Is that you?*"

The silence lasted so long she finally decided both her and her eVi had dreamt the comm. She flopped down on her pillow as the rush of adrenaline seeped away—

"*Is this the Human who tried to rescue me?*"

And back up again!

"*Yes, yes it is. Are you okay? I worried you'd been captured.*" Or killed, but she kept this part from making it into the comm.

"*No, I...I ran into the swamps. A long way. I heard them searching for me, but I hid.*"

It had been nine days since their escape attempt. The thought of nine days hiding in that awful swamp...she shuddered and wrapped the covers tighter around her shoulders.

"*Vaihe, you are so brave. I'm proud of you. Why didn't you answer my messages before now?*"

"*When I heard your voice the first afternoon, I believed I was hallucinating. Driven mad from fright. Then last night I found this strange device on my clothes. I thought about it all night. And I decided it wasn't a Savrakath tool, so it must be a Human tool. And I thought I would try to talk back to it."*

Marlee leapt out of bed, pulled on a loose top and hopped around the room wiggling into her pants.

"I'm so glad you did. I'm going to help you, okay? Are you safe where you are right now?"

"Safe? I...I think so. I haven't seen any guards in two days. I haven't seen anyone. I am hungry, but...I will be fine, I think."

"Stay where you are for a little while longer. I'll get you out of there. I promise."

"How can you do such a thing?"

"Just trust me. I'll be in touch soon."

She shoved her bare feet into shoes and rushed into the main room of her apartment and over to her hard-lined workstation. CINT was a spy organization. Surely they maintained the ability to track their active comm devices.

She maneuvered to her backdoor into CINT systems and started rooting around. She usually tried not to so flagrantly violate Concord security systems from a workstation that in theory could be traced, but the exigent circumstances called for an exception. Let's see...agents on assignment...field equipment...unassigned—there!

Query: Location of CINT Comm Module #D17e4s

Coordinates spit out onto the screen, and she plugged them into the SuperGalactic Coordinate System. On Savrak, obviously. Zoom, zoom, zoom closer...

...damn. Vaihe really had run a long way. She was located sixteen kilometers from the spaceport, smack in the middle of swamp nowhere.

Marlee drummed a rhythm on the desk with her palms—then leapt up, left the apartment and went down the hall to knock on Eosha's door. By the time she arrived, she had her plan.

Despite the time of night, the Novoloume woman opened the door looking like she was heading out to a fine dinner party; then again, she always did. "Marlee! This is a pleasant surprise. Do you not sleep at these hours?"

"Sometimes. I need your help."

RW

The Cavare spaceport couldn't be characterized as bustling at this time of night, but it was far from deserted. The business and pleasure of Concord's not-an-empire never stopped completely, and certainly not on one of its most important worlds.

Eosha hurried after her as she wound through the various wings to reach the Caeles Prism Hub, where permanent wormholes to a variety of popular destinations, mostly but not solely human worlds, operated.

A security officer sat bored at a desk in one corner. Anyone already on Seneca didn't need authorization to go to the locations accessed by the Prisms, and his presence was a mere formality.

Marlee leaned in close to Eosha's ear and pointed out the portal leading to the Senecan Federation world of Krysk, where she'd briefly lived when she was young. "Stand next to that portal. If anyone tries to use it, say it's down for maintenance. We can't have some poor civilian ending up in a Savrak swamp."

"No, that will not do. What if the guard challenges me?"

"You can speak diplomat-ese, can't you? Convince him you were sent by Cavare Central Maintenance. I know at least one or two Novoloume work there as part of the exchange program."

"I shall do my best."

"You'll be awesome." She headed back out of the portal room. From the hallway she took a left, out of the public-access area, then a right, and broke into the hub control room using another tool she'd swiped from CINT storage. Their gadgets were just full of uses.

Once the door closed behind her, she took a minute to study the setup and decide on a method of attack.

Soon, breaking into maintenance corridors and evading security guards wouldn't be necessary. She was working on a comprehensive rewrite of her cybernetics programming, which she hoped would elevate them and her to a level where she'd be able to open her own wormholes without needing to become a Prevo and chain herself to a separate intelligence, one with its own needs, desires and bossy opinions.

But she wasn't finished designing the rewrite yet, so for now this was the only way.

She sat at the empty chair in front of the input panel. The Caeles Prisms may be fairly new, but the system running them was based on old Federation technology, and in seconds she had hacked into the security control system and found the connection instructions for the Krysk portal. She reprogrammed the destination using the coordinates from Vaihe's comm device, then set it to loop back to its regular destination after twenty minutes. This way, she wouldn't need to return here and change it manually.

Satisfied, she backed out of the system, left the control room and returned to the Prism Hub. She paused outside the entrance long enough to adopt an expression befitting a young woman out for a night on the town, then walked casually inside. Eosha lounged next to the Krysk portal like she owned it, and Marlee strolled up to the Prism, winked at Eosha and walked through it.

It wasn't the sweltering heat or sopping humidity that nearly knocked her back through the wormhole all the way to Cavare; it was the stench. Out here in the raw wilds, the swamp *stank*.

She instinctively covered her mouth and nose with a hand and peered around while she waited for her eVi to dampen her olfactory nerves. It was late dusk, and the sky radiated a pea-green color. Also, she was standing knee-deep in half a meter of muck. She dragged a leg forward. "Vaihe? Are you here?"

A rustle in the underbrush to her left drew her attention. A wide face with enormous eyes peered out from between two reeds.

"Vaihe! Come here! We need to leave."

The Godjan cautiously stood and slogged through the muck toward Marlee a step at a time. "How did you—? You made a hole in the world." Her progress stopped. "Are you a god?"

"Oh goodness, no. It's only technology. Come on. You and I are going to go back through the...hole...and then you'll be safe."

Vaihe took another two tortuous steps before stopping again. "I don't...where will it take me?"

Marlee wiped sweat off her forehead. She hoped the wormhole hadn't been detected this far out into the wilderness, but Savrakath technology was pretty good, so she couldn't afford to assume it hadn't been. "Someplace clean and cool. Someplace with lots and lots of food, where no one is enslaved and no one will hurt you. Someplace safe. Now please, we don't have much time. Come with me."

She held out a hand.

Vaihe stared at it for several seconds...then slogged the final steps and took it, and Marlee guided her through the wormhole.

RW

Vaihe shrieked when she saw Eosha, and Marlee had to hold tight to her hand to keep the Godjan from fleeing back to Savrak.

The guard started, stood and began to approach them. "What's wrong?"

Marlee laughed and fell against Eosha's shoulder, slurring her words. "Just a little too much of a good time on Krysk. Who knew such a thing was possible on that rock, right?"

"You're covered in mud."

"It's raining on Krysk." Which it must be doing *somewhere* on the planet. She let her gaze drift blearily around. "And we couldn't find the street. So mud."

The guard regarded them suspiciously, but his steps slowed. "Is everyone all right?"

"Sure, sure. We're headed home. No more drinks for us tonight." She and Eosha each took one of Vaihe's arms and gently began guiding her toward the exit. The girl looked utterly terrified, but at least she didn't shriek when Eosha touched her.

When they were almost to the exit, Marlee glanced over her shoulder. "Oh, the guard on the Krysk side said...he said something about..." her face scrunched up in concentration "...some technical issues they were having and to not...um...not let anybody through for ten minutes. Or was it fifteen? Fifteen. 'kay?"

The guard paused halfway to sitting back down. "Got it. Fifteen minutes."

"Yep." She smiled sloppily and helped everyone lurch out the door.

RW

"You live here? All by yourself? It's so *big*."

Marlee shrugged as the door to her apartment closed behind her. "It's nice enough for now. So, I bet the first thing you want is a shower."

The Godjan kept staring wondrously around the apartment. "A...?"

"A bath? To get clean. Wash the swamp off of you. The lavatory is in here." She confirmed Vaihe was following her, then went into the lavatory and turned on the shower water.

Vaihe made a squeaking noise behind her. Did the Savrakaths not allow the Godjans to shower? She did the mature thing and bit back a rousing tirade; the important thing right now was to make Vaihe feel safe.

"I'll step out, so you can have privacy. Leave your clothes on the floor, and we'll worry about trying to clean them later. I'll bring you some fresh clothes and set them outside the door here. Then I'm going to step down the hall real fast. I'll be right back. But you take your time in the shower."

Vaihe nodded vaguely and reached a tentative hand into the water, then smiled.

Marlee left her to this new adventure and went to her closet, where she dug out a plain gray t-shirt. It would swallow Vaihe whole, but it would be comfortable and cover the important parts. She folded it on the floor outside the lavatory as promised, then jogged down the hall to thank Eosha again for the help.

The Novoloume was as gracious as ever, though she did have questions about why they had snatched a strange alien girl through a wormhole and escorted her to Marlee's apartment. Marlee promised fulsome answers in the morning and excused herself due to not wanting to leave said strange alien girl alone for too long.

When she returned to her apartment, she found Vaihe curled up on the couch, in the t-shirt, fast asleep.

RW

CONCORD HQ

CONSULATE

It was early afternoon the next day by the time Marlee had gotten Vaihe fed, more appropriately clothed and convinced her to come with Marlee to Concord HQ.

The Godjan trailed Marlee through HQ in a daze, her eyes locked in wide orbs and her mouth hanging slightly open. Probably a combination of awe and fear. Intellectually, Marlee understood how such a place must appear terrifying to someone who had been oppressed and kept poor and isolated since birth. But Marlee had grown up running wild through the halls of buildings and stations such as this, and to her, this was home as much as her apartment or her mom's house.

She only hoped the Godjan didn't get spooked and bolt, though the consequences of her doing so stood to be much less severe than if she'd done it on Savrak.

When they reached the door to Mia's office, Vaihe froze cold. Marlee reached out and took her hand. "It's okay. We're going in here to talk to my boss."

"Boss...like Ambassador-sir?"

"No. Nothing at all like that cretin Darhk. She's a very nice lady, I promise."

Vaihe's double eyelids blinked. "Nice lady?"

"That's right. A very nice lady."

The girl's chin bobbed, and Marlee opened the door.

Mia looked up from an aural. "Marlee? Did we have a...." Her gaze quickly took in Vaihe, and she painted on a gracious, welcoming countenance as she stood. "You've brought a guest, I see. Hello, I'm Mia Requelme. You're a Godjan, yes? From Savrak?"

Marlee, how much trouble should I prepare for?

A fair to middling amount.

"This is my friend, Vaihe."

"It's a pleasure to meet you, Vaihe." Mia gestured toward the couch off to the left. "Why don't we sit over here. It'll be more comfortable than the desk chairs."

Vaihe's stare darted between Mia and Marlee, so Marlee placed a hand on her elbow and guided her toward the couch. When they arrived, Vaihe half-perched awkwardly on one of the arms.

Marlee sat down beside her, and Mia moved a chair closer and sat opposite them. "Now, what can I do for you today, Vaihe?"

Vaihe turned to Marlee in question, and she gave the girl an encouraging smile. "All you need to do is tell Mia your story. Tell her about what all the Savrakaths have done to you, and to your people."

"But...be punished? Okshakin?"

"No. No more dungeons, no more shock collars. No Savrakath will ever be able to lay a hand on you again. We will protect you. You're safe here."

Vaihe still looked terrified, but she took a breath and lifted her shoulders, and her gaze grew reasonably focused on Mia. "I never knew my parents. I was taken from them by Savrakath soldiers when I was two years old...."

RW

Vaihe gulped down a mug of cold cider, which she held between both hands in a vise-grip. Her legs were pressed tight at the knees as if for protection, but she'd made it to a proper cushion on the couch.

Marlee watched the girl from where she propped against the viewport near Mia's desk. "She can stay with me for now. I think it's the only place she feels safe. Maybe in a few weeks, we can set her up in an apartment of her own in the building. Right now, though, I need to get her some clothes and a portable translator. She'll need credits, and eventually a job? When she's ready."

Mia entered a few commands in her control panel. "If you're comfortable taking care of her, I agree your apartment is the best place for her. The Consulate will of course pay for everything. I'll have an account open for her in a few minutes."

"I appreciate it."

"What job skills might she have? Do you know?"

"Well, she worked as a helper to—" Her mouth slammed shut. *Dammit.*

"A helper to who?"

"To...Ambassador Darhk."

Mia exhaled and stepped back to lean against the wall. "She's the reason you were arrested."

"Yes. Because of me, she ended up lost, alone and hunted in the Savrak wilderness. I owed it to her to finish the job of rescuing her."

Mia fell silent for several interminable seconds, then nodded mostly to herself. "I understand. I can't approve in an official capacity, but I do understand."

"And that is why I love working for you!"

"Don't push it. How did you get her here?"

Marlee huffed a quiet laugh. "It's better for both of us if you don't know. Trust me. The important thing is, she's here now. And you're going to do something about her mistreatment, aren't you? About the mistreatment of all the Godjans?"

"Yes."

"What?"

"It will depend on—"

"No, no depending. What are you going to do to hold the Savrakaths accountable?"

Mia gave her an austere look that reminded Marlee too much of her mother's scoldings. "That's a far more complicated question than you realize, but I promise you they will be. Please trust me and let me do my job."

Despite her best efforts, Marlee wilted under the weight of the woman's innate, unassailable *authority.* "I do. Thank you."

29

CONCORD HQ

Daayn Shahs-lan droned on about a decline in the quality of platinum-group metals in the last two Theriz shipments. The Barisan representative's voice was a nasally, pinched affair that never failed to set Mia's nerves on edge—so much so that two minutes into his speech, she'd quieted her aural receptors in the offending range and let Meno replace Shahs-lan's voice with a lovely tenor. The adjustment made for a more pleasant Senate meeting, to the extent such a thing was possible.

Most of the other representatives served as the elected or appointed leaders of their species; as the Senate met in regular session only once a month for a single afternoon, the position didn't warrant a full-time dedicated appointment. The Anaden representative, Ferdinand elasson-Kyvern, marked an exception of sorts, however.

Fourteen years after the elimination of the Directorate, Mia still wasn't entirely clear on how the Anadens governed themselves. From the outside, it seemed to be via a mish-mash of Dynasty-specific *elasson* boards and local planetary leaders. Ferdinand spoke with the most authority—and certainly with the loudest voice—but he was not the leader of the Anaden people. Not the undisputed one, in any event.

So long as the Anadens obeyed Senate directives and the Code of Rights, the situation continued to suffice, but it was not ideal. Humanity's stated preference was for the Anadens to learn how to oversee and guide their own people for themselves—in a fundamentally free and democratic manner being tactfully implied.

Granted, the removal of the Directorate might have left them ge-netically and psychologically unable to accomplish it, but if so, they needed to adapt and overcome.

Mia was not the leader of humanity either, though she was its recognized and endorsed voice at Concord, for their discrete gov-ernments survived The Displacement. The Earth Alliance, Senecan Federation and IDCC continued to exist and oversee domestic mat-ters on their respective planets.

The power dynamics were now radically different, of course. The GDCA had stepped up and adapted its purpose to the new re-ality, and both its political and military purview had grown in kind.

The various governments were free to do as they wished within their territories—and within Concord protocols—but when it came to external matters, they must present a united front. The Alliance and the Federation would not be going to war against one another ever again. At least, this was the hope. Thus far, it was proving to be a well-founded one. The ways in which The Dis-placement had changed humanity for the better were subtle but real.

Separate militaries for all intents and purposes no longer ex-isted, with the former EA, SF and IDCC forces now comprising the AEGIS military. And Malcolm led them.

She smiled to herself; he wasn't always comfortable in that role—forever undervaluing his skills and accomplishments—but he did excel at it. To the outside world, they were the ultimate power couple, but the reality looked a bit different. Their daily lives were so hectic that the time they did get to spend together was invariably quiet, intimate and too rare.

Despite the Senate meeting only once a month, Mia neverthe-less spent the majority of her days at Concord HQ serving as the diplomatic head of the Concord Consulate. Every now and then, tensions arose between her role as humanity's representative to the other member species and Concord's representative to everyone else, but it was nothing she couldn't handle.

Theoretically, the Consulate role rotated among each of the member species every five years, but the Efkam, Barisans and Naraida had expressed no interest in serving. This meant that in eight months' time, the role was due to pass to the Anadens for the first time. No one was quite sure what this was going to mean, Mia included. Could humanity trust their former enemy to speak for them? To speak for all the species they had worked so hard to free from the yoke of Anaden oppression?

Unlike her current dual roles, this question *did* keep her up at night.

"Let's move on to the next item, lest we miss the banquet this evening. Senator Requelme, what's the status of the Savrakath negotiations?"

She'd missed the last minute of Shahs-lan's rant, but Meno reeled off the highlights in the second she took to respond to Dean Veshnael's question. "In a word, dreadful. The Savrakaths continue to exhibit difficulty grasping—or accepting—the reality that in order for them to become a Concord ally, they must make concessions to rise to our standards. In particular, they remain unwilling to acquiesce to restrictions on the authorized use of force and to the institution of basic rights for all sentient inhabitants of planets they control. In this case, with respect to the Godjans in particular."

"Is it true they're developing antimatter weapons?"

Her expression didn't flicker at Ferdinand's baiting question. "CINT is investigating those reports."

This was a lie, or at a minimum not the whole truth. But CINT and Command had asked her to delay engaging the Senate on the issue until they had finalized a plan to respond. Ideally, until they had already responded, as legally Command possessed the authority to take action to prevent the use of antimatter weapons without needing to seek prior approval from the Senate.

Her obfuscation was being made harder, however, by the fact it appeared CINT had a security problem, since Ferdinand seemed to know everything they did by the next day. Still, she did her best. "If the reports prove true, it will be a matter of grave concern, but we will wait until the conclusion of this investigation, as well as others, to determine how best to respond."

"Others?" Now Ferdinand was practically snarling, a mien best reserved for Barisans.

"We have received a credible report alleging that, far from treating the Godjans as equal citizens, the Savrakaths are in fact subjecting them to severe mistreatment, including forced servitude, internment and denial of basic rights. Slavery, in effect."

"We need to call off negotiations immediately and fire a warning shot across the lizards' bow."

For once she agreed with the Anaden. "A likely course of action, yes. We simply need a little additional time to uncover all the facts. For now, we have a potentially far more serious situation to address. I trust everyone has received the information packet on the species known as 'Rasu'?"

RW

COMMAND

Mia rubbed at her eyes. The strain of maintaining a mask of perfect composure for the entirety of the four-and-a-half-hour meeting had taken its toll. Entire years had gone by where the Senate contributed nothing of note to the functioning of Concord society. Now two burgeoning crises churned in the shadows, and it wasn't abundantly clear whether the Senate was *capable* of contributing to their resolution.

She gave Malcolm a weary smile, then turned her attention to Miriam. The three of them sat at the small table to the left of Miriam's desk. If Ferdinand were to observe them, he would doubtless accuse them of abusing their positions to orchestrate Humanity's domination of Concord.

A ridiculous notion. You are not abusing your positions to do so— you're abusing your relationships with one another to do so.

Meno! We're not abusing anything. We have a responsibility to act to further the safety and protection of all Concord species, and it so happens we also have the power to do so.

I understand, Mia. I was being trenchant in order to provoke a reaction.

Why?

Because you are in danger of falling asleep, and the others need you to be present in mind as well as body right now.

She chuckled silently. *Oh.*

She accepted a cup of Miriam's tea, because apparently she also needed a caffeine boost. "Not to be uncharitable to my fellow senators, but both of you could predict their reactions to the Rasu dossier without any help from me. The Novoloume are highly concerned and advise cautious gathering of additional data, while the Naraida are more curious than frightened of these strange shapeshifting aliens. The Efkam wish to study them, the Dankaths to eat them. The Khokteh are ready to bomb them into oblivion today, while the Barisans wish us to keep our distance in the hope of not being noticed. The Anadens are anxious to bring the Rasu to heel—but only after we allow them to wipe the Asterions out."

Miriam's teacup clattered to the table. "Ferdinand actually *said* that?"

"Oh, yes. Tact has never been a tool in his skill set. As far as I'm able to determine, most of the Anaden *elassons* continue to hold a grudge against the Asterions. It will not be easy to bring them around to the idea of an alliance."

"Well, they don't have to be brought around. The Anadens only get one vote of eight."

"True, but you know if they disapprove they will cause trouble."

Malcolm scoffed. "And this differs from the standard state of affairs how?"

His lack of patience with the Anadens was probably due more to her constant pillow-talk ranting about them than his own personal experience, but since she agreed with him…. "Fair point. I'm merely saying that as we move forward with the Asterions, we will need to be on guard for incidents, whether they be public defiance or private insurrection."

Miriam got an intriguing expression on her face for a second, but it swiftly vanished. "As Malcolm said, the standard state of affairs. But thank you for the warning."

"There's something else. I mentioned it at the meeting today, but you both need to know the details, as they may impact your decisions concerning the Savrakaths—or perhaps reinforce them." She hesitated briefly, then elected to shield Marlee as much as she could. "A Godjan refugee was brought to my attention by a good samaritan, and she had a most disturbing tale to tell."

RW

MACHIM IMPERIUM DELTA

LGG REGION V

"Engage privacy mode." Torval elasson-Machim maneuvered around his desk in the captain's cabin, pulled out his chair, and sat rigidly while the surveillance blocking field enveloped the room. Then he waited another five seconds before initiating a secure comm to Ferdinand elasson-Kyvern.

"I received your message. You've obtained confirmation of the Savrakaths' development of antimatter weapons?"

Ferdinand nodded curtly. "Confirmation of development and assembly. A CINT team infiltrated a facility outside Savradin and acquired visuals and copies of the research data. The Savrakaths have overcome the last challenges in the science and are moving ahead apace. Our analysts estimate they'll complete deployment-ready missile assembly in the next ten to fourteen days."

"I see. Do you possess any information regarding CINT's next steps?"

"No. They are withholding details of their plans behind a Sensitive Intelligence classification. I assume they must be planning to do something, however."

"I don't assume any such thing. The Humans have done nothing but lick the Savrakaths' boots for the last year. They won't act."

"Perhaps not, especially while they're distracted by their new Asterion friends."

Torval leaned in closer to the cam. "Asterions? Are you kidding me?"

"I am not. Apparently, a ragtag group of the rebels escaped our grasp all those millennia ago and holed up in a distant galaxy. Now they've shown back up to beg for help in fighting some supposed inorganic species they call 'Rasu.' I tell you, the Humans would make friends with the Dzhvar if the bastards were to ever poke their heads out of the ether again."

"Ferdinand, they really have gone too far now. Their refusal to use force against enemies who flaunt our rules and laugh at our demands not only humiliates us, it leaves us all exposed and in danger. We need to act."

"I understand your concerns, but there are rules to be followed."

Rules! Godsdamn Kyvern and their worship of bureaucracy.

"We have rules in the military as well. They require us to remove the Savrakaths' ability to harm us."

Ferdinand's lips narrowed into a thin line, giving him the look of the weaselly politician he was. "Which is outside my purview. I leave it to you to decide the proper course of action. Do as you think best."

Torval ended the conversation without a farewell. He'd cultivated the relationship with Ferdinand because it granted him access to information Casmir and Commandant Solovy did not deign to share, and because it always paid to have allies in positions of power. The man's vague declarations had granted Torval license to act—and also absolved Ferdinand of all responsibility for any negative repercussions that might result.

This was fine, as he didn't need the man's permission or his blessing. He did not take orders from a Kyvern; no Machim ever had.

Still, such bold action should not be undertaken lightly. Torval stared at the surface of his desk for several seconds, then initiated a new comm.

"Casmir, the VI-2B Regiment is preparing to begin a new circuit of the Briseis Dwarf galaxy. Can I expect any change in its orders for this circuit?"

"Negative. Continue to observe and conduct passive scans, with a focus on any Savrakath fleet movements."

"But there is strong evidence the lizards are—"

"It is not your role to judge the nature or strength of 'evidence' on anything. Those are Concord Command's orders, Torval. You will not deviate from them."

His nails dug painfully into his thigh beneath the desk. "Yes...sir."

He ended this comm as rudely as the last one and leapt up out of his chair to tear around the cabin. To the Styx with Concord Command! The Directorate would never have acted so cowardly toward a threat. The Machim Primor would never have dawdled while an enemy-in-the-making thumbed its nose at his demands. He would have struck first, and in such a manner that ensured he wouldn't need to strike a second time. He would have lobbed a host of Igni missiles at their capital city to show the Savrakaths what antimatter weaponry was truly capable of, thereby ensuring the Savrakaths were never again a problem.

But the Machim Primor was gone, murdered by those who now claimed authority over Torval and his kin. The Humans had slaughtered the entire Directorate and over eight billion Anadens for sport, then forcibly taken the reins of power for themselves. Once in charge, they hid behind their impenetrable warship hulls and their empty platitudes about democracy and freedom.

It had taken more years than Torval had expected, but now their cowardice was going to destroy what remained of the Empire. If someone didn't step up and counter their timidity with strength.

He didn't want to rule. He was a soldier, not a politician. But not just any soldier—an exceptional one, bred through thousands of generations into a perfect specimen to fulfill his purpose. And as an *elasson*, he enjoyed something few other Machims did: judgment. The ability to assess a situation and the wisdom to decide on the proper course of action without the need for orders from on high.

If Concord Command didn't want to give the order, so be it. He had assessed the situation, and he knew what must be done.

30

MIRAI

MIRAI ONE

Adlai grabbed a salami sandwich at the deli down the street from the Justice Center on his way back to work. He was scheduled to have dinner with Perrin, Dashiel and Nika tonight at Dashiel's flat, but that was hours away, and in his rush to get into the office this morning, he'd neglected to eat breakfast. In fact...he returned to the sweets section and grabbed a peanut butter cookie, then scanned through the checkout terminal—

"Error. Insufficient funds."

He stutter-stepped to a stop—he'd been halfway out the door—and backed up to scan his ID again.

"Error. Insufficient funds."

The service dyne tending to the deli came over. "Do you require assistance?"

"Yes. The system is claiming I don't have the funds to pay for my food, which is clearly a mistake."

The dyne instantiated a pane in front of it. "Allow me to process the transaction for you."

"Thank you." Adlai provided his ID and scanned the food a third time.

"I'm sorry, Advisor, but your bank is reporting insufficient funds in your account."

"That can't be." He sighed and set the food down on the counter. Wherever the glitch originated, the dyne would be no help in correcting it. "I understand. I'll check with the bank."

He hurried out of the deli and jogged down the sidewalk. In one small break, his bank maintained a branch office two blocks away. Three leads on the Justice Center server breach waited back at the office for him to run them to ground, and he did not have time to deal with a bureaucratic mistake, dammit.

RW

The bank's dyne clerk uttered words, but they were so nonsensical that Adlai's OS refused to process them. He stared at the clerk in confusion. "Would you repeat what you just said?"

"You withdrew all funds from your account at 8:48 today. They were transferred to a financial data weave, and you departed the bank with it in your possession. Do you need to see the footage from the security cam?"

"Yes—no." Apprehension made its first appearance of the day via a sour taste in his mouth. He swallowed through it. "I need to speak to your supervisor."

The bank's Duty Officer was a short man with spiky silver hair and a handlebar mustache. He welcomed Adlai into his office with effusive eagerness. "The clerk has alerted me to your issue, Advisor. I'm certain we can take care of any problems and get you back on your way."

"I'd appreciate it." Adlai sat stiffly on the edge of one of the guest chairs and waited while the man entered a couple of commands in his central pane. The apprehension had migrated to an itchy tightness in his throat. He continued breathing past it.

The Duty Officer's mustache bunched up as a perplexed frown grew on the man's face. "I'm terribly sorry, Advisor Weiss, but the transaction does appear to be genuine. Here's the security footage." He nudged the pane around so Adlai could view it.

A man who was the spitting image of Adlai entered the bank and walked up to the transaction counter. The man presented proper identification, and two minutes later left the bank with a weave chock full of credits. Alongside the footage, a series of system

245 | G.S. JENNSEN

entries displayed the ID and passcode information entered by the man, followed by the transfer of funds out of Adlai's account.

He motioned for the pane to go away. "That wasn't me."

"I understand, Advisor. We'll institute a fraud investigation and alert Ju—well, I guess we've already alerted Justice, haven't we?" The Duty Officer laughed awkwardly, then cut himself off under the weight of Adlai's glare.

"Your security is supposed to be better than this. It's supposed to keep our funds safe." But even as he said it, Adlai recognized his hypocrisy. How dare he expect a private bank to have superior security to Justice, which had suffered an outrageous breach mere days earlier?

The mustache vibrated. "No security is perfect, sir."

"Improve it. What about my funds?"

"We can, um, let's see. Given your position and obvious trustworthiness, we can deposit an advance of up to thirty thousand credits into your account pending the recovery of the stolen funds. If your salary continues to be deposited here—and we do hope it is—the deposits should pay off the advance in nine weeks. Obviously, better for all of us if the funds are recovered and returned to your account. And let's add an additional layer of security for you going forward. We offer a hardware token system, as well as triple-factor authentication."

RW

Adlai dragged down the hall toward his apartment. He'd never had to file his own Notice of Crime before, and he'd walked away from the experience with a long list of changes in dire need of being made to the process. Then he'd spent all afternoon trying to do his job and work the server breach leads while being interrupted every ten minutes by another useless update to his personal case.

By the time he'd left the Justice Center, the apprehension had spread to the base of his skull in the form of a persistent tickle, like a fraying wire sparking as electricity flowed through it. It made it increasingly difficult to concentrate. He'd find an hour somewhere to have it checked out at a clinic, but his heart told him it was all 'in his head.'

He wasn't the panicking type—his job forbade it—but stress and worry nevertheless found inventive ways to wear him down, body and soul.

He was far too exhausted to go to Dashiel's for dinner, but he couldn't bring himself to cancel and disappoint everyone. Perrin had pinged him earlier to let him know she'd be heading straight to Dashiel's from work, so he could at least clean himself up before seeing her. Run through the shower and don a fresh shirt and a happy face for the evening.

He toggled the door lock and—banged into the door.

He pressed his fingertips to the lock pad again, but the apprehension whispered that he already knew how this story was going to unfold, and as a result he wasn't particularly surprised when the door failed to open.

Someone had changed the lock information. Presumably the same someone who had successfully posed as him earlier today, when they stole all his money.

His shoulders sagged as he slouched against the wall beside the door. He could ping Perrin and ask her to come home and let him in, or...he hurriedly reached into his pack and pulled out a multimodule. Being a Justice Advisor, even a broke one, did have its advantages.

He attached the module to the lock pad, entered a command, and in seconds had brute-force overloaded the system. The door slid open.

Of course, now he'd need to get a repair service out to reset and reconfigure the lock. Maybe dinner tonight simply wasn't going to work out. He'd shower first, then decide. He tossed his jacket on the couch and his pack on the floor and began unbuttoning his shirt—

—the blow to the side of his head sent him slamming into the kitchen divider wall. His mind reeled, but training, instinct and programming brought his hands up to protect his head from further strikes while he put the wall to his back. "Lights maximum!"

Nothing happened. They hadn't solely modified the door lock. All control of and rights to the apartment had been stripped from him.

> *Hq   (visual) | ((scan.infrared   &&*
> *scan.thermal)(240°:60°))*

He surveyed the shadowy living room, but no heat signatures flared and no motion cut across the background. Had his attacker fled, or was he wearing some type of advanced kamero filter? Adlai unlatched the Glaser at his hip and brought it up—

RW

Forensics officers and drones crawled through every centimeter of Adlai's apartment. Perrin sat on the couch with her elbows on her knees and hands at her face; after an initial frenzy of panic, it was as if all the animating air had left her person, and she'd simply crumpled in on herself. Nika sat beside her, one arm around her shoulders and the other trying to squeeze her friend's hand while she murmured assurances.

When Adlai hadn't shown for dinner and all pings went unanswered, Perrin insisted they go to his apartment to check on him. They'd arrived to find the apartment door open and signs of a struggle inside—a chair overturned in the middle of the living room, a table knocked crooked against the wall, Adlai's jacket hanging haphazardly off the edge of the couch.

They'd immediately contacted Adlai's second-in-command, Bron Walosky, who had immediately contacted his predecessor, Spencer Nimoet.

Dashiel leaned against the wall by the door with his arms crossed, watching as Spencer conferred with one of the officers. He hadn't known the man long, but he was predisposed to like him.

Spencer exuded a sober air—earnest, much like Adlai, but display-ing a more practical and worldwise bent. He also had shown an independent streak in helping Nika and NOIR when it could have cost him his job and his freedom.

Dashiel couldn't decide whether the fact that Maris was sleep-ing with him counted in the man's favor or as a strike against him; he and Maris were playing nice to one another these days, but they'd yet to mend the bridges he'd set fire to over the First Gen lies.

Adlai clearly trusted Spencer, having recommended his pro-motion to the Justice Advisor position on Synra. But he was still a brand-new Advisor who was arguably out of his depth in what had now become the most important investigation of his career.

The officer hurried off to give instructions to one of the drones, and on seeing Dashiel brooding in his direction, Spencer came over. "We've picked up a couple of skin flakes and two hairs. Light, so they could be Adlai's. No prints or other identifiers so far. The assailant was careful, no question. Any evidence we might have obtained from the door lock was obliterated when it was over-loaded."

"So, the attack was carefully planned by someone who is not an idiot."

Spencer stared at him for a moment. "Yes. And that's a large pool of suspects. But it also means the person or persons had a rea-son to come after Adlai specifically. Odds are, the culprit will be from one of the cases he was working on. Or less ideally, from a case deep in his past." The man glanced around the living room, checking on all his people and equipment. "Earlier today, Adlai filed a report of identity theft. Did he talk to you about it?"

"No, we didn't speak at all today. What happened?"

"Someone emptied his bank account and, it now appears, changed his locks. If you weren't an Advisor, I wouldn't be telling you this, but early last week they had a security breach at the Mirai Justice Center. Someone sliced and delved the primary server. They didn't diverge any of the data, so they were looking for something.

As of ten minutes ago, my working theory is they were looking for Adlai's personal information. The server breach was a precursor to his identity theft and kidnapping."

"But you can uncover who breached the server, right? There must have been a thousand cams and security checks between the front door and the server room."

"Two thousand. But there are complications."

Dashiel arched an eyebrow in question.

Spencer turned away to review a pane presented by an officer. After a few seconds he sent the man back to work. "Adlai was personally overseeing the investigation, which means now someone else needs to get up to speed on it. I'd assign Walosky to it, but he's got to run Mirai Justice in Adlai's absence, so I'll likely put one of my guys from Synra on it. The investigation could probably benefit from fresh, outside eyes."

"And you?"

Spencer gestured around the living room. "This is my life now."

"Good." Dashiel rubbed at his jaw, concern for Adlai gnawing a hole in his gut. "Just find him, okay?"

"He's my friend, too. Nobody wants to see him safe more than I do."

"Find him, and we won't need to hold a competition."

"Right. Listen, we're going to be another several hours here." Spencer canted his head toward the occupants of the couch.

Dashiel took the hint and went over to kneel in front of them. "We should get out of the officers' way and let them work."

Nika's eyes cut up to him, churning and strangely hardened. "What did Spencer say?"

"That's he's on the case, and he won't rest until they find Adlai."

She squeezed Perrin's shoulder. "Dashiel's right. Come on, let's go home. You're staying with me until…until Adlai gets back."

Perrin nodded weakly; her hair had spilled messily over her face, obscuring her features. "Okay. But are you sure we ought to leave? What if…?"

"I'm sure. You need some food, then some rest."

"Ha!" A cackle burst up from Perrin's throat as she acceded to Nika's urging and stood. "I didn't sleep half a wink when Joaquim was kidnapped. How the hells do you expect me to sleep now?"

Chemical sedation?

Dashiel caught the slightest hint of a dark smirk as it flitted across Nika's lips in time with her ping.

Let's start with a cup of hot tea and go from there.

It took another minute of urging, but they finally got Perrin out the door. Dashiel stopped and took one last look around the apartment, consumed by a question with no answer: what had happened to his friend?

31

UNKNOWN LOCATION

ASTERION DOMINION

The odor of scorched hair stung Adlai's nose. By the time he'd recognized it for what it was, however, his attention had been overcome by excruciating and all-encompassing pain. His head, his jaw, both shoulders, his chest...he soon lost track cataloging all the places that screamed in agony.

He forced his eyes open.

He was in a featureless, nearly empty room with exposed beams and piping. No windows allowed in sun- or starlight, but the room was harshly lit. He turned his head, forcing it to move past the strain in his neck. Okay. He was strapped into some kind of full-body rack, held in an upright position against a wall behind him, his arms and legs spread wide and his head held up by a strap across his forehead. He was naked, and electrodes were taped to various parts of his body. Some, not great parts.

He tried to send a multitude of pings; all bounced. The room was warded against communications, because *of course* it was. What dungeon-master let the object of their torture send messages to their friends?

A man—presumably the dungeon-master in question—paced deliberately across the far half of the room. Adlai blocked as much of the pain as his OS allowed him and focused on absorbing every detail he could. Tall, with a thin, lithe frame. Fair, almost pink skin. Straw-colored hair in need of a trim. The man wore beige, baggy utility coveralls. His motions were energetic but deliberate, indicating he exercised control over his movements and actions. So not strung out on a bad trip or aggressively insane.

It took several seconds for the man to notice that Adlai had awakened. When he did, he pivoted and marched closer, then stopped a meter and a half away. Adlai studied his face…and he felt confident he had never seen the man before in his life.

Adlai licked his lips, which were already dry and splitting. How long had he been here? "Who are you? Why have you kidnapped me?"

"You let me die."

"I try very hard not to let anyone die. If you'll tell me who you are—"

"But before you let me die, you let me suffer. Suffer unspeakable torture for weeks. Months. *Unspeakable.*"

There weren't many circumstances that fit such a description and only one in recent memory. Adlai might have managed to appear sympathetic, were he not naked and strapped to a torture rack. "You were a victim of the Rasu, weren't you? Your former incarnation was convicted of a crime and sent to Zaidam Bastille, and from there delivered to the Rasu. I'm so sorry. But it was not my doing."

The man's thin lips curled into a sneer. "It *was*. Justice didn't care about how I'd been infected with a virutox against my will. They convicted me of assault anyway and locked me away. Justice didn't care what happened to me in my icebox at Zaidam. Justice did the Guides' dirty work for them and sold me to aliens to be experimented on!"

The man reeled his rising voice back in and paced in circles until he'd calmed himself. "Justice woke me back up in a new body and said, 'we're sorry you lost the last four months of your life. We've cleared your conviction, but you still have to pay the repair bills for the man you beat up.' But I wasn't me when I did that. None of it was my fault."

Gods, his head hurt—and an oddly specific spot beneath his left ribs. "Agreed. It wasn't your fault. The virutox caused you to assault the man, and the Guides and the Rasu did the rest. But this *is*. Kidnapping an Advisor? Emptying my bank account? Breaking into my apartment? No virutox is making you do these things."

"I know. It's called justice—*real* justice for what you did to me." The man's thumb moved over an object in his right hand, and pain shot through Adlai's body riding waves of sizzling electricity. He gritted his teeth to keep from biting his tongue.

When the waves of white-hot power finally subsided, he forced his eyes open again and tried to talk past a suddenly thick tongue. "Wha...what's your name? What can I call you?"

"Oh, you can call me 'Master.'"

Well, hells. He might not be *aggressively* insane, but the man had psyche issues that went well beyond a temporary virutox infection. Adlai's brow knotted, pulling at the strap over it, as he struggled to piece the right words together through a muddled and reeling brain.

"I'm not going to do that. I'll call you 'M' instead. M, if you've done your research, and I suspect you have, then you know that the instant I found out about the virutox, I acted to prevent its spread. And as soon as I found out about prisoners being taken from Zaidam Bastille, I stopped sending people there. I have done every single thing within my power to repair the harm done by the Guides. I'm sorry I didn't learn what was happening before you were caught up in it. I truly am. But I am not your enemy."

The man's throat worked in an exaggerated manner for several seconds, until an ugly scowl overtook his gaunt features. "You allowed it to happen. You allowed the Guides to manipulate and control Justice. You were nothing more than their lackey. You let them take me. You let the Rasu torture me then kill me. Now, it's time for retribution."

32

MIRAI

MIRAI ONE

Perrin had woken up after a fitful few hours of sleep insisting that she wanted, *needed*, to go to work today. So Nika had filled her friend's stomach full of pancakes and blueberry muffins and accompanied her to the Pavilion.

Once there, she'd loitered on the top floor of the Initiative for almost an hour, chatting with various people and reviewing project updates while she kept an eye on Perrin. Finally, one of Personnel's part-time employees showed up and seemed to engage Perrin in actual work. Nika dropped by to hug Perrin, tell her she'd be back in a few hours and insist for the four-hundredth time that she ping Nika if she needed anything at all. *Anything.*

Then she went to the cafeteria, for no particular reason. The last eighteen hours had been emotionally draining, and in truth she hadn't gotten much more sleep than Perrin had. Worry for Adlai clouded her every thought, and though she now had the afternoon to herself, she found she had no idea what to do with it. Go to the Justice Center and harass Spencer about finding Adlai? Go to Dashiel's office and ineffectually vent about everything, thus preventing him from accomplishing whatever work he'd otherwise be able to get done? A thousand Initiative items could use her attention, but she couldn't work up the desire to see to any of them.

So she grabbed a banana and wandered around the Pavilion until she located Maris in a conference room on the third floor. The Culture Advisor stood alone in the middle of the room, dressed in a champagne silk pantsuit and scowling at a row of panes floating in front of her. Each one displayed a different…Nika squinted…slogan?

She cleared her throat, and Maris spun around. "Ah! Nika. You are a most welcome sight." She gestured to the panes. "Which one do you like best?"

"What's the intended purpose of the statements?"

"To inspire the populace to greater effort in the Initiative. To give them hope for our future, and to engender pride in the Dominion."

She considered the choices. "I like, 'The Omoikane Initiative: Taking the greatest wisdom and knowledge of the Asterion people to the stars and the future.'"

"Fantastic. That's my favorite, too, I think. I can't be certain. I fear I've been finding it difficult to concentrate today. Is there any word on Adlai?"

"Your lover would know better than I would."

Maris flinched, albeit almost imperceptibly. "Spencer has not been overly…available since the kidnapping. For which I do not blame him."

"Nor should you. Anyway, no news."

Maris' face fell. "I see."

They stared at the slogans together for a minute…then Nika had an idea. It might stretch her promise to Perrin of 'a few hours' to the limit, but she'd gotten quite adept at using the *Wayfarer's* Sukasu Gate to leap across megaparsecs; they'd be back by evening.

"Can you get away for an afternoon?"

"If it's important, absolutely."

"It's not important to the Initiative, if that's what you mean. It is important to me, though, and I think possibly to you as well."

"Yes, then. Frankly, even if it wasn't. I need a distraction. What is it?"

"A surprise. That's what it is."

Maris' hand came to her throat. "I adore surprises. Am I dressed appropriately?"

"Maris, you are always dressed appropriately. Unless you're going to a siege."

"Are we?"

Nika winced and headed for the door. "I deeply hope not."

ASTERION PRIME

MILKY WAY GALAXY

When they stepped out of the spaceport into a mid-morning sun, Maris gasped as dramatically as a stage actress stunned by the play's big reveal. "Precious stars, this is Asterion Prime!"

"It is. Does it look the same as you remember it?"

Maris started walking down the staircase. When she reached the bottom, she gazed in both directions then took the left sidewalk. Nika quietly followed for several steps, until she couldn't stand it any longer. "Well? Does it?"

"No, not at all. I assume this is the capital city, but none of the buildings look as they did. I can make no sense of the street layout."

"Yet you knew where you were instantly."

"Of course I did." Maris breathed in deeply. "It smells right. Like pine and cedar. And the sky is the color I remember—turquoise dipped in glistening powder. Gods..." she hurried over to a bench on the perimeter of a tiny park and sat down "...I am home."

Nika sat beside her. Try as she might, Maris' joy evoked only melancholy in her. "I wish I could view it that way. But even in the earliest memories I saved, I had already left Asterion Prime for the final time. And the journals? They began around the time the rebellion did, when home became no longer safe. I have no true recollection of this place, only the vague yearning of missing it."

"It may be a blessing. I am deluged with emotions right now, and many of them are not happy ones."

"I'm sorry. I didn't mean to make you sad. I thought you'd want to see this."

"Oh, I do! Thank you. Thank you so very much." Maris sighed wistfully and contemplated the passersby for a moment. "No one acts surprised by our presence. We've received a few brief, curious glances, but nothing more."

"I suspect they assume we're some variant of Humans."

"Do Humans all look alike? I mean...you know what I mean."

Nika chuckled. "No, they display as much diversity in appearance as Asterions do. Plus, there's a wide disparity in their extent and presentation of cybernetics. Hence us being mistaken for a variant."

"What do you mean by 'disparity'?"

"Well, all Humans have some level of cybernetics embedded in their bodies, but they seem to span the full range from the most basic of functionality to SAI-level capabilities. Except there's no SAI involved, because the cybernetics have all been grafted onto the Human's neural system. Then some people have a minimal connection to a separate SAI—they're called, um, Mélanges, I think. Also, there are the Prevos, who enjoy full neural integration with a SAI."

"Similar to what we did during the Rebellion?"

"Exactly. Or close enough. Then there are free, stand-alone SAIs. They live in hardware, mostly, but many of them also have dolls they use to interact with the world."

"And they're allowed to simply walk down the street, like a normal person?"

"They are."

"I wonder if they had to rebel to earn the right to do so."

Nika shrugged. "I don't know. There were some troubles around their development, but I haven't asked about the details. If they did, their rebellion went better than ours."

"Did it, though? Would you give up everything we've had these last seven hundred thousand years in exchange for having won our freedom here?"

Nika studied the water fountain at the center of the park, where stone birds hovered above crystal pillars. "Is this where I remind you how I don't actually remember those countless years? I've now read every journal I wrote—many of them twice. Enough to feel as if, in most respects, I lived through it all. But no matter how hard I try to make them so, journals will never be memories."

Maris gave her a sad smile overflowing with empathy.

"Besides, knowing what the Anadens became in those intervening millennia? No. I would not have wanted to be a part of that descent into cruelty and oppression."

"But who can say? If we'd been here, perhaps we could have nudged our leaders onto a kinder path."

"You think so?"

"Since we'll never know, I choose to believe it."

Nika laughed faintly. "Fair enough."

Maris peered at a couple passing by them on the sidewalk. "But all these people are Anadens, yes?"

Nika scanned the vicinity. "Everyone I see, yes. Anaden cybernetics present differently—more visible, less elegant—than what Humans use. My impression is that Anaden-settled planets remain rather insular. Other species have the legal right to come here, live here and work here, but that's not the same as being made to feel welcome."

"I'm not surprised." Maris leapt up and grabbed Nika's hand. "Come, let's walk. I think I've regained my bearings."

They strolled for several blocks, during which time Maris guided them through several unexpected turns. Abruptly they arrived at a much larger urban park surrounded entirely by tall buildings constructed of a gloomy pewter metal. Maris' lips morphed into a pout. "Alas...it's not here. I mean, of course it isn't. It's been seven hundred thousand years. I expect every building has been torn down and replaced eighty or a hundred times by now."

Then Maris pulled off her heeled sandals and marched barefoot into the park. Nika gave her a dubious glance but followed suit. "What isn't here?"

"My apartment building. Where I lived for, oh, at least two hundred years."

"Really? What about me?"

"You lived across town, on the periphery of the urban jungle."

Nika plopped down on the grass and curled her legs beneath her. The cool blades slid between her toes with a pleasant tickle. "Can I ask you something?"

"You may ask me anything, always."

Nika chewed on her bottom lip. "We had parents, didn't we? I mean, at that point in history, Anadens were still having children—not the physical birthing part, as I assume they had synthetic wombs and whatnot. But they got married and had children, and the children had siblings and children of their own. Families."

"Oh, my dear." Maris sat on the grass beside her. "Yes, we had parents. You had a brother as well."

"A brother...." Nika shifted around and pulled her knees up to her chest. It had been a while since she'd felt the poignancy of her lost memories so powerfully as she did at this moment. Her heart ached with a sorrow she feared would never be healed. *So much lost.*

"His name was Loshi. He was a systems engineer—and a tinkerer, as I teasingly called him. Gods, I haven't thought of him in fifty millennia, but he was a lovely man. Truly lovely."

"Was he part of the rebellion?"

Maris nodded tightly. "He was killed in one of the later skirmishes. And since the Anaden government denied regenesis to the rebels...."

"Oh." She hastily wiped a stray tear from her cheek. Crying over the aeons-past loss of a brother whom she did not remember.

"We were trying to get our own regenesis lab up and running. Nearly succeeded, but the government traced some of the equipment we needed to purchase for it and promptly bombed it flat." Maris paused. "Your parents, though...they stayed out of the rebellion. I won't say they didn't approve, exactly, but you encouraged them to keep their noses clean, for their sake. Do you think..." Maris gazed around at the buildings surrounding them "...is there any chance they could be...?"

Nika shook her head. "My understanding is that once the Directorate seized full control of the government, every Anaden underwent frequent and repeated...the equivalent of our Retirement & Reinitialization. There could be two people walking around with their names, but in their psyches there'd be nothing left of the people they once were."

"I'm sorry."

"I'm sorry for you, too. What about your parents?"

Maris hesitated as she picked at a blade of grass at her feet. "My parents disowned me after I joined the rebellion. We were the wealthiest family on Asterion Prime, you see. Valerian and Salash Idoni—those were my parents' names. The scandal created by my reprehensible actions became far too much for their honor to bear, so they stripped me of my surname, my inheritance, my apartment and all my funds." She smiled quickly. "You helped me break into their bank account and abscond with eight hundred thousand credits so I wouldn't be destitute."

"I'm glad to hear it. Still, it must have been so hard for you."

"I wouldn't have joined the rebellion if I hadn't wanted to shake up my life. It was what it was, and so terribly long ago."

Nika fisted her hands at her chin. "I'm honestly not sure why I wanted to come here. There's nothing left of that life, and I don't even remember it, anyway. The only thing we share with this place now is a name."

Maris reached out and grasped her hands. "But we named ourselves Asterions for a reason. It does have meaning. A meaning I can't yet craft into poetic words, but give me a little time. You were right to bring us here."

Nika stood. "I hope so. Nevertheless, are you ready to go back to our real home?"

"We should. Perhaps we will return to find Adlai safe and sound, lounging at the Initiative with his head in Perrin's lap."

"That would be something, wouldn't it?"

33

MIRAI

MIRAI ONE

Grant hurried down the hall toward Maris' loft. He was running late, hence the running. Late because he'd gotten held up at DAF Command on Namino. Late because he was *working.*

He'd never lacked for a work ethic; he just hadn't used it for the benefit of others instead of himself in a long time. And it was exhausting.

Grant slipped in the door and collapsed on the couch next to Charles Basquan. The man's regened body featured a shock of hair even more gloriously ginger than before. It was his pride and joy, far beyond his considerable wealth.

Charles jerked a nod in greeting. "I haven't seen you at the Pavilion lately."

"They'd have to unchain me from the DAF Design Department first for me to get by there."

"I'm not surprised to learn that Lance is a slave-driver of a boss."

"I heard that, Charles." Lance emerged from the kitchen carrying a half-eaten brioche. "Mesahle's working no harder than the rest of us."

"Actually...." Grant leaned forward, eager to take umbrage at Palmer's dismissal of his contributions, but Maris made her usual grand entrance then, and he let it go.

She surveyed the room as she pulled a chair out from the dining table, slid it over to the couches, and took a seat. "Thank you all for coming tonight."

Grant didn't bother to glance around before directing a frown Maris' way; he didn't need to. "Where's Nika? Are we not going to wait for her?"

Lance sat on the couch opposite Grant. "Nika wasn't invited to this particular gathering."

"Why the hells not?"

Maris extended a hand. "I'm not entirely comfortable with it either, Grant, but there is a reason, and we'll get to it shortly. As I was saying, thank you for coming. Part of me wishes there were more of us here, more members of the First Generation who had chosen to step up and lead in this time of transformation for our people. But I'm also heartened, for I believe you all represent the best of us."

The void created by Nika's absence grew with Maris' first words. He didn't care for this, because Maris wasn't wrong in her declaration. Too many members of the First Generation had re-fused to heed the call of service to a greater cause. And while he wasn't necessarily proud of it, if not for Nika, he'd probably be one of them. She'd fought for the freedom of other Asterions even when she couldn't remember why she was driven to do so, and to hold this meeting without her already felt like a betrayal.

But he couldn't conceive of Maris betraying Nika, so he decided to give the woman the benefit of the doubt—for five minutes.

"I realize it is not our habit to congregate, but nothing is usual or ordinary about our circumstances. The Dominion is changing, because it must, and I'm so grateful to each of you for the role you're playing in guiding those changes. As members of the First Genera-tion, we have a unique obligation to ensure our society never loses its soul.

"To that end, we need to discuss our new relationship with what is now known as Concord, but which we all remember as the Anaden Empire.

"Fourteen years ago, the Anaden governing body was deposed by a species known as Humans. Like us, they share their genetic origins with the Anadens. Like us, their society has developed sep-arate from and free of Anaden oppression. Now they rule alongside

Anadens and numerous other species. Peacefully, to all appearances. We have made contact with their leaders and engaged in several discussions with them about the Rasu and other matters. Now we stand on the cusp of forging a more substantial relationship with them."

Maris paused to let a portentous sigh escape her lips. "I visited Asterion Prime yesterday with Nika. Yes, it continues to stand, and beneath the new buildings and new landscapes, the soil and the sky are unchanged. I cried tears of joy and sadness, and my heart ached in a way no words exist to express. For me, after this visit, the wounds of the SAI Rebellion burn fresh and raw, as if inflicted anew.

"But they aren't fresh, and we must be careful not to follow a grudge off a cliff to our own end. And so the question we must grapple with is, do we trust these Humans? Do we trust an empire still glutted with Anadens? Do we dare hope that a relationship of equals can possibly be forged?"

Charles leaned back and crossed a leg over a knee. "You have me at a disadvantage. I haven't met any of them. What are the Humans like?"

"Lance, you've spent more time with them than anyone here."

"Reasonable, so far. Friendly but reserved, accommodating within tight strictures. Keeping their secrets close to the vest. And fielding a mighty armada of warships."

Grant frowned again. "Isn't that a good thing? Isn't it what we're looking for?"

"In theory, yes. But it also gives me pause. They play at peace, but they seem awfully ready for war."

Maris shrugged delicately. "They did fight a war against the Anadens barely over a decade ago. It's possible they believe they need to be on guard for a while longer yet."

Lance conceded the point. "And fought a war against the Sogain—they call them Kats—a few years before then."

Charles choked on his drink. "Against the Sogain? How the hells?"

Lance gestured dismissively and finished off his brioche. "It's complicated to the point of absurdity. They're allies now. The Humans seem to make a habit of befriending their former enemies the minute the shooting is over, which raises some questions about their judgment.

"But, frankly, I'm not so concerned about the Humans. I mean, I *am*, but my far greater concern is the Anadens. They're still the dominant population in this 'Concord.' There are *trillions* of them. And the Humans let them *keep* their military. The last time the Anadens saw us, they were trying to kill us. Forgive me if I'm not in a hurry to welcome them to try again."

Grant decided he might as well adopt a semi-permanent frown for the evening. "They didn't disarm the Anaden military? Seriously?"

Maris stepped in. "According to Nika, the Humans claim their war was always with the Anaden ruling body, this 'Directorate,' and never with the Anaden people, who were in fact slaves to the whims and wishes of the Directorate."

Lance snorted. "That much is accurate. The Directorate used something called 'integrals' to impose top-down control of thoughts on their trillions of minions."

"How very Anaden of them." Grant stood to pace behind the couch. "So what does Nika think? She's spent the *most* time with them."

"Exactly. She's been busy cuddling up alongside the Humans ever since she met them. She's completely bought their spiel and is rapidly making herself at home in Concord. I wouldn't be surprised if she's already leased property there."

"Lance exaggerates, but it is true Nika has voiced an overwhelmingly positive opinion about Concord in general and the Humans in particular. She is in favor of a closer alliance with them." Maris directed a piercing gaze across those present. "The question we have to answer is whether we agree."

So this was the reason for her absence, for Maris and Lance going behind her back. Grant stared at the door. He wanted to walk out now, and only a simmering and mostly inexplicable sense of obligation to his people—one Nika had reawakened in him—kept him in the room.

Charles arched a ginger eyebrow. "And if we don't agree?"

"Then we advise caution in the ongoing negotiations. If it comes to it, we endeavor to see to it that the Advisor Committee votes against any such alliance." Maris retrieved her glass of sherry from the floor and took a contemplative sip. "I don't know whether the Anaden people have changed. I don't know whether they whisper in the shadows of their own nascent rebellion against the Humans.

"I only know that yesterday, I sat on a bench on Asterion Prime and watched Anadens go about their lives. None of them challenged my right to be there or inquired as to my species. I believe the Humans mean well, and it's at least possible they're wearing off on the Anadens."

Grant stopped brooding long enough to ask a question. "What about these other species? Who are they?"

Lance grunted. "Not relevant. They've spent millennia living under the boot of the Anadens, and fourteen years is not enough time for them to remember how to stand up for themselves. A couple of the species have decent military fleets, but they'll use them when and where they're told to. The question is whether it's the Humans or the Anadens who will do the telling."

"And it's really all about the fleets, isn't it?" Charles asked. "No disrespect meant toward the hard work you're all doing, Lance and Grant especially, or toward the miracle you pulled off at the Rasu stronghold, but the ugly reality is, we have a mountain of catching up to do. If the Rasu show up here in force anytime in the next decade, we're all dead. Lance, what does a Concord fleet at our side when they show up do for us?"

"I won't lie. The Human military force is damn impressive. Their ships are constructed of some allegedly indestructible metal. I assume the Anaden ships are similarly formidable. If Concord sends a real war-ready fleet to fight alongside us? It changes every equation."

"Then I'm not certain what it is we're debating. We need them. You all are free to keep an eye out for knives in our backs *after* we survive the next Rasu attack, but our first and currently only responsibility is to make sure we do survive it."

RW

Lance stopped Grant as he was on the way out the door. "Hey, I want you to do something for me tomorrow."

"You know, tonight's not the best time to come seeking favors."

"What is that supposed to mean?"

"It means I don't care for you shutting Nika out of this conversation. You should have given her an opportunity to make her own case."

"I'm sorry if you still have a boner for—"

"If you want me to show up for work tomorrow, you'll stop right there."

Lance's mouth opened...then he shrugged. "Okay. As I said, I want you to do something for me tomorrow. Not a favor—work."

Grant groaned and dropped his head against the wall. "What is it?"

"Concord is sending a guy to DAF Command in the morning—Commandant Solovy's husband, which I guess counts for more than any military rank. Ostensibly, it's a quid pro quo visit. They showed us their goods, now we show them ours. Which is fine. We're happy to do so.

"I want you to give Mr. Solovy the full tour. Make us look good, but not too good. As everyone agreed back there, we need their help. Much as it pains me, therefore, we ought to appear as if we need it."

"All right. But why me? Why aren't you doing it? You so crave being in charge."

Lance sighed. "Because I've been told I come off as...abrasive. Also caustic and irritating."

"And?"

"For reasons that escape my comprehension, people like you. The few minutes I've spent with this guy who's coming? He's a real character. You two should get along great. And I need for you to make certain that's exactly what happens."

34

UNKNOWN LOCATION

RASU-OCCUPIED TERRITORY

K iernan lay sprawled on his back, his eyes closed, as the lukewarm rain soaked into his long-ruined pilot's uniform and splashed across his face.

He stuck his tongue out and let it fall into his mouth. He'd topped off his canteen earlier, and Toshke was fashioning a sort of bowl out of the broad leaves of the ubiquitous crop grown here. Starvation would kill them slowly, but dehydration would kill them fast, and water was at a premium.

Kiernan had offered to help with the bowl, but once they'd gathered enough leaves Toshke had waved him off. And it wasn't as if 'weaving' was one of Kiernan's top skills listed on his resume, so he'd acquiesced and collapsed to the ground to soak up the rain.

They'd come across eight alien bodies this afternoon, providing them the first hard evidence that someone had called this planet home before the Rasu invaded. The corpses were tall, long-limbed grasshopper-looking creatures, and they'd been torn joint from joint and tossed aside to rot. A hundred meters from the corpses, the burnt-out remains of what might have been a tiny village lay in sooted ruins.

He *really* disliked the Rasu.

"There." Toshke presented his bowl for inspection. He'd woven the tough blades into an intricate and surprisingly sturdy pattern, then dug up a chunk of damp clay and caked it along the outside. "Once the clay dries, it will hold water most efficiently."

"Great work, sir. I mean, we'll have to carry it around, but we weren't doing anything else with our hands."

"True enough." Toshke's wings fluttered briefly behind him. "We will head toward what appears to be a forested area to the west tomorrow in search of more substantial food. Perhaps if we are successful in our search, we will fashion a shelter beneath the trees and use it as a home base."

As if on cue, Kiernan's stomach grumbled. A starvation diet sucked in so many more ways than he'd expected. "Until the Rasu show up to raze the forest."

"Yes." Toshke's wings stilled. "Until then."

Kiernan sighed and sat up. A snarky attitude helped him to cope—or run from coping—but Toshke was stolid, stalwart and resolute, and it wasn't doing a damn thing to help the Taiyok. "Maybe they'll finish taking what they want soon and leave. I mean, other than some roughage crops, I haven't seen anything on this planet a species like the Rasu has any reason to be interested in. We can hide and wait them out. Then, when they're gone, we can build a real shelter. Start a farm. Domesticate some critters."

"You mock me."

"No, I don't. I don't want to die here, but if that's my only option, then I'd prefer to do it several decades or centuries from now."

Toshke studied the drying clay on his bowl. "I don't understand why you bother to struggle to live. When you die, won't you simply awaken in a new body on your home planet?"

"Nope. That's not how it works. Believe me, I wish it was. If it did, I would've made sure I didn't survive the crash." He groaned and dragged a hand through rain-soaked yet somehow still filthy hair. "Truth is, they've probably already awoken a new me in a new body. But *this* me? It's the only one of me I've got. Besides, I can't leave you here alone."

"Please do. You are nothing but a burden to me, Kiernan."

He blinked. Opened his mouth, then closed it. Blinked again. "Was that a joke?"

The Taiyok's hollow cheeks shifted in what he'd come to recognize as a smile. "Indeed, my friend. I trust I would not be alive today were it not for you, and should you depart, I would miss you."

"Well...thank you. I'd miss you, too." The rain had lessened to a faint drizzle in the last few minutes, and Kiernan stood, searching for a way to distract them from the sudden awkwardness of comradery. He pointed off to the west. "So this forest in the distance?"

"Yes. I think—" Toshke slammed into his back, and he landed face-first on the muddy ground with a jarring *oomph*.

"What?"

"Rasu. Moving fast."

"Shit." He lifted his head, wiped mud out of his eyes and craned his neck around, then zoomed his vision in the direction Toshke was fixated on.

Four—no, five—vehicle-sized Rasu sped across the field in formation. They'd made motors for themselves and looked to be clocking around one hundred fifty kph. Their course, if it didn't alter, was going to bring them about three-fourths of a kilometer to the south of his and Toshke's location, headed the way they had come from earlier today.

Toshke's voice was a low, raspy bark at his ear. "We don't have time to move without risking attracting notice. We stay low and still."

"Right. Okay. Fuck!"

"And silent."

Kiernan pinched his lips together and tried not to inhale mud. He scanned the crappy map of the region he'd been constructing in his head. If these Rasu stayed on their current heading, it would take them worryingly close to the crashed ships.

He and Toshke had talked about fully dismantling or even burning the ships, but they'd decided against it. One, burning them risked attracting Rasu attention. Two, they might find themselves in need of parts or metal or components or...something. It seemed short-sighted to destroy what were presumably the only pieces of non-Rasu technology on the planet.

So they'd let the wrecks be, obscured as they were by a growing coat of mud and dust and some tree limbs they'd tossed over them as camouflage.

Now he worried it had been the wrong call. These Rasu weren't harvesting the fields or collecting other resources; they were in a hurry to get somewhere. What if they were from the crashed Rasu ship? It was logical that if any pieces of the leviathan had made it through the wormhole, they could have landed in the same region of the planet as he and Toshke had. If they found their wrecked vessels, they could...he didn't dare guess the extent of what the Rasu could do with an Asterion and a Taiyok vessel, but nothing good.

Fear gripped his chest. The same arguments and scenarios he'd run through a thousand times spun up again in his mind, followed by a suffocating feeling of helplessness. Not only was he stuck here, he couldn't do a damn thing to warn the people back home. Assuming there even were any people back home. For all he knew, they'd been wiped out by the Rasu the day after the assault on the stronghold.

"They have passed."

Kiernan pushed up to his knees and dragged his hands down his jaw. "We should follow them."

"We cannot begin to keep pace with the machines."

"No, but if they find the wrecks, we should at least know."

"What will knowing accomplish?"

"Not a godsdamn thing."

Toshke stood and flexed the shoulder muscles controlling his wings. "So back to the east, then?"

"Back to the east."

35

SAVRAK

E ren bounded through the open wormhole, and the crisp, dry air of the CINT secure storage warehouse hit him like a blast from an arctic cold front. He closed his eyes and exhaled with rapturous joy.

"Eren—"

He held up a hand, eyes still closed. "Give me a minute." He brought the hand to his hair and twisted it up around his head, letting the artificial breeze created by the ventilation system waft across the bare skin of his neck. "Oh, this is glorious."

A hand swatted him on the rear, jolting him out of his nirvana. "Get your Idoni ass in gear. We don't want to leave the wormhole open for any longer than we have to."

"Drae, you are a humorless bastard. One day you'll experience true joy, and when you do, you'll think of me."

Drae snorted as he picked up a crate of UDHE explosives. "Trust me, I won't be thinking of you."

"Yep, you will be. I'm in your head now." He turned and delivered a flourishing bow to Richard Navick. "Sir."

Navick tried not to look amused. "Eren. Any updates to report?"

"Yes, in fact. General Jhountar paid the facility another visit last night, and this time without his usual pomp and hordes of lemmings in tow. Because we left one teeny-tiny surveillance cam inside when we infiltrated it, I can tell you he spent the entire forty minutes meeting with two individuals we believe are the facility's manager and the head scientist."

His boss nodded thoughtfully. "Assessment?"

"We're almost out of time."

"Agreed. Nevertheless, don't rush the op. Take care when placing the explosives and even more care planning the detonation."

"Sir, when it comes to placing explosives, there is simply no one better."

"So I've heard. I've also heard you enjoy watching the show, but not this time. For God's sake, get you and your team out of there before you blow the facility."

Eren frowned as a tickle of humidity raised the hairs on his neck. The fetid Savrak atmosphere was already seeping through the wormhole into the warehouse to ruin his brief luxuriation. "No worries there, sir. I admit I'd relish seeing the fireworks, but we are all beyond ready to come home."

"You've all earned it." Navick patted him on the shoulder. "I know this has been a tough assignment. Give the team my thanks."

"Will do." Eren bestowed a big smile on his boss and grabbed the last crate, then lugged it back through the wormhole into the swamp. A second later, it closed behind him.

They carefully arranged the crates in a square pattern on the ground in one corner of the camp. The explosives were conventional in nature, if highly sophisticated conventional, but they still needed to be careful with them.

He got why antimatter weapons had been banned, but not using them really did make some things more difficult. Mostly, it took *more* explosives to get the job done. A belt-length of antimatter would blow not only the facility but most of the capital city and twenty or so kilometers of swamp. UDHE explosives wielded the highest density of any conventional material, but it was going to take sixty kilos of the material to level their target and around a kilometer of the surroundings in every direction. Couldn't happen to a nicer swamp.

Granted, there was a non-zero chance that the initial explosion wouldn't obliterate the matter/antimatter stores instantly, in which case the two would likely commingle and obliterate one another themselves. If that happened…he cast a gaze toward the city in the distance. Well, this was what the Savrakaths got for playing with the universe's version of hellfire.

He ambled around the assemblage of crates. "Gather around, everyone. Here's the plan: we've got enough explosives to place two charges inside—one in the lab and one on the assembly floor—and four outside, on each corner of the building. I'll be handling the interior placement. Drae, you'll be responsible for the west side, Cosime the east.

"Felzeor, go on and hit the skies now. Keep a solid eye on the entrance. I want to know about any variation in schedule or routine and any unexpected arrivals or departures. Cosime, go check over our ship and make sure it's ready to get us out of here from a cold start. While you're gone, Drae and I will divvy up the charges and get the packages ready."

Felzeor and Cosime departed without sassy commentary—everyone was ready for the mission to be done—and he and Drae set about the delicate process of unpacking the crates, attaching remote detonation modules to the blocks, and wrapping them in a heavy canvas-like metamat. The wrapping should keep any critters out as well as shield the packages from detection by security scans.

Eren didn't intend to start the remote detonation sequence until all the blocks were placed and the team was safely on board the ship. Then he'd start the five-minute countdown and fly the fuck off this Athena-forsaken planet.

They'd detonate during the night shift. For one, it was the only time he'd be able to sneak inside and place the explosives. For another, it should keep casualties to near zero (unless the antimatter blew, which, again, their own fault). Political optics and all.

Cosime (mission): "The ship looks good. I'm considering firing it up now and bailing."

Eren (mission): "Get your ass back here. You wouldn't leave me."

Cosime (mission): "Eh, I guess not. Can I take a shower first?"

Eren (private): "Nope. I want to do that with you."

Cosime (private): "I'll be happy to take a second shower."

Eren (private): "Ass. Here."

He chuckled to himself. Their camp was tiny and offered zero privacy, and he'd had to content himself with little more than a few kisses, snuggles and furtive gropes for days and days and days. He was too hot and grimy to be horny at the moment, but the instant they were off this planet....

Felzeor (mission): "The evening shift is beginning to depart. No deviations so far."

Eren (mission): "Roger that, Felzeor. Keep me posted."

Eren grinned at Cosime as she jogged into the camp. "And now, the words I've waited for thirty-three days to say. Let's pack up the camp and get ready to go home."

Cosime sprang into motion like a cat, rolling up sleeping pouches and stuffing them in bags with a speed, grace and efficiency of movement he could only admire. Next came the insect nets, then the cooking unit, then the surveillance gear. The Veil module hiding the camp would have to wait; he'd snatch it on the way to the ship after the explosives were set.

He considered the stack of bags and containers now littering the camp. He didn't care to lug yet more heavy objects in this heat, but proper mission leadership demanded he suck it up. "Let's go ahead and get all this gear inside the ship, on the off chance that we're running for our lives to escape after we plant the charges."

RW

Eren crept up the stairs and into the main lab for a second and final time lugging a heavy pack stuffed with explosives. Having twenty kilos of high-powered explosives strapped to his back didn't particularly bother him, seeing as it basically defined his career. Still, he'd be glad to be rid of them.

He contemplated the sealed containers of materials along the wall, each one decorated with bright red 'X's and many exclamation marks. He could gather a few samples, prime them and place them in proximity to one another, and the problem would take care of itself.

But, no, he was a proper CINT employee now, and he'd do it the way CINT wanted it done. He crouched in front of one of the cabinet-lined workbenches and eased the pack off his shoulder to the floor. He'd hide the payload deep inside the cabinet, in case something went wrong tonight and they had to wait to detonate. Odds were decent the package wouldn't be discovered right away, if at all.

He nudged a set of replacement lab equipment to the side and slid the wrapped explosives all the way to the rear of the cabinet, then rearranged the equipment in front of it. *There.*

One down, one to go.

RW

The second set wasn't quite so easy to hide, and his attempts were complicated by needing to evade the roving lizard mech. He settled for stuffing the package behind a monitoring station near one of the missile assemblies.

He felt the pressure of time urging him onward now, and he had to force himself not to sprint down the hallway and out the maintenance door, where he was, unsurprisingly, stopped short by the thick, oppressive heat. News flash: he would not miss this place.

Eren (mission): "Drae, Cosime, report?"

Drae (mission): "Placing the second set on the northwest corner now. ETA two minutes."

Cosime (mission): "Same on the northeast corner. ETA two-and-a-half minutes."

It was taking them longer than it had taken Eren to place the charges mostly because they had to trudge through the swamp to get to the far corners of the building, whereas he'd been able to glide around the spartan and cool interior.

Eren (mission): "Roger that. Rendezvous a hundred meters south of the facility—"

Felzeor (mission): "Alert! A large ship is descending from the southeast and appears to be on an intercept course with the facility. I think...it resembles a Machim Imperium!"

Eren (mission): "Zeus' marbles! Also, the fuck? Everyone double-time it! Forget about securing the explosives. Just drop them by the building and get to the rendezvous point!"

He pivoted and took off running for the east side of the building as an inky shadow encroached across the swamp, blotting out the stars. He spared a sideways glance up, and his heart dropped into his gut at the sight of the underbelly of the Machim warship. Fourteen years after the end of the anarch rebellion, it still sent dread rippling through him, though they were supposedly on the same side now.

Except possibly not.

When he got to CINT headquarters, he was going to raise the dead with his ranting.

Cosime (mission): "Moving now."

Eren (mission): "Move faster now. I'm on the way to you."

Cosime (mission): "How's that going to help anything? Get to the rendezvous—"

A flash of blinding light flared from above, briefly turning night to day. The façade of the facility shook, then the ground beneath his feet. Cracks opened wide to race along the structure's exterior.

Eren had seen more than one or a hundred explosions, and in the nanosecond warning he had, he tried to brace himself. Even so, the shockwave sent him tumbling through the air. Flames filled his vision as he landed on his back in the mucky, filthy mud. Something broke inside him, but he ignored it to shove himself immediately to his feet and begin running back toward a facility now engulfed in raging flames.

Eren (mission): "Cosime?"

Nothing.

Eren (mission): "Drae?"

Nothing.

His throat tightened then closed up as secondary explosions—from *their* explosives—boomed outward, ripping the already crumbling building off its foundation and shooting the remains of the walls out across the landscape.

Eren (mission): "Cosime, answer me! Felzeor, pull up Drae's locator and find him."

Felzeor (mission): "Eren, I don't think—"

Eren (mission): "Just find him!"

He stumbled forward, blinking blood out of his eyes, for all the good it did him. Smoke and flames billowed forth to consume the landscape, and he could barely make out the outline of where the building had stood seconds earlier. He veered to the right as debris rained down on him. Not fast enough, and a chunk of façade whacked him in the head. He fell to his knees...and pushed himself up again.

Cosime's locator blinked in his virtual vision. It wasn't moving. Of course she'd been injured. Obviously. But he'd get her out.

A hundred thousand meters later, he climbed across smoking debris and through a rain of fiery soot to fall at her side.

She...*arae anathema.* Blood coated her hair and half her face...and her chest...but it could be debris. And a little shrapnel. He leaned down close and pressed his cheek to her lips. She wasn't breathing.

Okay. They'd been here before. He'd saved her before, he could do it again. He pinched her nose and began performing resuscitation, thanking the gods that she no longer needed special air to fill her lungs. But when he went to pump on her chest, he cried out as his hands found only mushy skin and bone. *Nonononononononono!*

Debris began raining down on them with greater urgency. He had to move. He gathered her up in his arms and held her close against his body, then began picking his way over uneven chunks of burning debris. All he had to do was get her to the ship.

Felzeor (mission): "I found...part of Drae. He's...he's gone."

A string of curses lined up on his tongue, but he didn't have the breath or energy to mutter them.

Eren (mission): "Get to the ship."

Felzeor (mission): "What about Cosime?"

Eren (mission): "I've got her."

Felzeor (mission): "Is she...?"

Eren (mission): "Just get to the godsdamn ship!"

The hundred thousand meters became a billion, then another billion as he struggled relentlessly forward. His hair caught fire from descending embers; the humidity put it out. Cosime was as still as...she didn't move in his arms.

Savrakath sirens rang out in the distance behind him as he at long last reached their ship, lurched up the ramp and fell inside.

PART III

TRIBULATION'S ORBIT

36

AKESO

Caleb rubbed at his beard and tilted his head, but neither did a damn thing to improve what he was staring at. Their probes had finally completed a circuit of NGC 55 and reported back nothing but bad yet still inexplicable news.

Rasu structures clogged the galaxy to such an extent their presence was affecting the galaxy's rotation. Further, they had indeed constructed *something* encircling the entire galactic core. Whether it was a Dyson ring or something else, they couldn't determine without closer study.

"It could be an antenna array for talking to Rasu on the other side of the universe."

He grimaced at Alex. "I seriously hope there are not Rasu on the other side of the universe. Sure, they might be boosting the signal to reach farther, or a greater number of targets. But a ring ten kiloparsecs long? I can't conceive of what manner of communications would require that much equipment."

"Other side of the universe? I'm just saying. I'll put it to the Noesis. I've no doubt they can collectively conjure a plethora of nightmarish possibilities." She sighed. "I don't think it's power-related. They've constructed Dyson lattices around thousands of stars in the galaxy. A megastructure such as this has to have some other purpose."

"Maybe this is how they're altering the galaxy's rotation. Maybe they're trying to...move it?"

"*Ebanatyi pidaraz.* They really could be doing that. To where? Closer to other galaxies they control—?"

Guests enter our awareness.

Caleb's head jerked toward the windows in time to see the Caeles Prism brighten above the landing complex. "Someone's coming through the Prism."

They left the data table behind and hurried outside, since no one was scheduled to arrive today. But he recognized the small ship as a CINT vessel, which narrowed it down to only a few possibilities.

The ship bypassed the landing complex and plummeted to the ground near the house, landing with a rough thud. An instant later, the hatch opened and Eren emerged carrying a form in his arms...Caleb's heart seized up.

Eren sprinted down the ramp, then spotted them and started running toward them. The next second, Felzeor flew out of the hatch to dart along behind. Late-evening shadows obscured the details, but the Anaden was covered in mud and blood and limping badly. Cosime hung bonelessly in his arms, her head lolling against his chest.

They met him halfway across the meadow, and Eren thrust his arms out toward them. "Help her."

"God, what happened? Are you injured?"

"The fuck do I care? Just help her!"

Caleb took Cosime from his arms and eased her to the ground. Her chest was shredded from collarbone to navel, more meat than skin. By the time her head rested on the grass, he knew she was dead. Nothing else felt so unsettling as the limpness of a body no longer infused with life. He looked up and worked his throat until it produced words. "Eren, she's gone. I'm so sorry."

"I *know* she's gone—why do you think I brought her here instead of to HQ Medical? Bring her back. You and your planet do your thing and *bring her back.*"

A yawning emptiness opened up in the pit of his stomach. *Sorrow death pain All aches mourning.* "It doesn't work like that."

"It did for you."

He brought blood-covered hands to his face and dragged them down his jaw. "I already had Akeso's essence living inside me when

I died. It was that essence which enabled Akeso to rekindle the spark of life in me. But—"

"But *nothing*. Naraida are, like, half plant, right? It'll work. It *has* to work."

Alex placed a hand on Eren's arm. "Please, it's not Caleb's fault—"

He threw her hand off, which was when Caleb realized Eren had a piece of metal shrapnel sticking out of his side between two ribs. "It is if he won't bring her back."

Guilt ripped through him as he braced his hands above his knees and stood. "This is not within my power."

His friend reached out and grabbed him by the shoulders; Eren's hands were shaking, and the skin on his fingers had been all but burnt off. His parched and cracked lips curled into a snarl. "Then what good are you?"

His response scraped past a throat that had turned to sandpaper. "At this moment, none whatsoever."

Eren's eyes widened into wild and bloodshot orbs. He squatted on the other side of Cosime's body, touched her arm and stared up to meet Caleb's gaze. He resembled a madman, and a half-dead one, hanging on by an unraveling thread. "*Try.*"

Caleb breathed in through his nose. "Okay. I'll try."

"Caleb—"

He gave Alex a tight, tragic smile. "I'll be fine. He's right. I won't know for certain until I try." He retrieved a blade from his belt and cut open his palm, then knelt opposite Eren and drew it over Cosime's palm. He set the blade aside and grasped her hand—

Death absence soulless bones and flesh empty empty empty tendrils of death writhing out to choke off life death dead everywhere every cell death spreads to swallow—

He gasped in air and fell onto his back. Black dots swam through his vision as his stomach roiled. If felt as though vines reached out from the soil beneath him to entangle him in their grasp and drag him into the depths of the underworld. He couldn't breathe.

All across the meadow, the grass wilted, turned brown and sagged flat upon the dirt. The creek fell silent and still. In the forest, birds wailed.

"Caleb!" Alex dropped beside him and touched his face. His vision blurred in and out of focus, but he saw the frantic worry animating her features. "Are you okay?"

"Not...not so much." He tried to clear his throat, but death clogged it until air scarcely made it past. He crawled to his knees and lifted his head as much as he dared. "Eren, I am so, so sorry, but there's nothing left of her. She's gone."

Eren's mouth opened, then closed. As they watched, the last frays unraveled into stark desolation. Tears cut rivers through the blood and grime coating his features.

He leaned in close over Cosime's body, whispering unheard words as he tenderly moved blood-soaked feather locks of hair away from her face. His lips brushed across her still lips and back again.

Abruptly he stood; his expression had transformed into frozen stone. "Take care of her for me." Then he pivoted and ran for his ship.

"Eren, wait!" Alex leapt up and shouted at him, but he ignored her. As soon as he cleared the hatch, it closed behind him, even as Felzeor rushed to catch up.

Felzeor jerked to a stop a meter from the ship as it rose into the air. In seconds it had traversed the Prism and vanished.

Felzeor hovered in the air where the ship had been for a moment, then settled to the ground and sluggishly picked his way on foot back to them, as if he lacked the strength to fly any longer.

Caleb rocked back and dropped his head in his hands as a headache bombarded his brain, throbbing so violently against his skull he nearly passed out right then and there from the pain. *Empty empty empty dead death sorrowful agony woe we drown beneath its pain....*

Alex knelt in front of him and gently caressed his cheek. "Go inside. I'll take care of everything."

He wanted to refuse her, but he could barely think and could no longer conceive of speaking. So instead, he nodded shakily and let her help him to his feet. His vision focused in on the façade of their home, and he put one foot in front of another across the *dead dead dead* grass until he reached its sanctuary.

RW

Alex made sure Caleb made it inside without collapsing, but once he reached the foyer he motioned her away. She continued watching while he pulled his shirt off over his head and stumbled out onto the rear terrace.

She imagined him and Akeso had a few issues to work through...so she reluctantly turned to revisit the tragedy waiting for her by the creek. Weariness crept through her bones, weighing down her steps. It seemed as if this night had already lasted a thousand hours, though she feared it had scarcely begun.

She wouldn't say that she and Cosime had been close friends exactly, but the woman had always brought energy and excitement to every room she entered. The skinny little waif of a Naraida was a force of nature, and she had made Eren happy, which was no small feat. Now Eren was...but she couldn't worry about him right now. She had plenty to worry about in the here and now.

Felzeor was lying next to the still form with his head resting on Cosime's shoulder. Alex's hand clasped over her mouth to muffle a gasp. To call it a heartbreaking scene didn't begin to do justice to the grief rippling out in waves across the meadow and soon, the stars.

She crouched beside Felzeor and gathered the Volucri up into her arms. He didn't resist as she stood and cradled him against her. "I'm so sorry. We'll take care of her together, okay?"

Felzeor nodded against her chest, and she stroked the feathers of his neck. "Can you tell me what happened?"

The Volucri's voice warbled with sorrow, but he lifted his chin. "Someone attacked the facility we were watching on Savrak. We had no warning."

"You don't know who attacked it?"

"It was chaos, and everything turned bad so fast, but it looked like a Machim warship. An Imperium."

She groaned with so much visceral disgust that Felzeor launched out of her arms to land on one of the branches above. "Bastards!"

"Indeed. I do not understand why a Machim warship would attack the facility when CINT had already ordered us to destroy it."

"We'll find out." She sent a pulse to her mother, one she anticipated would serve as the first spark in a coming firestorm. Next, she sent one to Richard, so he could join the list of people whose night was about to be ruined.

You've got five seconds before I invade your privacy.

My...what?

She stretched out her arm, let the miniature Caeles Prism on her wrist gather power from unseen, infinitely folding dimensions, then opened a wormhole into Richard and Will's living room and stepped through it.

Will sat in a cushioned chair wearing a cable-knit sweater and sipping on something dark and steaming, while Richard was buttoning a woolen shirt from the door to the bedroom.

"Sorry to intrude, but we have a...problem. A...will you come with me? Both of you?"

Will stood and set his mug aside. "Of course." Richard studied her gravely but joined them, and they both followed her through the wormhole to the meadow.

Will cried out and fell to his knees beside the body. "Richard, go back to the house and get our med kit—"

Alex placed a hand on Richard's arm. "You don't need to. She's gone."

Will glanced up at her, his features screwed up in concern and uncertainty. "Are you sure?"

"Caleb tried...he...I'm sure. She was dead before she got here."

Will stared back at Cosime's blood-streaked face. His shoulders sagged, and he slowly stood.

Richard stared at them both. "I don't understand. How *did* she get here? She's supposed to be on Savrak with Eren, or possibly on their ship leaving it behind by now. They were going to—something went wrong with the plan to blow the antimatter facility. Where are—"

Felzeor flitted down from his limb to hover among them. "We had almost finished placing all the explosives when a warship, I think a Machim Imperium, arrived out of nowhere and bombed the facility. Cosime and Drae were still right next to the walls of the building and they...Eren was injured, but he found Cosime and got her to the ship. We came here."

Alex cleared her throat; it felt dry and scratchy, and she wished she'd brought some water out with her. "He wanted Caleb to bring her back to life, but...."

Recognition dawned on Richard's features, and he gazed at the body and the dead grass surrounding it with new eyes. "But it doesn't work like that."

"No, it doesn't. So Eren said for us to take care of her and left."

"He just...left in the ship? He didn't say where he was going?"

Alex couldn't rightly blame Eren for anything he'd done tonight, even the misery he'd inflicted on Caleb. He was blinded by grief and desperation and rage and pain, and in his place she doubted she would have comported herself any better. But at the moment emotion was leaving logic in the dust, and she found she was quietly, profoundly furious with him. "No. He simply left."

"Is Caleb all right?"

She stared back to the house, but nothing moved beyond the glass walls. "He will be." *He has to be.*

Richard tried to smile as he motioned Felzeor closer. "Felzeor, I'm so glad to see you're uninjured. What about Drae? What happened to him?"

Felzeor cooed sadly as he landed on Richard's shoulder. "They...there wasn't enough of him left for Eren or me to..." a cry escaped his beak "...it was so awful, he was blown to pie-pieces and...."

"Okay, okay. Don't forget, Drae's Anaden. You'll see him again soon." Richard tried to soothe Felzeor, sounding more like he was trying to soothe himself. "Damn this all to Hell. An Imperium, truly? Miriam needs to know."

"I sent her a pulse. I expect she'll be hunting for details soon, but she's aware."

"Good." His gaze fell to the body once again, then to Will. "I need to bring a small forensics team here, as well as medical personnel. Can you—"

"Just tell me where."

"CINT offices at HQ. The Forensics department, if you know where it is. If not, it's fine, we can walk a few steps."

The next hour passed in a hazy blur. People arrived and did things to the body she didn't watch, then left. More people arrived to do more things before finally securing the body on a gurney, draping it in a white sheet and departing with it.

Its absence wasn't as much of a relief as she'd expected. The mark it had left on the planet and on the souls of those present—and absent—wouldn't soon be erased.

Richard returned through the wormhole and crouched in front of Felzeor, who had huddled up beneath the canopy of a nearby tree. "Will you come back to CINT with me? I need to take your official statement. I realize it's going to be hard for you to relive these events, but we need to learn what occurred tonight in as much detail as possible. So we can get justice for her."

"I want to stay here. I want to comfort Caleb. But I must do my duty. People need to know about the travesty committed tonight. So, yes, I will come with you." Felzeor flapped his wings to rise into the air and land on Alex's shoulder. "I wish I could be here when Caleb gets to feeling better. Tell him I'm sorry I had to go."

"He'll understand. You're doing right by her, as a friend should." She kissed him on the head and urged him toward Richard, to whom she sent a quick pulse.

Once he's fulfilled his obligations, you'll make sure he gets to wherever he wants to go, won't you?

Of course. We'll look after him.

Will finished gathering up the last of the gear the teams had left behind, then came over and grasped her hands. "Get some rest."

"I'll try. Thank you, both of you. I'll, um, touch base in a few hours."

Then everyone was gone, and she was alone. Full dark had long since fallen, and clouds drifted sluggishly above, obscuring all but the occasional star. She trembled and rubbed at her arms. The silence felt oppressive, but...it wasn't total, she realized. The creek gurgled quietly as the water flowed smoothly over the rocky bed, which hopefully meant that Akeso, and thus Caleb, were beginning to recover from the ordeal.

She breathed in deeply, trying to hold herself together for a little while longer, and went into the house. "Caleb?"

She received no answer. She checked the bedroom upstairs first; on finding it empty and the bed still made, she returned downstairs and headed out onto the rear terrace.

Caleb lay on his back in the grass beyond the stone-paved area, his shirt discarded to one side. He must have been this way for hours now, and a flare of worry sparked in her chest. But this was hardly the first time she'd found him in this state.

She dropped to her knees beside him, relieved to see the steady, calm rise and fall of his chest. She touched his cheek; he wasn't shaking or sweating. All good things, atop an ocean of terrible. A weary sigh escaped her lips. "I could really use your company right now, *priyazn.*"

She got no response, and hadn't expected one, so she kissed his forehead and stood. She grabbed a throw from the bench, dragged herself to one of the adirondack chairs and collapsed into it.

RW

Caleb opened his eyes to a clear, star-filled sky above him and cool grass beneath him. He breathed in, and somewhat to his surprise, it didn't cause him intense physical pain. A dull lament filled his soul, but it lacked the sharp sting of agony or the fervor of panic.

He turned his head, and his gaze fell on Alex asleep in one of the chairs. That did elicit a stab—of guilt. He'd had a vague sense of people arriving, of equipment and conversations, then sometime later of friends and strangers alike leaving, but it had remained on the periphery of his senses, an idle note by Akeso of all things that occurred upon its soil.

He'd abandoned Alex and left her to deal with all of those awful tasks on her own, left her with a corpse and a grieving Felzeor while he crawled off to wallow in the agony of having touched Death.

It had been necessary, even required. Death had rarely visited Akeso in any real way, and the shock of it had reverberated from root to leaf, from core to atmosphere, and every one of those pangs mirrored themselves in Caleb's anima. Not by either of their choice; it was merely the nature of their shared existence.

This existence brought with it many benefits and a few drawbacks, and tonight he'd experienced perhaps the worst possible of them. And after the waves of terror and panic and suffocating anguish had subsided, he was left to work through the sorrow of a friend's death and another's devastation.

He pushed up his knees and crawled over to the chair where Alex slept. Overwhelmed by exhaustion, for these last hours had been anything but restful, he dropped his head in her lap and wrapped his arms around her legs. In seconds, he had fallen asleep as well.

37

CONCORD HQ

Security officers brought Torval elasson-Machim into Miriam's office. His hands were bound in front of him, and he still wore his uniform. Casmir entered after the entourage, saluted her and adopted a parade rest stance to the left of the prisoner and his guards.

"Commandant Solovy, as requested, I present Navarchos Torval elasson-Machim to you for the filing of charges against him. He has prepared and signed a full confession stating that at 14:22 CST on day 238 of year 6,157, 12th Epoch Proper, he breached the atmosphere of the planet Savrak and ordered his Imperium to fire on the structure designated SS 12B. The ship did so fire, destroying the target."

Miriam stood and walked deliberately around her desk, returned Casmir's salute, then came to a stop directly in front of Torval. Her stance, like her expression, was formal and professional, displaying none of the frustration and anger churning through her mind. "You freely admit to your actions, without coercion or duress?"

The man had the audacity to look smug. "I do. I'm not ashamed of what—"

"Very well. Torval elasson-Machim, you are hereby stripped of the title of 'Navarchos' pending a judicial determination of the following charges: disobeying the orders of a superior officer; dereliction of duty; involuntary manslaughter of Concord personnel; voluntary manslaughter of members of a non-Concord species and conduct unbecoming a Concord military officer. Additional charges may follow at the conclusion of a thorough investigation. You are to be remanded to CAF Detention, where you will await a preliminary hearing in front of the Concord Armed Forces Disciplinary Board."

Torval growled and lunged toward her, though in the officers' grip he stood no chance of breaking free. "You don't have the right to take my title or my ship from me!"

Casmir stepped over, but not so far as to block Miriam. "Yes, Torval, she *does*. We agreed to abide by the Concord-established laws, regulations and chain of command when we decided to serve in the Concord military. You took an oath, and you broke it. You had to realize there would be repercussions."

"Fuck you, Casmir. You fucking bootlicker. If not for you, the Humans would all be dead, our Primor would be alive and we'd be rulers instead of servants."

"Enough," Miriam snapped. "I don't care if you respect me. I don't care if you like me. But you *will* obey me. And when you don't, you will endure every single consequence."

"At least I fucking *did* something. You're ready to invite the disgusting lizards into Concord with open arms. Spineless bitch." Torval spit in her face.

The officers yanked him back another two meters, but she didn't move a centimeter. Her teeth gritted together painfully, for rarely had maintaining control over her demeanor and actions been so difficult. "We had people on the ground. People you killed."

Torval blinked. "I didn't know."

"It's not your *right* to know the details of our clandestine operations. If or when it became relevant to your duties, you would have been told, and not before."

"Well, I'm sure your people will be back in action soon enough."

"You arrogant ass—" Too far? She drew in a deep breath through a clenched jaw. "Has it never even occurred to you that not all of them might be Anadens? That other species work and serve and *die* for Concord? The fact that you, ignorant of a thousand details, took it upon yourself to declare war on another species makes you unfit to command so much as a ground squad. No matter the findings of the Disciplinary Board, you will never serve again."

"How dare you! I am Machim. I am a soldier. It is my calling and my purpose."

"Not any longer it isn't. You can contemplate a new one while you rot in a prison cell." She jerked a nod at the officers, and they hauled him out of the office.

Casmir started to follow them out, then hesitated and turned back to her. "I want to express my condolences regarding the personnel who were lost, and to apologize for Torval's actions. He has been troublesome of late. I should have recognized the danger and taken a heavier hand with him."

"Yes, you should have. Though I suspect it would have had little effect. He's a cocky hothead with zero respect for authority—mine or yours."

"In the absence of the Primor, I fear this is an accurate estimation, ma'am."

"The Primor is fourteen years dead, and Torval has long been a serving officer in a military claiming hundreds of millennia of rigid tradition. He knows better."

"Yes, Commandant." Casmir hesitated. "But the loss of the Primor, and with him the loss of our integral, has fundamentally altered this dynamic. I fear Torval is not alone in his beliefs. Many officers in the ranks are struggling with disciplinary issues."

"Again, I question how this came to be."

He relaxed his rigid stance a fraction. "Machim soldiers followed orders without question because the integral made it literally unthinkable to do otherwise. They weren't *taught* discipline and obedience; they simply *were* obedient. In the absence of the integral, I fear there is no ingrained training and no long tradition upon which to rely."

Miriam went back around to her desk, pausing briefly to wipe the spit from her cheek. Then she called up an aural but nudged it aside to give Casmir her full attention. "I suggest you start instilling it post haste. Rework your training programs from the ground up. If you need assistance, I'll instruct Fleet Admiral Jenner to provide it to you, as we have quite a lot of experience at grooming disciplined officers and those who serve under them.

"Also, if you have identified any other officers in positions of authority who are exhibiting similar tendencies to those Torval has displayed, fire them. Today. It will send a clear message that insubordination will not be tolerated and..." she shrugged minutely "...fear will suffice as a workable substitute until you can properly teach discipline."

" 'Firing' a Machim soldier is not a concept that exists in our...tradition."

"Then it's time for you to introduce it."

"I..." his throat worked "...yes, Commandant. I understand."

RW

Miriam sat quietly at her desk as her mind navigated through a maze of variables and competing interests and branching courses of action and their ramifications.

With a single rash action, Torval elasson-Machim had taken control of events away from her. Now steps must be taken in response to this calamity on both sides, with new ramifications and consequences following henceforth. She needed to wrench back command of the situation, and swiftly. Even if she didn't like the choices doing so would force upon her.

She sent a message to Mia, asking her to come by the office when she had a free minute. Then she refilled her teacup and took a long, soothing sip.

Thomas, a moment please.

The Artificial who served as the heart and soul of the *CAF Stalwart II* instantiated in front of her desk in the hazy, amorphous shape of an amber-hued giant cat. A cougar perhaps, or an albino panther; the details weren't sufficient to say. Thomas rotated his avatar amongst a variety of animals, but he invariably chose intelligent, savvy hunters. She'd considered worrying over what it said about the Artificial's state of mind, but decided that since he *was* the Artificial of a military flagship command vessel, she shouldn't expect anything less from him.

"Good morning, Commandant, though I doubt it has been any such thing. My condolences over the loss of the CINT team."

"Thank you. You're aware of recent events, then?"

"I doubt I am aware of every recent event of note, but I do make it a point to stay up on activities relevant to Concord governance and your duties here at Command."

It didn't fall within his job description, but with the *Stalwart II* in dock much of the time, he had plenty of opportunities to do so. Right now, she found herself grateful for his display of initiative. "I want to begin a full shakedown of the *Stalwart II*. Confirm the functionality of every system and schedule swift replacements or upgrades for any components that fail inspection. I also want to make certain the ship is fully stocked with a selection of all authorized weaponry. Further, I'm issuing an order requiring the crew to remain on standby so they will be able to report for duty within two hours if recalled."

"Yes, Commandant. I'm seeing to it now. May I ask if you have particular plans in mind for the near future?"

His tone was notably somber, lacking his usual veneer of cheeky humor. Then again, little about today deserved humor. "No. But this strikes me as an excellent time to ensure we are fully prepared for anything."

"So it does. Is there anything else? If not, I will get to work."

"Nothing further. You're dismissed."

The avatar faded away, and Miriam was preparing to turn to the next matter when Mia requested entry. She opened the door and motioned the woman in. "Thank you for coming so quickly. You've been briefed about what happened on Savrak?"

"Of course. Everyone's in shock over it. But you and I can't afford to be, can we? You have thoughts."

"This is not how I wanted our interaction with the Savrakaths to play out, but this is the hand we've been dealt. To that end, I have a proposal regarding our diplomatic response."

RW

CONSULATE

Mia stood with her back to the viewports in her office; the fields of ships acting as a backdrop served not as an implicit threat—her words would do that—but as a warning of how easily and thoroughly Concord could make good on the threat, should it choose to do so.

A holo materialized in front of her. Ambassador Darhk stood as well, adorned in full military dress regalia, though with only his desk as a backdrop. "Senator, I assume you have contacted me to explain the grievous insult Concord has committed upon the sovereign world of Savrak and to offer reparations for the damage inflicted and lives lost?"

"Not exactly. Ambassador Darhk, on behalf of the Concord Consulate, I am hereby formally terminating all negotiations regarding the Savrakaths' application to become a Concord Allied species. The reasons for doing so are as follows. In continuing to develop antimatter weapons after negotiations began, you have not shown good faith progress toward complying with our Code of Rights. Therefore, in destroying your antimatter research facility, we have removed what we viewed to be a clear and present threat to our people and yours.

"Further, you have actively misrepresented your compliance with our protocols regarding the treatment and legal rights of sentient species under your rule. Your abhorrent practices toward the Godjans violate not only the Concord Code of Rights but natural law. We will not tolerate slavery under any circumstances."

Darhk made a hissing sound that escaped through the gaps in his razor-sharp teeth. "While Concord continues to tease us with the lure of its riches, you give us nothing in exchange for emasculating our sovereign rule. We must be allowed to protect ourselves and our traditions as we see fit."

"Not at the expense of innocent life. If you wish to avoid further repercussions from your infractions, you will agree to the following conditions. First, you will not deploy antimatter weaponry in any way against any target, foreign or domestic. Ever. Second, no Savrakath vessel will enter Concord space without prior authorization from the Consulate. Any vessel to violate this condition will be subject to being fired upon.

"Third, Concord is now extending an offer of asylum to any Godjan who wishes to leave Savrak. You will allow Concord-flag humanitarian vessels to land at any and all spaceports under your control for the purpose of accepting asylum seekers and bringing them to Concord soil. You will allow every Godjan who expresses a desire to accept our offer of asylum to leave on these ships and will inflict no harm or other adverse action on them or their families.

"A physical record of these conditions is being delivered to your office as we speak. Do you understand the conditions as I have presented them to you?"

"Duplicitous, arrogant Human. What happens if we don't bow down and submit to your demands?"

Mia canted her head the tiniest bit toward the viewports. "As I said, there will be repercussions. Our response will be commensurate to the nature and extent of the transgression, but we reserve the right to act as we deem necessary to protect Concord lives—and Godjan ones. To this end, I'm informing you that Marlee Marano will not be returning to Savrak to answer to any charges, nor will she be further punished by the Consulate. Her actions in the face of blatant mistreatment of multiple Godjans were justified under Concord law."

Spittle gathered on Darhk's bottom lip. "You will regret so callously disregarding our sovereignty, Senator." With a sneer, he severed the connection.

Mia pinched the bridge of her nose. All they had to do to avoid further bloodshed was be decent sentient beings and comply, but she feared their pride outweighed their good sense. She sent Miriam a message.

Well, that went about as well as we expected. Be prepared for not merely noncompliance, but retaliation.

I understand. Thank you for trying.

She settled back against one of the viewports. She felt no compunction about delivering the demands to Darhk, for she believed in the fundamental rightness of each and every one of them.

But people were dead. Those deaths didn't rest at the feet of the Savrakaths...and she couldn't help but wonder if they rested at hers. At Malcolm's and Miriam's. Her mind drifted back to the meeting the other day in Miriam's office. Meno had joked about them abusing their positions *and* their relationships to do as they wished, but had it truly been a joke?

Yes, Mia.

But maybe it shouldn't have been.

Torval elasson-Machim was unequivocally in the wrong for acting as he did, and she could already hear Malcolm's coming tirade about military discipline and following the chain of command. But had their insistence on secrecy and their blithe belief that they possessed—deserved—the right to act without consulting the Senate or any other Concord leaders, ultimately caused the series of cascading disasters that now befell them?

Had their hubris caused Cosime Rhomyhn's death and started a war?

Meno didn't speak up to disagree, which seemed like answer enough.

38

CONCORD HQ

COMMAND

Miriam finished conferring with Mia Requelme about the continuing Savrakath *khrenoten'*, then checked to make certain Torval elasson-Machim had made it to a confinement cell. Then she went over to the cabinet behind her desk and set her teacup under the dispenser, her shoulders relaxing in profile when aromatic steam wafted out.

When the cup was full, she brought it to her lips, closed her eyes and let it hover there.

David's heart warmed as he watched her draw much needed comfort from her rituals. Despite the calm, collected exterior she projected, he knew well the conflict raging inside her. But this was why she was who she was, and he took his own comfort from being allowed on the inside.

As she finally took that precious first sip, she wandered to the front of her desk and leaned against it. "The obedience of the Machims has always been a tenuous affair born out of an arrangement of convenience. They chafe under rules that are more strict than they were accustomed to, but for the most part, they have played along. But now?"

David offered her a sympathetic smile. "But now they're acting rather like Ch'mshak denied a chance for blood sport." The smile faded. "I'll be honest, Miri. The Machim *elassons* worry me. I've no doubt you can handle whatever they stir up, but I worry they'll make your life a living Hell doing it."

She sat down opposite him and cradled the teacup in both hands. "My job, maybe, but not my life."

He recognized that she hadn't always drawn such a distinction, and it meant a great deal to him that she now did. "I heard there was a scene at Alex's after the bombing. Is she okay?"

"As much as can be expected. She and Richard handled what was a terrible situation as best they could."

"And Caleb?"

She sighed. "Complicated."

"When is he not?"

"True." Another sip of the tea. "Torval is now in the brig, and I've ordered Casmir to clean house. None of this will matter to the Savrakaths, however. Mia preemptively delivered a severe list of demands to their ambassador, none of which I expect him to agree to. Despite all our exhaustive efforts, we're headed for war against them anyway."

"All because one Machim thought he knew best."

"No. With the revelations about their mistreatment of the Godjans and their development of antimatter weapons, the negotiations were doomed to failure. One way or another, I suspect we were always ending up here."

He scoffed and dropped his elbows to his knees. "Do you know what I think? I think you need to get Lakhes in this office and inform them the Kats need to clean up their own mess. They created the Savrakaths to be aggressive and militaristic. They created them to make war, and the blood from the other night—the blood that's yet to be spilt—is on their ethereal hands."

"Would you ask Lakhes to send in a fleet of superdreadnoughts to wipe the Savrakaths off the map? So far as I'm aware, that's the only way the Kats have to address dangerous problems of their own creation."

He brought his hands to his jaw and, after a second, chuckled wryly. "No. Of course not. You win. This is the hand we've been dealt."

She shrugged in agreement. "As for Torval, I fear he's a symptom of a larger problem. Ferdinand denies any knowledge or involvement in his actions, but...."

"But he's lying."

"Likely so. Torval is a firebrand, but I have difficulty believing he would take such radical action entirely on his own initiative. The truth is, without their Primor, the Machims have no direction. Without their integral, they have no discipline. It makes for a hazardous combination." She exhaled ponderously. "We should've disarmed them fourteen years ago."

"You know it would have been impossible, and attempting it would probably have kicked off a renewed war when what we needed most was peace."

"I do know." She leaned across the space between them and kissed him softly. "But that's a problem for later. Tell me what you learned on your trip to the Asterion Dominion."

He let a hand linger along her cheek for a long moment, savoring the warm, reassuring softness of her skin, before relaxing back in his chair. "The Asterions are immensely clever, industrious and determined. They appear to be working with unlimited funds, man-and-machine power and, except for kyoseil, unlimited resources. Their entire society has dedicated itself to protecting itself from the Rasu."

"And?"

"And..." he spread his hands wide "...today, they're not ready. They can field a fleet of impressive ships that is growing by hundreds of new vessels every day, all of which will perform admirably in a clash—equivalent to a Novoloume fleet at a minimum. They are deploying some fancy new weapons and defenses that should make a real difference. They also downplayed some of their capabilities, presumably so I wouldn't conclude they'd be fine without our help. But even allowing for what I didn't see? Given another year or two, I might begin to like their odds. But not today.

"And honestly, another year or two may not make a difference. I agree with Lakhes on this point. As a people, they do not strike me as being ruthless enough to do what it takes to defeat an enemy the likes of the Rasu."

"Are we?"

He huffed a laugh. "Fair observation. I realize you try so hard not to be, but yes. Some of us humans can be brutally ruthless if it's required to protect those we love. Also, this is one area where having the Machims on our side—if we can keep them there—will be useful."

"Assuming they're amenable to protecting the Asterions, which is a huge assumption. Ferdinand has not reacted favorably to their overtures."

"The SAI Rebellion was seven hundred thousand years ago. Surely the Anadens haven't held a grudge for so long."

"Remember, SAIs were still banned when we arrived fourteen years ago. They've accepted our Artificials only under duress, and even putting aside the historical context, I doubt many Anadens will be willing to fight to protect synthetics."

"At least the Asterions look organic...mostly. Hopefully, this will help the Anadens get over their backward prejudices."

"Perhaps." She set the teacup aside and steepled her fingers at her chin. "So your professional assessment is that in the near-to-medium term, the Asterions will not be able to defeat a Rasu assault on one of their worlds?"

"A few Rasu vessels, yes. But not an assault of any real size, no. Not yet and not soon."

She nodded thoughtfully. "Thank you for doing this. The information is most helpful, if not particularly surprising."

He arched an eyebrow. "You're very welcome, *dushen'ka*. What are you going to do about it?"

39

OURANKELI STELLAR SYSTEM

BEYOND THE BOUNDARIES OF CONCORD SPACE

"T he Ourankeli are the most advanced species I ever encountered in my travels, and by a wide margin. They give shame to the greatest Anaden technological monuments and expose the lie of our believed evolutionary superiority. Remembering their worlds, I remain in awe."

"Are they more advanced than the Katasketousya?"

"It is difficult to say. The Katasketousya keep their technology shrouded in mystery, as if we are therefore expected to believe it is alchemy. The Ourankeli's technology is real, tangible and massive."

Her grandfather was not an easy man to impress, but Nyx did have to wonder if nostalgia might be sprucing up the memories of his time with the Ourankeli a smidge. Either way, she would find out soon enough. "Yet they treated you well? With respect?"

Danilo shrugged mildly. "Hmm. With decency. I never sought their respect."

An interesting answer. From what she knew of him and his tumultuous history, he'd rarely if ever needed to seek it; respect flowed as a natural consequence of his every action. "Did they know of us before you encountered them? Of the Anaden Empire?"

"They knew of every Type I-B or higher species for megaparsecs. They recognized what I was and soon ascertained that I was a lone traveler rather than an advance scout. Not that they had anything to fear from the Empire. They did ask me not to share what I saw and learned of them with my leaders, and I agreed to keep their confidence. An easy promise to make, given I expected never to speak to an Anaden leader again."

"So maybe they *were* a little afraid of our strength."

"I suspect they simply didn't want to be bothered by us. They likely viewed us as brutish and belligerent—which we were—and thus a pest they'd as soon not waste time swatting away."

A tiny pang of defensiveness flared, even after all this time, but she hurriedly tamped it down. She'd had the wool ripped from her eyes when the *diati* revealed to her the Primor's treachery, and she'd come to understand the width and breadth of the Anaden Empire's egregious sins in the months after leaving it behind to travel with her grandfather. But she had been a Praesidis Inquisitor for millennia upon millennia, and pride clung tenaciously to her soul. She'd worked diligently to mold that pride of station into pride in herself, into pride in her own worth instead of in her species or dynasty. It remained a work in progress.

She also grew frustrated from time to time with his utter dismissal of the considerable good the Empire *had* effected, as well as the good that flowed from his own leadership. And the good the Humans might well be doing now. He acted completely uninterested in checking in on how the new state of affairs was working out, much less in playing any sort of role in it.

She understood the pain he had endured. She understood how much he'd lost, over and over again. But he was a *leader,* in a way few individuals ever achieved, despite the fact he couldn't see it in himself any longer.

She tried to reengage in the conversation. "But they are not violent themselves?"

"Not in their dealings with one another, nor with me. I saw no warships—at least no vessels I recognized as such, but their technology is so advanced they might not need vessels to deliver their firepower. But I also saw few aliens among them. They must have encountered many species over the millennia, and how they treated them, I cannot say."

Her gaze traveled across the HUD to check their progress. They were going to arrive in the Ourankeli stellar system in a few minutes, so she settled back to prepare herself for the encounter.

Danilo had saved several images he'd captured all those hundreds of thousands of years ago, so she knew what to expect in terms of physical form. The Ourankelis' skin had a mushy, gelatinous texture, the bones within it more akin to tendons. It would be a stretch to call them 'shapeshifters,' but they adjusted their bodies quite a bit to suit their needs at any given time. Their limbs and digits shortened and lengthened on command, stretching and bending across the full range of motion, and their torsos did the same. Three eyes floated like blobs of pectin in a wide band above a single breathing orifice, and all three were able to spin in a full three-sixty circle with ease. The Ourankeli moved in long, fluid strides that resembled gliding more than walking.

Their gender was apparently as fluid as their motion, and they displayed either many or no genders except when they were pregnant. Danilo wasn't clear on the details of how that happened, thank Athena.

"Exiting superluminal in five seconds. We'll arrive some distance out from the core worlds, in case they've added long-range defenses since you were last here."

Stars snapped into clarity as normal space greeted them once again. She began the usual battery of scans to ensure nothing natural or artificial nearby displayed designs on killing them.

After a few seconds, she frowned. "I'm not detecting any technology signatures. Does their tech operate extra-dimensionally?" So far as she knew, it was the sole thing standard scans wouldn't pick up.

"I'm confident they're skilled in manipulating nonspatial dimensions, but they use the normal ones as well." He leaned in and studied the readings. "Perhaps they've needed to shield themselves for some reason. From some threat."

"Then we will as well." She activated the cloaking field.

"Yes." He peered out the viewport, though nothing was visible from here. "I recall they inhabited several moons of one of the outer gas giants, as well as orbital habitats of the gas giant itself. Those should be the closest settlements for us to reach."

She pulled up the astronomical scans of the stellar system and reviewed them. "We're only detecting a single gas giant in the system."

"No, that's not accurate...but, fine, let's visit it and see what we can learn."

RW

Two megameters from the coral-and-lemon gas giant, the shattered remnants of a rocky moon lay amid an expansive field of debris. A full third of the moon's mass was gone, and the jagged crevasses marking its new surface suggested the removal had not been gentle. A high metallic content in the orbiting debris indicated it could include the wreckage of structures, but nothing large enough to be identifiable remained.

Danilo leaned into the dash vehemently. "No, this isn't right. This moon was covered in biospheres and encircled by a docking and power ring."

"Maybe Caleb Marano came through here."

He whipped around to glare at her sharply, and Nyx shrank deeper into her chair. "I'm sorry. That was inappropriate of me."

Disapproval lingered in his eyes as he returned his gaze to the broken moon.

Fine, the remark had been in bad taste. But the moon did look as if someone had lobbed it about like a bludgeon. "Possibly a large asteroid struck it, though the Ourankeli should have been able to divert such an object with little trouble, right? What of the other moons?"

It didn't take them long to scout an additional three moons, all of which were in similar or worse shape than the first. This ruled out an asteroid impact. Again, she couldn't shake the impression that they had been used as weapons...or shields.

"The crown jewel of the system was a halo ring encircling the star at 0.8 AU. A habitat for three hundred billion Ourankeli, with solar receivers built into the facing edge to provide sufficient power for all. The ring itself spanned fifty kilometers in width and stretched for seven hundred fifty thousand megameters. Whatever happened to these settlements, it will not have damaged such a magnificent structure."

"Setting a course." She didn't know what else to say. His dark moods were often impenetrable, and she sensed one descending now as surely as a fog rolling in across the moors of space.

RW

The ring did still exist, but only in pieces. It would take them several hours to follow its circumference to completion, but from their current vantage they were able to detect two complete breaks in the structure.

They slowly skimmed five kilometers above the star-facing side, searching for any signs of life. But the solar receivers were dead and the shield keeping an atmosphere captured gone. Scattered buildings stood for up to a few dozen meters before crumbling away, but most were reduced to dust. If there had ever been greenery—and Danilo insisted there had been—it too was now dust. Whatever happened here, a quick scientific analysis said it had taken place a minimum of two centuries earlier.

Her heart ached, because even in its utter destruction she could see the majesty of such a creation as the halo ring. It had taken Anadens almost a millennium to build triple Dyson rings around the stars of the Dynasties' homeworlds. To build something such as this would take them a hundred hundred millennia.

"I want to land. I need to see the destruction up close."

Nyx hesitated before burying an objection. There was nothing to be learned from stepping on a surface that no longer supported life, but Danilo could be sentimental in the oddest ways. So she searched ahead for an area mostly free of jagged wreckage, slowed and lowered the *Periplanos* to the surface.

With the ring broken and its orbit decaying, only minimal gravity remained, so she fired two harpoons into the ground to keep the ship from floating away. They donned their environment suits and exited the ship, activating their magboots to keep themselves from floating away.

Danilo strode off to the left at a determined stride, and with a sigh she followed.

RW

They found no bodies. Most would have floated off into the void when the gravity and shield failed, but they spotted no bones trapped beneath debris or inside the few structures that held onto their semblances of façades. It was further evidence this catastrophe had occurred sometime in the past. Long enough ago for skin to dissolve into the soil and bones to join the dust.

Gloom settled around her in a shroud. The ring was silent, desolate and so dead it lacked ghosts to whisper its tale of woe.

Danilo picked up a milky glass-like shard half a meter long and turned it over in his hands. "Their buildings were all constructed of this material. It changed translucency as befitted the situation. Stronger than any metamaterial we can produce today, and at only two centimeters' thickness." He tossed it to the ground and stared up toward the star they orbited. "I don't understand—"

Nyx's suit alarm beeped, and an alert flashed across the inside of her visor.

Hazardous electromagnetic radiation detected. Suit integrity 94%.
93%
92%

"We need to get back to the ship."

He must be receiving the same warning, because he didn't argue. "Yes, of course."

She pivoted and headed back the way they'd come, setting a brisk pace, driven forward by the rapidly decreasing percentage on her visor.

Out of habit and training, due to the treacherous situation, her hand went to her firearm to unlatch it from the holster. When the automatic motion was interrupted before completion, she glanced down in surprise. The latch wouldn't release.

She'd inspect it once they were on the ship, as despite the instinctual response, she was unlikely to need the weapon here. Nothing lived here.

Suit integrity had dropped to 63% by the time they reached the *Periplanos,* and the quiet sound of the airlock sealing them in had never sounded so comforting to her ears. She quickly stripped out of the environment suit and placed it on the workbench for a thorough inspection later, then went into the cockpit.

There she hesitated, her hands hovering above the controls. "Are we okay to depart?"

"What? Oh…yes. The surface holds no answers as to what happened here."

She retracted the harpoons and engaged the engine, noting with concern several low-level warnings emitting from the ship's operational systems. Nothing immediately problematic, but they were a *long* way from help if the ship started failing.

"What now, grandfather?"

"Indulge me for a few more moments. Let's follow the ring for a while. I fear it's all destroyed, but we can search for evidence of how."

She set a course following the ring at two hundred kilometers distance, in case random broken pieces jutted out too far into space.

RW

Eventually, some three hundred ten thousand megameters later, the ring ended in a serrated stub, resembling an unfinished and abandoned bridge. According to calculations, this meant over a quarter of it was missing entirely.

"What could do this?"

Danilo's face resolved into a grim expression. "A weapon. It's the only answer. Someone more powerful than the Ourankeli, wielding weapons of incomprehensible power, arrived and destroyed a shining civilization that had stood proud for untold aeons."

An alert flashed on the HUD. One of the issues with the systems had been elevated in severity by the *Periplanos'* VI. She worried at a fingernail while she read through the alert. "We're getting a lot of destructive electromagnetic radiation from the star here, and our shields are having difficulty keeping it out. I'm sorry, grandfather, but we need to leave the system before our ship is damaged."

"You are correct. Our safety always takes priority." He seemed to ponder something unseen for a minute. "The Hoans are but two galaxies away. I visited them a mere fourteen years ago, but now I find myself concerned this enemy may have found them as well."

The Hoans had sheltered him after his son had thrown him into an arctic crevasse and left him for dead, and he'd spoken of the species often during their travels. Nyx tried to smile, but the gloom that had overtaken her on the ring clutched her like an omnipresent shadow. "We'll check in on them."

RW

It was several hours later before she was finally able to turn her attention to the environment suit and its associated gear.

A diagnostic scan reported the metal ring seals on the suit had suffered significant degradation. Not the corrosion one would naturally assume, but actual slippage in the seals. The ring connecting the air hose to the oxygen canister appeared slightly misshapen, as if someone had hammered on one section of it for a spell. How odd. She wasn't a scientist or an engineer, but she was fairly certain a few minutes in open space wasn't supposed to inflict this kind of damage on suits designed to operate in open space.

Hopefully, the workbench equipment would be able to repair the suits, because she didn't look forward to trying to convince her grandfather to visit Anaden space to acquire new ones.

She picked up the holster rig that still held her firearm and peered at the latch. Her eyes widened in disbelief. The latch had *melted*.

40

MIRAI

MIRAI ONE

Perrin leapt off the couch and tromped across the living room. Through the kitchen. Back to the couch again.

Justice had finally released Adlai's apartment five hours earlier, so now she had a proper place to be. Her home, more or less. But with Adlai gone, she felt like a trespasser. An interloper treading across hallowed ground.

Nika would chide her for being histrionic then insist Perrin return to her flat...but Nika wasn't here. Nika wasn't even in the local stellar cluster.

Spencer had rebuffed her pleas for information yet again this morning. They were pursuing every lead using every available resource, he'd assured her. They damn well better be—it was their job!

She was certain it was true. She trusted Spencer and had faith in his abilities as an investigator. But he refused to let her help search for Adlai, and if she didn't help, she was apt to go mad. Certifiably, irretrievably insane, worthy only of reinitialization or scrapping.

She groaned and took a sip of coffee from Adlai's favorite coffee mug. She'd only lived here for a few weeks, but she already knew his favorite everything. Eggs over-easy with burnt toast. The soft heather gray t-shirt and faded navy sweats. The middle of the bed, but they were working on that one. The umber glazed mug with a chip on the handle. Blacker than black coffee.

Hers had cream in it. She frowned and set it aside.

She helped people. It was her highest calling, her reason for being. She *had* to be able to help him somehow.

An idea bloomed in her sleep-deprived mind like the soft amber gleam of a meadow at dawn. Emboldened, she pulled on a sweater over her tank top and hurried out the door.

RW

Parc Eshett met her at the pub on Lakeview. He beat her there, which was surprising considering Adlai's apartment was only a few blocks away.

She hopped up on a stool at the high table by the front window. "I thought you said you were on Namino this afternoon?"

He paused tapping his fingers on the table long enough to shrug. "I was already on my way back. No worries."

"Okay." Her mind bounced around as scattershot as a ball in play; she tried to focus. "And you brought a routine I can use?"

"I always carry a routine for every occasion with me." He fished through the pack on his hip and produced a small module. "It comes with an adaptive algorithm pre-programmed for damn near any form of encryption, so all you need to do is stick it in an input slot and point it toward the folder you want to derive."

"And it has plenty of storage room?"

"You won't be able to copy out the entire Justice Center database onto it or anything, but it'll hold a few million files."

"That ought to be...sufficient." Her shoulders sagged as she deflated a little. "Maybe I shouldn't do this. I truly do believe Spencer's moving star systems to find Adlai. I simply need to find out what's going on."

"Of course you do! And since Spencer's gone full-on respectable, there are things we can do that he can't."

"We? Parc, I am not asking you to get involved in this. I mean, beyond loaning me the module."

"I know you're not. But I've got some bandwidth to help. And while I'm kind of ambivalent about this Adlai guy, you're on my squad. So I'm here for you."

Parc had been quirky when he was in NOIR, but he was amping up the peculiar these days. Presumably the result of spending much of his time with Ryan, a compatibly quirky dude if there ever was one. She also had no idea how he could possibly have any free bandwidth, what with all the work he was doing for the Initiative's ceraffin. But she was desperate, so she didn't challenge him. "Thank you. I appreciate it. I'll keep you updated on what I learn."

"Screw that. Come to the warehouse after you leave the Justice Center. We'll review the files together."

She started to protest, but the truth was she'd welcome the companionship, not to mention his keen and devious perspective. "I will."

RW

MIRAI JUSTICE CENTER

Spencer hid a grimace behind a mask of sympathy when he saw Perrin at the door to his office. "How are you holding up?"

"Shittily, that's how. Any updates?"

"Since we talked this morning? Two more leads evaporated, plus—" he cut himself off. "I'm sorry. Nothing so far. I wish I had better news."

"So do I." She wandered around Adlai's office—Spencer had left a deputy in charge on Synra and set himself up in the office to better run the investigation on Mirai. On the way over, she'd decided to give him one more chance before resorting to criminal actions. "You know, I've got a lot of friends out there. People who might not be comfortable talking to Justice. If you'd point me in the direction of some possible leads, I can track down information that you aren't able to access."

He sighed audibly. "Perrin, I've been a Justice Advisor for precisely ten seconds. I *can't* break procedure. Especially not on such a high-profile case. I've already got Selene and Harris and Julien peering over my shoulder every five minutes, anxious to leap in and shove me to the side the instant I screw up. I understand why you want to get involved, believe me I do. But I *can't*."

"I appreciate you being honest with me. I feel so helpless, and I'm not able to concentrate on anything else, and…" she swayed unsteadily, grasping out for the arm of a chair to steady herself.

"Hey, hey, are you all right?"

"I…haven't been sleeping. And I think I've forgotten to eat today."

Spencer urged her down into the chair. "Sit. I'll go get you some juice and a protein bar. I'll be right back."

She smiled weakly. "Sounds like a good idea. Thank you."

She sagged limply in the chair, closed her eyes and listened for the door to shut behind him. When it did, she was instantly out of the chair and at his—*Adlai's*—desk.

Spencer had left two panes open, and both contained information on Adlai's kidnapping. She resisted the urge to read them, because she had no time, and she needed *all* the data he had on the case. She found an open slot on the control panel beneath the panes and inserted the module.

Since the case files were already open, it only took a second for her to point the routine to the parent folder, then another seven agonizing seconds of waiting for the routine to do its work of unlocking and copying all files.

A bright green light told her the process had completed; she snatched the module out of the slot, scurried back around the desk and threw herself into the chair.

She was slumped halfway to the floor by the time Spencer returned less than a minute later, and she made a show of pushing herself up to sitting then smiling gratefully when he handed her a cup of juice and a bar. "Thank you again."

He crouched in front of her. "Perrin, you need to eat. And sleep, and generally take care of yourself. What is Adlai going to say when he gets home and sees you in this state?"

"I know, I know. I'll try. You'll ping me if anything happens on the case?"

"You'll be the first to hear when we find him."

That wasn't quite what she'd asked of him, but she stood while munching deliberately on the protein bar. "Then don't let me distract you any further."

RW

MIRAI ONE

Parc and Ryan had upgraded from Ryan's tiny apartment to a floor in an old warehouse in an industrial sector of Mirai One. Ryan had converted a third of the space into workbenches, storage and testing areas for his dynes and drones, and Parc had converted another third to housing for stacks of servers, quantum orbs and programming hardware. The sleeping area, kitchen and bath were all stuffed into the meager remaining space.

Two ceraff hubs glowed in prismatic color beside Parc's recreated command center, but he lounged on a couch by the kitchen drinking a beer when she walked in. Ryan was nowhere to be seen.

Parc stood and motioned for her to follow him to the command center. He took the module from her and dropped it in a cavernous recessed dock. "Let's see what we have here."

Data burst to life across five permanent panes. She blinked several times, taken aback by the glut of information. "At least they've been as busy as Spencer claimed."

Parc entered several commands, and the data rearranged into an outline structure, with neatly collapsible bullets lined up beneath orderly headings. "Better."

Invigorated, Perrin sidled up next to Parc's seat and began reading.

RW

"Hey, it looks as though they have a suspect..." she sighed "...or had one. The security cam at the entrance to Adlai's apartment building caught an image of this guy. He used Adlai's signature to get into the apartment, but he wasn't wearing Adlai's face when we walked in the building."

Parc zoomed the relevant bullet until it filled an entire pane. "The Justice algorithms pegged him as an 82.3% likelihood of being someone named Ian Sevulch."

She scanned ahead. "Spencer brought him in and questioned him. But it says he has an airtight alibi. He was working at a restaurant called *Ellison* in Kiyora Two during an eight-hour window around the kidnapping. He's got multiple witnesses and video and transactional proof. He never left the restaurant." She dropped her head into her hands. "Godsdammit."

Parc spun his chair in circles. "Eighty-two percent likelihood is damn high. Are they still interested in the guy?"

They scrolled through the file for several paragraphs. "Here! An investigative routine is double-checking the store logs for any evidence of tampering, and an officer is confirming the backgrounds of the witnesses. But barring one of those falling apart, he can't be the guy. It's impossible."

"Well…" Parc stood and went to the rear of the command center, making a show of checking the connectivity of a couple of wires "…not *impossible*."

She took a step back and crossed her arms over her chest. "What do you mean?"

He peeked at her through a gap in the panes. "There's always the possibility that he could be a Plex."

"A what?"

Parc nodded to himself and came around into view. "So you haven't heard about them yet. Good. Whenever you get your guy back, try not to spill the beans, okay?"

"Spill the beans on what? I have no idea what you're talking about."

"Right. Ugh, I'm going to regret this. A Plex is one instance of a person's psyche with multiple physical instances—multiple bodies—that are linked in a permanent ceraff structure."

Her eyes narrowed, then reversed course and widened. "But that would mean...wait, that's illegal. You can't get a psyche imprinted on a body without proof of body death, R&R or diversification."

"Of course it's illegal. What would be the fun in it otherwise? But it isn't difficult to pull off. You diverge the records the clinics access is all. Not a big deal. Not for a ceraff."

"Are there a lot of these people?"

"A few dozen instances. Maybe a hundred by now. It's spreading fast."

"And these people...they're connected to each other all the time?"

He reached over to one of the control panes and fiddled with a few impenetrable settings; she seldom understood his programming machinations. " 'Connected' is a seriously feeble word for what's happening with the psyche. It's literally the same person, expressed through multiple bodies and engaging in multiple simultaneous experiences."

"Stars, my head would explode."

"Nah, it wouldn't. Our operating systems are multi-threading masters. This merely involves using the infrastructure on a more conscious level. Oh, this will make sense—it's basically exactly what Nika did at the Rasu stronghold, only without all the dying."

She gazed at him suspiciously. "One would hope. You seem to know a great deal about these Plexes."

"Hey, I'm the inventor of the ceraffin that make them possible. Damn straight I do. Anyway, the point is, if he's a Plex, his 'alibi' is worthless. At every given moment, there's a minimum of one more version of him—and possibly a bunch more—walking and talking at somewhere elses."

She leapt up. "We have to tell Spencer about this right now—"

He slid over to block her path. "*Or*, we could not and investigate it ourselves."

"But Justice—"

"Will bollocks it up. If any Plex gets the slightest whiff of Justice poking around, they will go to ground before you can blink.

Probably every Plex will. It's an underground community, living out there on the ragged edge of progress. They realize proper society isn't ready for them, and they will do whatever they have to in order to survive until it is. Kind of like NOIR did."

"Hey..." her nose scrunched up in distaste "...perhaps it *is* an apt comparison. What do you have in mind?"

He returned to the command center, and data Perrin couldn't make out at this distance flew across one of the panes. "Interesting. This Ian Sevulch guy? He got infected with the virutox, trashed a high-end clothing store and beat up a customer. Was convicted of assault and property damage and sent to Zaidam, then...well, no need to relive the rest of that sodding sad tale. Justice overturned the conviction, but he had to pay recompense for the damage to the store and the victim. A few days after he was regened, he ostensibly moved to Kiyora and acquired the job he's using as an alibi." He glanced back at Perrin. "So this answers the motive question."

She left the data to him while she paced in increasing agitation. "You mean because of the virutox? Because of Zaidam and the Rasu lab? None of that was Adlai's fault. He fought to expose it."

"But maybe this guy doesn't realize that. Or maybe he doesn't care. We both know someone who has let his understandable hatred of Justice get out of hand more than once."

"Joaquim. Granted, I see how a certain type of person could overdose on vengeance to the point of ignoring logic and facts. It's still not right."

"Nope. Now, here's the thing, Perrin. If he *is* a Plex, I'd be willing to bet that at least one version of him didn't move to Kiyora at all. I'm sending you the address where he used to live here in Mirai One. It'll be worth staking it out for a few hours to see if he shows up. In the meantime, I'll find and shadow the Kiyora version."

"You'd do that for me?"

"Sure. I've got the time, and now I'm curious. Let's keep in contact. If he's got Adlai stashed somewhere, I bet he won't be leaving him unattended for long."

41

MIRAI

Spencer dropped his head into his hands and closed his eyes. He hadn't been home in several days, hadn't seen Maris in more. He'd chided Perrin earlier, but he'd scarcely slept himself since Adlai had vanished. He was only eating because every few hours, one of the officers in the building shoved food in front of him.

He allowed himself a few brief seconds of rest before he straightened his shoulders, blinked his eyes clear and reopened his notes. Lines and arrows slashed in every direction between names, bullets and images. But no matter how he rotated the scrawl, it never resolved to an answer.

The server breach had to be connected to Adlai's kidnapping. Years of experience had taught him that when coincidences did manifest, they were invariably explained away with the discovery of a few additional data points. Not so here, however. No other crimes or disruptions had occurred that could be blamed on the server breach, and no other evidence explained how someone was able to impersonate Adlai so thoroughly. But the five suspects in the server breach didn't exist, and they had no way to uncover the individuals' true identities.

He groaned and banged his head against the chair. He'd encouraged the use by Nika and other NOIR members of morphs when it served all their purposes, including getting his friends inside the Justice Center undetected. Morphs projected an altered physical appearance and voice print to all scanning and recording devices, which included surveillance cams as well as the eyes and ears of other Asterions. They didn't actually change a person's physical appearance, but in most scenarios, there was no practicable difference. Now their use prevented him from finding his friend and catching those who had captured him.

A wave of inadequacy churned in his stomach until he felt nauseated. Adlai had been wrong; he wasn't worthy of this position. Not if he couldn't solve a simple kidnapping!

He breathed in through his nose and reimposed a modicum of order on his psyche. This kidnapping was anything but *simple*, but he still had to solve it.

He refocused on the notes. The evidence from Adlai's apartment—

His door buzzed insistently, and with a frown he opened it. Erik Rhom, the lead forensic analyst at Mirai Justice, burst inside and skidded to a stop in front of his desk. "Sir."

"Mr. Rhom. It's been a while. Can I help you?"

"Since we cracked the virutox, I think. And yes, I believe you can." The man grabbed a chair and pulled it almost flush against the desk. "Our analysis-focused ceraff? They've had a breakthrough. It needs to be extensively tested and mapped and verified—"

Spencer leaned into the desk. "What is it?"

Erik gave him a weary smile; Spencer wasn't the only person putting in long hours. "They've developed an algorithm that can strip the signals a morph sends to a cam."

"Care to repeat that?"

"A morph has to override what a person or cam sees. It does so by sending out programmed EM patterns—"

"I know how they work...sorry, I'm not trying to be rude. Tell me how we're getting past the overlay."

"Yes, sir. The pattern a morph emits has to be stronger than what nature provides in order to override a person's outward appearance. That strength can be measured, separated and stripped out from the rest of the data captured by a surveillance cam."

"Leaving behind the original data?"

"That's correct. It was there all along, muffled beneath the signals from the morph."

The nausea in his gut was swept away by the flutter of dangerous excitement. Of hope. If true, this development would transform thousands of Justice investigations, but right now he only cared about one.

He hurriedly opened a new pane and entered several commands. "I'm having the original records from the surveillance cams the day of the server breach sent up. What do we need to do to run them through this new algorithm?"

Erik held up a plain gray box he'd brought in with him. "I've got it right here."

RW

It was a rare thing, watching magic unfold in front of one's eyes. Spencer rested one arm across his chest and brought the other hand to his chin.

A frozen image of one of the five suspects hovered in front of him and Erik Rhom. Gradually, the man's features began to blur and fade, as if he were being erased from existence. Scan lines raced over the image—the algorithm was still a raw, messy creation—as pixel by pixel, new features took their place.

Spencer's heart sank. "That's Ian Sevulch."

"You know who he is? Excellent."

"Not so much. He has an airtight alibi for both the server breach and the kidnapping. He can't have been here." Spencer motioned toward the magic box. "Let's take a look at the next suspect."

"Sure." Erik switched out the data weave with a different one, and the image updated to one taken at the lift leading down to the central server room. The scan lines' work didn't seem so magical this time as the man's features shifted and changed—

"What is this?" Spencer threw his hands in the air. "Tell the ceraff their algorithm is busted..." he willed himself calm "...and thank the members for trying."

Erik paced in front of the worktable. "Sir, if it's broken, okay. But how it could be broken in such a specific and relevant way?"

"You mean how could it turn every morphed face into the face of a man who coincidentally happens to be a suspect in the kidnapping?"

Erik spread his arms wide. "The odds are infinitesimal if not zero." He rummaged through a small drawer in the bottom of the box. "Here. I've got some of the test runs they did on the algorithm. Millions of faces, morphed and not. It was white-box testing, and it *worked*. Also, I'm almost certain none of the faces uncovered matches this one."

Spencer rubbed at his neck and scowled at the frozen image. "Run the other three."

"Yes, sir." Erik swiftly replaced the data weave again and started the process anew.

Spencer held his breath for a solid five minutes, until the last image had been analyzed. When it was done, they stood there staring at five different visuals, taken at five different locations at almost the exact same time.

All five revealed the face of Ian Sevulch.

He shook his head roughly, most of his processes refusing to believe his eyes. "How is this—" His incredulous train of thought was interrupted by the arrival of a priority message. He read the message twice, then went to grab his jacket and Glaser. "Document all of this and have it ready to put on the record. I have to go."

42

MIRAI

MIRAI ONE

Perrin ordered her third lemonade in half an hour before returning her gaze to the sidewalk outside. The one across the street in front of the third door on this block, to be precise. It wasn't a great neighborhood, and the half-eaten sandwich on her plate consisted of bland turkey squished between 3-day-old bread, but the dirty glass of the shopfront hid her surveillance-minded prying eyes. Or at least she hoped it did. It had to serve as better stealth than her sitting on a bench outside for two hours or crisscrossing the same block thirty times.

But the evening shadows were growing long; something needed to happen soon, or she'd need to come up with another plan.

Her new lemonade—she'd never call it fresh—had finally arrived when a figure exited the third door on the block. She zoomed in her vision enough to confirm he matched the description of Ian Sevulch in generalities, then slid off the stool and eased out the door.

The man turned right out his door and strode down the street at a brisk pace, hands stuffed in the pockets of a hunter-green jacket. Pedestrian traffic was fairly heavy, so she sped up and closed the distance as much as seemed prudent, tugging her hood down low over her forehead. She'd forgone her usual brightly colored attire for light gray fitted pants, a black tactical shirt and a charcoal hooded jacket. This Sevulch guy shouldn't know her, but if he'd researched Adlai's life enough to impersonate him, he might, and she didn't dare take the risk.

Parc, you were right. A man matching Sevulch's description just left the apartment.

Meanwhile, my guy's grumpily serving problem patrons in downtown Kiyora Two. Called it. You all right?"

I'm following him.

Yeah, but are you all right?

Yes. I...yes, I'm fine. I can handle this.

The man took a left at the next intersection, and the sketchy neighborhood took a nose-dive. But it wasn't a problem. She'd visited worst places when meeting potential NOIR recruits, and she'd brought a Glaser. *I can handle it fine.* She repeated the affirmation twice more.

A block and a half down, the man disappeared through a non-descript door.

Her steps slowed as she tried to evaluate the area, the vibe and the door. People were on the street, though not a lot of them. There was a skeezy club and a skeezier bar across the street, but she didn't see any commercial signage above this door. Had he gone into a residence, or was it something else?

When she neared the door, she felt the thrum of bass-laden synth vibrating along her skin. A club, despite the absence of a sign proclaiming its existence to potential patrons.

All they could do was deny her admittance. She opened the door and walked in like she knew what she was doing.

No one stopped her. No one seemed to be staffing the door at all.

At first glance, the space reminded her of every underground club she'd ever visited. At second glance, she began to recognize how wrong first impressions could be.

A prismatic globe rotated high above the center of the space, sending rainbows of light cascading through the room. A microsecond switch into the k-band confirmed its role as a ceraff hub.

329 | G.S. JENNSEN

Anyone in here was able to tap into the group consciousness of the other patrons who had joined it.

As she scanned the space, she realized many of them were doing exactly that. Vacant gazes, body posture relying heavily on bars and tables for support. A woman slouched in a chair in a corner, her hands tearing into her hair in an obvious state of ecstasy, but no one was located within a meter of her.

Perrin did a mild double-take at a man and a woman who wandered around naked, only neon body paint covering a few swathes of skin. She'd heard people musing about how spending time in a ceraff made you feel mentally naked, so perhaps this was the next natural step.

She jumped as someone bumped into her on their way across the room, then belatedly attempted to look as if she belonged here.

But she didn't. For reasons she couldn't quite articulate, this place made her deeply uncomfortable. No one here was experiencing what was visible, what was heard and seen. They'd chosen to turn inward, to scenes and sensations that couldn't be witnessed from the outside. It meant she had no *idea* what was going on in this place.

Which also meant she needed to find where her mark had gone, and fast.

Hq (visual) | scan (190°:100°) | Hr(Λ) = (parameters (hairHue(#FEE5AC +- 10%), height(195cm +- 4%), weight(75kg +- 6%), faceChar (/img_ ββθθ +- 5% pf)))

Nothing. She moved toward the far side of the room and tried again—

There. He stood at a table beside a man wearing waist-length unbrushed hair and a dirty white t-shirt. A dealer. Were the Plexes dose junkies, too?

She positioned herself where she could see the two men without staring at them and swayed absently to the music. After a minute, the dealer handed over a box full of doses to Sevulch in exchange for a thin film of untraceable credits. Sevulch stuffed the box inside his jacket and headed for the door.

She sucked in a breath and hurriedly adopted a course that would cross his own. Her fingers clenched the tiny tracker dot she'd retrieved from her pants pocket. She bumped into him with her shoulder, much as the patron had done to her by the door. "Sorry, man." She slurred her words a little as she patted him on the arm, pressing the tracker dot onto the fabric of his jacket.

"Whatever." His voice sounded clipped and nasally; he kept going, cutting through the crowd in a straight path for the door.

The dot wouldn't hold for long, but it would be invisible unless he looked directly at it, and it enabled her to pause and create space between her and her mark. She gave him a full thirty seconds before she departed the club as well. The virtual map in her vision told her he'd turned left, and so did she.

Perrin? Are you hanging in there?

I'm good. He went to some weird back-alley club on Macron for a few minutes.

The new ceraff club down there. Trashy place.

There are more of these clubs?

They started popping up a few weeks ago—about two minutes after the ceraffin did. Some are nicer than others.

Well, he bought a bunch of doses off a dealer then left. I'm tracking him now.

That's not a great neighborhood. Why don't you hold back? I can be there in ten minutes.

I thought you were on Kiyora?

I am, but my guy went to a restaurant near the transit hub and ordered a big meal. He's not going anywhere for a while.

She did the math in her head. That still didn't make it possible for him to get here in ten minutes. But she had bigger concerns.

No. I can take care of myself.

Sure, sure. But keep aware. Nobody in that neighborhood is your friend.

She rolled her eyes at Parc telling her how to act in enemy territory, then slowed as the dot on the map stopped moving.

Oh, he's stopped. What's at 182 Basille?

One second. It used to be a barely legal tech shop. Records say it was sold two weeks ago, but there's no new registration yet. Be careful. I'm on the way.

She started to insist he not, but the shadows had grown dark, and few lights illuminated the gaps between them. She shivered, and not from the cold. Still, she forged ahead, driven by purpose and desperation.

Sevulch was nowhere to be seen when she reached the door in question, but his tracker placed him inside. She pulsed the immediate area to get a basic schematic of the building. It returned the outline of an open room on the main floor and stairs down to a basement. Two thermal signatures were downstairs, and the whole structure gave off a higher energy signature than one would expect from a closed-down shop late at night.

Her heart seized. This was it. Adlai was inside.

She paused long enough to send an anonymous message to the district Justice office reporting the sound of screams from the address, then another one to Spencer's comm address reporting seeing Sevulch going into the building carrying weapons. Next she retrieved the slicing module from her pocket. It took her too long—slicing had never been her specialty—but she got the door unlocked. She cringed as it squeaked quietly on opening but slipped inside.

The main room on the first floor sported empty shelves and open boxes scattered across the floor, befitting its alleged former tech shop status. She cautiously moved toward the staircase.

Her Glaser had found its way into her hand, though she didn't recall removing it from her belt. She'd gotten it highly modified and tricked out after Satair's attack on the Pavilion. If she got a chance to take the shot, it would put her target on the floor.

She hurriedly primed all the NOIR combat routines she'd ever installed. One of them calmed her racing heart and flooded her veins with adrenaline, and suddenly she felt like she could take on a ship full of Rasu. One dosed-up man? Easy.

Her shoes were soft-soled and grippy; she was proud of thinking ahead on that one. So long as the stairs didn't squeak like the door had, she should be able to sneak into the basement.

Thudding noises echoed up the stairs as she started down, followed by a muffled voice. Harsh yellow light shone through an open door on the left at the bottom of the stairs.

"—until you fucking accept responsibility for what you did to me."

Four steps left. She raised the Glaser, and the combat routines ensured her hands didn't even shake.

"I...won't...." Adlai's feeble, broken voice drifted out the door and straight into her soul. *Three-two-one* steps and she cleared the door.

Sevulch stood to the right of the doorway, his fingertips on a floating pane. Against the left wall, Adlai was strapped into some sort of torture device, naked, bruised and bleeding.

Sevulch jerked toward her in surprise, then lunged for something on a small table. She shot him through the back of the head.

She barely noticed him collapsing to the floor in her peripheral vision as she dropped the Glaser and ran to Adlai.

His head lolled against his chest, but he struggled to lift it as she reached him. "Pe...Perrin? How?"

"Shh. Don't talk." She wanted to hug him so bad. She ran her hands over him, trying to be gentle so as not to unwittingly cause more damage. Because gods, there was already so much damage. His entire torso was one giant bruise, save for an open slash eight centimeters long across a rib where blood seeped out of mottled, infected flesh. His face was swollen almost beyond recognition, his lips a bloody mess and one eye sealed shut.

She breathed in. She had to be strong. For him. She had to be stronger than she believed she could be. "I need to figure out how to untie you, okay?" She peered up at the restraints cinching his right wrist then retrieved her Glaser and turned the setting way down. "I need to burn this restraint off. I'll try not to singe you."

"I don't…think…won't feel a…thing."

"Even so." She gave him her bravest smile ever, then held the Glaser a few centimeters from the restraint and oh-so-carefully began melting it.

His arm fell away, and his whole body sagged down to the right. His left wrist jerked against its restraint at an impossible angle, and she hurried over to the other side and quickly burned it away—

—Adlai fell into her arms, and she stumbled backward into something solid.

"Let me help."

She jerked in surprise as Parc appeared beside her and took most of Adlai's weight onto himself. She'd never heard him enter…and if he'd instead been another of the Sevulch Plexes, she'd be so screwed right now.

"Thank you. Let's ease him down to the floor. I need to get the ankle restraints, too."

"Yep."

There was nothing to do but lay Adlai at an awkward angle on his stomach, but he didn't seem to care. Perrin crouched by his feet and pressed the Glaser close to the restraints in order to avoid burning his bruised and swollen skin, but in a few seconds he was free.

She and Parc rolled him onto his back, and she leaned over him, gently caressing his cheeks. "Hey, sweetie. You're going to be okay."

"Perrin…." His eyes closed.

Loud noises reverberated from upstairs, followed by shouts. She raised her voice. "Down here! Hurry, please!"

Two Justice dynes clambered down the stairs and raced into the room, and she and Parc held their hands in the air. "Please, help. He's injured very badly."

One of the dynes went to check the body in the corner while the other continued to watch them suspiciously, *not* coming over to help.

More feet sounded—Asterion ones—and Spencer burst through the door, Glaser raised. His gaze swept across the room and back to them as he began issuing orders. "Secure the body over there and check for any other bodies and weapons."

He knelt beside Adlai. "We need a Class I Repair Team at this location stat." His hands roamed over Adlai's injuries. "Perrin, what in the bloody hells are you doing here?"

"Somebody had to rescue him."

"We...." He studied Parc, eyes narrowed, and after a second seemed to place him. "Oh. I see." He sighed and checked Adlai's pulse. "The three of us are going to have a conversation later, one I expect none of us will enjoy. But for now...thank you."

She nodded as the adrenaline evaporated and tears began streaming down her face. "Just take care of him."

43

MIRAI

MIRAI ONE

Nika rushed into the Hataori Renewal Clinic lobby and scanned the room without slowing down. Perrin was curled up in a chair in the far corner; Nika hurried over and dropped to a knee in front of her. "Gods, Perrin, are you okay?"

Her dearest friend peered up at her with tired, bleary eyes. "Nika! I'm fine. Only a few scrapes."

"And Adlai?"

Perrin glanced toward the doors leading to the clinic's treatment facilities. "He's not...great." When her gaze returned to Nika, it had grown dark and troubled. "They tortured him. Strung him up in a rack and abused him for over a week. It was the most awful thing I've ever seen."

"I can't imagine what it must have been like for you." She squeezed Perrin's hand. "Why didn't you ask me to help you find him?"

"You're busy. And you said you were heading to Toki'Taku to brief the Taiyoks on the status of our defenses and to talk to them about Concord."

"I could have *postponed* the trip."

"I know, but you've got so much going on, and it's all so important. I thought I could handle it myself. And I did! I mean, with Parc's help. I saved him."

"You really did." Though her words were upbeat, Nika struggled to force her expression to match them. There might not be any broken bones or open bleeds, but Perrin looked dreadful. She probably hadn't slept more than a few hours since Adlai was kidnapped.

She'd gone toe-to-toe with a crazed torturer, then cradled her lover's broken and beaten body in her arms. "Because you're amazing. Absolutely, no qualifiers amazing. I just wish I'd been there for you. I'm sorry. I've been distracted and...maybe a little impressed with myself and my new allies. I'll try to be a better friend in the future."

Perrin rubbed at her eyes. "Don't be silly. You're looking out for everyone, not solely me. And that's how it should be. Besides, you're here now."

"I am, but I'm going to send you home. You need a shower and a nap and hot food."

"No, I can't leave."

"I swear to you, I will ping you the instant Adlai's awake or the clinic shares any news whatsoever on his condition."

"You'll stay here at the clinic? No, you shouldn't, you have a thousand obligations—"

"I can work remotely for a few hours without straining any diplomatic muscles. Now—oh, here she is." Nika tilted her head toward the entrance, where Maris glided in wearing a soft ivory sweater and tan fitted pants. "Maris is here to take you home. Then she will cook you some real food and get you whatever else in the world you need."

She'd hadn't actually cleared any of this with Maris ahead of time, as they'd both rushed here mostly in the dark about the details of Adlai's condition and Perrin's state. But the woman accepted the pronouncement with her typical grace. "Why, yes I am. Today, I am your handmaiden." Maris reached them and extended an open palm. "Come. You can tell me all about your triumphant heroics on the way."

As Perrin stood, Nika mouthed a silent 'thank you' to Maris, who simply smiled and took Perrin by the arm.

Perrin's brow furrowed in a tight knot. "You'll ping me when you hear something?"

"Anything at all. Now go rest. You did well."

She nodded in weak acceptance, and Maris guided her across the lobby and out the door.

Nika checked in at the reception counter to let the staff know she was now the on-site contact for Adlai. Then she settled into the chair Perrin had vacated, opened several panes and tried to focus on work.

Her contacts in Concord had gone virtually radio silent for the last several days. Something had happened, something she wasn't close enough to the people involved to be informed of or possibly even understand.

This bothered her more than it ought to. She didn't care for being on the outside, cut off from what might be crucial information. At a deeper level, though, it reminded her that while she'd quickly bonded with Alex, Mia and the others, and while being paraded amongst Concord's riches was a heady experience, those burgeoning relationships remained on tenuous, uncertain footing. She needed to be careful not to mistake the natural empathy of skilled diplomacy for authentic interpersonal connections.

A strong alliance with Concord was important to the Dominion's future, but she couldn't lose sight of *why* she sought it—to protect what truly mattered. Her friends, her love, her people, her home.

44

HIRLAS

NARAIDA/VOLUCRI HOMEWORLD
PHOENIX DWARF GALAXY
LGG REGION VI

A gentle, almost delicate rain drifted through the treetops, clinging stubbornly to the canopy of leaves before wafting down onto the funeral attendees in a fine mist.

Alex shivered beside him, despite wearing a deep burgundy turtleneck and black wool pants. Caleb wrapped an arm around her shoulders, and she leaned into him to rest her head in the cradle of his neck.

Hundreds of people filled the vale nestled by forest on two sides and rolling mountains on a third. Naraida mostly, but also several dozen Novoloume and a smattering of other species. Eight Volucri flew in slow, reverential patterns above those gathered, while he spotted others perching within the limbs of the trees that lined the vale.

Richard and Will were here, as well as a few other people Caleb recognized from CINT. The final member of Eren's team, Drae Shonen ela-Machim, hadn't been cleared out of the regenesis lab in time to attend.

But no Eren. Caleb repeatedly sought him out in the crowd, and he'd already caught Alex doing the same several times.

Eren hadn't responded to communications from anyone since he'd left Cosime's body on Akeso and vanished. Everyone was worried about him, but no one more so than Caleb. He'd truly thought Eren would be here. Most of those present held some affection for the woman they gathered together to honor, but Eren had given her his heart. To an outside observer, his absence today would appear to be the height of callousness, but Caleb feared it meant something far, far worse.

As he and Alex walked toward the edge of the crowd, he reached out and grasped a dangling vine, running the pad of his thumb along the jagged leaf edges.

Alive, but no voice.

He let the vine fall by the wayside. *The planet is beautiful and bursting with life, but it's not like you. It doesn't have a beating soul.*

It would take but a single spark generously applied to free its voice.

His mind had become skilled at translating the amorphous thoughts of Akeso into meaningful words, phrases, at times sentences. It made for more natural conversation, if nothing else. He smiled a little. *How would that work?*

All will consider this question.

Alex shot him a perturbed look. "How can you be smiling at a time like this?"

He hurriedly schooled his expression. "Sorry. It's just...Akeso wants to bring Hirlas to life."

"It's a bit late for that now." She increased the space between them, though she kept a hold of his hand.

He didn't need to ask what she meant. If Hirlas were alive, no question the Naraida would have formed an even closer symbiotic bond with it than the one they now enjoyed. Were it alive, this planet might have been able to do what he and Akeso could not.

They settled on the end of a row of attendees near the front. On a raised platform, Cosime's body lay wrapped in loose cloth atop a wicker dais. Blooming flowers of emerald and rose with broad sage leaves encircled the body and trailed down the wicker to the grass.

Her face remained uncovered, her features frozen in a tranquil, serene mien. It bore no resemblance to how she'd looked the other night—

—tendrils of death writhing out to choke off life—

—he squeezed his eyes shut and breathed in through his nose. *Be still. Be at peace. It was an illusion, nothing more.*

Acid burned his throat as he reopened his eyes. He owed it to Cosime, owed it to Eren, to be present here in this moment. Owed it to Alex to not leave her alone with this burden yet again.

Thelkt Lonaervin opened the service with a Novoloume poem about the exquisite beauty of life, even in sorrow. Next, he said many kind words about Cosime, recounting a humorous tale of the first time he met her, then sharing all she'd done for the anarchs and how she'd nearly given her life for their cause time and again.

When he stepped aside, other people Caleb didn't know rose to speak, and the words, sincere and heartfelt as they were, began to blur together.

After the speeches came rituals, distinctly Naraidan in origin. His thoughts returned to the Taenarin rituals invoked at Beshai's funeral; the two species had more than DNA in common. He remembered the contrast of the dramatic, sonorous Khokteh rituals they'd witnessed at Cassela's funeral. Every species had developed their own customs enshrined in history and tradition, liturgies that strove to impart meaning and significance to death for the mourners.

A curtain of tiny leaves fell from the sky, released by the circling Volucri, to coat the body and the dais. When the leaves had settled, the Volucri descended, and as a prayer of sorts was intoned by many of those gathered, they wound their claws around the stilts jutting out of the dais and lifted it into the air. Ever higher, past the treetops, until the procession disappeared into the clouds.

Thelkt had told them of the symbolism involved, originating in ancient Naraidan mythology, and how the body was to be taken to a mausoleum in the mountains, where it would be entombed.

Thelkt returned to the now-empty platform and offered some final parting words, and the ceremony drew to a close.

As the crowd began to mill about, Alex half-turned to him to mutter quietly, "If we're all supposed to be immortal now, how come all we do is go to funerals?"

Dead death sorrowful agony woe we drown beneath its pain—

Black spots swam at the edges of his vision; he pinched the bridge of his nose to force them away. "Fuck immortality. I told you it was nothing but a curse." He gestured haphazardly toward the empty platform, his voice dripping with bitterness. "Welcome to its tribulation."

She flinched away from him, her shoulders jerking and her irises flaring strident platinum beneath falling lashes. Her gaze darted to the forest canopy, and her chest rose in a consequential breath.

"Alex, what is it?"

With the exhale, she returned a gaze to him that had grown uncertain and unexpectedly vulnerable. "Are we okay?"

Though delivered in a whisper, the words ricocheted through the vale to echo in his ears and roil across his mind. The rain, no longer a gentle mist, beat down upon them as if in impassioned grief. His brow furrowed into a rigid line, but he grabbed her hand tight in his. "Come with me?"

She nodded silently, and he guided her away from the crowd. Off to the left, following the natural flow of the flora until they reached a secluded alcove protected by low-hanging limbs of a towering beech tree.

Now he turned to face her and the question written on her features. He brought a fingertip to her chin, then splayed his hand across her jaw. "Everything feels wrong right now—everything except you. You can never feel wrong. I'm sorry. I'm frustrated, I'm conflicted, I can still…taste her death inside me. But I shouldn't have snapped at you. None of this is your fault."

"It's not your fault, either."

"I know."

"Do you, though? When I tell you it isn't, it's as if the words go straight through you, and you drift away until you're a ghost to me. This *isn't your fault*. Just like Solum wasn't your fault—"

His eyes flickered away to nowhere.

"—see? You're gone again. Caleb, I worry we're never going to be okay until you let loose of this self-imposed millstone you're dragging around behind you." Her throat worked. "And I really need for us to be okay."

He grasped her face with both hands and drew her closer, until their foreheads almost touched. "Baby, listen to me, please. Sometimes, like now, you're the only thing that makes sense to me in this world. But you always do. I love you. With everything that I am."

"I know you do."

But she was telling him this wasn't always enough, wasn't she? His lips drifted across the tip of her nose, her eyelids, her cheeks. "I hear you. No ghosting. This wasn't my fault. The scene at home was...horrific and drowned in despair, but nothing I could have done would have made it any less so. Some things can't be fixed. Not even by me."

He pulled back enough to catch her gaze. "Better?"

She nodded against him. "Better. I love you."

His mouth found hers and stayed there, because *this* was his home. His sanctuary and, when everything grew dark, his lifeline. Also because he might not get to hold her again for a while, and he wanted to refresh the imprint on his soul of how she felt in his arms.

The sound of conversation nearby drifted into their alcove. The mourners were dispersing, which meant they probably ought to as well.

He stepped back, letting one of his hands drift down her arm until it reached her hand. "Listen, I want to look for Eren."

She glanced toward the vale. "I haven't seen him anywhere. I don't think he's here."

"He isn't. I mean I want to *look* for him."

"Oh. I understand, but maybe he wants to be alone."

"Doesn't mean he should be. I shudder to think of how he must be suffering. If I..." he closed the distance between them once more to touch her cheek "...if I lost you, I shudder to think of what I might do. To myself, to the world."

"You won't lose me. You basically can't."

"Can't I?"

When the recognition that he wasn't talking about her dying dawned in her eyes, she shook her head. "No, you can't."

"I'll take you at your word for now, but I reserve the right to revisit the subject later, when the world has mended itself. Or possibly when it hasn't. Anyway, I couldn't help him the other night, but I have to believe I can help him now."

"If you find him, you will. He admires you so much."

"Why?"

"Are you kidding?"

He forced a laugh. "Sure. And honestly, finding him may well be the hardest part. I thought I'd talk to Thelkt before he leaves. And Felzeor, obviously. Damn, I treated him like shit that night—and don't say I didn't."

"I won't, but Felzeor understands. Everyone...except Eren...understands. And Eren is in another place right now."

"Which is why I need to find him. To drag him out of that place and back into the light."

"Do you want me to come with you?"

"Do you want to come with me?"

She stared at him oddly. "Of *course* I do."

"But?"

"But..." she took up meandering around the tiny alcove "...it feels as if our mostly halcyonic empire is revving up to spin out of control. I've lit a lot of fires recently—the Asterions, the Rasu, adiamene and Reor, and now the Savrakaths are lighting their own fire in our backyard—and it doesn't seem right to walk away and leave them unattended.

"Also, now I have the Noesis banging around in my head, shooting me all these lunatic ideas about how to combat the Rasu, and I need to sift through them and try to figure out what could actually be feasible and...I don't know, make a damn list then show it to someone." She dragged a hand through her hair. "Does any of that make sense?"

He gave her his most convincing smile, because she was making the correct decision. Not to mention making a mature, unselfish decision to take responsibility for the whirlwinds that inevitably spun out in her wake. "It does, and I agree. You can't let everything we've worked for go to waste. But I can't let this go, either. He's my friend."

"Nor should you. He's *our* friend, and he desperately needs saving. I wish I didn't have to send you off to do it alone."

He stepped out from beneath the protective canopy of the alcove and eyed the sky, where several Volucri soared above the vale. "I'm not sure I will be alone."

Then he reached for her, hugging her tight against his chest. "I'll let you know what I find out and where I'm headed. And Alex?"

The crush of her lips on his silenced him. "Shh. We'll be okay."

45

LETHE

MILKY WAY GALAXY

The strobing lights flashed straight through Eren's pupils and directly into his brain. Neurons flared in offense then shorted out in little pinpricks of pain. The thrumming beat of the 'music' tormented his eardrums, though they put up a braver fight against the onslaught.

He staggered away from the angry lights and angrier music to flee down a narrow, nameless street. With every stumbling step, the assault receded. It was darker here. Quieter. Also more dangerous, which he wouldn't give a shit about but for the fact that he had one last mission to complete before he surrendered to oblivion forever.

He forced one foot in front of the other for her memory, kept a blade ready in his left hand for her love.

One hundred eleven years had passed since he'd last visited this particular corner of the second-shadiest city on Lethe, and the shop was still located beneath a dingy awning decorated in a puke orange dragon/monster caricature. He ignored two thugs giving him carnivorous leers to shove through the door and inside.

The store owner was closing the deal with a customer, but he did a double-take on seeing Eren. His attention wavered then returned to his customer, and Eren sagged against the wall to wait.

His mind drifted in out of lucidity. In and out of nightmares of blood and flames—he fled for bliss, sunny beaches and glistening skin and glittering emerald irises. He clung ferociously to the illusion, but it always slithered through his fingers and out of reach—

"I remember you, though I didn't expect to ever see you again. To be honest, I assumed you fried your brain out and died a hundred years ago."

"Nooope." He lurched forward and dropped his elbows on the counter. "You did right by me, helping me burn out my integral. I went on to become a mighty and famous anarch, you know. Brought down that Directorate, yes I did. *Nos libertatem* fucking *somnia.*"

"All by yourself?"

"Well...." His eyes drifted closed and his head lolled—he jerked back to awareness. "A magnificent Naraida woman helped me."

"I see." The Erevna man—he hadn't gotten a name on his first visit and didn't want one now—nodded thoughtfully. "You won't hear many Anadens saying this aloud, but I appreciate what the anarchs did."

"Good, 'cause now I need you to do right by me again."

"If you don't mind me saying, you don't seem to be lacking in the hypnol department. Not sure what else I can offer you and less sure I should. You don't look good."

"Well, the brightest star in the universe just blinked out, so I wouldn't. I need...." He tried to meet the man's gaze, but it jerked across his vision like a Dankath trying to dance. He frowned and brushed hair out of his face. Greasy, filthy, alcohol-and-tear-soaked hair. A strand clung to his cheek, insinuating his skin, too, was damp. Sweaty and hot. He shoved the strand back until it stuck to other locks. "I need *dialele.* Five units of it."

The man stepped away from the counter and lifted his hands as if he were surrendering to a robbery. "*Dialele* isn't street legal, even here."

"The Hades does that matter? I can pay." He fumbled around in his pouch and tossed a platinum-laced thin film on the counter.

The man stared at it for several seconds, greed flickering hungrily in his eyes. Then he sighed. "Believe it or not, I do have a tiny nugget of a conscience, way down low in the back of my brain. You look like shit took a dump and rolled you around in it. I can't sell you anything in this state. Why don't you rent a room across the street and sleep this bad trip off. In the morning, you'll realize you were foolish to think you wanted anything from me."

Eren leaned over the counter with a growl, triggering a rush of vertigo. "I know godsdamn fucking well what I'm doing and what I need. And what I need is *dialele.*"

"It has a thirty percent failure rate on every dose. Do you understand what failure means with *dialele?* It drives you insane. You start tearing into your skin, cutting, biting, whatever you can manage to try to flay yourself alive. Eventually, somebody will put you down for a regenesis, but it's not a good time until then."

That wasn't going to be his fate, mostly because he'd already corrupted his link to the CINT regenesis data banks. When he checked out on life this time, it would be the last time. "I'll take those odds. Now put five vials on the counter."

The man cast a glance to the ceiling then went into the back of the shop, returning a minute later with a small, plain box. He reached under the counter and retrieved a second, smaller box. "If you somehow survive these doses with your mind intact, coming off *dialele* is one hellacious beast. This *immade* here will take the edge off and ease you out of it. A little." He paused. "The *immade* is on the house."

Eren grunted, shoved the thin film toward the man, snatched the two boxes up and wrapped his arms around them, and left the shop.

When the two thugs outside tried to rob him a minute later, he sliced open their guts and left them on the street to bleed.

RW

Dialele was, at its base, a potent alacrity drug. It sharpened the senses and mental concentration to a savant level. Physical reflexes naturally followed from the enhancements. It was the drug of choice for assassins, especially snipers, for so long as they survived it. The insanity rate wasn't anywhere near thirty percent if you took it correctly. Closer to eighteen percent. Mercenaries rarely took it correctly, hence its lousy street reputation.

One of the non-lethal side effects of *dialele* was an extreme dulling of emotional responsiveness. Empathy, affection, happiness...grief, depression, despair? They all flat-lined when one was on *dialele.*

This wasn't actually why Eren was taking the hypnol. No, really, it wasn't. Okay, it *was,* but only because he had no choice but to become an automaton in order to complete his mission. After it was done, none of this mattered, and he'd drown in an avalanche of grief all the way to his death. But he had to set aside his mourning for a few short days. Long enough to see justice served by his hand.

He dragged himself into the dingy hotel room, dropped his bag on the floor and kept going until he reached the spartan bathroom, where he tossed the boxes on the browning porcelain shelf. As he did, he accidentally caught a glimpse of himself in the smudged mirror. Red veins popped out of his eyes like rivers of blood. His skin glistened with hypnol-induced sweat, and the left half of his hair was one giant matted knot. Brown stains dotted the neck of his shirt, and he couldn't begin to guess what had created them.

The wretched sight seemed about right. He lowered his gaze to the counter shelf and concentrated on steadying his shaking hands long enough to get the larger box open. Inside it sat five vials of a rust-colored liquid and one injector.

He took one of the vials and tried to fit it in the injector. His fingers slipped, and the vial rolled to the edge of the shelf and teetered—

—he barely managed to get his hands beneath it in time and caught the vial as it fell.

"Arae!" Eren grabbed for the vial of charist *as it tumbled through the air toward a terrible fate. He succeeded in rescuing it, but doing so caused the* ferusom *to slip from his grasp and shatter on the hard floor.*

"Gods, Eren." Cosime hurried into his room and knelt beside him. "I'm sorry, I didn't mean to startle you."

He shrank away from her, pressing against the bureau while he remained focused on the floor. "Go away, Cosime."

"No. What's wrong?" Her voice dropped as she finally took in the full state of his room. "Are these all hypnols?"

"Just go. Leave me, please."

"What is—"

"Permanently, in fact. You don't want to be around me any longer. I'll poison your life." A glint of light flashed off to his left; it was reflecting off the vial of laevona that had rolled under the bureau. He retrieved it and hurriedly turned it up, dumping the contents onto his tongue unfiltered.

There. Soon enough he wouldn't even be aware of her bright emerald eyes gazing at him in naïve concern. She didn't know, and soon he wouldn't care.

She reached out and snatched the vial away while it was still a third full.

He shot her a glare and grabbed at her hand, but she held it out of the way. "I think I get to decide if I want to be around you."

"Don't be stupid. Leave and don't look back."

"Dammit, Eren! You're going to overdose if you keep this up."

He smiled vaguely as his vision blurred and he slumped farther down, closer to the floor. "Good. The point."

The sliding whoosh of the door closing sounded echoey and distant. It took a long time to close. Minutes, probably.

Sometime later she appeared beside his head, sitting with her legs wound beneath her among the spilt hypnols and random stains of blood. Her hands took hold of his shoulders. She guided his head into her lap. Soft fingers coaxed sticky strands of hair out of his face.

Glittering eyes stared down at him. Infinite facets reflected emerald light over and over and over…. "Let me help you."

He shook his head, he thought. "Can't. I'm a fiend, Cosime, fit for Tartarus. You should run."

"No, you're not, Eren. You're a good man with a few occasionally fiendish tendencies."

"What? Why do you…?" He squinted up at her, but it didn't help bring her features into focus.

"You think I don't know you have a dark side? In that case, you're also a very silly man." She bent down and kissed his forehead. *"My dear, sweet, mad, broken Eren."*

He touched his fingers to his lips and closed his eyes, letting the image of her fill his mind. "I'll be back for you soon, my love."

He jammed the vial into the injector and the injector into his neck, then stumbled out of the bathroom and fell across the bed as unconsciousness consumed him.

RW

Eren's eyes snapped open. He took in the grimy beige walls, the coarse bed linens, the putrid yellow light embedded in the creases. Noted. He breathed in, making certain his lungs functioned, then swung his legs off the bed and strode into the lavatory.

First things first. He removed the trimmers he'd bought from their case, held his hair back from his face, and without hesitation began cutting.

Ten minutes later, a lion's mane lay scattered on the floor around his feet. One tactical weakness that would not impede him any further.

Next, he stepped in the shower stall to scrub days of grime and sweat and filth off his skin. He checked the medical tape over his ribs to make certain it remained secure, trimmed his fingernails and toenails and washed his mouth out with scalding alcohol.

Once he'd finished cleaning himself up, he unpacked his bag and spread the contents out on the bed. He'd called himself collecting the tools he'd need for the mission ahead of time, but his grief-and-hypnol-addled brain had done a piss-poor job of it. He made a list of additional gear he required. Most of it he could acquire in the black-market district here, but he might have to make an additional stop or two. Quickly, because the clock was ticking.

He returned the few useful items to the bag and tossed the rest down the garbage chute. Then he retrieved the two boxes of hypnols from the bathroom, added them to the bag and left the room behind.

46

SAVRAK STELLAR SYSTEM

MACHIM IMPERIUM DELTA

C asmir stood at the captain's perch of Torval's Imperium. The Savrakath patrol currently ranked as the highest priority duty assignment in the Concord Armed Forces, and with Torval's arrest, Casmir had stepped in to cover it. He'd met no resistance since taking command of the Imperium, for Machim officers were bred to obey one of higher rank. Still, he kept on cautious guard. Torval was a dissident and a mutineer, and he may well have inspired others serving under him to take up his cause.

Given patrolling this region of space did not constitute his job, Casmir needed to promote someone to replace Torval. But how? *Elassons* and *elassons* alone commanded Imperiums and bore the rank of Navarchos. All the other *elassons* already commanded their own ships, and now was hardly the ideal time to retire such a powerful warship. Not with the Savrakaths provoking war and dire warnings of a yet more formidable foe approaching from the void.

The Humans promoted servicepeople through a system of meritocracy coupled with experience, as well as small helpings of nepotism and favoritism. The fact that a Human's role—their career and their station within it—did not originate from their genetic makeup had been made crystal clear in the last fourteen years, and emulating this practice should be a simple enough matter. But the Machim Dynasty remained stubbornly unable to adapt.

Did some officers perform their responsibilities with greater skill than others? Yes. Undoubtedly. Those who did so saw the genetic patterns believed to have produced such performance fortified on their next regenesis. After sufficient generations of precise genetic honing, they might be considered for elevation from *ela* to *elasson*.

Only the Machim Primor had ever awarded such elevations, however, and he was dead, his regenesis backups obliterated. Did it fall to Casmir to make those decisions now? To all the *elassons* as a group? By majority vote, or unanimity? Why had these questions not been answered?

Because no one existed to answer them. Every Anaden had spent these last years stumbling through a new reality no amount of genetic refinement had prepared them for: figuring out how to live without their integrals. Figuring out who they were...and at times who they were not.

The Directorate had left behind no script for them to follow. Casmir recognized that if he were not careful, he would still be standing on the captain's perch of this Imperium in a decade, merely through his own inaction.

But he'd been promoted to first among equals because fourteen years ago, he had *acted*. The capacity to do so again must lie within him.

"Navarchos, we are detecting multiple vessels departing orbit around Savrak. Initial analysis suggests they are adopting an intercept course."

He didn't acknowledge the XO directly, instead speaking the order with the understanding it would be followed. "Maintain our heading. All ships go to Threat Alert Orange."

In this respect, no decision need be made, for his orders from Command were explicit. He was to patrol the borders of the Savrak stellar system as normal and not take any action to provoke the Savrakath military. If attacked, however, he and his regiment were authorized to defend themselves to the fullest extent required.

The Savrakath fleet executed a superluminal jump to emerge barely ten megameters from the regiment's location.

"All ships go to Threat Alert Red. Move to a Sigma Five engagement plan."

The details of the approaching fleet populated a screen at his perch. A large formation, some twenty-two hundred ships, but his formation was larger. Machim formations were always larger than those of the opponent. The outcome of the coming battle was a foregone conclusion, so much so he questioned why the Savrakaths insisted on initiating it. The lizards were aggressive and prideful, though, and apparently that was reason enough.

"Sir, I've got multiple readings centered at S 68° 20° z E, eight megameters distance—the location of the Savrakath dreadnought. Suspected missile launch."

So be it. "Launch interceptors. All ships, you are weapons free."

The interceptors from the Imperium met the missiles 1.5 megameters out—

—the bridge jerked violently, sending Casmir to the floor. His head cracked against the corner of his perch, sending bolts of pain shooting through his skull and radiating down his spine. His vision swam beneath a shrill ringing in his ears.

He blinked and grabbed the vertical pole of the perch railing. Shouts and cries began to penetrate the ringing as he hauled himself to his feet. A hand went to the top of his head and came back bloody.

"Report!"

No one responded for several seconds, for confusion reigned on the bridge. Imperiums did not take hits, not from ordinary weapons. An impermeable shield prevented any missiles or weapons fire from ever reaching the vessel. And yet.

"Report, dammit!"

The XO struggled to get his screens to respond. "The outer shield took a massive energy surge and went offline for 3.2 seconds. The inner shield held, and the hull hasn't suffered any damage."

Casmir tossed an arm toward the rampart disarray on the bridge. "Then what the hells is this?"

"The shockwave, sir. The energy had to go somewhere."

He started to retort when alarms began cascading down his regiment status screen. He leaned in close and squinted to read it since his vision hadn't resolved to clarity. "Impossible."

"Sir?"

"We've lost contact with twenty-two percent of the regiment."

"Confirming. Initial scans, where they're coming in, indicate numerous ships were destroyed in the energy surge."

Casmir rubbed at his temples. His cybernetics should have suppressed this throbbing headache by now. "They were antimatter missiles."

The XO stared at him for too long before nodding. "A reasonable conclusion, sir. It's likely any antimatter that reached our outer shield resulted in a further energetic reaction."

"All ships, all weapons, fire on the Savrakath dreadnought." He hoped like hells someone remained conscious at the weapons station of the Imperium to execute on the order.

It took another five seconds, but the vessel's powerful lasers burned through the debris field separating them and the Savrakath fleet. Were any of the enemy vessels taken out by the antimatter explosions? No...this was why they were holding back a full eight megameters.

"All vessels, increase speed and close on the enemy fleet—"

"Missile launch!"

Casmir gritted his teeth. "Increase. Speed." He stood to lose most of the regiment with the gambit, but he intended to do everything possible to take the Savrakath fleet out with them.

"Sir, the—"

The bridge lurched thirty degrees to starboard. Casmir was ready this time and had grabbed the railing with both hands, since the captain's chair didn't come equipped with a harness. No Imperium captain had ever needed one.

His right hip slammed into the railing, and it felt as if his brain jostled around in his pounding head, but he stayed on his feet. "Report."

The XO had similarly braced himself, and he was already scanning a cascade of information flowing in. "We've lost another thirty-one percent of the fleet. The explosions occurred closer this time."

Casmir waved off the justification. "What about the dreadnought? It should be in pieces now."

"Um..." the XO frowned "...scans cannot locate the Savrakath dreadnought."

"Perhaps the pieces are too small to register on scans."

"Or any other Savrakath vessels. Sir, it appears they've retreated."

"Cowards."

It might be the headache and the blood loss, but right now Torval's arguments regarding the Savrakaths were making a great deal of sense. The urge to take the Imperium straight into the Savrak atmosphere and blast its capital city into dust was strong indeed.

He grimaced against the persistent throbbing in his skull. But this manner of thinking had driven his Primor to madness. Vengeance would be served, but it would arrive coldly, logically and with unstoppable force.

"Order two reconnaissance squadrons to patrol the system and report any movements of Savrakath forces. Set a course for Concord HQ."

CONCORD HQ

COMMAND

"You're certain they fired antimatter missiles at your fleet."

"Yes, Commandant. Analysis of the composition of the debris field confirmed a strong concentration of neutrinos throughout the field as well as pervasive gamma-ray radiation."

Miriam steepled her hands at her chin. "And the Savrakaths fired first?"

Casmir jerked as if insulted. "Yes. I assure you, we strictly followed the rules of engagement."

"I'm confident you did." Damnable aliens! Did they not appreciate the herculean efforts she had exerted in order to save them from themselves?

For a moment she considered, more seriously than she was proud of, contacting Lakhes and asking them to 'clean up' a problem the Kats had created, just as David had speculatively suggested. But she couldn't do it. The Savrakaths would be defenseless against a surprise superdreadnought assault. Well, unless they had a thousand antimatter missiles ready to deploy, which...she shuddered. All the more reason to address the problem head-on.

The Savrakaths had willfully violated the terms Concord had delivered, and she had a duty to protect trillions of innocent Concord citizens from their aggression.

Some of us must be brutally ruthless if it's required to protect those we love. Warfare never had been for the faint of heart.

"Commandant?"

She looked up to find Casmir waiting with increasing impatience for some further orders from her. She obliged him. "The Savrakaths will be red-flagged, effective immediately. The Imperium involved in the battle is undergoing repairs at present. You are to take command of the newest Imperium when it leaves the Section 31 Fabrication Center tomorrow. You will lead the II-1C, IV-3A and V-2D Regiments and institute a blockade of Savrak. Not merely the stellar system, but the planet itself. Let them see the shadows of our ships when they gaze up at the sky."

"But Commandant, if they deploy additional antimatter weapons...."

"In executing on this blockade, unrestricted Dimensional Rifter use is authorized."

Casmir's eyes widened, breaking his usual rigid demeanor. "Doing so risks missiles emerging from a rift inside the planetary atmosphere."

Of course it did. Dimensional Rifters tore a hole in the fabric of space, but not forever. Objects and energy that fell into the tear eventually emerged back into normal space. The formulas for determining where a given object or energy would do so were astoundingly complex, but they could be calculated by an Artificial—but rarely in the time between a weapon being fired and the captain of a ship needing to decide whether to activate a Rifter to deflect it.

"They picked this fight. They built and deployed antimatter weapons knowing full well their destructive capabilities. If they insist on firing them, they can face the consequences of doing so."

Casmir sank back in the chair. "Yes, Commandant. I understand. It's the right decision."

"I wonder. But right or no, it's the only decision I can make. Keep me apprised of any activity on the Savrakaths' part. Dismissed."

CINT

Miriam knocked on the open door frame of Richard's office.

Perhaps reading her expression, gave her a sympathetic smile and motioned her inside. "Bad day?"

"Challenging one." She sat in one of the guest chairs and folded her hands in her lap. "The Savrakaths are fielding working antimatter missiles."

"But we destroyed the lab."

"I know."

He dragged a hand roughly across his jaw. "No completed missiles ever left that facility—which means they're operating more labs hidden elsewhere. Labs that were further along in weapons development than the one we destroyed."

"It would seem so."

"Dammit!" His fist hit the top of his desk with a thud. "So Cosime died for nothing."

"Cosime died because Torval elasson-Machim is a criminal and a murderer. The destruction of the facility was still justified."

He scratched at his forehead and blew out a heavy breath. "I'll concede the point, but...dammit. We should have realized the extent of their weapons production."

"They've spent the last several months working very hard to hide much of what transpires on their world from us."

"True enough." He straightened his shoulders to reimpose order. "Okay. We need to find the other facilities."

"We do. Are the first Ghosts ready for deployment?"

"The ships have been cleared. The pilots are continuing to train, but four of them have passed all the certifications."

"Good. In that case, I'm authorizing a Ghost squad infiltration mission. Send them in with orders to scour every centimeter of every Savrakath planet, moon and space station until they have located every facility that so much as smells of a single antimatter particle."

"And once we find them all? What then?"

"Seeing as we're now at war, the need for discretion no longer applies. I'm thinking I'll let Casmir blow them up."

47

MIRAI

RIDANI ENTERPRISES

I'*m forwarding a set of files I received from Alex. Apparently, they're for you. I'm still at the clinic—no updates yet—but I'll see you in a few hours.*
— *Nika*

The relief Dashiel felt over Adlai being found couldn't be overstated, but now it competed with worry over his friend's physical and, once he woke up, psychological condition. No one deserved to be relentlessly tortured for days, but Adlai deserved it least of them all. Dashiel had never known a more earnest, sincere and forthright person. Not even Nika. He hoped they locked the perpetrator up for several eternities.

But with Adlai now in the care of capable professionals, for the first time in a week he believed he could actually get some work done. The files requiring his attention were stacked high, but instead of turning to them, he opened the ones attached to Nika's message.

They weren't in a format used in the Dominion, and he had to dig up a couple of translation routines to convert them into a readable format. Once that was done, Dashiel opened the file titled 'Overview.'

> *To Whom It May Concern,*
> *If ever asked, it would be fantastic if you said you never received these files. Or received them from an anonymous sender*

whom, despite the most exhaustive of efforts, could never be tracked down. Which might even be true! One can dream. But I digress.

I'm sending you this information because some of us believe the Asterions deserve every chance we can provide to defend themselves. Also because we despise bureaucracy and government over-regulation—but that's a whole other topic.

I am told you possess the knowledge and experience to understand the schem flows and formulas contained herein, so I will assume you do. No, it shouldn't work. Yes, it does. No, it isn't necromancy. Yes, it is as resilient and adaptive as promised. I've included scads of testing data, but I suspect you won't be convinced until you run your own tests. Please do so.

If you have questions or concerns...I'm afraid I can't help you with them. We can't be communicating back and forth like pen pals. Not at this time. Perhaps later.

So, in closing, I guess all I can say is...good luck! Kick the Rasu's asses!

The letter wasn't signed, which considering its content and tone, wasn't surprising.

Dashiel sank back in his chair and pondered the odd note for a moment. He had a good inkling as to its source, but barring unexpected complications he was fine with respecting their privacy.

Curiosity piqued, he opened the rest of the files.

RW

"So, this is why you missed lunch."

Dashiel looked up, startled to see Nika leaning in the doorway of his office. "Shit. I'm sorry. I lost track of time."

"Clearly." She came around the desk, kissed his neck and began massaging his shoulders.

They had grown tense and stiff from hours of concentration, and he moaned in pleasure. "How's Adlai?"

"He woke up long enough to refuse a regen. So he'll be in a tank for a while. Perrin came back to the clinic looking refreshed enough that I let her chase me out." She leaned in over his left shoulder to peer at the bank of panes arrayed in front of him. "Are these the files Alex sent?"

"Mm-hmm. I don't think they originated from her, though, unless she happens to be an accomplished materials engineer in her spare time. More likely Ms. Rossi, seeing as these are detailed instructions on how to manufacture their adiamene metal."

"But Concord refused to...*oh*." Nika chuckled. "I guess Alex really doesn't play by the rules, and her friends don't either. For which I am most appreciative. So, can we make it?"

He nodded as her hands moved to his neck with a gentle touch. "I think so. Vance is setting up a run on the prototype line at the plant in Mirai Two. He'll make a few meters' worth of it, then we'll subject it to every stress test ever invented, because there is simply no way it can be as resilient as these documents claim."

"They've outfitted tens of millions of ships using it while guarding its secrets with high-powered weapons. I doubt they'd go to such extremes if it didn't perform as advertised."

"I'm not saying it's not extremely durable. But nothing is *this* durable."

"Well, when will you know?"

"In around eight hours. So, how about a very, very late lunch? Want to go to *Komoko* for some noodles?"

She reached in her bag and retrieved a wrapped package, then handed it to him. "Can't. We're expected at the Initiative in twenty minutes."

"The concealment shielding. Right." He unwrapped the package to find a hot turkey and cheese sandwich. "I'll eat on the way."

RW

OMOIKANE INITIATIVE

With the entire top floor of the Pavilion taken up by the Initiative offices, the team members had converted a large conference room on the fifth floor to the control center for the planetary shielding program, dubbed 'Project Shirudo.' The equipment used to deploy and maintain the shield was located elsewhere, of course. Mostly in space, but also at multiple top-secret facilities far from any city.

They walked in to find Parc scurrying between three large control panes, typing in commands while he muttered to himself under his breath. Every few seconds his voice rose enough to bark an order at one of the two techs seated at a long row of equipment.

Lance stood in the corner of the room, his arms crossed tight over his chest as he scowled mercilessly at Parc.

Nika went over to calm Lance down. "This is just how he works. No need to worry."

"I know. Doesn't mean I have to care for it. There's no rigor, no discipline, no *order*. I should have had my division take charge of the project from the beginning."

"Then there wouldn't be any project to activate today!" Parc shouted over his shoulder without breaking his typing stride.

"He's probably right. Not to disparage what I'm sure are talented developers in the Military Division, but he's that good."

Lance grunted in response, and she gave up trying to mollify him, instead going to stand next to Dashiel behind the techs.

Abruptly Parc spun around to address the room. He took a deep, dramatic breath. "Today we will be activating the shield over Mirai for one hour, during which time probes both inside and outside the shield will take a plethora of readings. Then we will deactivate it and analyze those readings, because *someone* insists on being worried about negative atmospheric effects."

Dashiel made a face. "It's a valid concern. A planetary atmosphere is an incredibly complex ecosystem, even before you factor in the stellar interactions."

"But the shield is simply electromagnetic waves."

"So is sunlight, which we'd very much like to continue to receive down here on the surface."

Parc made a show of exhaling. "Fine, fine, fine. We'll measure and test. But it's going to work perfectly. Watch and see."

Nika smiled. "That's what we're here to do. Show us what everyone working on Shirudo has created."

"You got it." Parc spun around and lifted a hand high above his head, then twirled it forward and lightly tapped a button on his center pane. "Voilà, my friends."

Nika peered out the window behind her, craning her neck to gaze up at the sky. Cirrus clouds drifted by against a powder-blue sky. "Is it active?"

"See for yourself."

She reluctantly turned from the window, and found a sea of mostly green graphs spitting out data across the panes. "Those look positive."

"No, *this* looks positive." Parc instantiated a new pane in front of him. It displayed a basic tableau of stars, with no distinguishing features.

"Where's that from?"

"The view from one of the probes orbiting Mirai. Its cameras are pointed inward."

"You're kidding. It doesn't seem possible."

Parc shot her a smug smirk. "You need to expand your mind a little. Qualitatively, it's no different from a kamero filter, or the stealth device on the *Wayfarer*. It merely takes a hells of a lot more power and equipment to generate."

Dashiel rolled his eyes beside her. "*So* much more power and equipment."

Lance tried to continue sounding gruff, but he wasn't scowling any longer. "We'll see how the readings come back."

"They're going to come back in the green." Parc flourished a hand toward the panes. "This is *working*."

Nika acted dutifully impressed, but an unexpected wistfulness trailed through her mind. She didn't like the thought of hiding. Not because it was cowardly, but rather because it didn't solve the crisis, only delayed it. But until they were strong enough to overcome the Rasu, delaying a confrontation was the most logical choice they could make.

48

MIRAI

MIRAI ONE

Perrin scooted her chair closer to the tank and pressed her hand against the glass. After a few seconds, Adlai's fingertips pressed against the other side. It was as close to touching as they were able to manage for the time being.

She smiled, then brighter as he tried to return the gesture around the tube in his mouth. He looked so silly that she bit her lower lip to keep from giggling. That simple act tired him, though, and his eyes drifted closed once again.

He spent more time asleep than awake in the tank, by design. But she was here for the moments when he awoke, so he would know he wasn't alone.

She yawned and checked the time. Another sixteen hours before they'd consider releasing him from the tank, the med tech had said. Maybe she'd have someone from the Pavilion bring her a sandwich. And energy drinks. Lots and lots of energy drinks. She'd caught a couple of hours of sleep at his apartment under Maris' watchful gaze, but she'd racked up a staggering deficit in the last week.

A rapping sound to her left jerked her out of the reverie, and she glanced over to see Parc lounging on the door frame. "How's he doing?"

"Barely a third of the way through the repair cycle. The med techs tried to get him to retire the body and do a fresh regen, but he refused. He said he wanted to wear these scars."

Parc frowned. "There won't actually be any...."

"No. I assume he was being metaphorical." She chuckled briefly. "What's up? How'd your shield test go?"

"Perfectly, exactly as I foresaw. I wanted to stop by and see if all was well in your world now before I headed home to crash. I had an *awesome* meeting with Spencer a few hours ago."

"Ouch. I haven't yet had the pleasure. What's the verdict?"

"In exchange for no charges being filed against me for any alleged conspiracy to breach Justice data banks, I agreed to upgrade his personal security system so it won't be sliceable by a Chizeru toddler with a screwdriver from now on. And possibly to consult on further security upgrades to the Justice servers."

"Does he know about the Plexes?"

"Oh, yes. Ian Sevulch lying dead in a basement in Mirai One while also having a seizure at *Ellison* in Kiyora Two was kind of a giveaway. I imagine there will soon be all-Advisor meetings with copious wringing of hands as they try to figure out what to do about them. More worrisome, though, is that one of the Justice ceraffin has apparently devised a way around morph disguises."

"Ooh, I'm glad we don't need to use them any longer."

"Lucky for you if *you* don't, but I'm going to need to rethink some of my life choices."

She nodded thoughtfully. "Like how you're a Plex? Does Ryan know?"

Parc stared at her for several seconds...then huffed a wry laugh. "Maybe he's one, too."

"Is he?"

Parc's face fell. "No, he is not."

"How's it going over with him?"

"Well, it went over superbly the first mind-blowing night, let me tell you. But in the morning light..." he scratched at his nose, possibly to hide any telltale angst in his eyes "...yeah. I don't know."

"Is this why he wasn't at the warehouse when I came by?"

"Not technically, but he has been scarce of late. Ryan's a stubborn man, but I'm trying to bring him around."

369 | G.S. JENNSEN

"I'm sure it'll work out." She wasn't sure, not in the slightest. It didn't take much musing to conjure a long list of complications having multiple copies of one's lover out in the world would bring.

"We'll see." He cleared his throat. "How did you figure it out?"

"Come on, Parc. People are what I do."

"Granted, but I'm still me, whichever one I happen to be."

"True." She sighed and cracked her neck; weariness made her bones feel stiff and achy. "But you were on Namino shopping for tools, then on Kiyora surveilling Sevulch, then on Mirai helping me, all seemingly at the same time, and all while you were prepping for a crucial test run of Project Shirudo. You're damn good, but even you can't be in four places at once—unless you can be. Plus, you knew way too much about Plexes to be an idle observer of the phenomenon. And finally, when have you ever merely been an idle observer of any new tech phenomenon?"

He studied the ceiling for a minute. "Okay, that's fair. You're not planning to mention this little detail to anyone else, are you? Such as, say, Spencer, or your guy here when he wakes up for real, or Nika?"

She hesitated, then remembered again how epically he had helped her these last few days. She shook her head. "You helped me—helped Adlai—more than I can ever repay. So it's between us."

She stood and took his hands in hers. "Thank you. Thank you so damn much for everything. Let me know if you want me to talk to Ryan for you."

"Will you tell him how badass and amazing I am?"

"I suspect he already realizes it, but absolutely."

"Then I might take you up on that."

He started to go, but paused when she called out after him. "Out of curiosity, how many of 'you' are there?"

He just flashed her a wicked grin, turned and left.

49

CONCORD HQ

Mia waved Marlee into her office, then stood and went over to the paired couches on the left side of her office. "Sit with me. I'm about to head to the—"

Marlee squared her shoulders and stood purposefully in the middle of the office. She'd rehearsed her speech all morning, and she would not be denied the chance to deliver it. "Before we discuss whatever you have in mind, I have a proposition to put forth."

Mia studied her speculatively before clasping her hands at her knees. "All right. Tell me about it."

Whew. "Now that we're for all intents and purposes at war with the Savrakaths—now that we have no formal diplomatic relations with them—I believe long-recognized international law regarding humanitarian aid, going back to ancient Aurora history, now applies. Under these traditions, which again, hold the force of law, we can rescue the Godjans."

"*Rescue* them?"

"There are tons of historical precedents for it. I'm sending you a cross-referenced and fully annotated report now. This is a proper act during a time of war. And it's our moral duty to do so."

"Marlee, there are more than a million Godjans on Savrak. We can't rescue them all."

"We can try."

Mia interlaced her fingers and brought them to her chin. "How is Vaihe adjusting to her new life on Seneca?"

"She's still very timid and subservient, but her curiosity is gradually winning out—ha. Nice try distracting me. You know I'm right."

"What I know is that you are stubborn. Very well, I'll review your report. If I agree with your findings, I'll speak to Director Navick about putting together some mission scenarios while we're gone. We'll see what we can do, but no guarantees."

"While we're gone?"

"Yes. I want you to come with me on an official visit to the Asterion Dominion."

"Why are you going now? I mean, Gramps just got back."

Mia gestured again to the couch. "Please, sit."

Marlee's eyes narrowed, but she relented and perched on the edge of one of the cushions.

"This is confidential information, understand? You're obligated under your employment contract with the Consulate not to share it with anyone."

"I understand." She drew two fingers across her lips as a tingle warmed her chest. Clandestine matters were afoot! "All sealed up."

"Ensure they stay that way. The unofficial decision has been made to escalate our relationship with the Dominion. They face a grave threat in the Rasu, but the Rasu will soon threaten us as well. It's in our interest to support the Dominion in its fight against them. And, much as you pointed out with respect to the Godjans, it's our moral duty to do so."

So she'd won Mia over on the Godjans. Yes! "Unofficial? You mean you and Aunt Miriam have decided to help them, but you haven't asked the Senate for formal approval of an alliance yet."

"Commandant Solovy. This is work, Marlee."

"Right, sorry. You and *Commandant Solovy* have decided to help them. Gramps must've said the Asterions can't defend themselves on their own."

"There is a reason you work here. Either your instincts are spot-on, or you've bugged our offices."

"Or both."

Mia sighed. "I'm going to pretend I didn't hear you—then have CINT sweep my office for bugs."

"If you must. So we're visiting to accelerate the creation of formal ties between Concord and the Dominion and jump-start providing the help they need."

"That's my intent, yes. I do plan to raise the issue with the Senate before we leave, but the visit will occur no matter the outcome of the discussion."

This was why she enjoyed working here. Once Mia decided something was going to happen, it got done—which also boded well for the Godjans. "Why are you taking me?"

"You haven't had any interactions with Asterions yet, correct?"

She shook her head. "I've reviewed all the information we've collected on them and watched the recordings from their official meetings here. I mean, the ones I was granted access to. But not in person, no. Much to my disappointment."

"Well, I'm interested in your first in-person impressions of them."

"Nah. You've already decided you like them. What's the real reason?"

Mia stared at her oddly for a moment. "You truly are Caleb's kin. All right. The Asterions may well prove to be the most significant ally we've encountered since The Displacement. No question they will prove to be a crucial player in intergalactic politics. I want you to pay close attention as our relationship is cemented and takes shape from here. This represents an important learning opportunity for you. A step up in your diplomatic knowledge and expertise."

Marlee nodded seriously, trying so hard not to reveal the extent of her excitement. "And?"

"And, they're partially synthetic. I think you'll...frankly, I think you'll take to them. Also, you're likely to catch on to their technology faster than anyone else I could take with me."

"Because you'll be too busy playing polite with their government officials for Meno to inspect their tech."

"Correct."

"I get you. We need to understand how their tech operates."

"The better for us to develop common communication and re-lated protocols."

"Absolutely. Communication protocols."

"Marlee, you are not to attempt to hack any of their terminals or servers or whatever else we come across while we're there. Ob-servation only."

She rolled her eyes. "Can I at least deep-scan the equipment? No one will ever be the wiser."

"Yes. I suppose this is exactly what I'm asking you to do. But mostly, I want you to focus on the people. Get a feel for them—how they interact with one another versus how they present themselves to us. View them as a diplomat would."

Because that's what she was now. A diplomat. All but officially. "I can do it." She paused. "Will we get to meet any of their alien allies? The little mineral aliens? Chizeru?"

"I can't say for certain, but I doubt it. Based on what Advisor Kirumase said, I don't think any Chizeru live on Dominion worlds."

"Damn. What about the moth creatures? They sound so cool."

"The Taiyoks? Perhaps, but don't count on it. We need to con-centrate on the Asterions."

"Yes, ma'am. And when we get back, we'll help the Godjans?"

"We'll try."

50

CONCORD HQ

COMMAND

Malcolm rushed into Miriam's office two minutes after the scheduled start of the hastily called meeting. Transitioning a military the size of AEGIS to a war footing was no easy task, and he'd spent the afternoon and evening on the Presidio reviewing strategic plans and fleet assignments and issuing orders.

Miriam, Richard and Mia sat at the conference table by the viewports. He took the empty seat by Mia. They were among friends, so he touched her hand by way of greeting. "I apologize for being late."

"We've all had an unexpectedly busy day." Miriam drew in a sharp breath. "Suffice it to say the Savrakath situation has taken a hard left turn. And while I wish events had played out differently, perhaps it should have taken such a turn, because in their current state, the Savrakaths need to be contained so they aren't allowed to threaten our people—but those are matters for the red-flag operations.

"I asked the three of you here so we could coordinate one specific mission. As you know, we've announced a standing offer of asylum for all Godjans who wish to leave Savrak. However, given the rapid degradation in our relations, I don't expect the Savrakaths to allow any Godjans to depart. Mia has presented a compelling argument that we ought to take a more active hand in assisting them in doing so."

Mia shrugged. "In fairness, your niece did the hard work of putting together the proposal."

"I'm not surprised. Richard and I have sketched out a mission plan for the first of what will likely be a number of joint CINT-AEGIS missions to extract as many Godjans as possible from Savrak, starting with those most at risk. We've received intelligence indicating a group of Godjans—dozens, up to a hundred—are being held at a facility on the grounds of the Savradin Government Hall. The Godjans refer to it as 'Okshakin,' and it appears to be a brutal re-education camp.

"A special forces team will infiltrate the complex with reconnaissance assistance from a Ghost squad that is already in place on Savrak. The special forces team will free the prisoners in the camp and bring them to Concord HQ, where they will receive medical treatment and other aid commensurate with their refugee status.

"In so doing, we will rescue innocents from severe mistreatment and risk of death. We will also send a clear message to the Savrakaths that we will not tolerate humanitarian abuses, and to the Godjans that we are on their side and fighting for them. Which we will be."

Malcolm rubbed at his jaw. "It's a good plan. And it'll let us test out the counters to Savrakath security tech we've been developing."

Richard slid a tiny quantum cube over to him. "A few programming updates for the spikes we sent you last week."

"Thanks. I'll see to it they get rolled out before we move."

Miriam poured a glass of water and eyed the two of them. "Malcolm, choose your special forces squads carefully. This is a humanitarian mission, not a free-for-all kill sweep. They'll need to be prepared to counter armed resistance, but the priority is extracting the prisoners."

"Yes, ma'am. I already have some ideas on who to send."

RW

CONCORD RESIDENCES

Malcolm lay on the floor of their apartment at Concord HQ, staring up at the featureless ceiling. He'd kicked his shoes to the wall on the way in the door and unfastened his shirt on the way to the floor, but he otherwise remained in uniform.

He heard Mia walk in too late to scramble to his feet and try to look presentable, so instead he just stayed where he was.

She draped her coat over the back of the couch, kicked off her heels next to his shoes and lay down on the floor next to him. God he loved her for that.

"What are we staring at?"

"Mountains. Trees and lakes as far as the eye can see, and not a single person. Except you and me, of course."

"Hmm. Sounds nice. When are we going?"

"Probably not this century." He sighed and pushed up to a sitting position. "Sorry. I'd intended to get over myself before you got home, but I lost track of time."

She propped up on one arm and rested her head on his shoulder. "You don't need to apologize. You're worried about the Savrakath conflict. And the mission Miriam proposed. And the looming threat of a horde of shapeshifting aliens."

"Among a few dozen other worries. But it's my job to worry about those things. Nothing new there."

"Doesn't make it any easier, though." She kissed him, let her delicious lips linger against his for an extra second, then stood and went into the kitchen. "Marlee will be so excited to hear about the Godjan rescue mission, but I think I won't tell her about it until after everyone is safely in Concord space."

He followed her into the kitchen, where he found her digging out leftover chicken piccata from the refrigeration unit. Right, food. He took the platter of leftovers from her and stuck it in the reheater. "It's a good idea to wait, in case we run into complications."

"Exactly. She simply wants to save them all, without regard to how it might be an impossible goal. So full of fire and zeal and righteous indignation, but I kind of hope the world never beats that out of her. It's refreshing, and it keeps me on my toes...."

She let the sentence drift to a conclusion as she slowly turned to him, eyes brightening beyond their normally brilliant jade. "You said, 'in case *we* run into complications.' You mean in case your squads do."

He steeled himself. It wasn't like he hadn't planned to tell her; he'd merely hoped for a few more minutes of harmony first. "I've decided to lead the special forces team on the Savrakath mission."

"Malcolm, you are the AEGIS *Fleet Admiral*. You have no business involving yourself in a ground incursion."

"But maybe I want to do it. Maybe I miss it. Maybe I'm tired of issuing orders from an office on a space station."

"I know you are. I know you miss the action, and your heart's always remained welded firmly to terra firma. But you're Fleet Admiral for a reason, and you have a responsibility to perform your job to the best of your abilities. AEGIS special forces have never been stronger, better equipped and better trained than they are today. They don't need you at their side to get the job done."

He looked at her sharply, and she shrugged. "I'm sorry if that sounds harsh. But you haven't waded into a close-quarters combat situation in eight years. Even your considerable skills get rusty from disuse." She touched his arm and softened her expression. "Don't you trust your people?"

"Of course I do. But...Mia, I need this."

"Do you? And what if something happens to you?"

"When has that ever been the criteria by which we live our lives? Also, it won't. Like you said, I'm Fleet Admiral for a reason, and the reason is skill."

"And obstinacy."

"Yes. And a healthy will to live. I have something important to come home to." He smiled and drew her into his arms, but she refused to give in.

"I don't like it."

He brushed his lips across hers. "I accept that."

"But you're going to do it anyway."

He closed his eyes...and nodded.

He felt her shoulders sag in resignation, and she stepped away. "Marlee and I are visiting the Asterion Dominion after the emergency Senate session. I have something important to come home to as well, so make sure you're here when I get back."

He reached out to hug her once more, but she thrust a finger in his chest. "And update your neural imprint before you get within a parsec of Savrak."

"You know I'm required to. It's regulation. But you also know how I feel about it."

"Yes I do—you believe the imprint doesn't capture your soul."

"Not only that, but I'm fairly certain one's soul doesn't go around jumping bodies. And once it's crossed over, it doesn't come back."

"I don't care. Keep the imprint updated." She grasped his hand in hers, then rested it firmly against her chest. "I've got your soul right here."

He kissed her fully, relieved she hadn't fought him any harder. "I believe you do, so be careful with it. As I understand the situation, the Rasu could show up in the Dominion at any time."

"Which is one reason why I'm making the trip now. We've no time to waste." She danced out of his arms while twirling the orb she perpetually wore on a chain around her neck. "Besides, I can vacate the Dominion and be back at HQ in a matter of eight seconds."

"If the Rasu show up, you make sure and do that."

"I will." She handed him a plate full of chicken. "Now eat. You need your strength if you're going to run off and act like a Marine again."

51

CONCORD HQ

"I thought the Rasu menace lay far in our future—as far as the boundary of their empire lies from ours."

Mia tilted her head a bit to soften her rejoinder. "Tokahe Naataan, you know as well I do that distance means very little in a world where wormhole travel exists, which is a capability we've confirmed the Rasu possess."

Daayn Shahs-Ian uttered a low grumble of protest. "But they don't know we exist. We should endeavor to keep it this way."

"We don't believe they do, but we have no evidence to buttress this belief other than the fact they have not yet attacked us." She cleared her throat and tried to redirect the endlessly circular debate toward something actionable. "But when the Rasu might discover us is not the focus of this emergency session. We know a faction of the Rasu have previously discovered the location of the Asterion Dominion, and it's likely other factions will soon do the same. The question on the table today is whether Concord will provide military assistance to the Dominion when or if they come under attack by Rasu forces."

"I thought the question on the table was whether to extend an offer of a formal alliance to them?"

Mia acknowledged Dean Veshnael. "Of course. One is implicit in the other, as all our alliances come with the promise to rally to our ally's aid if an aggressor threatens them."

Veshnael frowned, though on the Novoloume's face it remained a gentle expression. "We just met the Asterions, and under most unusual circumstances."

"The Katasketousya introduced us. That's not so unusual."

The Barisan representative interjected again. "But how do we know we can trust them? They are former rebels, after all."

Mia gave Shahs-Ian a placid smile. "Rebels against the Anaden Empire, you mean. Trust me, that is not a disqualifying act for an alliance."

She felt Ferdinand's glare burning into the side of her skull. But somewhat to her surprise, instead of lobbing a veiled threat over rebels and rebellions, he tried to change the subject. "Are we going to discuss the latest Savrakath attack on our patrols?"

"Not at this meeting, no. The Savrakaths are red-flagged, thus addressing their transgressions is now a military matter. As I was *saying*, since our initial meeting with the Asterion representatives several weeks ago, they have shown us every courtesy and responded openly to all our requests. We've been granted full access to their planets and government institutions. No question asked has gone unanswered, and their laws and practices already comply with our Code of Rights.

"Therefore, after a thorough appraisal of their laws and customs, as well as in-person reviews by Concord officials, the Consulate is hereby recommending we offer the Asterion Dominion allied status. Further, after an investigation into the nature, history and reported practices of the Rasu, Command has recommended issuing a preemptive red-flag on the Rasu."

Shahs-Ian snarled—a toothless act at a conference table in the heart of Concord HQ. "The last one's obvious. If or when they do arrive, we'll meet them with force. But again I ask, why should we pick a fight with the shapeshifters?"

"That's not what we would be doing by forming this alliance. We would be helping the Asterions defend themselves."

"And why should we do that?"

Mia didn't raise her voice above a conversational level, though she wanted to, if only to drown out Meno's offended ranting in her head. "Because it is the right thing to do."

Dean Veshnael nodded solemnly. "Indeed it is. Despite my initial caution, you present a convincing case. I vote 'yes' on both proposals."

"Agreed. Also, we need to see these Rasu on the battlefield. Take stock of them." The Tokahe Naataan jerked his long snout. "I vote 'yes' on both proposals."

Ferdinand snorted. "I agree we need to see how the Rasu fight. This doesn't mean we need to fight back ourselves. Let them take the Asterion rebels down a few notches, if not destroy them entirely. We need to watch from afar and learn what we can about our future enemy."

Deja vu, anyone? The story went that when Alex Solovy first informed the Earth Alliance's military leaders about the approaching armada of Metigen superdreadnoughts, several of those leaders had suggested they allow the armada to attack Seneca, which lay directly in its path, before sending their own military fleets to meet the threat. A 'win-win,' they had called it, as an adversary would be weakened by the attack while the EA would have the opportunity to observe the aliens in action and identify weaknesses to be exploited.

In a few ways—not many, but a few—humans weren't always so different from their Anaden brethren.

But they *were* different when it mattered, because in humanity's case, better, more ethical voices had prevailed in the end. The Earth Alliance and the Senecan Federation had ultimately joined together in common cause to defeat a common enemy. Ferdinand, however, did not appear inclined to take such a route.

She couldn't rightly be disappointed when she hadn't expected him to rise to the occasion, but she could be outraged. "Senator Ferdinand, do I take your morally repugnant comment to mean you are voting against offering an alliance to the Asterion Dominion?"

"Senator Requelme, putting aside your morally sanctimonious exposition, you are correct. I vote 'no' in the strongest possible terms. In fact, if the Senate goes forward with this action, I will be lodging a formal protest and requesting an inquiry be opened."

"Noted. We have three votes for and one against. What say the rest of you?"

RW

CONSULATE

Damn, that was too close! Marlee had several Barisan friends who she thought the world of, but as a species they needed to grow a backbone. And if she ever met Ferdinand elasson-Kyvern in a deserted hallway, she'd ensure he didn't walk out of it under his own power....

But the alliance vote had passed the Senate, which was what mattered. Now she and Mia could get some real work done when they visited the Dominion.

A reminder beeped in her eVi, and Marlee groaned and hurriedly backed out of the surveillance system, where she'd been keeping an eye on the Senate session. She had eighteen things to do to prepare for the trip, virtually all of them dull bureaucratic boxes to check.

So instead of doing them, she set a helper routine running to take care of most of them for her and left her office to go grab lunch.

At the crossway outside the Consulate, she paused, then went left instead of right. The paninis at the deli in the Senate atrium weren't quite as tasty as those at *Elliptical*, but she didn't want to run into Ainye right now. By the end of their date after Gramps' birthday party, Marlee couldn't endure another minute of the woman's vapid shallowness. She'd excused herself with a vague promise of another date soon—a promise she didn't intend to keep.

She'd nearly reached the deli when a familiar shout drew her attention. "Tiny human!"

She spun around in delight, then hurried over to embrace Pinchu. "Oof!"

"Hin adzaa, Marlee Rosa Arrigucci Marano. Nitawa tsin ichaga doo-sagya?" (*Apologies, Marlee Rosa Arrigucci Marano. Your bones have grown no stronger?*)

She giggled. "Ndaga, ma'ichaga toeyas kut. Hait' eego mani Cassdenini?" (*No, I'm pretty much full-grown now. Speaking of, how is Cassdenini?*) She'd met Pinchu's nephew on her last visit to Ireltse, where she witnessed firsthand how Pinchu doted on his nephew like Cassdenini was the son he'd almost had.

"Unlike you, his bones are still growing. He won first place in the junior combat trials last week. He will be a fine warrior very soon now."

"Of course he will be. He's of your blood." She glanced back down the hallway he'd emerged from. "How did the Senate meeting go?" She already knew, but she valued his take on the political dynamics.

"Too many cowards in the room for my taste, but your Senator Requelme is not one of them."

"No, she isn't. She can in fact be rather scary sometimes."

"I believe you. It took much bloviating from the others, but I expect we will soon be heading to war on a second front." He breathed in deeply, puffing his stout, fur-covered chest out. "The Khokteh are ready to defend these Asterions, weak though they are. It is our duty as the strong."

She grinned. "It is. You will do your people proud as always, I've no doubt."

"I will endeavor. Now, run along. I snatched you out of a most purposeful stride, but I will not delay you further from your—" he gazed past her shoulder "—nourishment. Eat well, and perhaps your bones may yet toughen up."

She hugged him goodbye, trying not to wince when his powerful arms nearly crushed her ribs. "Ni deeni jiniya khiza. (*Be fierce in the battles to come.*) I'll see you again soon."

PART IV

RIVEN

52

UNKNOWN LOCATION

RASU-OCCUPIED TERRITORY

Hours of rain had turned the clay soil to a clingy mud soup, and their pace progressively slowed until it became a trudging crawl. They had plenty of water now, but their utterly rash and short-sighted abandonment of their plan to reach the forest meant food was minimal and making a beeline to non-existent.

Kiernan felt weak, papery thin. An aching weariness had seeped into his bones with the rain and the fading shadows of the Rasu speeding across the landscape.

Toshke must be in worse shape than him, but the Taiyok remained a picture of stoicism. Steady, plodding stoicism. His wings drooped heavily down his back, however, and Kiernan wondered whether his companion retained the strength for flight.

Gradually, the appearance of meager trees began to look familiar. Was it possible they neared the crash sites at last?

Toshke abruptly snapped a sopping-wet wing out in front of Kiernan. He bumped into it before coming to a halt, sending droplets of water flying into his eyes.

"What is it?" He'd learned over the previous weeks that Toshke's sight was obscenely sharper than his, particularly at picking out motion against the unremittingly umber landscape.

"Rasu."

"Here? Where?"

"At your ship."

His fears come to life, yet he refused to accept it. "No, that's not possible. We camouflaged it."

"Not well enough."

With rumbling dread, he peeked around the outstretched wing and zoomed his vision as far as his OS allowed. Two Rasu had taken on bipedal form and were using long, fluid arms to poke through the innards of his vessel. Above, another Rasu circled the wreckage in weaponized form.

What were they looking for?

His heart leapt into his throat as a terrible realization occurred to him, weeks later than it should have and now far too late. If these Rasu here were from the wrecked leviathan, which had been his and Toshke's working theory since first spotting them, it meant they knew about the battle in the Gennisi galaxy. They knew about Asterions and might even know that was who had attacked their stronghold. The Rasu who had camped in Gennisi had spent almost a decade experimenting on Asterions, and they understood not only Communis but the inner workings of Asterion programming. And they were a hive mind consciousness, or something close enough to it for the details not to matter.

If these Rasu were able to access and activate his ship's systems, they'd be able to read its data. Its *navigational* data. The ship had only ever flown around the Namino stellar system on training missions before heading to the Rasu stronghold, but that was enough.

He fell to his knees in the tall grass and dropped his head in his hands. The Rasu were going to find Namino, and it was going to be his fault. He had no way to get off this planet, no way to warn anyone. He would die here soon enough of starvation, while millions would die back home in far more horrific ways.

The urge to lie down on the ground, curl up into a ball and just *quit* overwhelmed him. Why bother to try to fight against such an enemy?

Toshke lowered to his knees beside him and touched a hand to his shoulder. "Kiernan, there is nothing you could have done."

"That's not true. Gods, I am such an idiot!" He gazed up at Toshke through splayed fingers as renewed rain dribbled down between them. "But there's something I can do now. We need to get to your ship ahead of these Rasu and burn it to ashes. They'll see the fire and find us and probably kill us, but at least we can keep them from discovering the location of Toki'taku. We can't save my people, but maybe we can save yours."

RW

Kiernan contemplated matters in greater depth while they fought through the mud and muck to reach Toshke's ship, and he decided that despite everything, he still didn't want to die. He'd do it if it was necessary to save even a few lives, but the strength of his survival instinct surprised him.

But a flaming ship was apt to draw Rasu attention in a big way, so they needed to, one, make sure it burned hot and fast and completely, and two, get out of the area with lightning speed once the blaze began.

Toshke was wary of fire, Kiernan assumed because feathers burned far faster than skin, but it also meant the Taiyok was quite knowledgeable about starting and controlling a blaze.

As soon as they reached the wreck, they ripped off every panel that protected wiring or anything circuit-based. Then they ripped off the panels protecting the engine core. Then they stuffed grass inside every crevice for kindling. Next they tore out the primary operating hardware, stomped it to pieces in the mud, then threw the broken pieces back in the ship and covered them with more grass.

Finally, they retreated twenty meters and fired their sidearms on the grass-stuffed wreckage until flames completely engulfed it. The rain meant the bonfire was unlikely to spark a larger inferno of the surrounding fields, but the ship contained enough flammable material to burn strong.

Toshke moved behind Kiernan and wrapped his arms around Kiernan's torso.

"What are you doing?"

"Carrying you. We need to be far away very fast."

"But they'll see us."

"This is a lower risk than them finding us here."

"Can you carry my weight?"

"For a time. Hold still."

Kiernan felt the heavy beat of Toshke's wings around him as they slowly, laboriously rose four meters in the air. They tilted downward until Kiernan was certain he was about to face-plant back into the mud, then flew off to the north.

RW

That night they slept on the cold, mucky ground of a small copse of trees five kilometers from the bonfire they'd created.

They'd drifted back over previously traveled ground, for want of other options. The rush from the bonfire had quickly evaporated, and it took with it what remaining fight he'd clung to. He wanted to live, sure, but these seesawing emotions were draining him dry. He was *tired*.

This had been a planet inhabited by primitives; there was no civilization for them to locate and seek a way off-planet. There would be no abandoned technology they could repurpose. Whether from the Rasu tomorrow or the next day or from starvation next week or from body degradation centuries from now, he would eventually die here.

Kiernan woke to the sun warming his face, though he couldn't honestly say if he'd slept, either. Nightmares of the Rasu turning Namino into a bloody killing field haunted his thoughts-turned-dreams, and they refused to fade away with the morning light.

Damn the Rasu. Damn their wormhole. Damn him for thinking he was a hotshot pilot who was going to single-handedly take out a leviathan warship.

Toshke nudged a pouch of berries over to him. The Taiyok had already risen and scavenged the area for food. Maybe sleep had reinvigorated a bit of his fight. Lucky him.

"Thanks." Kiernan stretched one arm across the other, but the kinks from sleeping on the ground for over a month were never leaving his muscles. He took a small handful of the berries and was about to pop one in his mouth when a glint off in the distance caught his attention. Rasu flying this way?

He leapt to his feet and shielded his eyes from the morning sun. Another glint revealed a span of silvery metal. Not aubergine. "Toshke, what do you see?"

The Taiyok drew up next to him and blinked several times. "A ship. Not a Rasu ship."

"It's descending, right?"

"Yes. To our northeast, perhaps near the remains of the massacred village we discovered earlier. Last week...or possibly the week before."

Kiernan grabbed his meager gear off the ground, stuffed a dozen berries in his mouth, and took off to the northeast at a jog. "We've got to catch up to them!"

53

HOAN STELLAR SYSTEM

BEYOND THE BOUNDARIES OF CONCORD SPACE

The *Periplanos* exited superluminal with a jarring *thud*, almost as if it had slammed into a wall in space.

Nyx heard Danilo stumble into something solid in the main cabin, but a second later he hurried into the cockpit. "What happened?"

Nyx shook her head while pulling up system diagnostics. "It says 'unable to reach programmed destination.' We exited superluminal...actually, only a few megameters short of the coordinates we targeted. The engine isn't displaying any errors, so I don't think it failed on us. Something kicked us off our course, however, and if it wasn't the ship..." she peered out at the seemingly ordinary scene outside the viewport "...it must have been something out there."

Scans returned a long-range image of a flaxen-and-caramel hued planet 1.3 AU out from the local star. Livad. Nothing looked amiss from this distance.

Nonetheless, her grandfather frowned and rubbed at his shoulder. "Let's do a complete battery of scans of the planet and the vicinity. This doesn't feel right."

She didn't question his instructions. She trusted his instincts, for they had been proved correct more times than she dared count; more than that, though, she felt it, too. Something was wrong here.

Twenty minutes later, they'd discovered several pieces of the answer. A closer approach to Livad revealed two large alien ships hovered in geostationary orbit above one of the major continents. A deep scan of the surface returned sporadic hotspots of electrical and other technological activity. Since the Hoans were a pre-industrial species, the logical conclusion to draw was the aliens owning the ships had invaded the planet.

The reason for their early expulsion from superluminal was a quantum interference field. It projected across the entirety of Livad and out to a distance of ten megameters. The field wasn't interfering with routine flight or standard sensor operation, but nothing extradimensional penetrated it.

The existence of the field vaulted the technological level of the aliens piloting the ships by several levels, possibly all the way to Type II-A or even higher. Who were they?

She watched Danilo stare silently out the viewport. His expression remained hard but neutral, but she could almost sense the speeding of his mind as he raced through weighing variables and competing arguments. She admired his insistence on approaching every scenario with the thoughtful application of logic drawn from history and experience, but she knew the outcome of this debate. He cared for the creatures who inhabited this planet; whatever the risk to them personally, they would be landing on the surface. Still, she forced herself to wait patiently until he had convinced himself of the rightness of this decision.

Finally he gave the viewport a sharp nod. "We'll engage the cloaking shield and perform an atmospheric entry on the opposite side of the planet, where the orbiting vessels are least likely to detect an anomaly. It will take us a few minutes longer to reach Hivam Village, but it's the safer course. Once we're planetside, we'll fly low and fast, but as quietly as we can manage."

"I agree. Are we ready?"

"I fear we are already too late. Let's go."

RW

Golden grasslands raced scant meters beneath the belly of the *Periplanos*. Thus far, they hadn't encountered signs of an invasion beyond a few scorched meadows and forests, but they were now approaching the region where spikes in electromagnetic activity had been detected—where the aliens had apparently concentrated their invasion efforts.

"Shift ten degrees to the northeast. Hivam Village is twelve kilometers ahead on the new bearing."

She'd preemptively been adjusting their course, but she didn't bristle at the gentle order. Her grandfather now displayed an emotion she'd never seen before from him: fear. Not for himself or for her, but for what waited a few short kilometers away. Renowned across mapped space for his exemplary control over his emotions, fear now radiated off him in turbulent waves.

Nyx was first and foremost a realist, and she accepted the inevitability of what they were going to find at Hivam Village. Not the grim details, because she'd never met a Hoan or seen the aliens who invaded here. But she knew what razing a planet looked like. Her grandfather insisted the Hoans had no defenses beyond personal weapons they used for hunting, thus they could not have put up a fight worth the name.

If the Theriz had chosen this planet for Cultivation, the Hoans would have been massacred without anyone even noticing.

The possibility that the aliens might be friendly, might be greeting the Hoans as explorers, she'd dismissed out of hand. Explorers arriving in ships such as those orbiting the planet didn't contact primitive species, not unless they desired to be treated as gods. And in those cases, the eventual outcome was the same.

Then there was the quantum blocking field. It was precisely the type of measure an invading force would deploy upon arrival at a target as a matter of course. The Hoans didn't possess quantum capabilities, but aliens such as these were not likely to take chances.

Halfway to Hivam Village, they passed over a perfect circle of scorched earth stretching 3.1 kilometers in diameter.

Nyx drew in a sharp breath and slowed almost to a stop above it. Danilo's gaze dropped to it, but his features didn't otherwise flicker.

"You're not surprised to see this?"

"I am mystified. But surprised? No."

He didn't add anything further, and she didn't comment as she increased their speed. The implications were beyond enormous to world-altering...but first they needed to confirm the Hoans' fate.

She slowed once again as the village came into sight. Or rather, what must have once *been* a village came into sight.

Danilo's fortitude finally broke with a horrified gasp. He pivoted and rushed into the main cabin. "Set down as soon as you reach the clearing."

By 'clearing,' he meant a swath of harvested farmland leading right up to the wreckage of several dozen primitive buildings. Broken wood and shredded fibers were strewn across a muddy expanse, but no building stood above a meter high.

She landed and secured the *Periplanos*, then grabbed her firearm and followed Danilo out the airlock.

The stench assaulted her nose for a microsecond before her cybernetics muted the odor. Death. Decay. Decomposition of bodies and spoiling food.

Danilo sprinted ahead to the outskirts of the village, then fell to his knees beside the first body.

She approached more cautiously, studying the body as she did. Long, reedy limbs lay spread out at all angles in a coagulated pool of pea-colored blood and gore.

"Why? Why would anyone do this? They were peaceful. Gentle. Kind. They possessed nothing of value to offer to anyone capable of inflicting such violence upon them. Why bother? Why not just let them live?"

Providing sympathetic comfort had never been on the list of desired traits for a Praesidis Inquisitor, and her skills in doing so were, in a word, dismal. But she had developed a rapport with him over the years, so she crouched beside him and made the effort.

"Some species do not comprehend compassion or mercy. They take and they kill, for they know nothing else."

He gestured wildly around them. "But what could they take? Bushels of wheat? Nutritious soil?"

"Whatever they could find, perhaps. Perhaps they did it for sport."

"There is no sport in slaughtering helpless creatures. Only cruelty."

He sank back to rest on his heels. "I am sorry I brought you here. Better for me to have lived another hundred millennia without knowing their fate. Now my heart will ache forever, but there is nothing we can do for them."

"That's not entirely true, grandfather."

"Oh?"

"We can exact justice for their deaths."

He stared at her strangely. "How—"

She leapt to her feet in a whirling motion, one hand unlatching her firearm and bringing it up to lead her focus as she swept the surrounding area. "I heard a noise. Stay behind me."

Her eyes scanned the ruins of the village and peered into the farmland surrounding it. The grasses danced on the breeze, obscuring any deliberate movement by a predator—

—suddenly two bipedal creatures sprinted out of the grasses and straight for them.

RW

Winded and exhausted by the time they reached the village, Kiernan paused only long enough to confirm the beings who had departed the small ship weren't Rasu before staggering out into the open. "Hey! We need help!"

One of the beings—they looked Anatype enough for him to just think of them as people—cautiously stood from where he'd been kneeling next to one of the corpses. The other, however, whipped out a weapon and had sighted it down on him in less than a second.

He held his hands in the air and slowed his steps. He had a Glaser, but if they weren't friendlies then he was fucked sideways anyway, so he didn't bother to reach for it. "We don't want to harm you. We need your help. Do you understand me?"

The armed one, a woman with jet black hair and arresting indigo eyes, glared at him suspiciously over her weapon. "Toss your sidearms to the ground. Both of you."

If he'd slept for more than a few hours in the last weeks, he might think it noteworthy how she spoke a dialect of Communis, but he was simply too drained and too grateful to care. He unlatched his Glaser and placed it on the ground, then confirmed Toshke had done the same.

"Good enough? Listen, I'd love to tip-toe our way through first contact protocols, but we are all—me, him, the two of you—in terrible danger right now. You have a ship that was able to land here, which I hope to hells means it can depart as well, because we need to do that ASAP."

The other individual, a distinguished-looking man with olive skin, dark hair and noticeably matching indigo eyes, took a step forward. "You're speaking Communis."

"And so are you. Small favor in a sea of bad. Did you hear what I said?"

"Why should we leave? There may be other Hoans alive elsewhere who we can help."

Kiernan groaned and shot Toshke an exasperated look. They did not have time for this! "The aliens who destroyed this village are called Rasu, and they are still here. When they find us—and they will, because I guarantee you if we spotted your ship they did, too—they will kill us faster than we can squeak out a few good bloodcurdling screams. Whatever weapons you have on your person or installed on your ship, I promise you they will not so much as scratch the Rasu here. We need to leave, *now*. Also, we desperately need to get outside this blocking field and get word to our people that the Rasu probably know where they are and will be coming for them soon."

"Your people? You two are clearly different species."

"Yes. I'm an Asterion, and he's a Taiyok. We're allies. Now we should—"

The man's brow knotted up in surprise. "Asterion? That's not possible."

"And yet. Can we focus here?" A low rumble echoed across the grassland behind them, and he pivoted to search the horizon. Nothing broke the skyline, but....

Toshke kept his attention on the direction the rumble originated from, so Kiernan turned back to the couple while pointing behind him. "Hear that sound? A Rasu, or more likely a horde of Rasu, are headed this way. When they get here, they'll slice us into tiny, fleshy bits like they did to those poor sodding creatures you were weeping over. Did I mention they're fast as well as brutally deadly? Now let's *go*."

The woman's gaze flickered to the horizon—and whatever she saw vaulted her into a flurry of activity. She nodded sharply to the man, holstered her weapon and motioned everyone toward the ship. "Leave your weapons. If you try to harm us, you'll be dead faster than you would have been if we'd left you here at the mercy of these Rasu. Now get on board."

54

MIRAI

RIDANI ENTERPRISES

Dashiel watched on a pane from his office as, inside a sealed incubator-style container in a lab ten floors below, dual robotic arms carefully extracted a series of kyoseil fibers from the block of Reor. The delicate, painstaking process had to be repeated for every single block, and using larger blocks didn't result in greater efficiencies. The amount of time and labor required to accomplish the extraction wouldn't be worth it for anything less than kyoseil.

It took two ceraffin ten hours of trial and error testing to hit upon a way to coax a Reor mineral block into giving up the kyoseil encased within it without destroying the fibers. The solution turned out to be pulsing a specific harmonic signal across the surface of the mineral, which for some reason triggered a softening of the mineral for a millimeter around the kyoseil, enabling the fibers to be drawn out from the block.

The ratio of pure kyoseil to Reor was 1:23, which meant they needed a great deal of Reor to net a usable amount of kyoseil—on the order of tonnes rather than kilograms. But Concord produced the mineral on demand, so the potential supply was effectively infinite.

A team had begun to explore uses for the left-over mineral, but while it was reasonably sturdy and resilient, its characteristics were comparatively unremarkable. At this point, the only rational conclusion to arrive at was that it served primarily to protect the kyoseil from the ravages of both space and people.

The robotic arm on the left deposited an eight-centimeter-long fiber in a vat of a gel solution then returned to the block to begin extracting another. Dashiel regarded the glittering fiber with what could only be described as lust, for visions danced in his head of what an unlimited supply of kyoseil stood to mean for his business and his people.

Not for the first time, a twinge of guilt chased the lust. Kyoseil was *alive*, yet they continued to treat it as a tool and use it for their own ends. Yes, as he himself had pointed out to Nika, kyoseil died at the hands of the Rasu every time an Asterion did, thus whatever form its intelligence took surely wished to defeat this enemy the same as they did. And according to Alex Solovy, the Reor helped them to defeat the Anaden Directorate by displaying a level of deliberate agency that sounded too incredible to be true, except for the fact that it had happened. The Reor had *chosen* to fight for the good guys, as it were.

And if it were as alive as the evidence suggested, it had similarly *chosen* to bond with his people long, long ago. Theirs was a partnership, even if Asterions didn't realize it until recently. He owed it to the kyoseil to honor and respect their partnership by using it responsibly and with full awareness of the impact of his actions.

Satisfied the extraction process had been properly designed and was being correctly executed, he went back to his desk and turned his attention to a spread of reports on his other new project, adiamene.

Every test the Industry Division's Conceptual Research department had run on the metal confirmed the preposterous numbers his mysterious benefactor had asserted regarding its performance. The metamaterial they had been using for their ship hulls represented the state of the art—highly resilient and feather-light—but adiamene surpassed it in every single respect, by several sigmas.

The numbers and the testing bore out its capabilities, and however unbelievable, science rigorously applied didn't lie.

Mass producing the material wasn't a simple matter, but he'd specialized in manufacturing advanced and finicky materials for thousands of years. Anything was doable with the proper application of money, resources, time and learned expertise. Now the question became, how to best introduce the metal into their designs?

He'd forwarded the metal's key characteristics to Grant for him to brainstorm ideas on how its use might alter their ship designs, and he assumed Grant was using a ceraff to share the workload. Which was fine, because it was a thorny problem. They couldn't simply slap adiamene outer shells on existing ships. Retrofitting key sections of certain hulls might be viable, though even determining what sections on what ships constituted a project in and of itself.

But mostly, the promise of adiamene was in the ships to come. It was a foregone conclusion that at some point, they'd switch over to it for all their military ship production. The trigger point would be when they'd manufactured enough adiamene for it to be practicable—and when he managed to convince Lance to stop the lines long enough to complete the change-over.

Not just ships, either. Dashiel believed the new planetary shield satellites should be the first to use adiamene. They'd already spent millions of credits getting thousands of satellites in orbit above Mirai, but in a matter of weeks they'd be able to switch to adiamene for constructions of the remaining satellites for Namino, the planet next on the list for the shielding.

He drummed his fingers on the desk. Then there was the Vault. The cost to replace its hull with adiamene would be astronomical on an order of magnitude that made his head swim; worse, it would delay the Vault's launch by more than a month. But he was on the verge of deciding it was worth it to ensure the safety and security of their most prized treasure and the key to their future if armageddon won the day.

He set a routine running to analyze the most time- and cost-efficient manner of retrofitting the entire outer hull of the Vault. Then he grabbed his jacket and left for the Pavilion, with a quick stop on the way to check and see how Adlai was doing. Rumor was that Senator Requelme would soon be arriving bearing what Nika had sought so hard to obtain—a formal alliance with Concord—and he wanted to be there for her victory.

55

SAVRAK STELLAR SYSTEM

AEGIS DAR VESSEL

Fourteen Marines gathered in the main hold of the tactical DAR, or 'drop-and-recover,' vessel. In theory they could have departed for the mission from anywhere—the EASC training grounds, a supply warehouse on the Presidio, the cafeteria at Concord HQ. Wormholes on demand were handy that way. But wormholes were technology controlled by people and machines, and all three of those remained fallible, so the better to have a physical backup on call for when the system failed.

Malcolm grabbed a brace-bar above his head and opened a large aural beside him. It showed the below-ground levels beneath the Government Hall in Savradin. "Here's the layout of our target location as captured by a Ghost reconnaissance pass. The first two levels are devoted to facility maintenance for the complex, such as structural girding and water pumping equipment."

One of the Marines, a bulky young man with sepia skin marked by elaborate non-glyph tattoos, interjected. "Trying to keep the swamp out of the building has got to be like Sisyphus and his boulder, eh?"

"I imagine so. But this is why the contents of these levels matter to us—we'll need to be careful with explosives. We bust the pipes connecting those pumps, and the lower level is underwater in minutes and us along with it. Now, the walls, floors and ceilings of all the underground levels are thick and sturdy, but we can't take any chances. Grenades are to be used only as a last resort."

He zoomed in on the bottom-most level of the complex. "This is our goal. The Godjans call it 'Okshakin,' which means 'reformatory' in Savrakan, which means 'dungeon' in English. Godjans who cause trouble or otherwise disappoint their Savrakath superiors are sent here for re-education or, in some cases, simply for torture. They are who we're rescuing tonight. On that point, does everyone know what the Godjans look like?"

Someone raised their hand near the rear of the hold, so he flashed a visual of one of the aliens.

"Ugly little frog-looking S.O.B."

"That is a subjective opinion, and also irrelevant to our mission."

"I know, I'm just saying. And, hey, those giant eyes are kind of pitiful-looking. Damn, now they're tugging at my heartstrings like a sad puppy. They *definitely* need rescuing."

The Marine took a few punches in the shoulder from his squadmates for the remark, but Malcolm had no good response, so instead he zoomed in farther to the northeast side of the level. "The dungeon only has one point of ingress and egress: a lift approximately ten meters wide located here. This will be our chokepoint." He pulled the perspective out to display the entire level and activated a filter to emphasize the interior walls.

"Ah, fuck."

And this was the reason for the small squad. Their target location turned out to be a cramped, claustrophobic maze, and if Malcolm had brought any more Marines, they would've risked clogging the halls and tripping over one another trying to move prisoners.

"Thank you for the color commentary, Captain Harris. It's a fair assessment. But if this were easy, they'd let the cadets do it."

"Instead of the Fleet Admirals?"

It was probably for the best that Malcolm couldn't determine who had shouted the remark. "Yes. Now, the dungeon is organized in an almost labyrinth design. From what we can determine, each Godjan is kept isolated in their own cell. Unless some of these rooms are supply closets, we've got fifty-two cells and only one way out."

One of the Marines he knew from back in the day stepped forward to get a closer look at the map. Colonel Odaka had worked for the IDCC RRF under Brooklyn Harper. As part of the military shakeout that took place after The Displacement, he had formally joined AEGIS and now oversaw a division of special forces squads. But for Malcolm's presence, the man would be in charge of the mission today.

"I've been hearing rumors touting these new Ghost ships, but they sounded like fairy tales to me. What, did it hover two meters outside the ambassador's office to get images this detailed?"

"Possibly. But the details of the Ghosts' capabilities are highly classified, so for tonight, let's merely be grateful they exist and not worry about how."

Odaka arched an eyebrow in silent challenge but resumed his position along the port hull.

The Ghosts were the newest project out of what used to be called ASCEND, but now went by 'Concord Special Projects.' Tiny, one-person vessels adapted from the Eidolon configuration, they represented the height of stealth technology. They carried the usual EM dampeners, ship-rated Veils and defensive lattices that caused seeker pings and scans to slide off the hull, but in addition, they were constructed of an adiamene variant that adapted its physical characteristics to the surroundings. It did so without the need for a dedicated power feed, circuitry or programming.

Initially, some had called it 'living metal,' but the descriptor now seemed reserved for the Rasu.

Two weeks earlier, Malcolm had stood three meters from a Ghost and would never have known it if the hatch hadn't opened and the pilot disembarked while he stood there—and this was without any electronic stealth measures active. Add in state-of-the-art sensors and scanners and a whisper-quiet next-generation engine, and the vessels held the promise of being the perfect stealth reconnaissance tool.

Something had to give, of course, and that duty had fallen to weaponry. A Ghost sported only a single weak laser weapon, one strong enough to take out a person or a light vehicle but nothing larger. The Ghost's defense was its ability to vanish.

Three Ghosts were currently on the planet. Their primary mission was to locate the additional antimatter facilities the Savrakaths kept hidden away, but Malcolm had borrowed one to swing by the Savradin Government Hall and do initial reconnaissance for the mission. Savrak was their first active combat support mission, but so far their performance had been exemplary.

Malcolm moved the aural out of the way. "Major Rodriguez, you're up. Show us what we're heading into tonight."

"Yes, sir." The Prevo came up beside Malcolm, projected his own aural, closed his eyes and slipped into sidespace.

The aural showed a narrow, dimly lit hallway. The walls were constructed of a dark plastic composite that seemed to absorb what little light shone into darkness. "Increasing infrared vision."

The washed-out scene brightened as the viewpoint shifted to reveal a wide recess in the wall—the lift. It pivoted again and started moving down the hall. Almost immediately, a new hallway branched to the right; two meters later, another to the left. The viewpoint traveled down the left branch, stopped at a solid door and focused in on the latch. "Card-activated electric lock, looks like."

Malcolm found the supply officer in the hold. "Corporal Bachn, we need five Jimmies out of the equipment locker."

The viewpoint returned to the main hallway and moved forward until it encountered a Savrakath in military attire carrying a shock rod and sporting a mid-weight firearm on his hip. "One guard." The viewpoint passed the guard to speed along the narrow, twisting hallways. On the first aural, their progress was tracked by a tiny dot; the dot was forced to backtrack multiple times, as most of the halls ended abruptly after three or four cells.

Finally the aural faded, and Major Rodriguez opened his eyes. "Four guards in total. Lighter than we expected, but I assume they don't meet with much resistance from the prisoners. Every cell I peeked into was occupied, but I didn't check all of them." He frowned. "Sir, it's dangerously dark in there. With full NV you'll be able to see well enough to move around, but you'll miss details. It's not ideal."

"Understood. Everyone—"

The Marine who had joked about keeping the swamp out earlier raised a hand, and Malcolm did a scan of the roster to come up with a name: Lieutenant Diya. He indicated for Diya to speak his mind.

"Major, can you drop back inside real fast and increase the UV band on your vision?"

Rodriguez checked with Malcolm, who nodded. The dark hallway reappeared, then lit up in a splash of fluorescence.

"Thank you, Major. Good enough."

Malcolm gestured to the Marine. "Care to explain, Lieutenant?"

"Yes, sir. Admiral. The Savrakaths are descended from a branch of lizards, right? Or that's where the Kats got the DNA from, anyway. Lizards' night vision sucks ass, so it didn't make any sense that the dungeon is dark. But many types of lizards have excellent UV vision."

Malcolm dipped his chin. "Handy knowledge there, Lieutenant. So the Savrakaths keep the dungeon dark to increase the prisoners' sense of isolation, but they can see fine."

"Yeah, but it's still stupid of them. Sir."

"Why is that?"

"Well, sir, frogs have about the best night vision of any animal. Now, maybe these Godjans don't, or maybe the Savrakaths are so arrogant they never thought to check."

"I wish this helped us more than it does. Good work, Lieutenant." Malcolm scanned the room. "Prevos, Mélanges, Enhanced, or general tech junkies. Who can whip up a script modification to our NV program that enhances UV vision without blinding us—and do it in five minutes?"

Two hands rose, and he waved toward them. "Get to work." He turned to Rodriguez and pulled the primary aural between them. "I want our wormhole here, eight meters in front of the lift. I'd put it farther back to give us more space to react to guests, but then it's in the maze." He indicated for Odaka to come over and join them. "Colonel, choose your two best shots. The three of you are going to be our blockade. Anyone who comes down the lift is taken out before they reach the extraction point."

"What if guards transport a prisoner to the dungeon while we're there?"

Malcolm suppressed a scowl. He understood if Odaka felt usurped by his presence, but a passive-aggressive attitude didn't help the mission. "Then try not to shoot the prisoner."

"Yes, Admiral."

"Got it!"

They all turned toward the shout to find one of the Marines who'd raised their hand wearing a shit-eating grin. "The script mod. With your permission, sir, I'll go ahead and push it out to everyone."

These people were the best the Marines had to offer, so the odds the mod would fry anyone's eVi were minuscule. "Do it.

"Attention everyone. Our field of play is a nightmare, but it's what we've got. We will move in teams of two, fanning out from the extraction point here." He circled where he'd marked the wormhole on the aural. "Use the Jimmies to open the cell doors. Rescue two prisoners then get them to the extraction point, and Corporal Bachn and Major Whalesk will secure them on the DAR. Go back for two more. Tech officers, you will send drone units ahead to disable each of the four guards, and back them up if necessary.

"Everyone's progress will be tracked on the TacMap, so nobody is checking empty cells. Everyone has Savrakan queued up in your translator? Good. The Godjans are likely to be submissive but also terrified, and we want to avoid any incidents. Get them through the wormhole onto the ship, and we get out of there. Any questions?"

RW

SAVRAK

SAVRADIN

A blast of heat surged through the wormhole the instant Rodriguez opened it. Suffocating humidity followed it, and Malcolm made a face as he shouted toward the cockpit. "Major Whalesk, crank up the air filtration system a few notches, or it's going to get real sticky in the hold real fast."

"Yes, sir," the pilot responded.

Malcolm removed his Daemon from its holster—due to the close quarters and water piping above them, they were going in carrying small arms only—and led the squad into the dungeon.

He blinked until the modified NV kicked in to bathe the hallway in a sickly glow. The hallway was barely wide enough for the wormhole, and Rodriguez had to shrink it down for Odaka's team to slip around it and take up positions covering the lift.

Admiral Jenner (mission): "All teams, fan out."

He paired up with Captain Chacko, a tall man from the South Pacific Islands, and they took the first right. When they reached a cell, Chacko positioned a Jimmy over the lock and activated it. Two seconds later, sparks flew as the lock shorted out.

Malcolm held his Daemon out to the side and slid the door open. Inside, two enormous glowing eyes stared at him from the corner. At first he thought the Godjan was sitting, but then it scurried along the far wall; it stood less than a meter and a half tall. "We're not going to hurt you. We're here to rescue you."

The Godjan whimpered.

Malcolm held out his free hand and took a careful step inside. "Please, come with me. We'll take you someplace safe."

The Godjan's shining, watery eyes darted between him and Chacko twice. Then the prisoner leapt forward and hugged Malcolm around the hips.

He tried not to stagger in surprise and placed a hand on their shoulder. "Yes—safe. But we need to go now. Stay close to us."

They nodded against his uniform, and he maneuvered them out the door. Chacko took the lead on the cell opposite them. The prisoner inside short-circuited its own panic attack when it saw its brethren hugging Malcolm, and they hurriedly ushered both down the hall and around the corner.

Nails dug into Malcolm's thigh when the Godjan clutching him saw the wormhole, and he tried to pat them reassuringly. "It's a shortcut to someplace safe. I'll walk you through, okay?"

They didn't resist when he began walking forward, and after a few steps they breached the wormhole and stepped into the hold of the ship. He waved the second prisoner onward. Following a brief hesitation, they tip-toed across the threshold.

Malcolm gently moved the Godjan's hands off of him and gestured to the waiting Corporal. "This man will take care of you." He spun and rushed back into the dungeon.

Damn, he'd missed this.

RW

Lieutenant Diya (mission): "Drones are down! Need backup in Grid C!"

Malcolm nudged his newest charge toward Chacko. "Get them to the extraction point."

Admiral Jenner (mission): "Hold tight. I'm on the way."

He knew where Grid C was because he'd memorized the layout, but he needed to keep the TacMap open to determine where *he* was and how to get from here to there. He raised his Daemon and cleared the next hall intersection, ran three meters, then repeated the actions at the next turn. Then the next.

He bumped into two Marines with two Godjans in tow and motioned them onward. "To the wormhole. I've got Diya."

Five seconds later, laser fire sliced past his ear. He flattened against the wall, blinking away the strange inverse floaties that muddled his vision in the fluorescent light.

Admiral Jenner (mission): "Diya, flash your position."

On the TacMap, a green dot blipped. Eight meters and two turns away. Between them waited at least one Savrakath guard. But nobody made defensive shields the way AEGIS did. He readied his Daemon and charged around the corner.

Laser fire washed over him and eVi alarms disappeared behind the light flooding his virtual vision as he plowed ahead and landed shoulder-first into the chest of the guard. They both crashed to the floor. But unlike the guard, Malcolm had been ready for it. He punched his Daemon into the guard's throat and fired.

The blood gushing across the floor shone purple in the false light as he climbed off the guard, checked the next corner and slid in next to Diya—which was when it belatedly registered that the big guy was a tech officer. Huh. "Report, Lieutenant."

Diya motioned to his leg, which glistened eerily above the knee. "Took one in the thigh after a guard caught the drone coming around the corner and whacked it with a shock rod. Not that guard, sir—there's one more active."

"Understood. Can you walk?"

The man sighed shakily. "I can limp, sir."

"All right. Tighten up your tourniquet and be ready to move. I need to take out the last guard."

"Yes, sir. I'll be ready."

Admiral Jenner (mission): "Odaka, report."

Colonel Odaka (mission): "Forty-three prisoners have come through. Five empty cells."

Admiral Jenner (mission): "We've got one free guard on the grid. Everyone be on your toes. Get your active prisoners onto the DAR and hold position. Odaka, send one team to clear through Grid C. Chacko and I will cover the last four cells."

He reviewed the TacMap. One corner of the maze remained uncleared. No live fire echoed in the claustrophobic hallways, which put the guard in that direction.

Admiral Jenner (private): "Chacko, meet me at the northwest corner of Grid C. Weapons hot."

Lieutenant Chacka (private): "Yes, sir."

Malcolm checked on Diya again, who gave him a weak thumbs up. "I'll just wait here until you get back."

"You do that." He moved out into the hallway.

This deep in the dungeon, even the plastic walls sweated, and under the fluorescent light they seemed to shimmer and writhe. The air felt laden in his lungs and pressed against his breastbone from both directions.

A dot in motion warned him of Chacko's approach, and a second later the man appeared beside him. Malcolm held a finger to his lips, then pointed to the left then the right. They crept toward the final branching hallway.

At the crossway they each swung in opposite directions, Daemons raised. A shadow cast upon the fluorescent backdrop raced forward, shock rod leading. Malcolm fired twice. The shadow fell at his feet.

Admiral Jenner (mission): "Last guard down. Prepare for evac when we arrive with the remaining prisoners."

He and Chacko quickly got the last cells open. Only two were occupied, and both Godjans were terrified into zombie-like compliance.

They met the team Odaka had sent to Grid C after a few meters and handed off the Godjans to them. "Take them to the extraction point. We need to get Diya."

Diya was standing when they arrived, though he leaned heavily against the wall and sweat soaked his face. "Admiral, ready as requested."

"Good job, Lieutenant. Let us help you out." He and Chacko each slid an arm around either side of Diya to support him—

Colonel Odaka (mission): "We've got activity at the lift. Hurry your ass up, Jenner."

No time to get miffed at the over-familiar attitude on an open channel. He grabbed the waist of Diya's pants to keep him upright. "I know this is going to hurt, but we've got to move."

The three of them trudged out into the next hallway. Diya grunted but kept dragging one foot in front of the other as staccato fire erupted in the distance.

"Faster, sir. I can do it."

Said the man with blood gushing freely down one leg. "All right, Lieutenant." He picked up the pace a touch.

Thirty-eight meters. Four turns. A blast shook the walls, and he instinctively glanced up at the ceiling, willing water not to start pouring out through racing cracks.

"Sir—"

"Whatever self-sacrificing thing you were about to say, Lieutenant, don't. Not when we're this close."

Shouts reverberated around the last corner. "Stop that grenade!" "Don't let them—"

"Around this turn, it's fifteen meters to the wormhole. At five meters, I'm shoving the two of you through it."

Diya protested. "But, sir—"

"Let's go!" Malcolm forced everyone around the corner.

The ring of the wormhole shone luminous gilt against a tableau of blacklight and laser fire. Blue flames licked just beyond it.

Admiral Jenner (mission): "All squad members, withdraw to the ship now. That's an order."

Not even Odaka would refuse an order from the Fleet Admiral, and human-sized shadows began slipping into the golden ring and the hazy ship on the other side.

Concentrated laser fire skimmed the rim of the wormhole to drive into Malcolm's shoulder; his shield hissed and burned. Eight meters. "Chacko, now!" He let go of his hold on Diya and shoved them forward. Chacko dragged Diya the last two meters and they fell into the DAR hold.

Malcolm jerked backward as the laser fire burned through his shield and his shoulder. Odaka's hand reached out from the space-time tear into the dungeon, urging him onward, and he sprinted toward it, his own hand outstretched—

—a blast tore through the dungeon walls and a rain of fire tore through the wormhole into the ship. The wormhole flickered out of existence. Something heavy and burning hit Malcolm in the head, and darkness consumed him.

56

MIRAI

OMOIKANE INITIATIVE

arlee followed Mia through the newly constructed permanent wormhole to the Asterion Dominion and
stepped onto another world.

Granted, she stepped through wormholes onto other worlds all
the time. But this was *another world*. Three megaparsecs from the
fringes of Concord space, home to a species who shared a vague
genetic legacy with humans but had lived apart from anything
Marlee had ever known for seven hundred thousand years. A culture and society that had shaped itself and bravely struck out on its
own path through the void.

The room they emerged in was an anteroom of sorts, and
someone—an actual Asterion!—greeted them and escorted them up
a lift into a much, much, *much* larger and more crowded room.

Her eyes swept across the space and the cacophony of energetic
activity it struggled to contain.

Snap impression: in many ways, despite the aeons-long distance and time separating them, it looked nearly identical to an
oversized Concord government meeting room. Tables, desks and
chairs. Screens that looked different in their physical details but still
displayed data in Communis. People talking and working, some
drinking out of bottles or mugs. A few discarded plates and jackets
scattered here and there.

Follow-up, more-considered-by-1.5-seconds impression: yet it
was different. For one, everyone in the room did indeed glow,
though en masse the subtle sheen nearly blended into the background and faded from active perception. And damn they were a

graceful species. They glided almost like Novoloume, but without reservation or formality, without pretense or presentation. Swiftly, too—their custom-designed limbs propelled them across spaces with impressive efficiency and speed. She doubted even a Barisan could outrun a one of them.

Marlee smiled, which coincided perfectly with Mia gesturing to her as she talked to a woman—Nika Kirumase. Alex's friend, and the reason they were here at all.

Marlee offered a hand in the slight Asterion variation on how humans shook hands, for she'd done the reading ahead of time. "It's such a pleasure to meet you, Advisor Kirumase. I'm Marlee Marano—I believe you know my uncle, Caleb." She didn't so much as flinch or scowl when she said it.

"Oh, I do. He and Alex have been wonderful to me."

"We'll endeavor to continue to do the same. Has Mia told you? We come bringing not merely aid, but an offer of a formal alliance. And not merely a formal alliance, but the first fruits of such an alliance."

Mia cleared her throat politely. "Yes, thank you for spoiling the not-so-big surprise." She produced a tiny crystal hexagon as well as a reader for it. "On behalf of the Concord Senate, I hereby present the Asterion Dominion with a formal invitation to enter into an alliance with the member species of Concord. The details of what such an alliance entails are on the data crystal. You can of course take as long as you need to review the terms and come to a decision."

"The Anadens agreed to an alliance?"

Mia's lips twitched. "The Anadens did not. But the Concord Senate does not require unanimity in its votes. Don't worry, the offer is presented with the full weight and authority of our government."

"I understand." Nika's eyes danced—Valkyrie was right, they *were* like bioluminescent oceans—as she took the reader and placed the hexagon in it. A virtual screen stuffed thick with boring government-ese materialized above the hexagon.

The woman studied it briefly. "A moment, please." Her irises sparked with tiny streaks of what looked an awful lot like genuine electricity, and her posture shifted a little. It didn't freeze exactly, but Marlee got the distinct feeling that she was no longer quite *here*.

In her peripheral vision, Marlee noticed several other people in the room had adopted similar postures where they stood. A handsome man with chestnut hair who had been approaching them; a blonde woman in a severe gray pantsuit; an androgynous individual with wavy white hair and bewitching fuchsia irises.

Less than ten seconds after whatever it was had begun, it ended. Nika blinked and gave them a brilliant smile. "Thank you. We accept. You'll have formal documentation on our part in a few minutes."

Mia took it all in stride. "Wonderful. I welcome the prospect of our long future together."

Marlee, however, fidgeted until she couldn't stand it another second. "Do you mind if I ask, what did you all just do? You went away, and so did he—" she pointed to the man who had now come up behind Nika to touch her waist in *that* way "—and several other people."

Nika huffed a laugh. "We have a technology where we can use our kyoseil to link together mentally. We call them 'ceraffin.' The Advisors have a ceraff hub here in the Initiative we use whenever there isn't time to get together around a table."

"That's fantastic. Can I see the hub? I mean, I'm curious."

Mia laid a warning hand on her elbow. "We have more important matters to discuss right now."

Nika shot her a wink. "Maybe later." She indicated the man who was positively snuggling up to her by now. "This is Dashiel Ridani, one of our Industry Advisors. You've already met Senator Requelme, but this is Marlee Marano, Caleb's niece."

"Nice to meet you." He offered her a hand and nod, then turned to Nika. "Can I borrow you for a minute?"

"Sure. Excuse me—and make yourselves at home."

As soon as they'd stepped away, Mia sighed. "Marlee, please try—"

"Do you think their ceraffin are similar to the Noesis?"

Mia's brow furrowed in mild exasperation, as it so often did with Marlee. After a second, though, her gaze drifted to consider Nika as the woman talked quietly with her lover. "No. I don't think they are. I suspect even us Prevos would be blown out of the water were we to experience a ceraff. I realize the Asterions look like us and talk like us, but...I'm not certain this means they *are* like us."

"But they're not different in a bad way?"

"No. Just in a different way. Something to remember." She schooled her expression as Nika returned.

"I'm sorry about that. We have a lot going on, as you can imagine." Nika clasped her hands together. "So, where do we begin?"

RW

"Dashiel's finalized a process for extracting pure kyoseil from Reor, so we're ready to begin receiving as much of it as you're able to send. Be warned, the volume requests might get very high very fast."

Mia shrugged. "I believe the supply chain was set up when we delivered the first shipment for testing, so tell Advisor Ridani he can open the floodgates."

"I will." Nika bit her lower lip. "I can't properly convey to you what a difference this is going to make for us. Thank you."

"This is what the alliance is for."

"It is. But I'll be honest with you. I need to revise my statement from our last meeting. Right now, the greatest gift Concord can give us—greater than a thousand tonnes of Reor, but don't tell Dashiel I said that—is ships. Or rather the promise of ships when we need them. Your people have toured our shipyards and military facilities. They know the deficit we're scrambling to dig ourselves out of."

423 | G.S. JENNSEN

"They do—we do. And you've seen something of what we can provide in that regard." Mia dug another hexagon out of her bag and slid it across the table. "This is from Commandant Solovy. It details our standard protocols and how we'll need to harmonize procedures when it comes to fleet requests, movement and so on."

"We should get this to Commander Palmer, where it can actually do some good—oh, speaking of." Nika stood and focused on a muscular man with close-cropped tawny hair as he hurried over to them, then frowned once he drew closer. "What's wrong?"

"Let's talk in private." He eyed Marlee and Mia warily before stalking away to wait impatiently.

Nika's expression darkened. "I apologize. Let me find out what's happened."

"Of course."

The instant Nika had left, Mia shifted to Marlee wearing an honest-to-god grin. "I have something to show you."

She perked up. "Then do show."

A small aural materialized between them. It showed one of the little-used lounge rooms at Concord HQ. In it, dozens of Godjans huddled on couches or sat on the floor against the walls. Military officers knelt beside several of them, while one handed out blankets and water bottles.

"Oh my god. What is this?"

"I didn't want to tell you until the mission was a success, but a few hours ago, we sent in a special forces squad to rescue the prisoners from the Okshakin facility. They'll be granted refugee status. They'll be taken care of."

"Ah!" She leapt up and grabbed Mia in a hug. "Thank you!"

"You're welcome." Mia patted her on the shoulder then urged her back into her chair. "It's only a start. We know there are a lot of Godjans to rescue, but these were some of the worst off and most in need."

"They look dreadful." Marlee studied the aural. "A couple of those Marines don't look so great, either. Did they meet resistance from the Savrakaths?"

Something unreadable passed across Mia's glittering jade eyes. "I assume they did. I don't have the details of the raid yet. I arranged for the visuals to be sent to me as soon as the Godjans arrived at HQ. Hopefully we'll know more soon. The important thing is, these refugees are safe."

Marlee felt as if her heart were about to burst out of her chest. "They really are. I think we—"

Nika returned to the table appearing so grave and agitated the vibes she gave off sent chills racing along Marlee's arms, and joy turned to trepidation. "I hope you meant everything that data crystal said."

Mia lifted her chin. "I assure you we did. What's happened?"

"One of our pilots who was unaccounted for and presumed dead after the Rasu stronghold battle just reappeared on our radar. His fighter fell through a wormhole and crashed on a distant planet, as did one of the Taiyok fighters and part of the Rasu leviathan that created the wormhole in an attempt to escape. Skipping over the details for now, the Rasu found his fighter and disassembled it, and he's concerned they were able to read the navigational data it held."

"Which would lead them here?"

"Maybe not here, but almost certainly to Namino, where our military forces are headquartered."

Mia stood, as others in the room began drifting closer to the table. "How long ago did the Rasu discover the ship?"

"The time differential is a bit fuzzy, but at least several days ago."

Commander Palmer showed up again with Ridani in tow. "We need to move on multiple fronts, right now."

"I realize we do. Dashiel, how long until the cloaking shield is ready to be deployed over Namino?"

Ridani shook his head. "Deployed? Two weeks. Ready for limited testing? Three or four days."

"Is there any way in the stars you can make that be three or four hours?"

His gaze darted between Nika and Lance. "I can move some mountains and maybe get it down to two days from now. But hours? No. Only sixty percent of the satellites are in orbit, and the power generators are still being assembled."

"Move those mountains. We'll have to hope we have two days."

"I'm on it." Ridani pivoted and rushed off to one of the many workstations dotting the room.

Commander Palmer grunted. "Hope never won a battle. I'm returning to Namino, to DAF Command, with the intention of getting the rest of our fleet in the air."

Mia took half a step forward. "If it's permissible, we'd like to join you there. If events move quickly, I can communicate your needs to Concord Command faster and more accurately if I'm on the scene."

"Considering you have a direct line to Commandant Solovy, I won't disagree." He gestured toward a row of shimmering portals along the back left wall. "Luckily for both of us, it's but a few steps away."

Nika grasped Mia's hands in hers. "Contact me if you need anything at all, and come back here whenever you need to. I don't know what the next hours will bring, but we'll get through them better working together."

"We will." Mia motioned to Marlee, and they followed Commander Palmer toward the row of portals as Mia sent her a pulse.

It looks as if this visit is going to get uniquely interesting. I hope you're ready.

I put on my big-girl pants this morning and everything. I'm ready.

RW

NAMINO

ASTERION DOMINION

DOMINION ARMED FORCES COMMAND

DAF Command was basically a grumpier, more utilitarian version of the place they'd just left. Military officers manned workstations and gruffly studied maps and charts. Everyone kept their posture rigid and saluted every thirty seconds.

Mia huddled up next to Commander Palmer to talk requirements and procedures, and Marlee considered the room with a sigh. She'd told Mia she would get deep-scans of working Asterion technology; everything had moved so fast on Mirai that she hadn't had a chance to get close to any of the equipment, but this seemed to be as good an opportunity as any.

She idly wandered past several workstations in use, surreptitiously zooming in her ocular implant to capture high-res visuals as she passed. One officer noticed her, but he simply gave her a curt nod in response before burying his head back in his work.

An empty but active workstation stood a few meters away, and she drifted closer to trail a fingertip over the virtual input panel, hoping to pick up dormant electrical signals or input receptors—

—a hand landed on her arm. "Committing espionage so soon? We've only been allies for a few hours."

She jumped in surprise and spun to the speaker—at which point she plastered on her most winning smile for the beautiful man standing in front of her. Dirty-blond hair fell beneath a sculpted jaw to frame lustrous eyes that reminded her of the fine aged whiskey Gramps enjoyed (except for the nanocircuitry) and an easy, enticing smirk.

"Hi. I'm Marlee Marano, and I promise I'm not stealing anything."

"Only borrowing, then?" He stuck out his hand. "Grant Mesahle. You're from Concord."

What was Concord again…? "Yes! I work with Senator Re-quelme at the Consulate." She tilted her head toward the large center workstation where Mia and Commander Palmer murmured in animated gestures. "The conversation got a bit too technical and grim for me, so I was merely looking around. I probably shouldn't have touched the equipment. I'm sorry."

He shrugged like his shoulders were always meant to move in such a way. "I won't tell, so long as you keep your bounty under a petabyte in size." He reached in his pants pocket, produced a small case containing a thin weave of nanofiber coated in a translucent material, and handed it to her. "Consider it a thank-you gift for sending your fleets our way."

"And that we will be doing." She accepted the mysterious case and tucked it away. "Hopefully we won't need to for a little while yet. I guess a lot is still up in the air."

He nodded sagely. "Doom upon the world or some such, but we don't know when."

"Maybe it won't be doom. Concord's military is *really* awe-some—and I'm sure yours is as well."

"Hmm." He frowned toward the center workstation. "If I stay in here much longer, Palmer is going to notice and yell at me about something, when at this point in the game there's nothing more I can do to alter the outcome. Would you like a tour of the complex?"

She hoped her face didn't light up too over-much. "Absolutely."

He motioned to the door, and they tip-toed out into a small lobby area and took a left.

"Hey, are there any Taiyoks here by chance? My specialization is in interfacing with various alien species, and I was hoping to meet one."

His mouth quirked around as he thought on it. "Not in the building, but there are a couple of Taiyoks working down at the market a few blocks south. Want to go there instead?"

She stared back at the door, where inside Mia was doing the diligent work of crisis diplomacy. Her boss was a master at it and didn't need her help. "I'd love to."

57

CONCORD HQ

COMMAND

Alex pulled a knee up to her chest and sank deeper into the chair opposite her mother's desk. "The Senate legitimately voted to provide military support to the Dominion if they're attacked by the Rasu? I confess, I'm shocked."

Miriam refilled her teacup and came around the desk to sit beside her in the second chair. "They did. Everyone had their own selfish reasons for doing so, naturally. The Khokteh are always itching for a good fight. Though they'll never admit it, I think the Novoloume like the Asterions' style, and the reality is the Naraida still vote with the Novoloume ninety-five percent of the time."

"And the Anadens?"

"Voted no in the most strenuous terms. I worry about the fallout to come...but it's my responsibility to worry. On a related note, I'm told all the kinks have been worked out and the first large shipment of Reor, all ten tonnes of it, is being delivered to the Dominion today."

Alex smiled gratefully, which she was. For once, the bureaucratic obstacles had melted away before she'd needed to resort to blasting through them. "It will be a huge help to them."

"So it seems. And they have the schematics needed to produce adiamene now?"

She blinked, stunned into silence. Her mother had caught her completely off guard with this one. *Well played, Mom.* "I don't know what you mean. They shouldn't."

Miriam took a casual, nonchalant sip of her tea, and Alex swore she detected a devious glint in her mother's eyes as she did. "Fifteen years ago, Kennedy sat in my living room in Vancouver and pronounced that she would sell adiamene to whomever she damn well pleased, governments and bureaucrats be damned. Your bad influence on her, I assume. Not long after that, she sold it to me—to Volnosti—when I most desperately needed it. A great deal has changed since then, for her, for me and for our governments. But I suspect her cavalier spirit isn't quite dead and buried." Miriam paused for effect. "Especially if you asked her to do it."

Alex groaned and dragged her hands down her face. Damn her mother for being savagely insightful!

"So that's a 'yes,' then?"

She leaned forward and dropped her elbows to her knees to stare up at her mother. "Please, please, *please* don't share your suspicions with anyone. Anything that might or might not have been done by anyone was all executed under cover of darkness using extreme spycraft, and I promised Kennedy it wouldn't come back to bite her this time. She has a family to protect now, not just principles."

"I won't do any such thing. As you said, they're only suspicions, and policing the sale of adiamene no longer falls within my job description. But what is she going to do when Asterion ships with adiamene hulls start showing up?"

"Hope no one notices through the haze of Rasu weapons fire?"

"I see."

"Then blame thieves. I expect Vii has worked up a theft report to be backdated and inserted into Connova records if or when it's needed."

"This isn't, as they say, your first rodeo."

"No, Mom, it isn't." She chuckled faintly, thankful in a thousand ways that they were friends now. Once upon a time, this conversation would've gone very differently, replete with shouting, expletives, thrown objects—on her part anyway—and overdramatic exits.

"How was the funeral?" Miriam grimaced. "That's such a terrible question, I'm sorry. Never mind."

"No, it was...sweet. Lovely. Sad."

"And Caleb? I haven't seen him since the Rasu meeting."

"He's searching for Eren. Eren didn't come to the funeral, and no one has seen or heard from him since he left Akeso that night. He's disabled his personal and ship trackers and his regenesis feed."

Miriam nodded thoughtfully. "Grief does terrible things to people. I suspect none of this has been easy for Caleb, either. I don't want to intrude on personal matters, but is it good for him to be alone right now?"

"Oh, he's not alone. Felzeor's with him."

"Oh, well then. This actually does ease my mind. The bird could bring sunshine to the seventh level of Hell."

"Right? I think he—" A message arrived from Nika in her priority feed; she was leaping up from the chair as she scanned it. "I hope the Senate is ready to make good on defending the Asterions."

"Why? Are the Rasu already there?"

"Not yet, but the Asterions have reason to believe some Rasu have learned where Namino—one of their Axis Worlds—is located. I'm sure you'll be receiving official word in the next few minutes. It won't be long now." Alex grabbed her coat from where she'd tossed it on the way in.

"Where are you going?"

"To the fight, of course."

Miriam pursed her lips and set the teacup on her desk. "Would it make the slightest difference if I asked you not to?"

"I mean, I'd appreciate the thought, but...no."

"Very well. I will see you there."

"You'll be taking the *Stalwart II* to the Dominion?"

"When the time comes, yes."

Alex found herself surprised by her mother yet again today. "Thank you. Your presence will make for a tremendous morale boost."

"For whom?"

She shrugged. "Everyone, I assume."

"Perhaps, but that's not why I'm going. I won't cower here while I send my forces against a new and unknown foe. I need to be at their side and take the measure of this enemy for myself."

"Okay. Point taken." She took a couple of steps toward the door, then glanced back. "Thanks for the talk. Kill lots of Rasu and come home, or I'll never hear the end of it from Dad."

Her mother smiled, though her fingertips were already racing over a screen. "Same to you."

58

LETHE

Old reflexes sputtered and stretched the instant Caleb exited the *Puddle Jumper's* airlock and entered the Lethe spaceport, but meeting instinctive resistance on his part, they quickly retreated into hiding once more.

There was a good reason for the gut response. He was stepping into the lawless fringes, the ragged frontier where civilization hadn't quite won the battle over barbarism.

To the extent this planet was lawless, of course, it was only because the Anadens allowed it to be so. Lethe was an ancient Anaden world, one nominally run by an Idoni *elasson* but mostly run by the gray- and black-market interests said *elasson* granted free rein.

Caleb suppressed Akeso's shiver; he needed to steel himself for what awaited him. A spaceport was where a planet presented the best version of itself, and the world outside its doors would hardly be more pleasant.

Felzeor clucked disapprovingly on his shoulder as they passed a vendor selling exotic pets restrained with chains and manacles, and Caleb reached up to stroke his pelt.

"Listen, I don't think it'll take me long to check out this hotel. Why don't you stay here in the spaceport? You can ask around if anyone has seen Eren come through here recently, then try to find a food establishment we can eat at and not get food poisoning."

"Noooo." The protest ended in a warble. "What if Eren is still at the hotel? Whatever state he's in, I want to be there when you find him."

"I'm sure he's not. I'm afraid we're following a cooling trail. I merely want to see if he left any clues behind as to where he's headed next."

Eren had used his registered account to pay for the hotel room, which meant either he was too out of his mind to think to conceal his movements or he didn't care if anyone followed in his footsteps. Neither option filled Caleb with hope.

"You are trying to protect me. But if I stay here, who will protect you?"

Caleb opened his mouth, but found he had no good response to that. Instead, he laughed in a way he hoped sounded reassuring. "I think if we're both on our guard and very careful, we can each protect ourselves. This is a dangerous place for the unwary, but that isn't us."

"No, it isn't. I am most definitely wary."

"Me, too." He patted Felzeor's tail and nudged him along. "Off you go. I'll be back soon. And remember, no food poisoning!"

RW

The dirty façades lining the dank, too narrow streets threatened to close in on Caleb from both sides. Out of the shadows, tripped-out revelers, the dealers and thugs who managed them, and worse leered out at him.

He belatedly tried to coax those old reflexes back out to help him track every movement, every potential threat to come ahead as well as those he hadn't quite cast aside, but they had already faded back into slumber.

All senses Your deep unease. Your blood crackles and pops, and your muscles strain in anticipation of extraordinary action. Come home, so that All may soothe.

I can't come home yet. Soon. I have a debt to repay first.

Akeso was justified in its anxiousness. There had been a time when he would have owned a place such as this—known every lackey and street corner boss, known precisely who to pressure and

435 | G.S. JENNSEN

who to bribe to get the information he needed. Once upon a time, he'd stalked streets like these, cocksure and righteously convinced of his own physical and moral superiority.

If a junkie thug jumped him now, would he even be able to emerge victorious from the melee? He kept his cybernetics updated with the best new routines, and his muscles had never forgotten how to move to protect him when threatened. But did he have the drive—the heart—required to win a fight when everything hurt and the injuries started piling up? What might happen if the other person wanted to win, *needed* to win, more than he did?

He wasn't a killer any longer, not in his Akeso-warmed soul. But could he still kill when it became the only option left to him? He wanted desperately to believe that if Alex were in danger, if Marlee or Isabela or Felzeor were threatened, nothing could hold him back from committing the most extreme violence imaginable if it meant saving them. Not even Akeso's boundless love of all living things.

But what if he was wrong? What if Akeso's repugnance toward violence overpowered him and left him cowering in horror, helpless to save either himself or those who mattered most?

A pernicious gloom dragged his mood toward the gutter with the junkies, but he tried to reason it away. This melancholic brooding he was in danger of wallowing in...was he *missing* the man he used to be?

Perhaps a little. So he acknowledged it, reminded himself of his own advice—*we don't get to choose what happens to us, but we always get to choose how we react to it*—and put it aside. This was the man he was now, and in the grand scheme it was an easy price to pay for being alive.

The grimy hotel sign ten meters ahead saved him from further torturous introspection, and he gladly left the street behind for the lobby.

Though the lobby was scarcely better. Two threadbare chairs framed a broken table, and a sweaty Idoni man slouched behind a dimly lit counter. "What do you need, Human?"

"I'm looking for a guest who stayed here recently. Eren Savitas asi-Idoni." In recent years, many Anadens had started using their lineage name as a surname, though most hadn't yet taken the leap of dropping their Dynasty altogether.

He flashed an image of Eren in the man's face.

"That burnout? Yeah, he was here. I haven't seen him since yesterday, but he paid through tomorrow. Probably jacked-out in the bathtub in his room."

"Can I get access to the room? If he is in a bad way, I want to help him."

The man peered at him lazily for a few seconds. "Sure, why not." He wiped crumbs off his mouth. "For a small fee."

It wasn't worth the time or effort to haggle. "How much?"

"Two hundred credits."

And that was extortion, but, again, not worth it. "Here. Tell me the room number and key code."

"Uh-huh. Room 443. If he's rotting in there, you're paying for the clean-up."

RW

Caleb hesitated at the door. Part of him did expect to find Eren's cold body inside. It would be far from the first time his friend had died, and not even the first time Caleb had borne witness to it. But while everyone else was mourning at Cosime's funeral, Eren had logged into the CINT servers and deleted his regenesis record and his connection to the servers. Unless they could find a way to reinstate a saved copy of the man's consciousness, this would be the last death.

He understood why Eren wanted it; he genuinely did. Right now his friend was trapped in the darkest pit of despair and saw no path by which he might ever crawl out.

But this was why Caleb had traveled to this forsaken place, why he chased a man who didn't want to be found.

He readied himself and opened the door.

437 | G.S. JENNSEN

There was no body. The bed covers were mussed, and the room smelled faintly of sweat and alcohol, but he'd frankly expected far worse as a best case.

An empty hypnol vial sat on the bedside table, and he went over to inspect it. The vial bore a plain label, '*Xanthecra Dialele C,*' but lacked any other identifying markers, like a vendor of origin or ingredients. He pocketed it and checked the closet, which was empty.

When he opened the door to the lavatory, he stopped short. A mound of tangled copper curls lay scattered across the dingy tile floor.

Perplexed, he crossed his arms over his chest and considered the scene anew. Was something other than what he'd thought going on here? The only thing Eren had ever loved as much as Cosime was his golden locks. And now he had neither.

Grief made people do strange, often baffling things, but it should take something stronger than grief to elicit *this* response.

If Eren was trying to disappear, he could have easily changed the color of his hair and skin; he'd done it many times before as an anarch. No, the most rational explanation for losing the hair was if it had become a liability for some reason.

But it had always been a liability in combat situations. Eren had crafted a dozen different ways of pinning it up, back or otherwise out of the way when he needed to move fast and be nimble and deadly. But he'd never, ever cut it.

So why now? Was it possible he simply didn't care any longer? Or….

Caleb dug one of the empty hypnol vials out of his pocket.

Valkyrie, can you run a check on 'Xanthecra Dialele C'? It's an Anaden hypnol, but this is likely the pharmaceutical name for it, not the street name.

One moment. 'Xanthecra Dialele C,' also known as dialele, *is a hypnol used to increase mental concentration and acuity and physical discipline. Though strictly illegal, it is often used by assassins for hire. The primary side effect is reduced emotional responsiveness. In a non-trivial number of cases, however, it can cause extreme logical degradation leading to self-harm. In layman's terms, it can drive the user crazy.*

Oh. Thank you.

You haven't located Eren yet.

No. But I have an idea of where he's going.

He left the room without further inspection.

Felzeor, why don't you get that food to go? We need to get back to Concord HQ.

As he hit the street and retraced his steps to the spaceport with a new urgency, he sent a priority message to Richard Navick.

59

CONCORD HQ

"CINT Agent Eren Savitas asi-Idoni to see the prisoner in Cell 18. Director Navick wants me to have a little chat with him."

The guard—a Human, not a former Vigil officer—scanned Eren's ID then nodded. "The prisoner is under Level III lockdown, so you'll need to interact through the barrier. No opening the cell without two armed guards present. Do I need to get some of those?"

"It won't be necessary. Like I said, I'm merely here for a chat."

The guard motioned him toward the entrance to Detention's high-security wing. More of a hall than a wing, really, as on the whole, there hadn't been too much need to lock up highly dangerous military personnel. "Press the button beside the inside of the door when you're done."

RW

Eren didn't care that with every action he took he was leaving a trail, that in the aftermath Director Navick and anyone else who showed interest would know he'd been the one to perform this transgression—and not solely because he currently had the emotional range of a teaspoon. By the time they discovered what he'd done, he'd be gone, and by the time they caught up to him, he'd be dust in the proverbial wind. And they'd understand.

He strode calmly down the hall and pivoted to face the glass barrier of Cell 18. "Torval elasson-Machim, stand and approach the glass."

The man—Machim to his core with dishwater-brown hair shorn in a buzz-cut and rippling muscles straining against the prison garb—offered a sneer as he made a show of reluctantly pushing himself off his cot to slow-saunter to the glass. "What do you want?"

Eren slipped a narrow tube down his sleeve into his left hand. With a quick flick, he brought it up to eye level and slid it through one of the air-holes in the barrier. A long needle shot out the end and plunged into the Machim's eyeball. Just as quickly, it retracted.

"What did you...?" The man blinked twice and collapsed to the floor.

Eren watched him coldly for another five seconds, then returned the tube to the notch in his sleeve, sprinted down the hall to the door and banged on the button. "Help! We've got a medical emergency!"

The door opened as the guard hurried toward him. "What happened?"

"The prisoner stood up to greet me when I reached the cell, then suddenly fell out on the floor. I don't know what's wrong with him."

The guard frowned. "I'm calling a medical response team to Detention, but I can't leave my post."

"I understand. I'll stay with the prisoner."

Eren hurried back down to the cell and squatted in front of the barrier. Torval had landed with his right arm trapped at a nasty angle beneath him. It might even be broken; if so, that was a decent start. Drool pooled below his half-open mouth. Sprawled on the floor, he didn't look like a strong, stalwart Machim soldier, though neither did he look like a cold-blooded murderer. Here he was weak and helpless—and those he would stay.

Four minutes later, two medics and two armed guards arrived. The cell barrier slid away, and in less than a minute the medics had the man strapped and chained to a powered gurney. They guided it down the hall and out through the Detention entrance into one of the many atriums at Concord HQ. Eren followed.

One of the guards pivoted to him. "Can I help you, sir?"

"CINT Agent Eren Savitas asi-Idoni. I need to accompany the prisoner to Medical. Director Navick will want to know what's wrong with him as soon as possible."

The guard peered at him in suspicion for a breath before accepting his explanation, and Eren trailed behind the procession as they crossed the atrium and boarded a levtram for Medical.

Once they departed the levtram, he drew beside the gurney. He brushed against the guard on the right and injected a fast-acting sedative into the skin below the edge of his protective vest. As the guard started to fall, the second one whipped toward Eren, weapon rising, and he got a less friendly projectile needle in the throat.

It had barely landed when Eren had grabbed one medic from behind and delivered the sedative to the side of his neck. The second medic opened his mouth to shout the same instant Eren fired another projectile, and the needle shot inside the man's mouth to lodge in his throat. Ouch.

He took over control of the gurney and increased its speed to leave the four unconscious bodies behind. At the next intersection, he dropped a portable Veil onto the sheet covering Torval to conceal him and the gurney and took a left, toward the docking platforms and his ship.

CINT VESSEL
CONCORD SPACE

Torval sagged limply beneath outstretched arms. His wrists were held tight in dual metal and force-field restraints. Eren had welded the metal latches into the port wall of the ship's small cargo hold. The man's legs were similarly bound together and chained to the opposite wall. Before hooking him up in the restraints, Eren had stripped the man naked to ensure he couldn't reach anything he'd be able to use as a tool or weapon. Surrounding him shimmered a CINT-issue force-field cage.

That last measure deprived Eren of the ability to inflict physical abuse on the man. In his both heightened and drastically restricted chemically induced state, he felt only the mildest, detached regret at the necessity of this limitation.

He leaned on the hold's drop-down ladder and considered his prisoner. The recent increase in respiration and heart rate indicated the man would be waking up soon. Eren started to run a hand through his hair, but his palm found only bare skin. Right.

The ship drifted in the black 6.5 parsecs from his eventual destination. Getting there in the middle of a flaring war was going to be a mission all its own, but that would come in time. First....

Torval's chin bobbed off his bare chest. His eyelids fluttered twice then popped open. Instantly he yanked at the restraints, pulling them taut as he struggled against them. He stared upward at where the wrist restraints met the wall, then followed his bound legs to their conclusion.

Finally his gaze settled on Eren, dull chocolate irises burning with impotent hatred. "*What is this?*"

Eren propped a hand under his chin. "I believe the most applicable term is 'vigilante justice.'"

"What the fuck does that mean? Who are you? I demand to be released this instant!"

"It means what it means. Who am I? Your worst nightmare, for now. And no."

Torval gave a hard jerk to the restraints. "You? One skinny, junked-up Idoni, *my* worst nightmare? You're nothing. I've squashed scarier than you beneath my boot on the way to breakfast."

"Sorry. No breakfast for you today. Honestly, you might not see breakfast again. Ever."

"So, what? You're going to torture me? Peel off my fingernails one by one? Burn my skin with a torch? Ram nails into my feet?"

"Those all sound like fabulous ideas. Thank you for the suggestions."

Torval sneered. "Do it. I am a Machim *elasson*. A Navarchos. Built from every DNA strand to be a warrior. Your petty tortures will not break me."

Eren shrugged. "Probably not. But I'm not interested in breaking you. You have nothing to tell me worth hearing."

"Then why take me?"

"Punishment."

60

NAMINO

DAF COMMAND

"Yes, pull the 3rd and 4th Wings at Kiyora and Synra off patrol and move them here. Thanks to the new long-range buoys, we'll get advance warning of any incursions elsewhere, but right now we have advance warning of an incursion *here*. Let's godsdamn use it." Lance turned to the DAF Command Operations Director, Colonel Lawrence Rogers. "The planetary defense lasers?"

"Fully powered and operational, sir."

"Noted." He found the Justice Advisor, Selene Panetier, across the room, knee-deep in reports. "I assume you're ready to pull the trigger on the evacuation protocol the minute a Rasu signature shows up."

"Yes, Lance, I am ready and able to do my job. Stop wasting time checking on mine and do yours."

"Screw you, too, Panetier." He pivoted to the Human diplomat—Requelme. "What about you? How long will it take Concord ships to arrive once they've been called?"

"I've already alerted Commandant Solovy to the fact their services may be required at any time. Now that they're on alert, sixty-eight minutes."

"All right. Good." He shifted to stare at the tactical map. Ninety-one percent of his available forces were in position, staged in high orbit above Namino or on the way there. A threadbare fleet waiting for what would likely be a monstrous armada.

He'd gotten word that around eight minutes ago, Jerry had abruptly spun up and fled E183-31B at breakneck speed. The surveillance probe was following, but it felt like the Rasu was getting out of town while it still could. In this respect, Lance didn't blame it.

So the enemy was definitely coming.

If only they'd had more time. If only the Guides had listened to him and started preparing for a foe such as this one millennia ago. If only no one had survived the wormhole at the stronghold, Kiernan included. If only Supreme Commander Praesidis had developed a single empathetic bone and let Lance's people live. But that was another war in another time, notwithstanding the Anadens' sudden reappearance at this most consequential of moments.

Now he needed to win this one...and deep in the hidden recesses of his indomitable psyche, he recognized that he had no idea how to do it.

He'd readied plans for how to use the Concord forces if or when they arrived, but he wasn't going to leave holes in the defenses from the start and assume they'd get filled in later. Taiyok forces were promised to him as well, but the same went for them. More defenders would always be better, but he didn't dare count on them.

Except that without more defenders, he was royally screwed, of course. But it was what it was. For weeks now, every day had meant more ships and better weapons; these were the ships and weapons he had on the board today.

If the Rasu took their time wandering this way and Dashiel was able to get a cloaking shield up and running to hide Namino from their shapeshifting eyes? Well, maybe when the Rasu did arrive, they'd look around and decide they must have read the navigation data wrong and take their leave. Or maybe they'd fire their crystal laser beams anyway, just for kicks, and expose the lie of the shield. Hope never won a battle, so he didn't bother with it now.

RW

"Sir."

Lance spun to Rogers. If the gravity in the man's voice hadn't warned Lance of what was to follow, the somber look on his face would have. "Tell me."

"The long-range sensor buoys are detecting a Rasu signature spike from beyond the outer asteroid belt."

"Thank you." He gestured to his guest. "Sixty-eight minutes? Make it happen."

Requelme's eyes flared. "It's done. Commandant Solovy will be in touch with you directly from here on out."

"Understood. Panetier, flip those d-gates. Rogers, I'm needed up there now, so DAF Command is yours. Senator Requelme, you've done your job here, so feel free to go home. We'll be doing everything we can to hold a line, but it might not be safe on the ground here for much longer."

The woman grasped the orb dangling around her neck. "Thank you for your concern, but we..." abruptly she scanned the room, a frown pulling her lips downward "...can be home in a matter of seconds. I'm sorry, has anyone seen my assistant? She seems to have wandered off."

"I'm sure someone here can help you locate her. Rogers, they're all yours." Lance saluted Colonel Rogers, turned on a heel and hurried out.

61

CONCORD HQ

COMMAND

Miriam received the details, such as they were, of the Rasu arrival in the Namino stellar system from Mia a few hours after Alex departed.

She'd already issued a recall order for all active-duty personnel across the Concord fleets, but now she sent an updated message to Thomas.

Thomas, prepare the Stalwart II *for immediate departure at full combat readiness. I'll be on board in eighteen minutes.*

Yes, Commandant.

Next, she issued departure and rendezvous orders to the 3rd, 4th and 6th AEGIS Assault Divisions. A message to David would have to wait until she was en route.

Less than thirty seconds after Mia's communication arrived, she had initiated a holocomm conference with the leaders of the various Concord fleets.

"Gentlemen, as I'm sure you've heard by now, the Senate recently approved a formal alliance with the Asterion Dominion, including military aid in the event the Dominion comes under attack by the Rasu or any other enemy. I regret to say the Senate acted none too soon, as I've just gotten word a Rasu armada is advancing on one of the Dominion's primary worlds.

"I realize that we have many forces committed in many places, all the more so given our current need to protect civilian targets from a possible Savrakath antimatter attack. Nevertheless, we will honor our duty to our new allies.

"As Fleet Admiral Jenner is currently on a classified opera-tion—" an assignment she hadn't known he'd awarded to himself until half an hour ago, much to her dismay "—I will be taking com-mand of the AEGIS forces. I leave it to each of you to determine the precise makeup of your fleets. However, Navarchos Casmir, I need you to send no less than four Brigades to aid in the Namino defense. Pointe-Amiral Thisiame and Tokahe Naataan, if you will contrib-ute no less than two percent of your active forces.

"Commander Lance Palmer, who I believe all of you have met, is not on this conference as he is preparing to lead the defense of his homeworld. When you arrive, I urge you to follow his or-ders...unless or until they become contrary to your good judgment, at which point you will confer with me before taking any action.

"We've all had some time, though not as much as we would like, to study the limited information we've collected on the Rasu. Despite the unknowns we'll face on the battlefield today, we have extensive experience working together, and I trust we will deploy our forces to best utilize our strengths against this new enemy."

Casmir cleared his throat. "Commandant, I must inform you that in the last few minutes, I've received a communication from Senator Ferdinand expressing his vehement disagreement with the alliance vote and ordering me not to comply with any directives implementing it."

She'd had cause to worry, then. But it was a headache for after the battle. "Senator Ferdinand is free to express the specifics of his disagreement with the Concord Grievance Board, but he does not enjoy the right to disobey legislation duly passed by the Senate. And, respectfully, you don't take orders from him. You take them from me."

"Yes, ma'am. I recognize that. As I said, I merely wanted to make you aware."

"Thank you. We will rendezvous at the provided coordinates in the Namino stellar system in sixty-one minutes."

RW

SENATE OFFICES

Democracy—as well as its black-sheep sibling, republicanism—represented the worst of all forms of government. Mob rule imposed actions on an unwilling and disenfranchised minority, stripping them of their free will.

Except in this case, the Anadens weren't actually the minority, for they outnumbered all other Concord species combined by almost a trillion citizens. Yet neither their greater numbers nor their millennia of successful rule counted for a damn thing under this farce of a government they'd been bullied into joining. One vote in the Senate, granted the same weight as votes by the barely technological Barisans, the frivolous Naraida and the incomprehensible Efkam.

Ferdinand and his fellow *elassons* had tolerated the arrangement these last years in the hope that they could maneuver themselves into gradually obtaining more power, then effecting an eventual quiet takeover. The Humans, however, had proved stubbornly resilient to their attempts at inroads. When it came to manipulating the budding Concord bureaucracy, they exhibited the skill and finesse of a Kyvern.

He'd spent some time contemplating what and when might be the tripwire that led him and the other *elassons* to give up on this experiment and take back what was rightfully theirs. He'd relied on the certainty that he'd know it when it happened, and so he had. Ally with and defend the rebel *Asterions*? They might as well invite the Dzhvar to come to dinner and feast on their flesh.

Ferdinand slipped into the conference room, engaged the anti-surveillance field and opened the holo system. Over the next several minutes, eighteen representations materialized in the room with him. Four other Kyvern *elassons*, two Idonis, a single Theriz and Antalla, three Erevnas, two Diaplas and a full five Machims. Torval had been on the cusp of winning enough support among his fellow

Machim leaders to unseat Casmir when he'd been arrested for doing his job. None represented a majority of their Dynasty—and no Praesidis had been invited—but Anadens hadn't operated as a democracy in hundreds of millennia.

"Thank you all for coming. Yesterday, the Senate voted 5-3 to form an alliance with the Asterion Dominion, including the provision of military and logistical assistance in their defense against a Rasu attack. An attack that is now on the verge of commencing."

"We will not spill blood in defense of the SAI traitors."

"Correct, Otto. We will not. But we must move quickly, as Casmir has capitulated to Commandant Solovy's demands and will be ordering numerous Machim forces to the Dominion any minute." He singled out the two strongest Machim *elassons* present. The other Machims would follow their orders without question. "Otto and Hannah, I need you to assign a Vigil team consisting solely of Machim officers to my authority. I will use them to relieve Casmir of command and secure him at a secret location under our control."

Otto nodded sharply. "Done. What about Torval?"

Ferdinand scowled. "Torval experienced a medical incident while confined to his cell. He disappeared en route to Medical for evaluation."

"What? The Humans have kidnapped him to keep him out of our reach!"

"Likely so. We will deal with Torval in due time, but for now, we need to focus on removing Casmir's ability to act. Our forces will not do the Humans' bidding. Let their warships burn, and the Asterions' alongside them."

RW

DOCKING PLATFORMS

Casmir strode purposefully through the docking wing toward his new Imperium. The rest of the crew should already be on board, and as soon as he arrived they'd rendezvous with the other brigades in MW Sector 38 before jumping to the Gennisi Galaxy.

He wasn't thrilled at the prospect of coming to the aid of the former rebels and pseudo-SAIs, but the rules and his chain of command were both clear: he took orders from Commandant Solovy, and she took orders from the Senate. Concord had decided to come to the Asterions' aid, and so he would.

He rounded the corner and stopped short. Ferdinand elasson-Kyvern stood blocking his path to the Imperium's airlock. Flanking the senator were eight Machim Vigil officers. "Casmir elasson-Machim, you are hereby relieved of command of all Machim forces. Surrender your sidearm and present yourself for confinement pending charges."

The absurdity of a Machim surrendering themselves to a Kyvern rang a dissonant chord in his mind, and he almost laughed. "On whose authority?"

He sensed the arrival of more bodies behind him, he assumed additional Vigil officers under Ferdinand's control. The man was *serious*. If the Primor were here...

...but the Primor was fourteen years dead thanks to Casmir. All the Primors were dead, and now their children, freed from reason and order, ran wild.

"Currently, the authority of superior firepower. Take him into custody."

Two of the Vigil officers hesitated. "But he outranks—"

"You have your orders from the Machim *elassons* whom you report to. Execute on them or be arrested yourselves."

Casmir reached for his personal firearm—too late, but he decided he might as well null out fighting. His fingers were wrapping around the grip when a sharp sting flared in the back of his head and everything went black.

62

ADV DAUNTLESS

L ance strode onto the bridge of the *Dauntless* without fanfare but full of resoluteness. The clock had run out on formalities and games ten minutes ago.

He jerked a nod at Major Valden, his XO. "Close the airlock and depart. Let's get up there and defend this planet."

The standard departure routines proceeded around him with rapid Asterion efficiency. In less than twenty seconds, they were leaving behind the cinnabar plains of Namino for its skies and, within minutes, the stars beyond. Namino was the second planet in its system, and the blue-white star at the center burned radiant in the distance.

His tactical pane updated with the latest formation movements since he'd left DAF Command, and he studied it briefly.

Commander Palmer (ADV Dauntless): "2nd Wing, 2nd and 3rd Regiments, shift five degrees relative and spread out an additional twelve degrees. We can't leave any gaps for the Rasu to slip through. 5th Regiment, flank the 1st Wing on heading E 22° -2° z N until such time as the Rasu deviate from their current trajectory."

The regiments had barely begun to adjust their positions when, somewhat to his surprise, ten thousand Taiyok vessels arrived. He'd only summoned—requested—them twenty-eight minutes earlier. The sneaky bastards were fast when they wanted to be. Today, he was grateful they wanted to be.

Commander Palmer (Dauntless): "Generale Rhanxe, your presence is much appreciated. Our purpose here is to prevent any Rasu from reaching the surface of the planet beneath us. You are free to use your ships as you see fit to best assist in that purpose." Despite extensive efforts on this front over the last month, he still knew very little about the abilities and limitations of Taiyok warships, and if he tried to order them around, he felt certain he'd do more harm than good.

*Generale Rhanxe (*TF Phaolane*): "Acknowledged, Commander. Taking into account our observations at the stronghold, we will adapt in response to the actions of the enemy fleet."*

Lance rubbed at his jaw while he absorbed the increasing flood of information pouring into his conscious awareness. A week ago, several of his braver subordinates had suggested he create a ceraff to oversee battlefield tactics. He hadn't fired any of them for their heresy, but only because he couldn't afford to lose any officers.

His fleet had tripled in size in the last seven weeks. His number of pilots had not, but many of them volunteered to create siblings, which was damn generous of them. One class of the newer ships were installed with base machine intelligences and flown remotely by a small group of siblings of his best pilots. Further, new pilots had been training up as quickly as the flight and combat routines were able to be loaded up and integrated into their OSes. Nothing beat real-world experience, but they'd been drilling mercilessly since a few days after the stronghold victory.

What he didn't have, however, were experienced, educated, savvy and right-thinking senior officers. Lieutenants he trusted to direct formations and operations without his active oversight. Such individuals would rise through the ranks in time, but that might be time they didn't have. It represented yet another opportunity to rue the decision of the Guides so long ago to eschew a standing military for cultural reasons. If things had gone another way, he'd have a fleet of millions and a cadre of brigadiers and admirals at his command. But it hadn't, and he didn't, and he would manage.

"Rasu signatures have closed to thirty megameters, sir."

Minutes to go. "Systems, confirm the planetary defense grid has been updated to recognize Taiyok vessels as friendlies."

"Yes, sir...confirmed."

"Thank you." He called up a menu on his primary pane and entered a code.

Commander Palmer (Dauntless*): "All vessels, the planetary defense grid is now active and ready to fire when Rasu vessels come into range. Do try to stay out of the beams' way."*

"Eight megameters."

Damn, they were fast. The dots representing the approaching vessels on his battlespace pane more closely resembled a giant crimson blob. "Tactical, do we have good information on enemy numbers?"

"Greater than thirty thousand, sir. At present."

Well, that could be worse. Could be better. But assuming their new Concord friends got here in time to do any good, it could definitely be worse.

The Rasu fleet passed across the shining face of the sun, exposing a great dark horde advancing upon them, and Lance reconsidered. It could also be better.

But this was why he'd gone to all the trouble of staying alive for seven hundred thousand years. "Prepare to open fire on my mark."

63

CAF STALWART II

The 3rd, 4th and 6th AEGIS Assault Divisions exited multiple Caeles Prism wormholes twelve megameters distant from the planet of Namino. Even so, they arrived into the midst of an arena on fire. The planet itself didn't appear to be on fire just yet, but much of it was obscured by crisscrossing weapons fire, exploding missiles and ships in pieces, so Miriam hesitated to draw any rash conclusions.

Commandant Solovy (CAF Stalwart II) *(Namino Command Channel): "Commander Palmer, Concord forces have arrived. Give us fifteen seconds to get acclimated."*

Commander Palmer (ADV Dauntless) *(Namino Command Channel): "Acknowledged."*

"Thomas, what are we looking at?"

'We've arrived on the rear flank of a heavy concentration of Rasu forces. Attempting to ascertain a firm enemy number…this is proving difficult, as the number of vessels keeps changing. Asterion forces have formed a blockade of the planet, with the aid of a dozen planetary defense turrets and some additional non-Asterion vessels. Likely Taiyok.'

The Artificial hadn't used a single decimal-point percentage in his presentation; she was proud of him. "How are they doing?"

'Not great, ma'am. The blockade's holding for now, but without reinforcements, it won't continue to do so for much longer.'

She smiled to herself. "I need specifics. What does 'not for much longer' means?"

'47.2 to 61.3 minutes.'

"Thank you, Thomas." The Rasu had made so many inroads so quickly? They couldn't have engaged the Asterions more than thirty minutes ago.

Commandant Solovy (Stalwart II)(Concord Command Channel): "Pointe-Amiral Thisiame and Tokahe Naataan, take advantage of our starting position and draw some of these Rasu away from the planet. Navarchos Casmir, sweep your forces around front, toward the Asterions, and create a wedge through the middle of the attackers where they are thickest."

Pointe-Amiral Thisiame (NF Eshtaina)(Concord Command Channel): "Acknowledged and executing."

Tokahe Naataan Pinchu (KAF Yuanwoh Vneh)(Concord Command Channel): "Affirmative."

Miriam studied the developing tactical map and—she frowned. Why hadn't Casmir responded?

Commandant Solovy (Stalwart II)(Concord Command Channel): "Navarchos Casmir, acknowledge receipt of communication."

Silence.

"Thomas, locate the Imperium Alpha."

'It is not registering in the region. Checking...no Anaden vessels have arrived in the Namino stellar system.'

Perhaps there had been a hiccup at the staging point in MW Sector 38. She sent a direct message to Casmir, but didn't dally waiting on a response.

Commandant Solovy (Stalwart II)(Namino Command Channel): "Commander Palmer, with your permission, I will be bringing the bulk of the AEGIS forces in to reinforce your blockade. I'm willing to replace your ships altogether. Mine can weather the assault, but yours are getting torn to pieces. Get them out of the direct line of fire and moving to where they can do more good."

Commander Palmer (Dauntless)(Namino Command Channel): "Permission granted, but I won't leave the planet unguarded for a single second. Bring your ships into position and then we'll talk."

Commandant Solovy (Stalwart II)(Concord Mission Channel): "All AEGIS vessels, flare wide of the Rasu vessels to the extent possible

*and proceed to Namino high orbit consistent with the positioning of the
Asterion defensive forces."*

But getting around the Rasu was not quite so easy as she'd made
it sound, for they already nearly encircled the planet in an ever-
tightening noose, which left going through them. A speedy gauntlet, then. Easy enough for fighters and Eidolons, but not so much
for a dreadnought.

"Shields to maximum. Navigation, plow us a path straight
through the Rasu to the following coordinates." Roughly above the
largest city and home to Asterion military command.

Where was Casmir, dammit? Eighty thousand Anaden warships were sorely needed right now. His message had gone
unanswered for too long. Something was wrong. She sent a pulse
to Mia.

> *The Anaden fleet is a no-show at Namino. I'm wondering if
> this might be Ferdinand's doing.*
>
> *Slimy rat. I'll send Ferdinand a message and see if I can root
> out what's going on.*
>
> *Wait, are you still in the Dominion?*
>
> *I am. It's resembling bedlam down here, and they need someone
> to help coordinate a lot of activity. Also, your niece has wandered
> off chasing new aliens to befriend.*

Miriam couldn't help but chuckle.

> *Of course she has. Be that as it may, the Concord fleet—absent
> the Machims—is engaged at Namino now. I advise you to wrangle
> Marlee by whatever means necessary and return to the safety of Con-
> cord HQ.*
>
> *I'll do my best.*

The ship shuddered from the first impact of Rasu weapons fire,
which turned out to pack a significant punch. "Stay on this heading.
Weapons, do not return fire until we're in position." Lest they
never make it to their intended position.

No, that was a ridiculous thought. This ship had survived the
full brunt of the Earth Terrestrial Defense Grid. It had survived the
destruction by antimatter missiles of a massive wormhole gate and

its adjunct Arx. It had survived countless hours of battle against Machim Imperiums and battlecruisers, and the ravenous pull of a hungry and expanding black hole. It would survive a smattering of Rasu weapons fire.

She forced herself to tune out the sea of roiling aubergine metal and bright flares of lasers outside the viewport for a brief span. She had no choice but to assume Casmir and his brigades would not be arriving today—and she didn't dare ruminate on what that meant. Instead, she had to compensate for the loss, and she had to do it now.

Commandant Solovy (Stalwart II)(*AEGIS Command*): *"Field Marshal Bastian, please report to my coordinates in the Gennisi galaxy accompanied by a minimum of two divisions."*

Bastian had been kept apprised of events, and he had the temerity not to sound surprised when he responded several seconds later.

Field Marshal Bastian (AFS Leonidas)(*AEGIS Command*): *"Acknowledged. We are not at combat readiness, so expect us in sixty-five minutes."*

Too long.

Commandant Solovy (Stalwart II)(*Concord Command*): *"Thank you."*

What they could really use right now were a few hundred Kat superdreadnoughts. But the Kats were not members of the Concord military forces. In fact, they had not used their AI-driven warships since the final days of the war against the Directorate fourteen years earlier. It was possible they'd dismantled them or converted them all to cargo vessels.

Still, the Kats were acting deeply interested in saving the Asterions and defeating the Rasu, so this would seem like a worthy battle for them to make an appearance.

"In position, Commandant," the XO announced.

"Excellent. Prepare to be a damage sponge—but one that fights back. Let's see what kind of wounds we can inflict on these shapeshifters."

Commandant Solovy (Stalwart II)(Namino Command Channel): "Commander Palmer, consider yourself relieved of blockade duty."

As her ships settled in position around the planet, she ordered the Eidolon squads to begin peppering the Rasu formations with negative energy bombs up to a demarcation line two megameters out from the blockade.

Commander Palmer (Dauntless)(Namino Command Channel): "Much appreciated."

The Asterion vessels—the ones that had survived until now—began peeling off from planetary orbit to vanish into the sea of Rasu pressing in on it.

From this vantage, the Rasu appeared as a dark cloud consuming the space around them. She saw now why they couldn't get a solid fix on the number of Rasu ships. They continually divided and combined to best handle a given target, then the next.

The *Stalwart II's* primary weapon cut a broad swath into a large Rasu vessel dead ahead, and she felt a surge of pride. But it gave way to dismay as before her eyes the damage immediately began healing itself. In seconds, no hole in the vessel remained. To their starboard, she watched as a Sabre blasted a Rasu vessel with its devastating railgun weapon; the impact ripped the Rasu vessel in two...for all of ten seconds.

One hand came to her mouth as the magnitude of the task in front of them began to reveal itself.

Commandant Solovy (Stalwart II)(Concord Mission Channel): "Our adversary today is proving most resilient. Report any successes causing permanent or longer-term damage to their vessels to Thomas, so we can get the word out to the fleet."

'Commandant, thus far negative energy bombs and missiles are faring well against the enemy. Any Rasu vessel caught in the primary blast radius is being atomized, though damage outside that radius is repaired.'

"Thank you, Thomas."

Commandant Solovy (Stalwart II)(AEGIS Command): "I'm requesting all AEGIS Eidolon flights not on active Savrakath patrol or *other operations to reinforce our fleet in the Gennisi galaxy. Come with all due speed, but not before your holds are filled to capacity with negative energy bombs."*

RW

The Eidolons began arriving even before the Field Marshal's forces, and within minutes they were making their presence known. Miriam made a mental note to, in future battles against the Rasu, bring all the Eidolons. Also, to build more Eidolons.

In the past, keeping clear of the negative energy bombs would have been a difficult, if not impossible, task for the two hundred thousand ships across the battlefield. But for most of the vessels, the intricacies of such tasks were now handled by Prevos and Artificials with a level of precision no purely human mind could achieve, and it saved countless lives.

She did advise Commander Palmer to warn his own pilots to stay clear as well, but they didn't seem to have any difficulty doing so, either, perhaps for the same reason. The Taiyok vessels, when they could be spotted, flitted about with the grace and dexterity of airborne hawks, so she had to assume they were successfully avoiding the deadly bombs just fine.

There was a moment, as there was in all such battles, when Miriam sensed the tide shift in their favor. It had taken over an hour of pitched combat and constantly shifting tactics before the moment arrived, but when it did, she allowed herself to take a breath.

She was going to zero out Concord's supply of negative energy weapons today, but in doing so they were going to destroy this fleet of invaders. She could feel it in her bones—

Commander Palmer (Dauntless)(Namino Command Channel): "We have a problem. Our long-range sensors are detecting additional Rasu signatures arriving in the stellar system."

And like that, the feeling evaporated.

Commandant Solovy (Stalwart II)(Namino Command Channel): "How many?"

Commander Palmer (Dauntless)(Namino Command Channel): "Too many."

She exhaled through her nose and sent a directed message.

Praetor Lakhes, if there is any possibility of the Katasketousya making an armed appearance at Namino in the Asterion Dominion, your presence would be most welcome. And most needed.

Silence lingered in her head while the multi-species fleet of old and new allies continued to fight the good fight.

I regret to say that we are unable to send any vessels at this time.

Unable, or unwilling?

No response arrived.

64

NAMINO

DAF COMMAND

*M*arlee, get back here this instant. In case you didn't notice, the planet is under attack. It's not safe on the streets.

The streets are fine! And Grant's about to introduce me to a Taiyok. I'll be back soon.

Grant?

Yeah, from DAF Command.

Now, Marlee.

No further commentary was forthcoming, which meant Marlee was going to do whatever she pleased.

It was stunts like this that had gotten her arrested on Savrak. The girl's heart nearly always resided in the right place, and she acted out of a desire to help people, but she had no regulator. No voice in her head that counseled perhaps her latest scheme wasn't the best idea to pursue.

They'd talked about her becoming a Prevo several times, as her cybernetics skills were exceptional. But Marlee fiercely resisted the idea, insisting she didn't want to share mindspace with someone else, Artificial or otherwise. Mia was of the opinion this was precisely what she needed...unless the Artificial turned out to be as reckless and willful as Marlee.

But fire didn't yet rain down from the heavens, and if she was with someone from DAF Command she should be safe for now, so Mia rubbed at her jaw and looked around. Colonel Rogers was doing an admirable job of controlling chaos made manifest, and the other person of note in the room, Justice Advisor Selene Panetier, had rebuffed all offers of assistance.

She'd badly wanted to ask Miriam about the status of Malcolm's mission to Savrak, to seek assurance all was well, but she'd refrained, because Miriam had far greater concerns at present.

Her fingers twitched from the effort of not simply messaging Malcolm and finding out for herself. She'd long obeyed a policy of never messaging him during missions; though he could ignore her or even filter out personal messages entirely, she didn't dare risk distracting him at a crucial juncture.

We know the mission is complete, though, don't we? The Godjans are safely being cared for at HQ.

It doesn't mean the mission is complete, Meno. Some of the Marines could have stayed behind to rescue more prisoners or destroy the facility.

Of course. I'm sure he's okay. He always is.

Yes, he is.

So she needed to put it out of her mind and do her job. She went over to a corner, squared her shoulders to mentally brace herself, and sent a holocomm request to Ferdinand elasson-Kyvern.

She was a little surprised when he accepted it. He stood in front of a plain, unadorned wall—not his office. "Senator Requelme, what can I do for you?"

"The Machim fleet seems to have lost its way en route to the Gennisi Galaxy. You wouldn't happen to know where it is, would you?"

Ferdinand gave her a bored expression. "Conducting its regular patrols, I expect."

"Navarchos Casmir is also not reachable, when Commandant Solovy ordered him to report to the Asterion Dominion with several brigades. Do you have any information regarding his whereabouts?"

"He is unavailable due to an internal Anaden matter. A realignment between our leaders and our priorities, as it were. Commandant Solovy will be notified when a new Lead Navarchos is appointed. Or not. We'll see how events play out."

Mia locked her jaw to retain control over her demeanor. The snake! "What have you done with Casmir? Senator Ferdinand, are you disobeying a directive passed by a majority vote of the Senate?"

"I reserve the right to refuse to follow any directive I believe is against the best interests of the Anaden people."

"That's not how this works."

"It's exactly how it works."

"As a member of the Concord Senate, you cannot act in contravention of its laws. You will be arrested for treason."

Ferdinand licked his lips as they curled into a noxious sneer. "Oh, I *do* encourage you to try."

She cut the communication and pressed her fingertips to her temples. Ferdinand, and likely a fair share of the Anaden *elassons*, were calling humanity's fourteen-year bluff. At the worst of all possible moments.

With conflicts raging on two fronts, with many of Concord's leaders away from HQ and otherwise engaged, the Anaden leadership was making a play for power, and in doing so, pushing Concord to the brink of civil war. Ferdinand's parting challenge meant he had security protection, whether they be Machim soldiers, former Vigil officers or both, while the comment about Miriam implied they intended to attempt a military coup at a minimum.

How long had they been planning this? Quietly building support among the *elassons*, gathering resources and building connections...or perhaps it was spur of the moment, brought on by an ancient and irrational hatred of the Asterions. She hoped it was the latter, for a disorganized endeavor they would be able to subdue without much difficulty. But if not? How far were they planning to take this? Thousands of humans worked at HQ, many of them directly alongside Anadens. How far and wide did the insurrection go? HQ Security consisted of a wide mix of Concord species. Could they be counted on to secure it against a coup attempt?

Right now, in the middle of a war zone, she needed to do everything possible to keep events from spiraling out of control. Then she needed to get back to HQ—and have a *human* security detail waiting on her.

Commandant Solovy, I know why the Machim fleet hasn't arrived at Namino.

RW

STALWART II

NAMINO STELLAR SYSTEM

The *Stalwart II* shuddered from the impact of repeated Rasu fire. It splashed brightly across the defensive shields, which diverted the bulk of the energy out and away before it ever came close to reaching the hull, and the ship continued to successfully perform its primary role of a damage sponge that shot back.

Miriam planted her palms on the perch railing and stared down at the empty space between them as Mia's words rang in her ears more loudly than the vigorous activity on the bridge.

She'd done everything feasible to prevent this day from arriving, and she didn't regret most of the choices she'd made to broker and keep the peace in the transplanted home where they'd found themselves. When they'd assassinated the members of the Directorate, she'd taken every step available to her to minimize the impact on the average, ordinary Anaden. She'd worked hand-in-hand with the leaders of the human governments as well as those of the other species to spread the belief in message and deed that the way forward for them all was one of cooperation and understanding.

And it had come *so damn close* to working.

Had she tragically underestimated the powerful influence of genetics and cultural legacy? Humans had proved time and again that they could change; they were far from perfect, but when given persuasive reasons and an example to follow, they could adapt; they could become *better.*

But perhaps it had been too much to ask for Anadens to change their core nature in a small handful of years. Perhaps the six hundred millennia of painstaking genetic tinkering of the Dynasties, reinforced in generation after generation by the integrals, were simply too powerful for more than the odd outlier to overcome. Perhaps it would take as many generations to undo as it had to construct.

She was the leader of the Concord military forces, not AEGIS, and until the Anadens got their act together, she would not let them harm the other species—they who had put their trust in humanity's promise to them, who had invested alongside humans in making the vision of a new peace and prosperity a reality.

She sent Richard a secure message.

> *Casmir elasson-Machim is off the grid. It's possible he's being held against his will by a group of insurgents led by Senator Ferdinand. Or it's possible he's one of the insurgents himself. Find him and either free him or arrest him as circumstances dictate.*
>
> *Revoke Ferdinand's access to all Concord facilities, including his office and the Senate wing at HQ, and work with Security to issue a warrant for his arrest on suspicion of treason. Also, increase the alert level for all Concord facilities to Orange. I'll explain what's going on when I'm not being shot at by the most confounding warships I've ever seen.*

Next, she sent a pulse.

> *David, I need you to go to my office right away. We need to implement the Lothering Protocol.*
>
> *I'm already there. No one is getting in this office.*
>
> *How did you know? Events are literally spiraling as we speak.*
>
> *As soon as I heard about Ferdinand trying to order Casmir to commit insubordination, I suspected things were going to take a nasty turn. I've got to look out for you while you're not here.*
>
> *I love you.*
>
> *And I you,* moya vselennaya.

She forced herself to refocus on the increasingly dire situation she and her forces found themselves in. Yes, the *Stalwart II* was doing its job, but it was just one ship—one of the most powerful ships in existence, and even it was barely able to dent the enemy. With the arrival of a Rasu reinforcement fleet far larger in size than the initial attacking force, the battle had begun its slow but inexorable drift toward defeat.

For the first time, she almost felt sympathy for the enemies who had faced AEGIS fleets over the last fourteen years. How could you hope to win a battle if you couldn't destroy the enemy ships? The Rasu had yet to be able to destroy her ships, but they not merely outnumbered the combined defensive forces, they'd doubled then tripled their numbers since they arrived, purely by splitting apart.

But they fought on, because the consequences of retreat were the massacre of an entire planet. Yes, the souls of most of the people on Namino would later be reborn, she assumed, but nothing justified the torture and suffering the Rasu would inflict upon them first.

*Commandant Solovy (*Stalwart II*)(Namino Command Channel):* "*Commander Palmer, I am open to any and all suggestions as to how we might avert calamity here. My ships can weather the enemy fire all day, but when we're the only ships left, the Rasu will simply go around us.*"

She received no reply. "Thomas, what's the status of the *Dauntless?*"

'A moment. It suffered a catastrophic hull rupture ninety seconds ago.'

"I see. Thank you."

*Commandant Solovy (*Stalwart II*)(Namino Command Channel):* "*All forces, this is Commandant Solovy of the CAF Stalwart II. I am taking command of the Namino defense. Commanders, report in with ship counts and weapons status.*"

65

CONCORD HQ

DETENTION

Felzeor clucked on Caleb's shoulder as they watched the cam footage of Eren passing through the security checkpoint into Detention. "Eren looks funny without hair."

"He does." Like an entirely different person, in fact. Which Caleb recognized was the psychology behind it, and he wondered who they would find when they finally caught up to Eren. But whoever it was, they'd work through it; there was no place so dark that one couldn't come back from it.

Richard hung his head. "We almost had him, thanks to your warning. Missed him by less than ten minutes. But now he, his ship and Torval are all gone, and he's disabled the ship's tracking." He spread his arms wide. "Unless he uses his account, which I doubt he will now, I can't think of a way to find him."

Caleb kept half an eye on the rest of the footage, which showed Eren disabling two guards and two medics in a blur of chemically enhanced movement then absconding with the gurney and its occupant. "He could have shot Torval dead at any point."

"Then the man would have simply regened and gotten locked up again. I don't think that was Eren's goal here."

"Good point. So Eren is taking him somewhere…or maybe just into the void where he can…" he paused, cognizant of Felzeor on his shoulder "…have his way."

"I'm betting on the latter." Richard sighed. "Drae will be up and moving later today. I'll talk to him and see if he has any ideas."

"Let me know what he says. I'm not willing to let this go yet."

"I understand." Richard's expression abruptly darkened; after a second he patted Caleb on the back. "I need to go. I'll be in touch."

They watched him hurry off, and Felzeor fidgeted on his shoulder. "Eren's going to hurt the Machim soldier, isn't he?"

"I suspect he is, yes. But you have to realize—"

"Oh, I realize most well. The soldier killed Cosime. I don't like the thought of Eren deliberately hurting someone, but...I already forgive him for doing it."

"That's good, Felzeor. You're pretty wise."

"I try to be. It's hard sometimes."

"Yes, it is."

Caleb wandered into the atrium outside Detention, and his gaze passed over the flashing directional sign as it helpfully noted how the Consulate offices were located down the left hallway. Guilt nudged at his conscience. He ought to apologize to Marlee for...arguably several things. For challenging her dating choice, for one—that plainly wasn't his business. For acting like an ass instead of trying to understand her, her point of view, her world. For being a grumpy old man who was no fun at parties.

Oh, how she was going to gloat. He cringed merely imagining it. But Cosime's death had brought home the inestimable value of those you loved, and of making sure they knew it.

He reached up and scratched Felzeor behind the neck. "Do you remember my niece, Marlee? She works with Mia just over this way."

"Oh, can we go say hello? She was delightful. She tickled me."

"It's been a few years, and she's all grown up now."

"Do you think she's forgotten how to tickle?"

"No, but you might need to remind her how much you enjoy it."

"I can do that."

Resolved to bury his pride and suffer through the gauntlet of gloating that awaited him, he took the left hallway and the levtram to the next inner ring, which housed the Consulate and the Senate.

66

SIYANE

NAMINO STELLAR SYSTEM

Alex arrived late to Namino, on account of having forgotten that she'd ditched the *Siyane's* missile loadout in favor of a suite of probes when they'd gone Rasu hunting in NGC 55. And the initial loadout had been minimal, so she'd needed to visit the Presidio to acquire a full complement of negative energy missiles. All indications were they constituted the only legal weapons guaranteed to permanently ruin a Rasu's day.

She and Caleb had been fighting dragons and force-fed memories on Portal Prime when the Kats had begun attacking human colonies sixteen years ago, so she hadn't witnessed firsthand the terrible sieges of planets like Messium and Sagan. Possibly if she had, she would've been more prepared for the scene that greeted her when she exited the Caeles Prism wormhole.

A dark sea of malevolent metal enveloped the planet below like a horde of inky spiders descending upon the dinner lying helplessly trapped in their web.

She leaned forward in dismay. She knew something of how tirelessly the Asterions had worked for the last two months to build advanced planetary defenses and a fleet to match. In a matter of a few hours, the Rasu had shredded all those defenses with relative ease.

She zoomed in the visual sensors to try to detect non-Rasu on the inside of the relentlessly tightening web. When she located them, the news only grew worse. She'd never seen a modern human fleet—girded with adiamene, flown by Prevos and Artificials and firing advanced weaponry—lose. Yet this was what she was seeing, wasn't it?

The luminescent Novoloume ships and more traditional Khokteh vessels were already decimated. She couldn't even find an Asterion ship flying. Nor a Machim one, interestingly. Virtually all that remained were AEGIS vessels and Rasu attackers, locked in a pitched battle.

And the AEGIS vessels were losing. Not because they were being destroyed, but rather because they were simply outnumbered and outpowered. Conventional weaponry wasn't stopping the Rasu, and their supply of negative energy weapons must be running dangerously low by now.

Well, at least she'd brought a couple of those. She accelerated forward but kept all non-Rifter defensive and stealth shields active.

They hadn't gotten this close to the Rasu vessels in NGC 55; now, what struck her most strongly was the depressing solemnity of their uniformity. A featureless, ceaseless cloud of black death devouring everything it touched. She shuddered, recalling the cavernous, soulless darkness of the interior of the Kat superdreadnought she'd boarded. It had been cold, empty, alien. She'd seen Nika's memory of the interior of the Rasu platform, so she recognized these vessels were anything but empty. Still, she couldn't shake the sensation.

"You know, you should really shoot one of them, Alex. While you're here and all." She rolled her eyes at her maudlin ruminations and selected a target, one of the comparatively smaller Rasu vessels chasing a squadron of AEGIS fighters.

The missile impacted near the strange crystal weapons hub sticking out of the belly of the ship and created a right proper explosion.

One down, four hundred seventy billion to go.

She quickly picked out an additional three targets and disposed of them, but her heart wasn't in it. Her actions were but four teardrops in a vast ocean.

She waded deeper into the heart of the battle, only to watch in horror as half a dozen Rasu ships evaded AEGIS fire to breach the crumbling blockade and enter the Namino atmosphere.

All right. What to do, what to do...she wished Caleb were here. He might not have any good ideas, but he'd make the bad ones sound good. Also, he'd hold her and murmur how it was all going to be okay, even if it wasn't.

At a loss, she finally sent her mother a pulse.

Mom, I don't want to distract you, but this does not look good.

So it is not.

What happened?

Beyond the fact that we're eighty thousand Machim vessels light? The Kats are also no-shows, and the Rasu are doubling the size of their fleet every ten minutes.

Fuck. What can I do?

Other than not get killed? Commander Palmer is down. Make sure Advisor Kirumase understands the deteriorating situation and is taking appropriate steps to minimize the impact on the ground when the blockade fails.

When, not if.

I can do that.

She stared out the viewport for another few seconds, until the scene it revealed became too much to bear.

Valkyrie, I need you.

'And I am here.'

She forced a smile, though it couldn't have been a pleasant one. "You're fabulous. Fly the ship, by which I mean make like a hole in space, and keep me updated on what's happening up here."

'What's happening up here is a massacre. This is...I have no words.'

"I know. Just keep me updated."

'Where are you going?'

"To give Nika the bad news." She left the cockpit, then with a flick of her wrist, opened a wormhole and stepped through it into the Omoikane Initiative at Mirai Pavilion.

67

MIRAI

OMOIKANE INITIATIVE

"They can't *all* be down. Is it a power issue? A communication one?"

"I don't know, sir."

"Try to figure it out. And quickly."

Nika waited until the exchange ended, then touched Dashiel's arm. "Dare I ask, what is it?"

Grimness seemed to have permanently settled into the deepening lines trailing out from his eyes and lips. "The Namino defense turrets. DAF Engineering says they're all down, but they can't determine what 'down' means."

"If the Rasu have gotten close enough to shoot out the turrets...that's close."

"It is." The pane behind him beeped, and he grimaced. "I need to deal with this."

"Of course." Nika took a step back and began searching a room in purposeful turmoil for where she might next help.

Was this what the battles of the SAI Rebellion had felt like? The energy and desperation—and yes, the rapid flow of adrenaline—did feel akin to her memory of the final hours of the Rebellion, when she and tens of thousands of her fellow rebels had raced for Starbase Archine as the clock ticked down toward promised annihilation. But at least then she'd been racing *toward* something instead of in helpless circles.

Despair gnawed at the edges of her every thought; she was keeping it at bay, but barely. Most of the people here worked determinedly at their responsibilities, and she couldn't help but envy them. A bit of purpose to focus on would drown the despair beneath necessity. But she'd already done her job. She'd brought the fruits of her diplomacy to bear on the crisis. And they had to be helping...surely they were helping. But now she was left to watch in horror as their best-laid plans began to slowly, gradually crumble.

No. No one else here was giving up, so she wasn't going to, either. She spotted Cameron returning to the room and moved to—

—a hand touched her arm from behind, and she jumped in surprise as a tiny part of her brain ordered her to reach for the Glaser that no longer resided at her hip. Some NOIR habits died harder than others.

She spun around to find Alex standing there. Damn but the woman's abrupt appearances were unnerving. The bleak expression that greeted her drained her resurgent determination away in a rush. "What's wrong?"

"You're about to lose Namino. Rasu ships are entering the atmosphere nearly at will."

"What about the blockade?"

"Overwhelmed by sheer numbers. Commander Palmer and the *Dauntless* are gone, along with most of the other Asterion ships. The AEGIS vessels are the only ones still standing, and they are now hopelessly outnumbered. Without a way to destroy the Rasu ships for more than a few seconds, they can't stop them from reaching the atmosphere."

"Lance is gone?" She pressed a palm to her forehead. "Okay. We've been evacuating people from Namino for several hours now. I'll see what Selene can do to try to speed the evacuation up."

"Yes, you should do that. But have you really thought about what's going to happen once the Rasu are on the ground?"

"Yes, I've fucking thought about it—they're going to blow up all our buildings and slaughter every single person who remains."

Alex pinched her lips together and glanced away, but Nika was too frustrated to apologize. After a second Alex met Nika's gaze once again, looking as resolute as ever. "And then?"

Dashiel appeared at her side, his arm sliding along her back until it reached her waist. "*And then* they will mine any servers they left standing for information. They'll learn everything."

"No. They won't be able to break the encryption on the Committee data banks. Will they?"

He slipped around to face her. "I can't say for certain. But there's a reason why all our efforts have been focused on keeping them from reaching the surface of any of our worlds—I mean, other than the obvious reason. They might not be able to access all the files, but they'll access enough. They'll get the locations of every Dominion world. The details of security procedures, defenses and weaponry. The science behind our d-gate technology. Our psyche backup methodology—"

Alarms screeched in her mind, and she grabbed him by the arm to cut him off. "The Vault. They'll learn of the Vault, and everything will be for naught. You need to get it in the air. Send it...I don't know. Into the middle of nowhere void."

Alex cleared her throat; she had backed away to the periphery of their conversation but, not surprisingly, continued to listen in. "I can't accomplish it using the *Siyane*, but if I can get a large enough Artificial-powered AEGIS vessel here to Mirai, we can open a wormhole and move this Vault of yours all the way to Concord space."

"And what makes you think it will be any safer there? You've got a nascent civil war on your hands, and I'd wager a lot of Anadens would relish nothing more than to blow a vault full of Asterion minds to smithereens."

"Been keeping up on all the day's events, have you?"

Nika shrugged tersely. "It's my job."

"Well, 'civil war' is an exaggeration...but admittedly not much of one. Fine. We could help you move it farther into the middle of nowhere void. Outside of both Dominion and Concord space and in the opposite direction from Rasu space. When we talked about it earlier, you said you'd be able to track its location, right?"

Dashiel nodded. "We can, so long as the equipment to receive its signals continues to function."

A thousand problems with each scenario ran roughshod through Nika's mind. "Say we let Concord take it somewhere, even non-Concord space. What if everything goes wrong? What if the Concord government falls to the Anadens? They won't be the first to do so. How will we get it back?"

"I will personally ensure…." Alex drifted off as her attention swung to the left. Nika's did the same, in time to see a swirl of ice-blue lights rush into the room and take up a position between her and Alex.

I will move the Vault and safeguard it.

Alex spread her hands wide in an overwrought gesture. "Seriously, Mesme, you pick *now* to suddenly show up? Also, how long have you been eavesdropping? Also, where the *fuck* are your super-dreadnoughts?"

So this was the elusive Mesme. The swirl of lights looked no different to Nika's eyes than those belonging to the Sogain she'd interacted with. She opened her mouth, intending to speak, when the lights shifted definably toward her.

Greetings, Nika Kirumase. I am Mnemosyne.

Oh. Mesme was a nickname. Because Alex. "The Greek goddess of memory? Intriguing choice."

Is it? I recognize time is short and options are rapidly narrowing on many fronts. Allow me to safeguard your Vault for you.

"I just met you ten seconds ago, and you expect me to trust you with the psyches of millions of my people? Absolutely not."

Alex's features rippled ethereally beyond the churning yet porous lights. "Nika, I totally understand your reluctance. But the truth is, there is no one in the universe more skilled at hiding things than the Kats. They will be able to keep it safe and return it to wherever you request in a matter of minutes."

Nothing about the Kat's unexpected entrance felt right. She tried to glare at the lights. "Mnemosyne, why did you show up now, for this? Alex, did you ask them to come here?"

She shook her head.

"Then you have been eavesdropping—yes, Alex has filled me in on many of your predilections. You listened, and you chose now to swoop in like some angelic savior and offer your assistance in our time of need. Why?"

Because all your other choices are sub-optimal. They carry risks, perhaps too high of risks. I am here because I am offering you a better option.

"Oh, believe me, your option carries its own risks." She peered around the lights. "Alex, your word vouching for them means a great deal. It does. And I appreciate that you have tremendous faith in the Kats in general and this one in particular. But they haven't proved themselves to me. None of them have. No. I can't do it."

The lights calmed their agitated whirling and approached Nika to envelop her. Her pulse raced toward panic, but this wasn't the harrowing grasp of the Sogain when they stole her from the *Wayfarer*. To the extent she actually felt a presence at all, it was...gentle.

Nika Kirumase, there will come a day when you trust me as much as Alex does. More so. Please, allow me to withdraw an advance on that trust and do this favor for you now.

"How can you possibly know what the future will bring?"

I do not need to see the future to know this will come to be.

A cryptic non-answer, and she could hardly trust a godsdamn ball of lights anyway...a crazy notion occurred to her, but no crazier than everything about this interaction, so she switched to the k-band visualization.

The undulating lights faded away to reveal a semblance of an elaborate winged creature. Alex had said each Kat had their own distinctive avatar form, usually expressed only in nonspatial dimensions.

This was the first time she'd been able to see something that wasn't kyoseil using the k-band, which didn't make much sense.

She shook off the spell, switched off the k-band and stepped deliberately out of the Kat's orbit before turning to appeal to Dashiel for help. "What do you think? Am I being unreasonable, or not cautious enough?"

His brow was furrowed tightly in consternation, and he kept glancing from her to the lights and back to her. "I have no idea what to think. I mean, they did help us with the Rasu, rather a lot when you consider it. And they brought us and Concord together. But..." he shifted toward Alex "...you trust this Mnemosyne?"

"With my life, which they have saved countless times."

Nika steeled herself and, for reasons she couldn't quite explain, plunged back into the Kat's embrace. "Do you comprehend the preciousness of this Vault? To me, to my people, to my civilization? If the Rasu destroy our worlds, it will allow us to begin again. If we lose it, we will be dust on the pages of history. If the worst comes to pass, it is everything we have and all we are."

The response reverberated in her head and vibrated across her skin with the Kat's gentle touch.

I would not be here were it otherwise. I comprehend what this Vault is. What you have named it, and more. I will protect it with my very life.

Jerry's unexpected and deeply insightful observation during its interrogation popped to the forefront of her mind.

"Trust—do you understand this word?"

"It is the other half of the whole created when joined with 'promise.' It gives 'promise' its power."

She lifted a hand and splayed her fingers wide, letting the lights dance through them. Such a strange yet compelling alien this was. "Do you promise you will keep it safe, no matter the cost to you?"

I give you my word.

She drew in a deep, portentous-laden breath...and nodded. "Then I will trust you. Take it."

68

STALWART II

NAMINO STELLAR SYSTEM

The Rasu leviathan barreled toward the *Stalwart II*, weapons blazing. It exhibited no fear of Miriam's vessel, which was understandable considering the *Stalwart II* had given it no reason to experience any. Still, this was new behavior on the enemy's part.

Sustained laser fire from the *Stalwart II* burned into the side of the Rasu, and a portion of its hull gave way. Yet when the weapons' fire ceased, the area around the hull melted and expanded, and in seconds the hole was gone.

What were they going to have to do to destroy these creatures? They'd run out of their replenished supply of negative energy weapons twenty-two minutes ago. The Sabres had proved able to blast apart the smaller Rasu vessels sufficiently to keep them blasted apart for the time being, but the Rasu had responded to this weakness by no longer fielding small vessels.

The bridge shuddered, and the XO glanced her way. "Shields at twenty-three percent and dropping."

The Rasu continued advancing, blotting out the system's star beneath a great shadow. Easily four times the width and breadth of the *Stalwart II*, the leviathan would dwarf an Imperium, dwarf even a Kat superdreadnought. And it seemed determined to ram them.

Rifter use was also off the table; Rasu fire sent into a rift here was likely to emerge on the planet below and inflict the very damage they were trying to prevent.

Miriam stood firm. "The hull will hold. Target all conventional fire at the weapons assembly of the enemy vessel."

Commandant Solovy (Stalwart II)(Namino Mission Channel): "All ships in weapons range of the enemy vessel marked T14A, target your fire at the weapons assembly."

Under the sustained onslaught, the crystals tucked up into the hull began to shatter and explode. As they'd suspected, the crystals weren't Rasu. At last, a true weakness.

"Shields at eight percent."

"Acknowledged."

A final weapons blast from nearly point-blank range rocked the *Stalwart II* at the same instant the crystal assembly ruptured.

"Defensive shields are down."

Adiamene, do not fail me today. "Continue firing."

Even if she had any in reserve, negative energy weapons were out of the question at this range; a single one would tear apart the *Stalwart II* alongside their target. She'd try to create some distance, but the Rasu had demonstrated they were as fast as AEGIS ships. And though they had now deprived the leviathan of the ability to fire on them, it remained far from toothless.

"Distance to vessel is thirty kilometers."

The Rasu intended to use the one weapon still available to it— its bulk.

Miriam forced herself to sit and strap into the command chair. "All stations, brace for impact."

As the leviathan filled the viewport, she blinked and shook her head, her brain reluctant to catch up to what her eyes were seeing. The leading edge of the Rasu had begun to split in two, or...open up in the center. What was it doing—?

She should have run. "Full reverse, maximum speed!"

The *Stalwart II* lurched 'backward,' but too late and too slowly. Semifluid metal extended outward from what had seconds ago been the hull of the leviathan to envelop the *Stalwart II* until the stars and the planet and the battle vanished into blackness.

The Rasu didn't ram them after all; instead, it swallowed them whole.

Miriam breathed out. "Weapons, continue concentrated firing. Try to burn us a hole out of here."

"Y-yes, ma'am." The normally unflappable Weapons Bridge Officer's voice shook. Miriam did not fault her for this.

"Navigation, be ready to initiate burst speed the nanosecond there's so much as a crack in that metal."

"Understood." The Navigation Bridge Officer, Captain Blatahn, was holding it together a little better.

The chatter on the mission channels erupted in confusion. Should they fire on the outside of the Rasu any longer? What about potential damage to the *Stalwart II*?

Yes! *Commandant Solovy* (Stalwart II)*(Namino Mission Channel):* "All ships, continue firing on the enemy vessel designated T14A. The Stalwart II can withstand any incidental damage. If possible, concentrate fire on..." how to designate the point on which her weapons were firing from the inside? "...just keep firing."

'Commandant, it appears the metal encasing us has thickened significantly from its state when it acted as the hull of a warship. I deduce the Rasu have diverted all internal metal to reinforce the shell.'

That explained why they weren't succeeding at creating any cracks. "Systems, work on getting our shields back up. Navigation, can we fire our thrusters at maximum power in our current situation?"

"Yes, ma'am, but I believe doing so will simply result in us ramming the wall of...metal...in front of us."

"Acknowledged. But we're flying a tank. If we're able to thin the metal enough, it might be worth a try." She paused. "What about engaging the sLume engine?"

Blatahn's eyes widened. "I don't believe the engine will be able to create a bubble in the space we have available to us. I can try— that's a negative, ma'am. The sLume engine is reporting multiple system failures."

She jerked toward the Navigation station. "What from?"

"I don't know, ma'am."

"Thomas?"

'I am analyzing the data from the failure alarms.'

She never thought she'd need to say this to an Artificial, but….
"Hurry."

The Systems Bridge Officer hurried over to the command perch. "Ma'am, I've got a report from an engineering team in Engine Control. They say a purple goo is oozing into the ship from around the engine block."

Her gaze whipped back to the viewport. Adiamene was indestructible…but it did have seams. Places where equipment needed to link into the ship while operating outside of it. Could the Rasu really be so adept as to be able to squeeze through less than a millimeter gap? She recalled Commander Palmer's comment at the Rasu conference: *every atom of a Rasu is a Rasu.*

'I can confirm that the sLume system failures are due to the intrusion of a foreign substance.'

Miriam tried to ensure her own voice didn't shake. "Security, send our Marine Detachment to Engine Control, weapons hot. Any oozing metal or…anything that isn't ours is to be destroyed or—" how would they do that? "—contained in a sealed area."

Commandant Solovy (Stalwart II *Internal Channel*): "All stations to alert level Red. All personnel, have your sidearm at the ready. We have been boarded by the enemy."

RW

"The Marine Detachment is about to engage outside of Engine Control on Deck 16."

She turned to the Security Bridge Officer. "Send the Marine feed to me."

The view from a cam situated outside Engine Control materialized on a screen to her right. Four undulating strips of metal poured through the minuscule seams running along the section door. Once through, they pooled on the floor and swiftly amalgamated into faceless shapes.

"Security, what's the status of the engineers in Engine Control?"

"We're getting no response from inside Engine Control, ma'am."

Laser fire erupted as the Marines entered the corridor, but the Rasu didn't so much as flinch. Amorphous limbs transformed into razor-sharp blades and other weapons as they rushed forward to engage the Marines. Screams erupted almost instantly, and she silenced the audio. Not so she couldn't hear the screams—it was her responsibility to suffer every one of them—but because the already shaken bridge crew didn't need to hear them.

The bright flares of weapons fire sputtered and died to reveal a massacre. Blood dripped down the walls and flesh...Miriam breathed through her nose to suppress a surge of nausea. The Rasu were nowhere to be seen.

"Thomas, use every internal system to track those Rasu's movements. We need to know where they are at all times. Systems, seal off every department behind blast doors."

"Every department?"

"You heard me."

She had no reason to believe the blast doors were going to keep the Rasu contained. Due to their emergency measure nature, they were made of adiamene, but the reality of their deployment mechanism meant there were seams. But at least they should keep some of the crew safe for a while and buy them some time. Maybe.

What could she do next? The Asterions had devised a blade that cut through Rasu metal, but she had none on hand. Why would she?

What else worked against them? Nuclear weapons, which were obviously out. Same for negative energy weapons. Antimatter was out for all the same reasons, plus they had none on board what with them being highly illegal.

"Ideas, anyone? I'm open to anything."

The Systems Bridge Officer spoke up. "If we can trap them in an exterior area with an airlock, we can vent them into...what space there is."

"They'll get back in eventually, but that will slow them down. Security and Systems, look into it. What else?"

The Security Bridge Officer shrugged weakly. "We could...well, ma'am, we could blow up the part of the ship they're in."

"And kill everyone in those sections? Not the kind of solution I'm hoping for, but we need to keep it on the table. That's one reason why we're tracking them. What else?"

"Ma'am, what are the consequences if they take over the ship?"

She gave the question from the Tactical Officer its due. "The Rasu are highly intelligent. This is the first time they've seen our technology, which I believe means if they're able, they'll take it and study it until they understand it." Including their navigational data, just like they'd done with the crashed Asterion vessel. That data had led them here, to Namino. The *Stalwart II's* data would lead them straight to Concord HQ.

She schooled her expression so the dark place her thoughts went wasn't broadcast to the entire bridge.

> *Thomas, start a silent countdown of the self-destruct system. Unless I give the order, pause it at five seconds.*
>
> *Given the circumstances, I calculate there is a 72.3% likelihood this will be our only option.*
>
> *I'm going to work on that other twenty-eight percent.*

She cleared her throat and projected her voice. "We need to make sure the enemy is not able to get their hands on our technology. Weapons, work with the other ships to break us out of this cocoon. Security, give me a plan to corral the intruders onto Deck 8."

"Yes, ma'am. But...ma'am, the watch officers on Decks 10 and 11 are no longer responding."

God, they moved fast! Her crew was dying beneath her feet.

"Thomas, show me everything we have on the state of our fleets and the Namino defense."

Data burst to life across her screens. Rasu descended into the atmosphere largely unimpeded. The Khokteh fleet was decimated, down to eighteen percent strength. The Novoloume ships fared slightly better, but only twenty-eight percent remained. The AEGIS fleet remained virtually undamaged, for all the good it was doing. Worse, three additional AEGIS vessels had now been surrounded in the same manner as the *Stalwart II*.

They hadn't had time to sufficiently integrate their data streams with the Asterions or the Taiyoks, but she hadn't registered the presence of a Taiyok vessel in over half an hour.

"Thomas, who is in command of the Asterion forces now?"

"Um, Lieutenant Bishop of the *Coruscant*, sir."

Lieutenant? "Thank you."

Commandant Solovy (Stalwart II)(Namino Command Channel): "Lieutenant Bishop, I realize you're in a difficult situation. What is the status of your fleet?"

Lieutenant Bishop (ADV Coruscant)(Namino Command Channel): "Fleet? Gone, ma'am."

Commandant Solovy (Stalwart II)(Namino Command Channel): "Take a deep breath and be more specific."

Lieutenant Bishop (Coruscant)(Namino Command Channel): "Um, we have forty-four vessels reporting in. Of those, twenty-six are heavily damaged."

Commandant Solovy (Stalwart II)(Namino Command Channel): "I see. Do you have a retreat rendezvous point established?"

Lieutenant Bishop (Coruscant)(Namino Command Channel): "Yes, ma'am."

Commandant Solovy (Stalwart II)(Namino Command Channel): "Then I suggest you use it. This battle is lost, and you need to preserve every ship you can for the next one. Concord will give you what cover we can for your remaining ships to escape. Also, inform the Taiyok commander of your intentions and invite them to do the same."

Lieutenant Bishop (Coruscant)(Namino Command Channel): "I...thank you, ma'am."

"Thomas, inform me when all Asterion vessels have left the system."

Commandant Solovy (Stalwart II)(*Concord Mission Channel*): "AEGIS 3rd Assault Division, provide cover to the departing Asterion vessels."

"Ma'am, Rasu reported on Deck 2."

"*2?*" Her eyes darted to the blast door. Having secured all engines and weapons, they were coming directly for the bridge. It was what any savvy invader would do.

Despite everything that she'd seen, some part of her had continued to think of the enemy as base, thoughtless metal. This had been a mistake.

"Understood." She went over to a compartment in the port wall and activated it. A door slid away to reveal a small stash of weapons. Everyone on the bridge was nominally armed, but nominally was not sufficient today. She attached a second Daemon to her belt. "Deck Chief, please distribute the weapons to the bridge crew."

"Yes, ma'am."

Outside the viewport, the Rasu metal roiled like a viscous liquid barely ten meters from the hull. It felt oppressive, claustrophobic. They were well and truly trapped.

"Thomas, transmit a full record of events to Concord HQ. Continue transmitting until the last moment you are able to do so."

She quickly composed a short report to herself, copying Malcolm, Thisiame, Pinchu, Richard, Kennedy, Alex and David, because later she wasn't going to remember the advice she would need to impart.

One, they must immediately change every security passcode and procedure across all Concord and AEGIS systems.

Two, they needed to build adiamene hulls without seams, though she had no idea how this might be accomplished.

Three, the next time they encountered the Rasu, they should bring hundreds of thousands more ships. Ships with unconventional weapons and no restraints, ships fast enough to ensure a Rasu never got close.

The Rasu were unlike any enemy they had faced before, and they were going to need a new plan if they ever hoped to defeat them.

She sent the message off, followed by too-short and wholly inadequate private messages to David and Alex, then readied herself.

Commandant Solovy (Stalwart II Internal Channel): "I trust everyone updated their neural imprints before leaving Concord space. I know opinions differ on what good that does, but we all deserve a chance at living again, should we choose to take it. It has been an honor serving with you all."

Now she projected her voice across the bridge. "When the bridge is breached, do whatever you can to slow down the enemy and protect yourselves for as long as possible." To emphasize her point, an ominous thud slammed against the blast door.

Commandant Solovy (Stalwart II)(Namino Command Channel): "*Tokahe Naataan, Pointe-Amiral, Field Marshal, I am placing the remaining Concord forces under your commands, as detailed in the instructions being transmitted to you now. In light of this new tactic by the enemy, we cannot afford to remain here and expose our vessels to Rasu capture. Do what you can to keep as many Rasu as possible off the planet below on your way out, but please see to an orderly retreat to Concord space. Survive to fight another day.*"

Finally, she contacted the captains of the three—now four—AEGIS vessels trapped inside Rasu cocoons. "*Captains, please execute the Scorched Earth Protocol on my mark. Godspeed.*"

MIRAI

OMOIKANE INITIATIVE

Alex, you need to see this.

Her assent didn't need to be voiced, and the next instant an inexplicable image filled her mind courtesy of Valkyrie on the *Siyane*.

A giant blob of Rasu metal roiled and heaved in the hazy shadow of Namino's outer atmosphere. Laser fire from AEGIS vessels punched tiny holes in the metal, all of which swiftly closed back up.

Valkyrie, what's inside that blob?

The Stalwart II.

Alex felt behind her for what she thought was a nearby wall; when her palm found it, she sank against it in horror. *It can blast its way out, can't it?*

Not thus far. Thomas says your mother is preparing to scuttle the ship.

What? No, she can't do that.

A message arrived in her eVi from her mother then, and she scrambled to open it—

The roiling Rasu blob exploded outward to expose a raging inferno at its center. Chunks of Rasu metal shot for over a megameter across the pitiful remains of the battlefield.

It took a powerful negative energy blast at point-blank range—or from inside—to disintegrate an adiamene hull, and in the wake of the explosion virtually nothing remained of the *Stalwart II* or the Rasu trapping it.

Alex let out a pained gasp and sank down the wall to the floor.

Mom?

No response.

Valkyrie...is she gone?

The Stalwart II has been destroyed with her on board, yes. I'm certain she updated her neural imprint before leaving Concord HQ, however. I'm certain.

I know, I just.... She closed her eyes as flashes of her father's death seared across her mind like flaming arrows. Of the weeks when she'd feared Caleb was gone forever.

Regenesis for humans was new and fraught with uncertainty. What if something went wrong? What if...? She couldn't go through a loss of that magnitude again. Her heart would disintegrate from the weight of the blow and be carried away on the wind.

"Alex, what's happened?"

She reopened her eyes to see Nika kneeling in front of her, her face wearing apprehension like a second skin.

She swallowed past a raw lump in her throat and blinked away tears to let them stream down her face. "The battle's over. We've lost. Whatever you're going to do to rescue those still on Namino, you need to do it right now."

69

MIRAI

OMOIKANE INITIATIVE

Nika strapped on a tactical belt as she returned to the top floor from the armory. She slipped her custom Glaser into its holster and her archine blade into its sheath, then dug a band out of her pocket and gathered her hair into a tight tail.

Alex had vanished through a wormhole seconds after her tearful declaration, and dammit but Nika simply couldn't worry about what any of that meant right now. What she could do was take the woman's warning at face value and act on it.

Dashiel spotted her as she hurried in, and she watched a cascade of emotions sweep across his features in the time it took for him to reach her. When they settled into resolve, she braced herself.

"What do you think you're doing?"

"Going to fight. I'm the only person who's faced Rasu in combat."

"And been killed by them eight thousand and one times."

"Granted. But there will be people who stay on Namino to fight for their home, or who can't get out in time, and they'll need someone to lead them. Dashiel, I can't stay here and watch impotently while our people get tortured and massacred. I know I'm supposed to be a diplomat, but in my heart I'm still a rebel. And a rebellion is about to be born on Namino."

The resolve never broke, but he added a little half-smile as he nodded. "Okay. We'll fight."

"We...Dashiel, no. You need to stay here. We need a whole new set of ship assembly lines, and getting the planetary shielding up is more important than ever—"

"Stop. That 'I need you to do the organizational work here' line worked once, but not this time. You taught me how to fight for a reason—to fight alongside you, which is what I'm going to do."

Further protests died in her throat. She tried so hard to summon them back up, because they were all true...but the thought of having him by her side in the fight to come evoked such pure, selfish joy.

Her shoulders sagged, and she reached out to pull him into her arms. "I'll be selfish for once. Dammit, but I'm tired of not having you with me. Go to the armory and gear up."

He glanced at the door, then at her.

"I won't leave without you, but don't dawdle."

He was headed for the door when much to her shock, Adlai staggered past him into the room.

Dashiel stopped to frown. "What are you doing here?"

"Fled the clinic a few hours early."

Dashiel clasped Adlai carefully on the shoulder and pointed at Nika. "If she tries to go through that d-gate before I get back, tackle her and tie her up."

"I'm a little gimped, but I'll try."

"You will not! Who's going where?" Perrin rushed into the room and to Adlai's side; Dashiel took a long look at them and left for the armory.

"Adlai, you should sit down."

"Yeah, yeah." With her help he hobbled over to the nearest desk and sank into the chair.

Nika studied him warily as she moved to one of the terminals and called up the full Guerilla Project plan for Namino and copied it to her internal storage. "You know, at this rate you'll end up back in the tank before the day's out."

"I'll muddle through. I'm needed here. Reaching out to Selene now to get the status of the Namino evacuation."

Perrin kept one eye on him as she moved to Nika's side. "Where are you going?"

"To Namino."

"What? To fight the Rasu?"

"Nobody's more qualified."

"And you've died every time you've faced them."

"So I've heard. What does that say about what's going to happen to the people stranded there? I have to try to help them."

An unexpected and most welcome ping arrived then.

Hey, where do we go to get in on the fight?

She chuckled to herself.

Hi, Joaquim. I don't know what you're talking about.

Sure you do. Namino. I tried the closest transit hub, but all the gates are in counterflow mode. So how do I get there, short of stealing a spaceship?

Come to the Pavilion. Dashiel and I are leaving in ten minutes, so double-time it.

Got it. Ava, Maggie and Carson are with me. Dominic and Josie are already on Namino. I told them to hunker down for now, and we can meet up later.

Her heart swelled in her chest. NOIR may be officially dissolved, but its spirit lived on undampened in its members. Now there was a new fight to wage, and they were choosing to step up and wage it. She grinned at Perrin. "And I'm not going alone."

"What does that mean?"

"Not you—you have to stay here and keep Adlai alive. But Joaquim...."

Across the room, several of Lance's officers stumbled in through the Namino d-gate. She went up to them and grabbed one by the arm. "You're evacuating DAF Command?"

"Yes, ma'am. Rasu ships have started landing in Namino One."

A row of panes along the rear wall switched over to cam footage from DAF Command and each of the Namino transit hubs. She didn't have to speculate as to why. At the first sign of Rasu in proximity to the transit hubs, the Committee was planning to shut down the Namino d-gates, cutting off everyone there and quarantining the planet. *Firewall.*

She checked the entrance. She truly didn't want to leave Dashiel behind, but she was getting onto that planet.

Two more staff members from DAF Command came through, and she went back to where Adlai sat. "Do not activate Firewall until I'm through the Namino d-gate."

He grimaced and eyed the panes. "We are absolutely going to wait until the last possible second."

"That's not what I said—"

Dashiel hurried through the entrance with Joaquim and the others in tow behind him.

She exhaled in overdramatic relief. "Cutting it close! We need to move." Then she squeezed Perrin's hands and forced a smile. "Keep the lights on here for me."

"Nika...."

"Got to go." When she pivoted to the row of d-gates, she found a steady flow of evacuees exiting from DAF Command and crowding into the room. She didn't want to impede others from evacuating, but, again.... She approached the d-gate technician. "I want you to reverse the DAF Command gate flow for a few seconds, just long enough for the six of us go through. As soon as we're out the other side, flip it back so the rest of the evacuees can get here. Understand?"

"Yes, ma'am. It'll take five seconds to transition on both ends."

"Thank you." She turned and gave her cohorts a smirk. "Last chance to do the sane thing and walk away."

Ava snorted, which she guessed ended the discussion.

"All right." She waited for another person to come through, then gestured to the technician. "Do it."

He entered a command on the control pane, and a ripple passed across the d-gate. "You're clear to go."

Joaquim didn't wait for her word to barrel through the d-gate ahead of her and disappear, Ava hot on his tail. She grabbed Dashiel's hand, took a deep breath and stepped through—

—and out the other side of the frame. She looked around in confusion. She was still in the Omoikane Initiative at the Pavilion. "What's wrong? Why did the d-gate go down?"

The man glared at the control panel. "I don't know. It's saying 'no such coordinates available to lock on to.'"

"What?" Her eyes rose to the larger panes lining the rear wall. Had the Rasu destroyed the entire planet in a matter of seconds? No, even they weren't capable of that. In hours, possibly, but not seconds. She spun and shouted across the room. "Adlai?"

He stood wearing a grimace. "It's not us. We haven't activated Firewall, though Julien and Harris are shouting for us to do it now."

The hells? She left Dashiel's side to crowd into the technician's space. "Reverse it back to outflow from Namino, just to re-establish the connection."

"I...it's not working either. It says it can't find the paired d-gate."

When she'd readied to traverse the d-gate, her hand had naturally gone to her Glaser holster and this time found its target, ready to start firing the instant she hit the ground on Namino. Now she forced her hand off the holster and to her side. Maybe DAF Command had been destroyed by Rasu weaponry. "What's the status of all the other Namino outflow gates? Every transit hub, everywhere."

A row of panes instantiated above the technician's station, and across them populated a series of red alerts.

All the d-gates were all down. *All* of them.

She instantly sent a ping to Joaquim.

Message unable to be delivered to intended recipient.

To Ava, then to Grant, who she thought was still at DAF Command.

Message unable to be delivered to intended recipient.

Her heart sank and her chest tightened to deny her air as the realization leveled her. Namino and everyone on it were cut off, and she was trapped here, unable to help them.

She barely noticed as Dashiel took her hand in his anew. What the hells were they going to do now?

70

CONCORD HQ

T he Consulate suite bustled with even more activity than usual, Caleb imagined due to the recent Senate emergency session, the ongoing Rasu attack in the Dominion, the Savrakath conflict, and generally all of the above.

For the tenth time today, he stewed on how he should be with Alex on the *Siyane* right now. In the thick of the fight against a daunting enemy, no matter how much personal discomfort it caused him. He should be at her side, fighting evil where they found it and defending those who deserved protection.

But Eren needed him, too. And Felzeor, whose beautiful, fragile little heart was broken by Cosime's death.

He sighed and pressed the button for entry into Marlee's small office. He got no response. It was possible she'd checked and seen who it was and was willfully denying him entry. He leaned in close to the door. "Marlee, I come in peace, I promise. And I brought a friend who wants to say hello."

Nothing. He went back out to the Consulate reception desk. "Do you know if Marlee Marano is in the office today?"

"No, she's with Senator Requelme on an official visit to the Asterion Dominion."

In an instant, those dormant reflexes and long-disused pathways in his body roared free from their slumber and flared to caustic life. All his senses sharpened into hyper-focus as adrenaline flooded his veins to drown out Akeso's perpetual calming presence in his mind. Time slowed down even as it primed itself to speed forward. The bright, welcoming lights of the lobby grew harsh against a tableau of jagged edges and too-crisp colors.

"She's *where?*"

"Um, the Asterion Dominion. Where the—"

"I know what it is. Are you certain they're still there? It's come under attack."

"Yes. Senator Requelme sent instructions regarding security measures here five minutes ago."

He pivoted and rushed toward Mia's office.

"What's wrong, Caleb? Your shoulder muscles have tensed considerably, and your breathing has...changed."

"I'm worried about her. About both of them." Without breaking his stride, he sent a pulse.

Mia Requelme, you get my niece out of that war zone this instant.

I'm trying, actually. She's not cooperating.

Open a wormhole to your office. I'll come to get her.

I...okay. One second.

He increased his pace to a rapid jog that approached running. When he reached the entrance to her office, he blew past Mia's assistant and vibrated at the door while the iris scan verified his identity in order to let him into the office. The adrenaline begged to be put to purposeful use. His muscles flexed in preparation.

"Felzeor, I need you to stay here at the Consulate. If I'm not back in twenty minutes, go see Richard about a new assignment, if you think you're ready."

"But what about Eren?"

Caleb's jaw clenched against the dueling urges pulling him in opposite directions. The idea of letting his friend down crushed his soul beneath a wave of desolation...but no scenario existed in which he could let Marlee die. "If I'm not able to follow Eren's trail any farther, talk to Drae. He might be willing to pick up where we've left off. I'll catch up with you as soon as I can."

"Okay, but—"

The door opened to reveal the shimmering air surrounding an open wormhole waiting in the middle of the office. He nudged Felzeor off his shoulder, though his hand shook from the effort of making the gesture a gentle one. "I have to go now."

RW

NAMINO

Marlee lurched around the street corner as the ground rumbled viciously beneath her feet, only to find that while she'd been down the block at the market, an elaborate security checkpoint had been erected at the entrance to DAF Command. Two quite large, well-armed and menacing-looking robots staffed the checkpoint.

What, did they think a couple of mechs were going to keep the Rasu out of the building? The only thing they risked doing was keeping civilians out of the best-fortified structure in the city.

She exhaled harshly, out of breath from the run. She'd lost track of Grant Mesahle when a panicked crowd had overwhelmed them and she'd stopped to urge a terror-frozen woman inside the temporary safety of a building, and there had been no time to try to find him again. And now there wasn't time to parcel out what the proper procedures were to befriend giant Asterion mechs.

Screams echoed off to the left, and she turned to see a ship—small by Rasu standards, but probably four hundred meters across—unleash a torrent of laser fire on a block's-worth of buildings half a kilometer away.

She palmed the hilt of her plasma blade and casually strolled toward the mechs. She'd studied the basic information Concord had received on Asterion machines, and her eyes scanned the one on the left in more detail now. A humanoid shape—made in the maker's image—meant the programming core resided either in the head or the chest. But the power and *oomph* for its considerable weaponry would take up more space, which put those in the sizeable barrel chest. Head it was.

When she'd closed to ten meters away, the mechs steadied their weaponized arms on her. "Halt. This area is off-limits."

That's what she'd thought they were going to say. She held her hands up in surrender—then vaulted off the balls of her feet to sprint the last two meters as speedily as her newly upgraded cybernetics allowed her. At the last meter she leapt up, activated her blade and shoved it into the narrow seam between the mech's head and neck. The mech jerked around roughly, but she hung on and even managed to twist the blade around a few times. She made a quick mental note to compliment Abigail on the quality of the new cybernetic upgrades when she next saw the woman.

As it started to topple, the other mech sighted down on her. She wrenched the tip of the hilt out from the metal casing, leaned over the shoulder of the disabled mech, and shot a new plasma blade directly into the eye socket of the other mech. Then another one to be certain.

Both mechs collapsed to the ground. Blocking the entryway, of course, so when she got her feet underneath her she crouched and began trying to lug one of them off to the side with a grunt. Crap, it was heavy!

A guard from the lobby rushed outside, his weapon drawn. "Ma'am, drop the dyne and raise your hands in the air!"

She rolled her eyes. "Can you grab the other side and help me get it out of the way of the entrance? We need to clear the way so people can get through."

"What?"

Marlee stood and grabbed the guard by the arm, ignoring his weapon. "This building has a basement, right?"

"Excuse me." He yanked his arm away and reaffirmed his grip on his firearm. "I don't want to hurt you—"

"Look, you're going to have a massive Rasu infestation here in about thirty seconds. This is the most fortified building I've seen in the city. *Does it have a basement?*"

"Yes, ma'am, it does. Did you say infestation?"

She pointed to the street, where an ominous shadow had grown to swallow the afternoon sun and bury the city in a malevolent dusk.

The guard peeked out past the gates and down the street, then stumbled back to her. "Oh, my gods."

"All these people are about to get slaughtered, so let's move the mechs out of the way and start directing everyone who comes by into the basement, okay?"

"Um...right. Okay."

"Fantastic." She shoved more than lifted the dead legs of the second mech off the walkway, checked to make sure the guard was doing the same with the other one, then hurried into the growing pandemonium of the street and began waving her arms. "This way! Get into the building and head downstairs! Hurry!"

RW

A thunderous roar shook the top floor of DAF Command, and Mia did the likely stupid thing and rushed to the window. Chaos spread out beneath her. To the left, barely two blocks away, a building collapsed behind a tsunami of smoke and debris swelling down the street. On what part of the street that could still be seen, people ran, as people tended to do in such situations.

Her mind flashed back to the night the Order of the True Sentients tried to burn Romane to the ground. They hadn't succeeded, but today the Rasu very well might.

And in the middle of the chaos below stood Marlee, ushering people into the entrance to DAF Command below.

Marlee Marano, get upstairs this instant. We have to leave now.

Or, you could get down here and help me.

Mia gritted her teeth, dug her fingernails into her palms and hurried out the door.

By the time she got outside, the situation had deteriorated yet further. A cacophony of sounds blended together into a discordant blare that assaulted her eardrums. People bumped past her in a panic, paying her no mind.

Meno, I can't hear anything—but I need to be able to hear important things.

I am working the problem.

Out in the street, Marlee was helping a bleeding woman to her feet.

She got it; she did. She wanted to help these people, too. But today's battle was already lost, and she didn't know what had happened to Malcolm on Savrak, and if Marlee got killed here, Caleb was merely the first in a long line of people who would have her soul on a spike for it.

Mia Requelme, you get my niece out of that war zone this instant.

It was as if he had heard her....

I'm trying, actually. She's not cooperating.

Open a wormhole to your office. I'll come to get her.

I...okay. One second.

Mia moved to the sidewalk near the entrance and opened a wormhole beside her. "Marlee, we have to leave."

"You go. I've got this." She flashed a long plasma blade in the air, then shoved a wavering man toward the building entrance.

"What? I am not leaving without you. And we are leaving now."

Out of the billowing smoke to the left emerged two...creatures. Mia had seen the visuals, so intellectually she knew they were the bipedal forms of Rasu. Few things in her life had ever truly frightened her, but now her heart shuddered in terror. Was this panic? She couldn't panic. "We are out of time. They're coming, dammit!"

Marlee's gaze darted down the street, and her bravado broke for half a second as her face blanched at whatever she saw. "Um, okay. Just let me—"

A man ran bravely in their direction as the two Rasu broke into a sprint behind him, and Marlee motioned him toward DAF Command. "Hurry, in here!"

The Rasu closed to forty meters away. Mia took a step nearer to the wormhole, felt its rippling energy on her skin. "Please, Marlee! Please!"

The man tripped and fell to his knees, and Marlee didn't hesitate to rush to his side.

No, dammit! Without meaning to do it, Mia backed through the wormhole, into the safety of her office—and into Caleb's arms.

He immediately pushed her out to arm's length. "Where is Marlee?"

She spun to the wormhole by way of answer, where through the tear in space-time, the slaughter was ramping up.

Marlee had gotten the man to his feet, and together they stumbled toward DAF Command and the wormhole—

A third Rasu rushed in out of the roiling smoke and sideswiped them both with a long metal arm shaped into a club.

Marlee flew twenty meters through the air before bouncing off the sidewalk, tumbling twice and coming to a ragged stop half on her side. She didn't move. The Rasu who had hit her kept running for some farther destination.

Mia gasped in horror as Caleb sprinted past her and through—

—the wormhole vanished, and he slammed into the far wall of her office.

What? She frantically tried to reopen the wormhole. Nothing happened.

Meno, what's wrong?

I do not know. We are unable to access those coordinates.

What about inside DAF Command?

No. We cannot access anywhere on the planet of Namino.

Caleb pushed off the wall and grabbed her by the shoulders. "Mia? Reopen the goddamned wormhole."

"I can't."

"I don't care what—"

"No, I mean I physically *can't*. It won't open. We can't access any location on Namino. It's as if something is blocking us from that region of space."

He staggered back, almost as if he'd been punched. "Get it open. You have to."

Her hand came to her mouth to stifle a cry. The image of Marlee crashing onto the sidewalk raced on a bloody loop through her mind.

Meno, what are we going to do?

Until we determine the nature of the block and a way around it, there is nothing we can *do.*

"Caleb...."

He holstered his Daemon and, with a sharp nod, headed for the door.

"Where are you going?"

He stopped short of the doorway and glanced back at her, revealing sapphire irises blazing, wild and savage. "To get my niece."

INVERSION
RIVEN WORLDS BOOK TWO

Coming In 2020

Author's Note

I published my first novel, *Starshine*, in 2014. In the back of the book I put a short note asking readers to consider leaving a review or talking about the book with their friends. Since then I've had the unmitigated pleasure of watching my readers do that and so much more, and there's never been a more rewarding and humbling experience in my life.

So if you loved *CONTINUUM*, tell someone. Leave a review, share your thoughts on social media, ask your library to get more copies, annoy your coworkers in the break room by talking about your favorite characters. Reviews are the backbone of a book's success, but there is no single act that will sell a book better than word-of-mouth.

My part of this deal is to write a book worth talking about—your part of the deal is to do the talking. If you keep doing your bit, I get to write a lot more books for you.

Of course, I can't write them overnight. While you're waiting for the next book, consider supporting other independent authors. Right now there are thousands of writers chasing the same dream you've enabled me to achieve. Take a small chance with a few dollars and a few hours of your time. In doing so, you may be changing an author's life.

Lastly, I want to hear from my readers. If you loved the book—or if you didn't—let me know. The beauty of independent publishing is its simplicity: there's the writer and the readers. Without any overhead, I can find out what I'm doing right and wrong directly from you, which is invaluable in making the next book better than this one. And the one after that. And the twenty after that.

Website: gsjennsen.com
Wiki: gsj.space/wiki

Email: gs@gsjennsen.com
Twitter: @GSJennsen
Facebook: gsjennsen.author

Goodreads: G.S. Jennsen
Pinterest: gsjennsen
Instagram: gsjennsen

Find my books at a variety of retailers: gsjennsen.com/retailers

APPENDIX

THE STORY SO FAR

View a more detailed summary of the events of the Amaranthe novels online at gsjennsen.com/synopsis.

AURORA RISING

The history of humanity is the history of conflict. This proved no less true in the 24th century than in ancient times.

By 2322, humanity inhabited over 100 worlds spread across a third of the galaxy. When a group of colonies rebelled two decades earlier, it set off the First Crux War. Once the dust cleared, three factions emerged: the Earth Alliance, consisting of the unified Earth government and most of the colonies; the Senecan Federation, which had won its independence in the war; and a handful of scattered non-aligned worlds, home to criminal cartels, corporate interests and people who made their living outside the system.

Alexis Solovy was a space explorer. Her father gave his life in the war against the Federation, leading her to reject the government and military. Estranged from her mother, an Alliance military leader, Alex instead sought the freedom of space and made a fortune chasing the hidden wonders of the stars.

A chance encounter between Alex and a Federation intelligence agent, Caleb Marano, led them to discover an armada of alien warships emerging from a mysterious portal in the Metis Nebula.

The Metigens had been watching humanity via the portal for millennia; in an effort to forestall their discovery, they used traitors among civilization's elite to divert people's focus. When their plans failed, they invaded in order to protect their secrets.

The wars that ensued were brutal—first an engineered war between the Alliance and the Federation, then once it was revealed to be built on false pretenses, devasting clashes against the Metigen invaders as they advanced across settled space, destroying every colony in their path and killing tens of millions.

Alex and Caleb breached the aliens' portal in an effort to find a way to stop the invaders. There they encountered the Metigen watcher of the Aurora universe, Mnemosyne. Though enigmatic and evasive, the alien revealed the invading ships were driven by AIs and hinted the answer to defeating them lay in the merger of individuals with the powerful but dangerous quantum computers known as Artificials.

Before leaving, Alex and Caleb discovered a colossal master gateway that generated 51 unique signals, each one leading to a new portal and a new universe. But with humanity facing extinction, they returned home armed with a daring plan to win the war.

Four Prevos (human-synthetic meldings) were created in a desperate gambit to vanquish the enemy invaders before they reached the heart of civilization; then they were given command of the combined might of the Alliance and Federation militaries. Alex and her Artificial, Valkyrie, led the other Prevos and the military forces against the alien AI warships in climactic battles above Seneca and Romane. The invaders were defeated and ordered to withdraw through their portal, cease their observation of Aurora and not return.

During the battle, hints of the consciousness of her deceased father manifested in the shared connection between Alex and Valkyrie. Alex reconciled with her mother during the final hours of the war, and following their victory Alex and Caleb married and attempted to resume a normal life.

But new mysteries waited through the Metis portal. Six months later, Caleb, Alex and Valkyrie traversed it once more, determined to learn the secrets of the portal network and the multiverses it held, leaving humanity behind to struggle with a new world of powerful quantum synthetics, posthumans, and an uneasy peace.

And in the realm beyond the portal, Mnemosyne watched.

AURORA RENEGADES

Following the victory over the Metigens, Alex, Caleb and Valkyrie set off to unlock the secrets of the Metigens' portal network. Discovering worlds of infinite wonder, they made both enemies and friends. A sentient planet, Akeso, that left a lasting mark on Alex and Caleb both. Silica-based beings attempting to grow organic life. A race of cat-like warriors locked in conflict with their brethren.

Behind them all, the whispered machinations of the Metigen puppet masters pervaded everything. In some universes, the Metigens tested weapons. In some, they set aliens against each other in new forms of combat. In yet more, they harvested food and materials to send through the massive portal at the heart of the maze.

But Alex and Caleb found yet another layer to the puzzle. In one universe, they discovered a gentle race of underground beings with a strange history. Their species was smuggled out of the universe beyond the master portal by the Metigens. They watched as their homeworld was destroyed by a powerful species known as Anadens; but for the Metigens, they would have perished as well.

Back home in Aurora, the peace proved difficult to maintain. The heroes of the war—the Prevos who melded their minds with AIs—found themselves targeted by politicians and a restless population desperate for a place to pin their fears. Under the direction of a new, power-hungry Earth Alliance PM, the government moved to cage and shackle them.

In desperation, the Prevos uploaded the AIs' consciousnesses into their own minds, fled from their governments' grasp and disappeared onto independent colonies. Devon published the details of the Prevo link to the exanet, unleashing its capabilities for anyone who wanted to follow in their footsteps.

Meanwhile, an anti-synthetic terrorist group emerged to oppose them, fueled by the rise of Olivia Montegreu as a Prevo. While the private face of Prevos was the heroes who defeated the Metigens, the public face became the image of Olivia killing a colonial governor and tossing him off of a building in front of the world.

Unaware of the struggles her fellow Prevos faced, Alex forged her own path forward. Rather than bringing the AI into herself, she pushed out and through Valkyrie, into the walls of the *Siyane*. Piloting her ship in a way she never dreamed, Alex was able to feel the photonic brilliance of space itself. Over time, however, that bond began to capture more of her spirit and mind.

On the surface of a destroyed planet, Mesme at last revealed all. The portal network, which the Metigens call the Mosaic, was above all else a refuge for those targeted for eradication by the Anadens. And the Anadens, rulers of the true universe through the master portal, were the genetic template upon which humanity was built. Aurora was nothing more than another experiment of the Metigens, created so they could study the development and nature of their enemy and the enemy of all life.

Alex and Caleb returned to Aurora to find a galaxy rocked by chaos. After the execution of Olivia Montegreu by Alliance and Prevo forces, Miriam had gone rogue. Under her careful planning, a resistance force, bolstered by help from inside the Senecan and Alliance militaries, moved to remove the despotic Alliance PM.

As Alex struggled with her growing addiction to an ethereal, elemental realm, she felt herself being pulled away from reality. Away from her husband, her mother, her friends. She watched as those she loved fought, but increasingly found herself losing her own battle.

When terrorists staged a massive riot on Romane, Dr. Canivon, the mother of the Prevos, was murdered in front of Devon and Alex. Overcome by her own and Valkyrie's grief, Alex unleashed the explosive power of the ethereal realm to destroy the terrorists' safehouse. Standing in the rubble of her destruction, Alex made a decision to sever the quantum connection between herself and the *Siyane*, choosing a tangible, human life. Choosing Caleb.

Miriam wrested control of the EA government away from the PM, bringing an end to the Prevo persecution. In the wake of victory, however, a shadowy Anaden hunter emerged from the darkness to attack Alex and Caleb. Caleb was gravely injured when the Anaden's power, known as *diati*, leapt into him, healing his wounds and helping him kill the alien.

Mesme revealed the ominous consequences of the attack. Soon, the Anaden leadership would discover Aurora. When they did, they would destroy it unless humanity could stand against them. Mesme told Miriam and the others to prepare, but knowing the end game was upon them, asked Alex and Caleb to come to Amaranthe. The master universe. The home and dominion of the Anadens.

AURORA RESONANT

In Aurora, Miriam led the formation of a multi-agency, multi-governmental (GCDA) and military (AEGIS) organization dedicated to meeting the imminent threat of the Anadens.

In Amaranthe, Alex and Caleb discovered an underground 'anarch' resistance movement against the Anaden Directorate. They made contact with an anarch agent, Eren asi-Idoni, and he helped them infiltrate the Anadens' Machim military command and steal secret information on the Machim fleets. Alex and Caleb were captured, but not before Valkyrie uploaded the information they sought. Eren 'nulled out' rather than being captured, for when Anadens died they underwent a regenesis procedure that returned their consciousness to a new body.

Valkyrie transmitted the data to AEGIS then returned to Amaranthe. When Eren reawakened, he joined Valkyrie and Mesme on the *Siyane*, and they rescued Alex and Caleb from the prison where they were being tortured for information.

The Directorate nonetheless learned the full truth about the Metigens/Katasketousya creation of Aurora and ordered a fleet to deliver a powerful weapon known as a Tartarus Trigger to Aurora and annihilate humanity. Forewarned, Miriam led a fleet of warships into Amaranthe to intercept them.

The battle commenced with the destruction of the one known gateway into the Mosaic, and Mesme sneaked onto the lead Machim warship and stole the Tartarus Trigger. Humanity used its Prevos, Rifts and other tricks to take the Anadens by surprise and prevail in the battle. Afterward, Alex, Caleb, Miriam and Mesme were summoned to a secret meeting with the leader of the anarchs, Danilo Nisi, and a tenuous alliance was formed.

AEGIS scored several early victories but also devastating losses. While the battles raged, Alex and the other Prevos developed a method for using sidespace to open physical wormholes, enabling AEGIS vessels to travel anywhere in known space without using the Anaden gateway system.

The AEGIS fleet attacked the Machim homeworld, destroying the Dyson rings encircling its sun and blowing up their orbital military command station. At the same time, Nisi broadcast an impassioned speech across the empire setting forth the Directorate's sins and the anarch's mission to free those oppressed.

In a flashback Caleb's *diati* showed him, it was revealed that Nisi was actually Corradeo Praesidis, the former leader of the powerful Anaden Praesidis dynasty. Many millennia ago, his son tried to kill him; thinking him dead, the son stole his name, face and power, and now served on the Directorate as the Praesidis Primor.

Valkyrie and her twin, Vii, had spent months rebuilding the consciousness of David Solovy that manifested during the final battle of the Metigen War. Using the Anadens' regenesis technology, they transferred his consciousness to a cloned body, and he and Miriam were reunited after twenty-five years.

The Directorate tracked an AEGIS vessel to the primary anarch base and launched a surprise attack, and a bloody battle followed in orbit and on the ground. To stop a Machim warship from bombing the base with antimatter missiles, Alex re-established her ethereal connection with the *Siyane* to bypass the warship's shielding and destroy it; in doing so, she found the connection no longer exerted the damaging hold on her it once did.

Alex soon discovered a way to use the supradimensional properties of the mysterious Reor mineral to access the contents of the Reor slabs used by the Directorate to store sensitive information. She uncovered the location of the Directorate's regenesis backups, and AEGIS and the anarchs devised a plan to take out the entire Directorate, permanently, in one massive strike.

For all but two of the Directorate members, the mission succeeded with minimal losses. However, the Machim Primor escaped his assassination attempt. Armed with the location of one of the Mosaic gateways, he acquired a new Tartarus Trigger and raced to wipe out the Aurora universe.

On Solum (Earth's twin), Caleb engaged the Praesidis Primor in a battle of staggeringly powerful *diati*, and the *diati* freed when the Primor died rampaged wild. Caleb couldn't wrestle it under control, and it killed millions before destroying the planet itself.

The anarchs learned that the Primors kept an additional regenesis backup stored on their secret space station, the Protos Agora, which orbited the Milky Way galactic core. The *Stalwart II* took the Tartarus Trigger Mesme stole at the start of the conflict and used it to destroy the station.

Just when they believed they had finally achieved victory, they discovered the Machim Primor's plans. The Primor had a head start, and the only way to try to prevent him from destroying Aurora was for the Kats to disconnect it from the Mosaic, rendering it unreachable forever. Caleb, however, instead used his now total control over *diati* to command the cosmic force to pull all the pocket universes in the Mosaic—including Aurora—into Amaranthe, then destroy the Mosaic.

He succeeded, but the energy the act required killed him. While Miriam and the others worked out what it meant for all of humanity to now exist in Amaranthe, Alex took Caleb to the living planet of Akeso and, via the deep connection they shared, Akeso brought him back to life.

ASTERION NOIR

On the planet of Mirai in the Gennisi galaxy, a woman woke up in a rain-soaked alley with no memory of who she was or how she'd gotten there. Two strangers found her and offered to take her in. When asked, she told them her name was Nika, though she didn't know why.

Fast forward to five years later. Nika, alongside her rescuers Perrin and Joaquim, led a group of rebels called NOIR against the despotic government of the Asterion Dominion. An insidious virutox was infecting people's programming, altering their personalities and causing them to commit inexplicable crimes. NOIR's investigation of the virutox brought them to Dashiel Ridani, who Nika learned was her lover in her prior life, before she lost her memory.

With her world thrown into disarray, Nika and Dashiel chased the threads of her lost identity while searching for the source of the virutox. Their search led them to the leaders of the Asterion Dominion, the Guides. Nika broke into the Guides' data vault, where she found they had ordered her psyche-wipe five years earlier after she pressed them on a series of disappearances.

Meanwhile, Gemina Kail, an Administration Advisor, traveled to an alien stronghold across the galaxy, where she delivered thousands of Asterions in stasis chambers to an alien species called the Rasu.

As the virutox spread, wreaking increasing havoc across the Dominion, Justice Advisor Adlai Weiss traced the source to the Guides' doorstep. They ordered him to drop the case and let the virutox propagate among the population. He disobeyed, developed a vaccine and contacted NOIR for help in distributing it.

Across the galaxy, Nika and Dashiel discovered the stronghold of the alien Rasu. A metal-based shapeshifting species of immense power, they'd constructed hundreds of thousands of warships and space stations. Armed with this terrifying information, Nika and Dashiel returned to Mirai.

One of the Guides, Delacrai, defied the others to help Nika. She shared how an Asterion scout ship encountered the Rasu eight years ago; the crew was captured and killed. The Rasu grew interested in the Asterions' unique bio-synthetic intelligence powered by kyoseil and quantum programming, and in return for not attacking Asterion Dominion worlds, they demanded a regular supply of Asterions to experiment on. The Guides agreed.

The other Advisors were told the terrible truth about the Rasu and the Guides' deal with the aliens. They scrambled to undo the damage eight years of the Rasu Protocol had inflicted while racing to find a way to respond to an impending Rasu deadline, when the aliens expected more Asterions to be delivered.

Nika's oldest friend from her former life, Maris Debray, revealed that both she and Nika were members of the "First Generation": Asterions who had never erased their psyches in the 700,000 years since they fled the Anaden Empire and created themselves as a new species by merging Anaden DNA, AI programming and the kyoseil mineral. Only a few dozen of the First Generation remained, and their history was kept secret from everyone else.

With time running out, Nika sought the help of the Sogain, an enigmatic species who once threatened the Asterions with extinction if they ever trespassed on Sogain territory. This time, the aliens disclosed the location of a single, stranded Rasu.

An Asterion team captured the Rasu and brought it to Mirai for interrogation. The creature revealed that the Rasu exhibited a collective intelligence when physically connected to other Rasu, but regained independent thought when they were separated. They intended to use kyoseil to control other Rasu over great distances, as kyoseil was supradimensional, deeply interconnected and one of the universe's oldest life forms.

Using this knowledge, the Asterions identified a way to link their consciousnesses together via kyoseil. They dubbed these connections 'ceraffin' and used them to develop a plan to face the Rasu.

They constructed volatile electricity bombs to be sneaked into the Rasu stronghold. The Rasu were expecting 8,000 Asterions in stasis chambers, so Nika used the ceraff structure to split her psyche into shards inhabiting 8,000 copies of herself.

The copies were delivered to the Rasu as expected, and they awoke inside the Rasu's lab on their primary space station. Chaos ensued as they fought to reach the power control center, even as they were cut down by the thousands. A mere dozen made it to the control center, and a single instance survived to override the power safeguards.

Dashiel detonated the electricity bombs, and a cascading power overload ripped through the stronghold. It destroyed the Rasu's Dyson lattice, which triggered an intense surge in solar flare activity, and all the Rasu stations and vessels were incinerated, save one vessel that escaped through a wormhole.

The Asterions recognized this was not the end of the conflict, but the beginning, and they needed to prepare for the Rasu's return. Nika was contacted by the Sogain, who informed her the Anaden Empire of old had fallen and suggested she might find allies among the new one which had risen to take its place.

Nika journeyed to the Asterions' ancestral home, the Milky Way. Before she arrived, however, a wormhole opened in the cabin of her ship, and Alex Solovy walked through it.

ACKNOWLEDGEMENTS

Many thanks to my beta readers, editors and artists, who made everything about this book better, and to my family, who continue to put up with an egregious level of obsessive focus on my part for months at a time.

I also want to add a personal note of thanks to everyone who has read my books, left a review at a retailer, Goodreads or other sites, sent me a personal email expressing how the books have impacted you, or posted on social media to share how much you enjoyed them. You make this all worthwhile, every day.

ABOUT THE AUTHOR

G. S. JENNSEN lives in Colorado with her husband and two dogs. She has become an internationally bestselling author since her first novel, *Starshine*, was published in 2014. She has chosen to continue writing under an independent publishing model to ensure the integrity of her stories and her ability to execute on the vision she has for their telling.

While she has been a lawyer, a software engineer and an editor, she's found the life of a full-time author preferable by several orders of magnitude. When she isn't writing, she's gaming or working out or getting lost in the Colorado mountains that loom large outside the windows in her home. Or she's dealing with a flooded basement, or standing in a line at Walmart reading the tabloid headlines and wondering who all of those people are. Or sitting on her back porch with a glass of wine, looking up at the stars, trying to figure out what could be up there.

CPSIA information can be obtained
at www.ICGtesting.com
Printed in the USA
FSHW010509280521
81918FS